FEAR THE FLAMES

FEAR THE
FLAMES

A Novel

OLIVIA ROSE DARLING

DELACORTE PRESS
New York

Fear the Flames is a work of fiction. Names, characters, places, and incidents are the products of the author's imagination or are used fictitiously. Any resemblance to actual events, locales, or persons, living or dead, is entirely coincidental.

A Delacorte Press International Edition

Copyright © 2022 by Olivia Iraci

All rights reserved.

Published by Delacorte Press, an imprint of Random House, a division of Penguin Random House LLC, New York.

Delacorte Press is a registered trademark and the DP colophon is a trademark of Penguin Random House LLC.

Originally self-published in the United States by the author in 2022 and subsequently published in hardcover by Delacorte Press, an imprint of Random House, a division of Penguin Random House LLC, in 2024.

ISBN 978-0-593-97507-7

Printed in the United States of America on acid-free paper

randomhousebooks.com

2 4 6 8 9 7 5 3 1

Design by Fritz Metsch
Map by Andrés Aguirre

For those who carry the weight of the world with a smile and never stop chasing dreams that others deem unrealistic, too big, or impractical. Every word is for you. Your dreams are alive, and so are dragons.

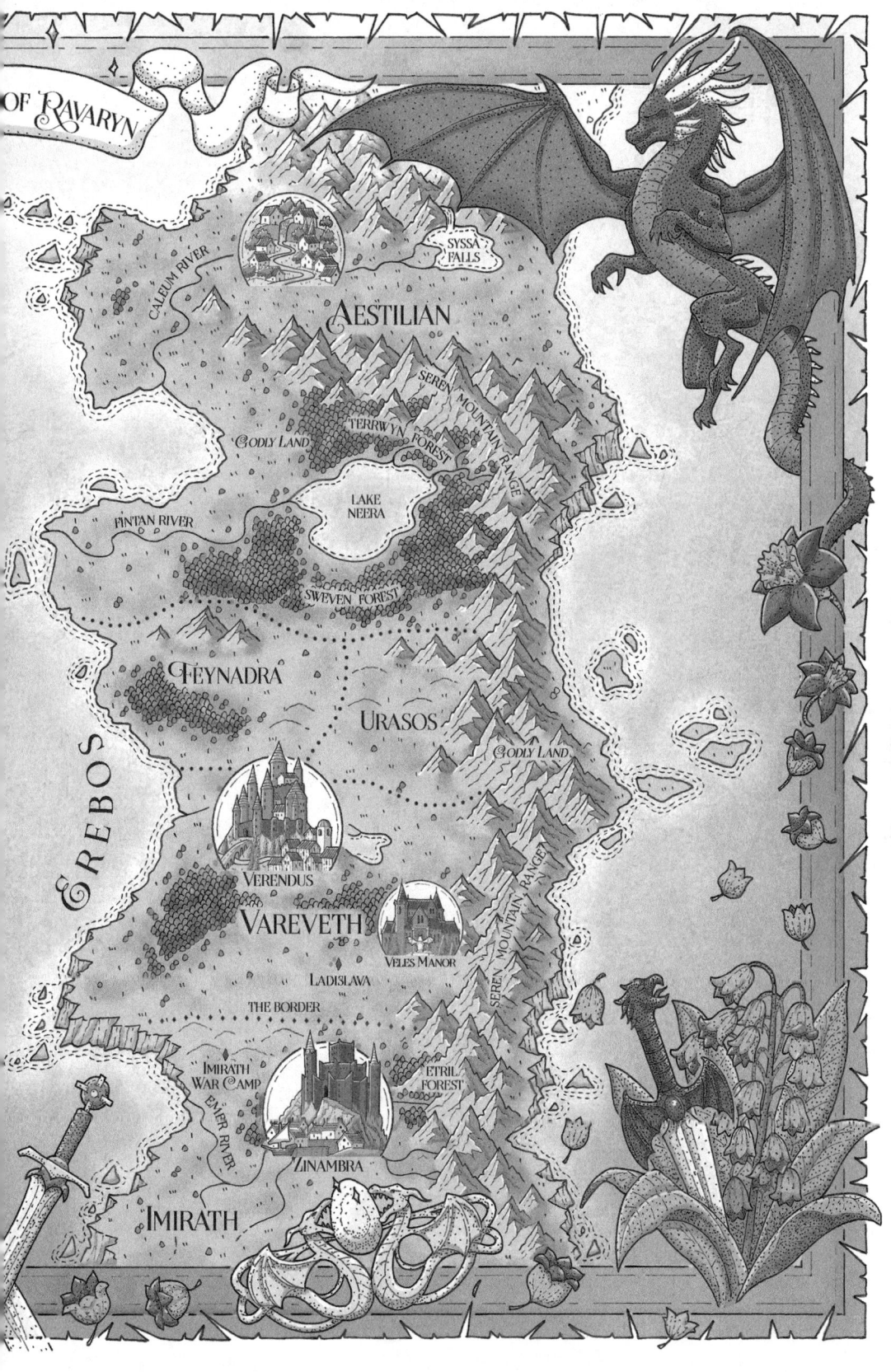

A NOTE FROM THE AUTHOR

This book depicts sexual assault (off page and NOT between the love interests), child abuse, graphic torture, castration, physical and mental abuse, and graphic sexual scenes that are entirely consensual.

FEAR THE FLAMES

PROLOGUE

There once was a princess born on a crisp winter night with enough fire in her soul to rival the frost that covered the earth. The sky wept as she did, and the stars burned brighter when she opened her eyes for the first time.

Dragons had not been seen in Ravaryn since the gods walked among mortals, or so the legends say. The gods had been resting for five hundred years, and yet the souls of dragons came alive and created light where there was once darkness.

The princess with hair nearly as dark as the night and eyes like two embers reflecting the fire within was a small thing, nothing anyone would believe could alter the fate of the world. But is it not the most unsuspecting people who do the most extraordinary things?

On her first birthday, the king and queen of Imirath held a celebration in honor of their daughter. They finally had an heir after trying for several years and cherished their baby wholeheartedly. Following the long-established tradition, they invited the rulers of Galakin, a kingdom far across the Dolent Sea, to join in the festivities.

They arrived, along with their retinue, bearing dragon eggs that some would see as tragedy wrapped in a bow. The queen of Galakin brought her seer to issue a piece of good fortune for the child, as was their custom. The seer claimed that the gods came to her in a dream and informed her that the dragon eggs that had been passed down through generations belonged to the princess. The eggs were so old, they were considered fossils, but they began rumbling on the night of the princess's birth. When the eggs were placed before the princess, five vibrantly colored baby dragons sprang free and perched around her cradle.

The princess and her dragons were one.

They were tethered by their souls.

If the seer had stopped there, perhaps all would've been well, but not all stories have happy endings. The seer proclaimed that the princess's soul was forged from the fire of the gods, creating a link to the five dragons that could not be broken by any mortal or god, and that she would be either the ruination or the glory of her kingdom.

The child grew, as did the dragons, and she could often be seen walking about the castle speaking to or cuddling with the tiny beasts. They slept where she slept. They ate when she ate. When she played, so did they. They were inseparable. Their love was like no other.

People are often threatened by love when they realize both the absence and power of it. What is love if not the one thing in this world that defies logic? Love is the emotion that can make someone run toward danger, but those threatened by it sometimes become the danger.

One day, nearing her fifth birthday, the princess threw a fit over dressing for a dinner, and her maid fetched the king. Surely he could calm down his precious daughter. But the king had become consumed by the prophecy, watching his daughter and her dragons with suspicion, fear, and jealousy. When she continued to defy him, he raised his hand to her, and the green dragon sprang forward, biting off his pinkie.

In that moment, the castle became a prison.

Shackles were locked around the princess's wrists, and the dragons were plucked from the air and shoved into cages when they refused to leave her side. The princess fought with all her might, slicing her wrists open on the metal, scarring her for life as she dug her nails into the floor to get back to her dragons.

Those who had treated her with kindness and deference became those who beat her for treason.

The bond was a curse to Imirath, but no matter what happened, that little girl never saw it as anything other than a blessing. The princess was everything to her parents . . . until she became their biggest regret. And in the dungeons of Imirath, the happy child became a creature of darkness. She morphed into her father's personal monster but never lost her kind heart, even if it was damaged. She gathered all the pain that was dealt to her and forged herself into a weapon that she vowed to one day turn on the kingdom, forcing them to suffer her wrath for all they had taken from her.

Vengeance is a promise signed in blood, but the princess believed that the blood of the dragon flowed through her. The dragons were her kin, and there was not a line she wouldn't cross to liberate her family.

Part I

THE DEAL

CHAPTER

ONE

R**AIN AND WIND WHIP AGAINST MY CHEEKS AS I URGE MY** horse to run faster into the dark forest with only moonlight and lightning to aid my vision. Thunder rumbles throughout the sky in tandem with horse hooves pounding the dirt. There are many reasons for a mission that requires riding through dangerous conditions—secrecy, desperation, curiosity, revenge, and haste, to name a few. I stopped trying to dissect my intermingling emotions years ago but can't deny the overwhelming sense of curiosity that courses through me tonight.

The steep mountainside resembles a maze of fallen trees, uneven paths, and slick rocks. My cloak does little to keep the chill from seeping into my bones, and several strands have ripped free from the braid that falls down my back, sticking to my face as if they're coated in syrup. But I'll never pass up an opportunity to gain information about the tension brewing between Vareveth and Imirath.

Hatred coils through me and a grimace contorts my face when I think of my imprisoned dragons. King Garrick will pay for what he's done in blood, and even that won't be enough. The patrol I sent out informed me of a sighting of soldiers from my father's enemy kingdom, and I want to know what they're doing so far from home and traveling in one of the most dangerous parts of the continent.

The Terrwyn Forest is filled with beasts, bandits, and several poisonous plants, and the mist that leaks down from the mountains is enough to send even the most seasoned explorer plummeting off a sharp cliff. If you keep your wits about you and follow the faint sound of trickling river water, you'll find my kingdom, Aestilian, hidden in a valley beside the Syssa Falls.

Finnian's horse increases its pace and strides beside mine. His ginger curls lie flat against his forehead, and his porcelain skin almost glows through the darkness. "Are you going to tell me why you ran into the house and dragged me out like a deranged goblin?" he shouts over the storm.

Technically I never told Finnian why we left, but we stopped clarifying details with each other years ago.

Wherever I go, he goes.

Wherever he goes, I go.

"A deranged goblin?"

"Yes." He clears his throat, and I already know he's about to imitate my voice. "*Finnian, make haste! Get your ass on a horse! A corpse moves faster than you!*" His voice cracks on the last word, which only increases my laughter.

"Vareveth soldiers were spotted at a tavern here, and it's a bit of a hike for a pint."

We slow our horses while passing through the weather-worn gate, their hooves sloshing in the muddy road. The scent of salt lingers in the air that wafts off the sea. I've been to this village before, but the dark wood houses, shops, and taverns look even drearier while shrouded in gloom.

I follow Finnian toward the rowdy establishment packed with soldiers, and we tie our horses off on a post. It's best to keep them close in case anything goes wrong. We're lined with weapons but no armor, for the sake of blending in as travelers. Knives adorn my waist corset and down my legs until they reach my boots; the only hint to my identity is the two dragon daggers I never go without.

Lantern light dances across Finnian's freckle-dusted cheeks. "What's the plan?"

"You stick to the lower levels and see what you can find out from the soldiers who are too deep in their pints. I'll spy through the floorboards on those of higher ranks."

He nods, straightening out his red tunic before disappearing into the tavern.

A few minutes later, I'm encompassed in a sea of off-key musicians as the creaky door falls shut behind me. I've never been a fan of noisy places, but Finnian thrives in them. It's what makes us a good pair. I peer through the crowd and spot him sitting at the bar, surrounded by several dark green cloaks. He throws his head back in a boisterous laugh, and even though I can't hear him, the song of his laughter is a melody that's stitched into my brain.

I steady my footing on the uneven floor while making my way to the dark staircase in the corner, keeping my head down as I weave through the mismatched tables filled with soldiers playing cards or shouting for another round of drinks. Nobody turns toward me. They're all too absorbed in whatever is in front of them.

The tavern is as plain on the inside as it is on the outside. There's no point in fuss and frills when everyone comes here for a single purpose—to get drunk while passing through. Wooden beams shoot up toward the ceiling to support the second floor, and the walls are completely bare aside from the rusting lanterns with hardened puddles of candle wax beneath them.

My eyes water as I walk through thick clouds of pipe smoke that waft through the small space. I stick to the shadows along the wall and take my first step up the rickety staircase. It creaks so loudly that if I hadn't done this ascent countless times, I would think the wood isn't strong enough to hold any weight. But I continue my journey without a second thought, dodging cobwebs along the way.

I pause at the top of the stairs, straining my ears for any signs of movement or breathing, but nothing reaches me. The open attic is filled with bags of grain, barrels of wine and ale, dust-filled furniture, and anything else the tavern may need. It's the perfect place to escape for dalliances in the dark. The only light infiltrating the space comes from moonlight trickling through holes in the roof and lantern light rising from cracks in the floorboards.

My steps are light even though nobody will be able to hear them over the noise. The last thing I want is dust raining down on one of their drinks, giving me away before I've even had the chance to acquire any information. I navigate the floor while picturing the layout of the tavern in my mind—maneuvering to the section where I know the generals sit, hoping they'll reveal something worthy of squatting in an attic. I cringe while looking down at the dirt- and dust-covered floorboard I always press my ear to. It's far dirtier than usual.

I take a knife from my thigh and rest my head against the small crack after wiping it with my cloak. The familiar steel is a welcome presence in my palm. Ever since I escaped Imirath, I've never gone a single day without a knife—even before I knew how to use them. I close my eyes and let all other noises disappear, zoning in on the conversation that drifts into my ears as smoke rises through the air.

"King Eagor may be a pushover sometimes, but he won't give up on this," a deep male voice rumbles.

"He knows this is in Vareveth's best interest, and Cayden won't let him," a sharp feminine voice answers.

Cayden.

Cayden Veles, Commander of Vareveth, is both the most feared and youngest warlord on the continent at only twenty-nine. He's as rich as a greedy god paired with the morals of a demon. Many even refer to him as the demon commander, or demon of Ravaryn.

"He's tired of losing soldiers at the border in pointless skirmishes. Tension's nearly at a boiling point already." The same male voice cuts through the music.

"Yes, but this war will be over before it even begins if King Garrick finds a way to control the dragons." My eyes snap open, and shock surges through my body. My heart pounds so rapidly that I worry it's knocking like a fist against the floor. Garrick doesn't let anything slip about the dragons. The only reason I know they're alive is that I would have felt their death. The bond I share with them would have broken, and it would be excruciating. The mere threat of the dragons keeps all of Ravaryn from his borders.

When I was born, my parents threw a ball in celebration of the Atarah heir, and all kingdoms were invited, including Galakin. Queen Cordelia brought her court seer to offer my parents a piece of good fortune in honor of their baby princess. Dragon eggs that should've been no more than stones were laid at the foot of my cradle, and five dragons sprang free.

The prophecy stated that my soul is forged in flames and bonds me to five dragons, and that I would either destroy Imirath or bring it immeasurable glory.

I was four when my dragons were ripped away from me and I went from being a princess to a prisoner overnight.

Shaking my head, I refocus on the conversation below me.

"Cayden has a plan for that. You know he's always scheming or plotting," the male voice says.

"Well, let's see what happens. Maybe Princess Elowen truly is out here." A chill creeps up my spine, and I inhale a breath so sharp that my face mask clogs my airways. One of my hands tightens around the hilt of my knife while the other pulls the mask below my chin.

Vareveth soldiers are here . . . because they're looking for me.

"Hear anything interesting, little shadow?" a deep voice drawls from the top of the stairs.

I pull my mask up before pushing myself to my feet. My eyes peer across the space, taking in a large male figure leaning against the entrance. He pushes off the doorframe and slowly walks in my direction, the wood creaking under his heavy footsteps.

"Not really." I shrug while twirling the knife.

"Do you often gasp at idle gossip?" he asks, coming to a stop a few feet in front of me. A shard of moonlight dances across one of his angular cheekbones as if it longs to reach out and touch him. A jagged white scar littered and framed with red stretches from the corner of his right eye, across his cheek, and ends close to the corner of his full lips.

"I saw a spider," I answer. He's dressed like an assassin in a black leather chest guard, and a cloak, pants, and boots to match. His staggering frame is clad with weapons. Several knives line his legs, a short sword and axe are strapped to his waist, and a broadsword rests across his back.

"Hm," he muses. "It's too bad I know you're lying, considering I know who you were listening to."

Fucking gods.

"Perhaps you should go back to them. Surely they're missing you much more than I will."

"Did you think I wouldn't notice you?" he asks, ignoring my previous suggestion.

Nobody ever noticed me before.

Even Finnian has commended my ability to move like a ghost through a crowd.

He's standing between me and the only exit from the attic. My only other option is the window. I've jumped from higher, but Finnian is still downstairs, and there are too many soldiers between him and the tavern exit. I assess his size, still twirling my knife . . . he's tall enough to make me tilt my chin up, but I've taken down monsters.

My hand tightens around the hilt, and I advance on the man a split second before he advances on me. I slam my fist into his jaw and ignore the throbbing sensation in my knuckles that follows. He hardly even flinches and grips my wrist. I shove my leg forward to knee him between his legs, but he senses my move and shifts away from the hit. He takes advantage of my off-balanced stance and pries the knife from my hand. Tossing it aside, he yanks me toward him, takes my other wrist, and slams my back into the wall.

"Now that we got that out of the way, what did you hear?" The light is just strong enough for me to make out an arrogant smirk and the intensity that laces his gaze.

"I think you should have pinned me to a wall in a bigger room. I don't think it's large enough to accommodate your ego." I strain against his hold.

He quirks a dark brow, and his smirk grows. "Knives, spying, and a sharp tongue. You're playing a dangerous game because I'm intrigued." His eyes dance over my face again but snag on my mask. "May I take that off?"

My heart skips a beat, but I don't let it show through my eyes. I already know the game he's playing. If I refuse, he'll know I'm a person who doesn't want to be identified, which isn't entirely true. I simply want to enter the game on my own terms, and I know he's part of the battalion looking for me.

"You have me pinned to a wall, and yet you're asking permission to remove my mask?"

"Chivalry's not entirely dead." He presses against me harder and angles his head closer to mine. If he thinks I'll crumble, he's sadly mistaken.

He slides my hand against the wall, bringing it closer to my right. His grip on me loosens, and I yank forward, breaking his hold and shoving him back. I knee him where it will hurt him most and swipe his legs out from under him, praying nobody below us heard him fall.

I climb onto him and cage his torso between my legs. We're still shrouded in darkness, but his calculating gaze blazes through the shadows. I grab another knife from my thigh, hold it to his throat.

"I much prefer this position." I place my free hand on his chest and lean forward to hover above his face.

"I can't complain." He lazily tucks a hand behind his head, and his voice is void of any anxiety one might have with a knife against his neck.

I ignore his comment and continue in my pursuit. "What does your commander want with the Atarah heir, soldier?"

His face shows no emotion. "Why would I tell you anything my commander wants?"

"You don't know the Atarah heir; I do. It's a rather simple concept if your brain can manage to work that hard."

He tucks his tongue into the side of his cheek. "The heir could be useful in the upcoming conflict."

"How?" I push the knife farther into his skin but not hard enough to draw blood yet.

"You said you know her?" His right brow rises slightly, and his scar moves with it.

"Yes."

"Would she be willing to meet with my commander?"

A tangled ball of curiosity, anxiety, and excitement clangs through me. I could have a meeting with the Commander of Vareveth—my father's enemy.

But what if it's to ransom me?

"Not yet." His eyes narrow, and he waits for me to name my terms. I open my mouth to list them, but I'm cut off by an inhuman growl coming from the roof. It's a sound I'm unfortunately familiar with.

A netherwraith.

The deadly creature drops into the attic from the largest hole in the corner of the roof. They can smell human blood from five miles away, and they crave it more than they crave water. It's a giant beast covered in thick white fur with blood-red eyes. As the netherwraith grows, so do two curved horns on top of its head, and they're sharp enough to pierce you if it decides to charge. A forked tongue hangs from its mouth, dripping in a frothy venom. It's a beast of nightmares, as are all the beasts that prowl the Sweven, Terrwyn, and Seren Mountains.

I scramble off the soldier and press my back into the wall while he rises to his feet. He unsheathes the broadsword from his back and a throwing knife from his thigh as his predatory gaze tracks the beast.

"Name your terms," he states without taking his eyes off the netherwraith. It prowls forward with its sights set on the soldier. I slide against the wall and move closer to the stairs. I need to get to Finnian.

"There's a clearing where the Fintan River meets Lake Neera. Meet me there tomorrow night with a token of good faith." The beast moves past me, still dead set on the soldier.

"A token of good faith?" He snickers. "My minuscule faith isn't placed in things many deem *good*."

"I won't send the heir to you only to be ransomed. Show me you're willing to work with her, and I'll judge whether you get to meet her. I'm not particularly fond of you so bring your charm next time, soldier." I now stand directly behind the netherwraith. It's the diversion I need to escape, but I can't let him die before finding out what Vareveth wants. I throw the knife in my right hand; the beast shrieks as the blade sinks into its back leg. I turn away, sprinting the rest of the way toward the stairs.

"There isn't a single place in this world where you can hide from me, you understand?" His tone makes me pause. I crane my neck in time to see him raise his sword toward the beast as he crouches into a perfect defensive stance. "If you run, I'll find you," he declares, taking one last look at me before swinging his sword at the beast that springs in his direction.

"Come alone!" I call out while rushing from the attic.

CHAPTER
TWO

Everyone must have heard the netherwraith's growl because most occupants are elbowing each other to get to the exit. My gaze whips around the room, trying to find Finnian through the commotion. It's not the first time I haven't been able to spot him, but the uneasy feeling that accompanies his absence never goes away. We've agreed to always meet up at our starting point rather than waste time trying to find one another in chaos.

My body pushes against the crowd that's moving toward the attic entrance. The soldier must be of high rank if others are rushing to his aid. Not that it seemed like he would need assistance. He oozed a lethal calm that only seasoned soldiers master after years of fighting.

If that's the case, it won't take him long to kill a wounded netherwraith. I must get to the clearing early tomorrow to ensure he arrives alone. A calming wave washes over my anxiety when I spot Finnian sitting on his horse. The reins to mine lie in the palm of his hand.

"I was about to come in and look for you." He drops the reins once I'm close enough. "A netherwraith?"

"Yes. A huge one," I answer while swinging myself up. Thunder booms above us as a growl turns into a whimper, and the attic goes silent. The soldier killed the netherwraith, and we haven't even left yet.

"I don't know if I want to ask this, but how much shit did you get into?" Finnian asks.

"No more than the usual amount." *Lies.* I think I've just gotten myself into an immeasurable amount of shit. I turn my horse toward the gates and nudge her in the side.

"If you run, I'll find you."

Chills snake up my spine, but it's not from the rain this time. I don't turn around, but I swear I can feel the heat of his gaze branding my back through the attic window. We keep pushing our horses through the dark, rain-sodden forest until I'm sure nobody has followed us.

"There isn't a single place in this world where you can hide from me, you understand?"

Another chill creeps up my spine.

We make it to the edge of the Terrwyn before we slow our horses. The rushing water of the Caleum River signals the start of our ascent up the mountainside. I dismount from my horse and bring her over for a quick drink after sprinting for the last hour.

I haven't stopped gnawing on my bottom lip since we left the tavern, and I taste the coppery blood on my tongue. There are too many thoughts flashing through my head. Too many possible scenarios that could end with me dying, or worse, back in an Imirath cell. I crouch by the river to splash cool water on my already freezing face before sliding my hands up and tangling them in the roots of my damp hair.

Just breathe.

In and out. In and out.

Find a way to control the situation before it controls you.

I sense Finnian's presence beside me before he opens his mouth. "You're going to need stitches if you keep biting your lip like that."

A halfhearted chuckle falls from my lips. "What did you find out?"

He sighs while sinking into a squat beside me and running his fingers over an arrow. "Their commander is making them look for something, but they didn't say what."

"They're looking for me, Finnian," I whisper. He sinks his fingers into the muddy riverbank to keep himself from toppling over.

"Most of the continent, *the world,* thinks you're dead," he protests.

"The assassins your father sent only found you outside our borders and stopped several years ago." A total of four assassination attempts occurred while I was wandering around unnamed villages when Finnian and I got separated.

"Most," I reason.

"Did you learn that from spying, or was someone in the attic with you?"

I'm careful with my words. "A male soldier followed me."

"Does he know *you're* the lost princess?" Finnian demands, shooting up and towering over me.

"No," I say while getting to my feet. He still towers over me, but Finnian towers over everyone.

"All I got out of him is that Vareveth is looking for the Atarah heir. The netherwraith cut the conversation short before I could learn more." Finnian visibly relaxes at my clarification. Guilt eats at me for keeping the meeting hidden from him. I know it's unwise to go alone, but I can't put Finnian at risk of an ambush. I don't trust the soldier; therefore, I won't bring Finnian around him. "What else did you hear from the soldiers on the lower level?" I ask, both out of curiosity and to take the attention off me.

"Vareveth is set on war. They're tired of making attempts at peace."

"They finally have a commander who knows you can't make peace with a tyrant. Good for them." Sarcasm drips from my every word.

Finnian continues while I walk over to where the horses nuzzle against each other, "They'll be in this part of the continent for about two more weeks. Their commander is with them—apparently he has a scar on his face that gives him away."

My blood chills, and I swear I stop breathing for a moment, my heart pounding like a war drum at the center of my chest, much like it did against the floorboards. It's a small blessing my back is to Finnian.

I was face-to-face with the Commander of Vareveth.

I held a knife to his throat.

Oh gods, I kneed the most feared warlord on the continent in the balls.

I suppress the deranged laugh that bubbles in my throat and resort to softly snickering as I grab the reins of Finnian's horse.

"The army is also pissed at King Eagor for not doing something against Imirath sooner," Finnian adds.

I stop a few feet before him and mentally prepare for how he'll react to what I say next. "I must do something about the food supply in Aestilian."

He flinches when he registers what I'm saying. "We can find another way."

Vareveth is a well-established kingdom. If I strike a deal with them, I can include sending food to Aestilian as one of the terms. "We're out of time. People are going to starve to death once the first frost hits. The rations are already dwindling."

We send out raids to bring supplies back to Aestilian. I only allow them to take from smugglers already traveling with stolen goods, but what we'll get is never guaranteed. We also have skilled hunters, but there is too much snow in the winter for them to get out of Aestilian safely. The population continues to grow, and every day that passes is another nail in the coffin of my sanity and puts my people at greater risk.

"Once you make yourself known, your father will never stop until he kills you."

"I can't hide forever. Tonight made that apparent," I state.

"They haven't found Aestilian," Finnian counters as his cheeks redden in anger.

"No, but there's a chance they might." My mind flashes to a sight only my nightmares have conjured—houses and stores burned to the ground, grief-stricken faces, my people fighting for their lives against an army with far more skill and weapons, children screaming for their parents, parents screaming for their children. "I won't wait until someone drags me from Aestilian. I'll leave on my terms after bargaining for a deal I want."

"I won't lose another sibling!" Finnian's hands shake at his sides, and his nostrils flare. His eyes blink rapidly, fighting to keep back his tears.

My temper dwindles. Finnian and I can yell at each other loud enough to wake a sleeping god, but once one of us cracks—it's over. My hands drop the reins, and I rush toward him, wrapping my arms around his torso and placing my cheek on the slick leather that covers his chest. His chin rests on top of my head while he wraps his arms around me, pulling me closer. Finnian rarely talks about the family he had before he came to Aestilian, just as I rarely talk about what happened to me in Imirath. But sometimes, when the darkness of night conjured up memories without our consent, we were always there to hold the broken pieces of each other together.

"You won't lose me, Finnian."

He sharply sniffles above me. "You've never been the Atarah heir to me."

That's why I love you.

"But that's who I am," I softly state.

"No. You're the girl who squishes fruit in the kitchen to make jam and gets excited over books," Finnian mumbles while giving me a squeeze. I laugh softly into his chest. "I won't watch you get locked up again."

"I won't let them." I swallow the lump in my throat while pulling my head back from where it rests. My teeth sink into my cheek to keep my emotions at bay. I don't want to worry him more than he already is.

I must go to that meeting.

I won't watch Aestilian burn to the ground.

I won't be a prisoner again.

I won't let Finnian starve.

I want too much out of this life and have too much resting on my shoulders to cower in the dark. I may keep to the shadows, but I also wield them.

"Come on." I poke him in the chest. "Let's get home."

CHAPTER
THREE

I HARDLY SLEPT LAST NIGHT, WHICH ISN'T UNUSUAL, BUT fatigue weighs on my tired bones and strained muscles. The heels of my palms dig into my eyes before I turn over and groan into my pillow. My face stays buried for a few seconds to avoid the light streaming through my windows.

I'm meeting with the Commander of Vareveth tonight. Cayden Veles wants me, and I have no idea why. I couldn't properly make out his features last night, so the only picture I have in my mind is a scarred, shadowy face.

I flop onto my back and kick the blankets off, tucking my feet into my slippers before they can touch the cold wooden floor. I tug the sleeves of my wool sweater to my elbows to run cold water over my face. Finnian always tells me I look intimidating until I smile, and then my entire face brightens. My tired eyes stare back at me in the mirror, and I pinch my narrow cheeks to bring some color into them, missing the slight glow I gain in the summer months while gardening.

We didn't always have running water here. Most places on the continent do, but it's a rarity for a makeshift kingdom like Aestilian. The tavern we went to last night doesn't have running water, nor do most of the villages in the Sweven Forest. You can always tell by the smell of the crowds.

I don't remember my chambers in Imirath, so I take pride in my room. It's the only corner of the world I have to myself, and I keep fresh flowers on my dresser when they're in season and stack books along the walls. The plush chair beside my hearth is well loved from all the nights I've spent reading till the sun came up, letting the words provide an escape route from my mind.

I enter the dining room, which is connected to the simple kitchen and living room, and realize our housekeeper must have been here because there's a steaming cup of coffee with two pieces of toast smothered in butter and raspberry jam waiting for me. Bless Galakin for providing Erebos with their caffeinated imports. Sunlight pours through the windows, warming the wood beneath my feet and illuminating the various weapons, blankets, and books strewn about the worn, mismatched furniture.

When I first came to Aestilian, before it was even Aestilian, I lived here with Ailliard and the four guards who helped me escape Imirath—Nessa, Esmeralla, Lycus, and Zander. They've all taken up quarters in the guardhouse, but Finnian and I chose to stay here.

I wish I could say I feel content, but I don't. The tide hasn't pulled back the wave of uneasiness that washed over me last night. I'm submerged, drowning in it. My hand rubs the back of my neck, and I lean my head against the chair. The urge to make a move is eating me alive.

A deep groan resembling a mother bear talking to her cubs sounds down the hall, pulling me from my thoughts. I laugh into my cup as a sleep-stricken Finnian with curls jutting in all directions trudges into the room. I remove my feet from the chair across from me before he flings himself into it.

"Go back into hibernation."

"I didn't want you to talk to Ailliard without me," he mutters, digging a fork into his omelet.

"I don't plan on talking to him today."

He pins me with sleepy eyes. "Do you really think this is something you should keep from him?"

"I'm not." I raise my palms in the air. "I just want to soak it in before I tell him. It doesn't feel real." My breakfast threatens to make a second appearance as the lies twist my stomach. I hate lying to him. I hardly ever do, not even little white lies.

As for Ailliard, he'll be on higher alert if I tell him Vareveth is looking for me. He'll send more soldiers to the border, making sneaking around harder, and I need to get to that meeting tonight. I'll leave slightly past midday to arrive at the clearing before Cayden Veles. It feels strange to name the shadowed face in my mind. He seemed more like a figment of darkness than an actual man.

I rest my hands on my lower abdomen and suck in a sharp breath, drawing Finnian's attention. "Menstrual cramps?"

"Mm-hmm." I press my lips together and give my best pained expression. He knows of the horrible pain that accompanies my monthly despite the tonic I take. Sometimes it's so bad I can't walk on the first day without limping.

His eyes fill with concern. "Do you need my help getting upstairs?" I make a mental note to buy him something from a bakery when all of this is over, or maybe new arrows.

"I'll be okay." I manage a small smile while channeling my inner emotional turmoil to present itself as physical pain. "I think I'm going to stay in my room for the rest of the day. Do you have plans?"

He shakes his head. "I was going to head down to the tavern later, but I can stay if you want me here."

"No!" I shoot out too quickly. "I've been dealing with this for years. Have fun tonight. Don't worry about me. I'm just going to sleep and read," I add to cover up my outburst.

"All right." He regards me with suspicious eyes. "Just tell me if you need anything."

"I will."

"No, you won't." His lips pinch in the corners. I can't help it; I don't want to be a burden.

"Okay, fine. But I promise I'll be perfectly content to sit in my chair by the fire," I say, staying at the table until he finishes his breakfast.

CHAPTER

FOUR

———

T**HE SUN SETS AS I BREAK THROUGH THE MIST OF THE** Seren Mountains, painting the sky in orange and pink hues. After Finnian finished his breakfast, I fake hobbled to my room and *technically* read a chapter from one of my books, so I didn't completely lie to him. I didn't absorb a single word, but the effort was there.

My horse continues at a steady pace as we make our way down the steep cliffside. I left early enough to arrive before Commander Veles but accelerate once we make it to somewhat flat ground, and ride through the dense forest without a single bloody encounter. It's still muddy from last night's storm, and the lake is so blue that it casts a glow throughout the clearing. Some people swear it's the work of the gods.

I unsheathe the sword from my belt and dismount, straightening my black leathers and cloak while I lead my horse behind a moss-covered boulder close to a cave opening. If there's an ambush we'll hide there, and symbols of the God of Water are chiseled above the entrance, which means no beasts will be lurking in the shadowy depths.

I peek around the rock and listen for signs of movement, but the commander is nowhere in sight. Darkness bathes the forest, and a crescent moon is framed by clouds. Something sends ripples through the water, but I don't have the chance to step forward before I'm yanked back. Quick hands pin my wrists behind me as I kick my assailant in the shin.

"Relax, little shadow. It's me."

"Oh, lovely." Anger bubbles in my veins. "That makes being tied up in a dark forest all the more enjoyable."

"You held a knife to my neck before running away." He finishes off the knot and spins me to face him. "Consider this a precautionary measure."

My breath catches in my throat when I tilt my chin to take in his features. I wonder if the continent believes him to be a demon because his alluring beauty is otherworldly. He's a harsh kind of handsome, something akin to jagged snow-covered mountain peaks, or an unruly ocean crashing against dark sand beaches.

The hood of his cloak is pulled down, and tousled chocolate waves spill onto his forehead and kiss the tops of his ears. I scan the scar on his angular cheek that stands out against his deep-olive-toned skin, but not before meeting the piercing emerald gaze that gleams through the night and dances across my features.

"You didn't seem to mind," I bite out.

"I never said I did." He steps to the side to wrap the rest of the rope around a tree, securing me in place like a rabid animal.

Sweat gathers on the back of my neck and I take in long, drawn-out breaths to keep calm. I strain against the rough ropes, but like any skilled soldier, he knows how to secure a prisoner.

"Did you bring what I asked?"

He saunters into my vision, stopping a few feet before me, and holds up a long clear vial filled with shimmering black liquid. "It's an elixir to generate crop growth on infertile soil."

"How did you know I would want that?" Because I do want it, but it's unnerving how well he guessed.

"If you live anywhere around here"—he waves a hand through the air, gesturing around the general landscape—"you won't be able to grow much."

He takes a steady step forward, followed by another. Our eyes remain locked together with every inch he covers. My nails dig into my palms for a sense of crescent-shaped clarity as his domineering presence fully enters my space, standing toe-to-toe with me. The corner of his lips turns upward after I narrow my eyes at him, morphing the shape of his scar as he tucks the vial into my thigh holster.

"Satisfactory?" he asks, tucking his thumbs into his pockets and putting some much-needed space between us. I purse my lips and rake my eyes over his muscular frame covered in the same assassin-like attire from last night, but somehow he looks even more threatening while cloaked in moonlight as opposed to shadow.

"Decent," I say, flashing my eyes to his again. "What do you want with the Atarah heir, *Commander Veles*?"

He quirks a brow. "Done your research, *Princess Elowen*?"

"How do you know who I am?"

"Call it a hunch."

"I applaud you for exercising your mind enough to come to that conclusion. I'm sure it was very hard for you."

He snickers. "You definitely have the prissy royal attitude mastered."

"You tied me to a tree!"

"Because I don't want you running away or pulling a knife on me midconversation, *princess*."

"Don't give me a reason to, *demon*." I pull against the ropes again. "Don't act innocent; you pinned me to a wall."

He shrugs his broad shoulders as if to say *Fair point* before moving on. "Have you ever thought about getting your dragons back?" His drastic subject change stampedes into me, and I would have stumbled if I hadn't been bound in place.

Every day.

I've thought about finding my way back to them every single day.

Guilt eats at my soul with every hour that goes by, knowing they're still locked in the castle. Whenever I wake up with a sore throat, all I remember is the night I escaped Imirath. I tried to throw myself off

Ailliard's horse while we rode away from the castle, screaming and crying until I couldn't utter another noise. I've attempted piecing plans together over the years, but nothing is good enough. If I die, nobody will rescue the dragons.

My bond has lain dormant in my chest, and I feel nothing. Emptiness. An endless pit that was once filled with light and love. All I have are memories of their vibrant scales and tiny bodies perched on my shoulders while we walked freely through the castle. But that was before they snapped their fangs at my father when he raised his hand to me when I was four years old. They were hatchlings, but a dragon's loyalty isn't swayed by rank or title. Once Sorin bit off Garrick's pinkie, life changed in an instant.

"You can't bargain with madness."

"I agree." Cayden brushes a thumb over his bottom lip before clasping his hands behind his back. "Why negotiate for something I can take?"

"A heist?" I tentatively ask. "You wish to free my dragons?"

"Correct."

"What's the catch?" I force my head down from the clouds but can't derail the hope swirling in my chest. Hope is a dangerous emotion. It renders us immune to logic.

"You stay in Vareveth after the heist is complete and use the dragons against Imirath in the upcoming war."

Shivers rack up and down my body, but I force myself to keep my tone even. The worst part about anxiety is trying to conceal it. "That's it? That's all you want?"

My decision was made the second I told Cayden to meet me here last night, even if I didn't realize it. I deserve more out of this life than hiding away. I love Aestilian, and I always will. But love shouldn't cripple you; it should flourish with you.

"You'll have to sign a formal alliance treaty, but yes," he confirms with a definitive nod.

"What about King Eagor and Queen Valia? I need to know where they stand." As the rulers of Vareveth, surely they have a say in this.

"They won't be informed about the heist if that's what you're asking."

"How is that possible?"

He pauses, weighing his words. "Vareveth has different military laws from most kingdoms. This is a militaristically motivated operation; therefore, I don't have to clear it with either of them."

"Okay," I say slowly, trying to wrap my head around everything. "What will they think I'm in Vareveth for?"

"Eagor thinks it may sway other kingdoms in our favor if you're with us. As of right now, they have remained neutral. You're next in line to the Imirath throne. Aligning with Vareveth would look good for us and bad for Garrick." I've gathered that Cayden isn't the type of person that people cross; he crosses them. He's talking about his own king and queen as if they're nothing more than pawns in *his* game.

"Untie me," I demand, needing time to collect my thoughts. I can't keep living for everyone else, and nothing will stand in the way of reuniting with my dragons. It shouldn't be seen as selfish to know what you deserve and to take it for yourself.

No more hiding.

No more being a ghost.

"You'll be coming on the heist with me?" I run my fingers over the irritated skin.

"Attached already?"

"You'll make an excellent shield." I summon the anger I felt when he first tied me up and slam my fist into his cheek. "Don't tie me up again, prick."

He slowly turns his head toward me and looks . . . shocked? Intrigued? I think it's both. "Yes, princess, I will be coming with you on the heist."

"There's still more we need to discuss." I pause, fidgeting with the bottom of my braid.

I can't tell my uncle, Ailliard, who got me out of Imirath, that I'm going back for my dragons considering they burned his sister—Queen Isira. I've brought up liberating them, but it's always ended in a screaming match. My father hired a mage when I was ten to physically break the bond, but the spell rebounded and drove the dragons into a frenzy. There were many casualties that day, my mother being one of them, and the flames only increased as a soldier dragged me out of the room by my shackles.

My mother wasn't cruel like my father, but every year on my birthday she sat silently on her throne while an interrogator hit me with a cane until I was unconscious, demanding I tell him how to break my connection.

"I have people to take care of. I need more of the elixir you gave me and a steady supply of food going back to Aestilian. I won't leave my people to starve."

"Aestilian?"

"It's my kingdom." I leave it at that. He doesn't need any more information other than the need for food and the name. "That has to be taken care of before the heist."

"Plan on dying in Imirath?"

"If I do, I promise to drag you down with me."

He fights back a smirk. "I'll take care of the elixir, and you have my word that Eagor will supply enough food for your people."

"Then you have a deal, Veles." It takes everything in me not to run around the forest like a drunkard at the prospect of seeing my dragons again, but I tip my head down until I can rein in my smile. If I don't leave Imirath with dragons, I won't be leaving at all. I've waited fifteen years for this, and I don't think I'll survive another year without them. "There is somewhere I need to be."

"Where?"

I narrow my eyes. "We may be allies but we certainly aren't friends. I don't owe you an explanation."

"You're no use to me dead," he states while untying my horse and handing me the reins. "We'll discuss further details while we ride. I want you in Vareveth within a week, and we'll be working together for months if not years to come, so we may as well start tonight."

"Forgive me, but if I had parents, I'm sure they would warn me against traipsing around forests with a stranger," I argue.

He pulls his sword free and lays it flat across his palms. "Elowen Atarah, queen of Aestilian and princess of Imirath. I, Cayden Veles, Commander of Vareveth, vow to protect you from harm from this day until my last." He briefly glances down at my parted lips. "Your enemies are my enemies. My sword is yours."

My throat tightens as I soak in his words. I can't trust him, I don't like him, but I can work with him. He needs me to accomplish his goals just as much as I need him to accomplish mine. It's a codependent, vengeance-based alliance, but it's still an alliance.

I'll have a steady food supply for Aestilian.

I'll have a chance to get my dragons.

I'll have a chance to stand against Imirath.

It's everything I couldn't stop myself from dreaming of.

I reach down and pull my dragon daggers free. "Cayden Veles, Commander of Vareveth. I, Elowen Atarah, queen of Aestilian and princess of Imirath, vow to fight beside you in the upcoming war as a true ally. My knives and dragon fire are yours," I say before tucking the twin blades back into their sheaths without removing my gaze from his.

Our breath mingles in the space between us, but the only sounds to be heard are the rushing current of the Fintan, owls hooting in the distance, and the rustling of leaves being carried by the wind.

"A book is easier than dragons." I've been tracking the fire cult's movement for the past few weeks and don't want to waste the opportunity of being outside Aestilian with no escort. Witnessing Cayden's skills in stealth will also be valuable knowledge considering the stakes of this mission are much lower than entering Imirath. "Consider this practice, demon."

CHAPTER

FIVE

———

Godly cults travel by the phases of the moon to avoid interacting with one another. There's bad blood between them considering their rivalries reflect grudges between the gods. They've been asleep for the past five hundred years, so I'm not sure what the rituals performed are supposed to accomplish.

"Where do you want to meet before we travel to Vareveth?" I begin, wanting to get this out of the way before we arrive. "I assume we'll be traveling into your kingdom together, considering I would have to pass through Feynadra or Urasos."

"I'll escort you directly from Aestilian with several of my best soldiers," he states as if it's obvious.

"No."

"No?" he questions incredulously.

"You're not coming to Aestilian."

"Elowen," he starts while pinching the bridge of his nose. The sound of my name on his lips—I can't tell if it feels like he's spoken it hundreds of times or a handful. "I vowed to protect you, and that includes your people."

"A vow forged from convenience is the first kind to be broken when it becomes inconvenient."

He grinds his teeth and grips the reins tighter. "Will you at least tell me where it is?"

"Not a chance," I state. He rubs a hand over his sharp jawline and looks like he wants to challenge me but doesn't.

"Do you know where the temple ruins for the God of Earth are?" he asks. Knowing where the temples are is vital to surviving a night in the Terrwyn or Sweven Forest. I nod in confirmation. "My soldiers and I will meet you there."

It's close to Aestilian. It's also the temple nearest to the tavern where we met. Which means it'll be a relatively short ride. I want to argue with him to choose a temple farther away but don't want to raise suspicion.

This is likely the first of many battles between our clashing personalities and priorities.

"Fine," I concede. "You said you want to be in Vareveth within the week?"

"I'll move my soldiers once I return tonight, but if you're not there by the end of the week I'll find you. My soldiers will serve as your guards while you're in Vareveth, and anywhere else we go, so you don't have to trouble yourself with assembling your own." His eyes rest heavily on my profile, and I twist my head to meet his gaze.

The relief I feel is locked away, far from any emotion he can gauge from me. Leaving Aestilian is something I want, but I won't assume anyone else wants to ride headfirst into war and political conflict. The only one I can guarantee is Finnian and probably Ailliard. Ailliard will be annoyed, but I doubt he'll stay in Aestilian if I'm not there. He'll be an awful grump, but I'll need him to attend political meetings.

Still, I ask, "Why should I trust that your soldiers will protect me?"

"Because I will personally punish those who defy my orders." He gives me a pointed look that translates to *Nobody wants to be on the receiving end of my wrath.* "You're the only person preventing my army being burned alive if the dragons are unleashed, and I have no intention of dying before I see this war through." A scowl mars his face, and he looks like a man hell-bent on revenge.

I tear my eyes away and face forward again. A slight tremor travels through my hands—the image of his contained rage is burned into my brain. Maybe we can find some common ground considering we hate the same person. But even imagining finding common ground with Cayden feels like stepping into complete darkness, unaware of where I'm supposed to be going.

"I won't enter Vareveth before signing a formal agreement. I know the alliance papers can't be drawn up on such short notice, but I want our vows written and signed with witnesses." The sound of drums floats our way beyond the stretch of my vision. Leather slides against leather as we drop to the forest floor beside each other. I jump back when his arm brushes against mine. Physical touch is something I like to see coming if I'm in the mood for it, but I'm shocked when he also quickly takes a step away.

Another unacknowledged truce.

"My word is as good as a blood oath, but I'll give you your fancy paper and signatures if that's what you wish, *princess*."

I laugh and cross my arms over my chest. "I would be a fool to take your word at face value. You either prove it to me, or I'm out."

"You're out?"

"I've lived as a ghost for fifteen years. I can easily slip back into the shadows. You'll never hear of me or see me again."

"As I told you before, I will find you in any corner of this world." He takes a step forward, eyes blazing with unrelenting promise and challenge.

"Don't let it come to pass, and you'll never have to fail." I tilt my chin up, not backing down. "Are you always this arrogant?"

"Are you always this demanding?" He chuckles. "You won't back out."

"Your presence is quite insufferable." We're a breath away from being chest to chest. "That's enough motivation to pursue other options."

"And you're as sweet as sugar." He shakes his head. "You want revenge just as badly as I do, and I'm the only person willing to help you liberate your dragons."

I force my lip not to curl at the mention of his aid. I'd rather suffer in silence than ask for assistance. It makes me feel like a burden, but with Cayden, it makes me feel inadequate. "You may be the only person who can help me, but I'm also the only person who can help you."

"You're not the only person who can *help me*." He bites out the last two words. "You're the only one who's worth it."

His words steal whatever retort I mentally prepared and make me acutely aware of how close he is. I fight the urge to step away and stay rooted in place, not wanting to be the one to retreat. Our breaths mingle with the war drums, and he takes a slow step back after several prolonged seconds but keeps his eyes on me.

"Is there a reason why you don't book shop like an ordinary individual, or does stealing from a cult enrich the story?"

I roll my eyes. "Feel free to stop speaking whenever you wish, considering I have no urge to answer any questions you ask."

"Right," he says, returning to silence until he stops short. "Did you see that?"

"See what?" I scan our surroundings before realizing the mistake I made and leave him snickering in my wake. "The book I need is in the tent belonging to the high priestess, and let's try not to kill anyone."

"Do you have any other issues, Your Majesty?"

I give him a cutting stare. "The only issue coming to mind is you."

"Being in the thoughts of the lost princess is an honor."

Tattered tents peek between the trees as we make our way to the edge of the camp, and flickers from a large bonfire illuminate the area. Fifty people, maybe more, surround the flames in large circles.

I sink to my knees and peer through a bush beside him. "Murderous, blood-drenched thoughts."

"Even better."

The high priestess stands at the center, closest to the fire, and chants a prayer while holding a chalice above her head. Her red robes swallow her frame, and she splashes a shimmering powder into the flames that sends them soaring. She bows and turns her palms to the sky as the scent of lemongrass is carried by the wind.

"Goddess, hear us!" she shouts as embers crackle at the base of the fire. I lean farther into the bush, eager to see what's happening.

I jolt back when a blinding orange light shoots up and smack a hand over my mouth to muffle a shriek. Something is forming in the flames—the powder must be made of magic. The priestess raises her voice in a powerful scream, and the rest of the cult sits back on their heels, eyes drawn to the sky. Another flame shoots up, followed by twenty others, all morphing into tiny dragons. Their fire-filled bodies flap around the bonfire, circling high over the prayer circle. It's a trick many merchants sell, along with all kinds of creature-conjuring spells. It has nothing to do with my dragons, but it's mesmerizing.

"That tent has the triple flame symbol," Cayden says. "We should move quickly."

I force my eyes away and move along the shadowed tree line until we're directly behind the cluster of tents. It's unorganized, but there's really no need for order when the cult constantly moves. We surge forward with steps so light I can't even hear them against the grass. I press my back into the first tent, and the reality of what I'm doing finally sets in. I press my lips together, so I don't crack at the absurdity of this night. Cayden gestures for me to follow after he's sure the coast is clear. We keep this pattern, each of us taking turns to listen before advancing farther into the camp.

We come upon the back of the priestess's tent and slip inside after Cayden peeks through the flaps. It's darker than I anticipated and only lit by a few candles. A floor bed topped with linen and wool blankets rests at the tent's center. That's the only piece of furniture besides the prayer table by the entrance and a few trunks strewn throughout the area.

"Keep watch," I command while hurrying over to the display. I remember the title from the day I spied on a traveler through the floorboards of a tavern: *The Flames of the Dragon*. She waxed poetic about the vivid depictions of the creatures, and I'm hoping to find a likeness to one of mine. The drawings may all be from the artist's imagination, but I can't stop myself from trying. I'd recognize their scales anywhere, and I need to see them, even if it's through a portrait.

But my desperation is too embarrassing to tell Cayden.

The book on the prayer table isn't correct, so I kneel by the trunks, picking the first lock and swinging it open only to find scarves and winterwear. I'm luckier with the second and hook my finger into the spine and place it beside me to lock the trunks again, but Cayden is behind me, ushering me to my feet.

He tucks the book safely under his arm and keeps us moving toward the exit. "Glad you got your bedtime tale, but the ritual is over."

We sprint into the night and the crisp air burns my throat as we cut sharp corners and make our way to the safety the darkness provides. But Cayden flies past me, not realizing I've stopped in my tracks.

"Elowen Atarah." The wind whispers my name.

"What are you doing?" Cayden growls while taking a few steps closer, drawing his sword, and staring beyond me.

"*Queen of Flames.*" The same cool voice drifts my way, and I know Cayden hears it when his head snaps in my direction. The cult members stand by their tents with their heads bowed and the high priestess walks before them. My senses tell me to turn around and bolt, but my mind forces me to stay in place.

"If any of you touch her, you die," Cayden declares while stretching his broadsword before me, "and I promise to make it painful." I'm taken aback by the defensiveness of his tone. I unsheathe my knives again, sharpening my senses and zoning in on my targets as I always do before a fight.

"We won't harm her." The high priestess continues her slow procession to close the distance between us. Her hood covers her face, so I'm unable to view her features. "I saw you in the fire."

"She saw us stealing a book in the fire?" I ask from the corner of my mouth.

"Top-tier security," he mutters back. I may not be a believer, but something about a high priestess watching me steal something through a vision seems sacrilegious.

"The dragon queen reborn from the ashes. I have waited a long time to meet you," she says while reaching into her pocket. Cayden shifts closer, angling his body in a more defensive position.

The high priestess holds up an amulet on a gold chain; it's beautiful. A diamond-shaped ruby dangles at the bottom with gold branches jutting out and tangling together, making an even larger diamond shape. "Hold out your hand," she instructs.

"I couldn't," I say, feeling guilty for stealing a book from her. The crowd standing along the edge of the camp is also unnerving, but at least their hoods are back. Seeing actual human faces makes the situation slightly less eerie.

"It was made for you." She takes another step closer. I sheathe a dagger and lower Cayden's sword. He complies but keeps it at the ready should anything change. "It is vital."

"Vital in what way?" I reach out, and she gently sets the amulet in my palm.

"When you're ready, you'll be able to put it on. Let it guide you," she answers. I wait for her to continue, but she doesn't.

I scrunch my brows and waver uneasily on my feet. "What if I put it on before I'm . . . ready?"

"The fire your soul was forged in will reclaim you, and to dust you shall return."

Oh, *just* death. Why would it be anything less than that? The amulet feels heavy in my hand. Cayden reaches over to take it from me, safely tucking it into his pocket.

"Thank you for the death jewelry, but we really must be on our way," Cayden states, guiding my stunned body away from the high priestess.

My steps crunch the twigs and leaves as we finally cross the tree line. Over my shoulder, I hear her say, "Make them fear the flames of a queen." She pauses for a moment. "We will meet again, Queen of Fire."

I step away from Cayden and tuck my arms around me as we walk farther from the camp. The more distance we put between ourselves and the priestess, the better I feel.

"Maybe she'll give me a soul-burning ring next time. I'd really like to wear a matching set when I meet my maker," I remark.

Cayden chuckles. "I'll keep the amulet."

"You're using the death jewelry as collateral? The reaper rock? Oh!" I clap my hands together. "The assassination amulet!"

Cayden blinks slowly and runs a hand over his face and through his hair, but not before I see the corners of his lips turn upward. "I'm taking *the assassination amulet* because I don't want to scour the continent for you and find a pile of ashes." He steps forward to hand me the book and I don't argue. "You truly won't let me escort you home?"

"No, but if you need something to occupy your time feel free to remove your boots and kick rocks." I swing myself onto my horse. "Careful, soldier. You're glaring at me as if you'll miss me."

"Don't hold your breath," Cayden calls out behind me. I don't turn around, just raise my middle finger high enough for him to see.

CHAPTER

SIX

THE CRACKLING FIRE MIXES WITH THE SOUND OF MY feet pattering against the floor as I pace the living room. I peeked into Finnian's room last night, eager to talk to him, but his snores had already infiltrated the space. He didn't stir when I propped him on his side, bordering him with pillows in case he had drunk too much.

I soaked in a hot bath, but the mixture of Finnian's floorboards and riding have given me the aches of an eighty-year-old. I'm so on edge that I know my outfit would be a mess if I hadn't laid it out the night before—a red shirt paired with a brown waist corset and pants always adorned with knives. The standard attire I wear when it's too cold for dresses.

"I see the pillows!" Finnian exclaims. My heart lodges in my throat when his door cracks open. "Darling, how many times have I told you, though I love you, you don't have to sleep on my—" His footsteps halt when he sees me. "What happened?" I build the courage to turn toward him, but his eyes fixate on the elixir and book I placed on the table. "You went somewhere last night?"

I clasp my clammy hands in front of me. "Just let me explain." He doesn't say anything, doesn't even look at me, just walks across the room to sit on the soft leather couch. "I met the Commander of Vareveth last night," I continue. He covers his face with his hands, and my heart squeezes. "I made a deal with him."

His hands drop away, and he finally looks at me with flushed cheeks. "Elowen, tell me you're toying with me."

He knows I can't. The evidence of my nighttime endeavor is displayed in front of him.

"You and I both know Aestilian can't stay hidden forever. We're already several times larger than I ever imagined. I needed to find a solution for the food shortage, and Cayden offered one." I desperately try to reason with him. I need to talk to Ailliard after this, and it'll be much easier if I have Finnian on my side.

He wrinkles his nose before leaning back, letting out a deep sigh. "Tell me everything. Starting from the moment you left here."

The crease between his brows eases as I rattle off more details. I inform him of what transpired in the attic, meeting Cayden in the forest, joining Vareveth in the war against Imirath, the cult, the amulet, and the book. I tell him everything except the heist. There's no point when I have no answers for his inevitable questions.

I won't lie if he asks me about the dragons, but I'd like to find the right time. We've remained hidden from the world since we met, and I hope to make the transition as smooth as possible if he chooses to rejoin society. His leg bounces and his fingers are peaked in front of his lips. "You deserve a life that doesn't force you to constantly stick your neck out."

I twiddle with the ends of my hair. "I'm not."

"You are."

"You don't have to come to Vareveth, and I understand if you wish to remain here. This is my choice, and I won't hold you to an agreement I made." I'll miss him terribly, but his happiness and safety mean more to me than any alliance ever could. "But I need you to support me when I inform Ailliard."

He looks at me as if I've grown three heads. "Of course I'll support you. I don't disapprove of the alliance; I merely wish you weren't the lost princess Vareveth wants."

"Well, I don't think there are many others hiding in Ravaryn."

"Is this what you truly want, or is it a means to an end?"

The sincerity in his question makes me pause, but my answer is instant. "Yes."

I've always known I'd never find something to light my soul on fire within the safety net I've been captured in. It's not that there hasn't been danger or solace within my hobbies, but I want adventure. I want my dragons in front of me and not just in my mind. No matter how hard I tried or trained, nothing ever filled me with a burning passion. I can't tend to my garden, heal our soldiers, or spy from the shadows forever.

I want to intertwine my fate with my dragons and alter the course of this world.

"All right," he says. "And you truly held a knife to the neck of the Commander of Vareveth?"

"I did."

"That's my girl." He stands up from the couch and pulls me into his chest. "When do we leave?"

"You don't have—"

"It's not up for discussion." He cuts me off, but I don't miss the nerves in his tone. "You know you always have me, witty remarks, arrows in necks, the whole package."

Emotion clogs my throat and I hug him tighter, holding him until I'm able to form a response. "Let's hope Ailliard takes it well."

He sighs while tying a blue cloak around his neck. "He'll adjust."

The kingdom is alive, as it always is when the sun comes up. Shutters are spread open and familiar faces smile down at me while hanging laundry or picking the final herbs of the season from window beds. The amount of progress we made in the past fifteen years still shocks me sometimes. Aestilian was merely a valley my guards deemed well-suited for exile, but now there's much more to it.

It's a small kingdom but a kingdom in its own right. There are houses and shops made of dark wood with peaked roofs, built with iron and resilience by the hands of myself and my people. There is now vibrancy where there was only wilderness, but wildflowers still paint the land in spring.

"Do you have a plan?" Finnian asks.

"I believe the tactic of improvisation is one of my greatest weapons." I lightly shove him after he scoffs. I have a vague, extremely cloudy sort of semblance of a plan, which is to tell Ailliard and brace for the storm. Perhaps I should've filled a trough with coffee and drunk from it like a horse.

Walking the path to the guardhouse doesn't bring me the same kind of peace it used to. The past few months, years even, have been plagued with an overwhelming sense of anxiety brought on by the rising tension within Erebos as well as our growing population and dwindling food supply. I haven't been able to be as mentally present as I used to be. I always do my duty, but too many uncontrollable factors follow me like a shadow.

The guardhouse is the largest building in Aestilian, followed by the orphanage, and is always being expanded, which is made apparent through the mismatched wood. The imperfection makes it feel more like a home, which Aestilian is for many people, but perhaps not for me. It feels wrong to want more, but ambition shouldn't be frowned upon. It should be encouraged.

I'm a few steps into the building when I hear a loud thump, followed by a curse. I spin on my heels to face my best friend, who's now rubbing a hand on his reddened forehead. "How do you manage to hit your head every time we come here?"

"I don't hit it every time," Finnian argues. I scoff and roll my eyes because he does, on the same beam every time. "Some of us grew after turning sixteen."

I laugh softly and stay the course to Ailliard's office. I'd rather not feed Finnian's ego; it's nearly as tall as him, and I reach just below his chin. My knuckles graze the door when a raspy voice speaks through the wood. "I could hear the two of you from the second you walked into the building."

"How does he always do that?" Finnian whispers.

"Maybe he's a wizard, or maybe he heard your head smack into a doorway." I push the door open and slip inside before Finnian can make a retort.

Ailliard turns away from the window and gestures for us to take a seat in front of his desk. He may be a blood relative, but the resemblance between us is slim to none. He shaved off his blond hair a few years ago, and a gray beard cut close to his face makes his sky-blue eyes stand out. My hair is the darkest shade of brown and falls to my lower back in loose ringlets, and my light brown eyes that appear amber in the sun are the fire to his ice.

The desk takes up most of the room, but cabinets filled with guard reports, financial records, population records, crop records, and more line the walls. The office is organized chaos, but we know how to navigate it.

"How was the raid?" Finnian asks, probably knowing I need a minute to gather myself.

"We've had better." Ailliard sighs, taking a seat and resting his elbows on the wood. "How was the midnight ride?"

Either of us could answer the question, but I know it's directed at me. Ailliard stopped reprimanding me for venturing outside Aestilian a few years ago. Not because he enjoys the idea of me leaving but because he knows he can't stop me.

"It was"—I take a moment to weigh my next word—"informative."

"Informative?" Ailliard's brows shoot up, deepening the wrinkles on his forehead. "Please, enlighten me."

I grip the teardrop-shaped moonstone pendant I always wear, moving it back and forth on the gold chain. "Did you get the guard report I left on your desk?"

"The one about Vareveth soldiers crossing the Fintan?"

"That would be the one," Finnian answers for me.

"Finnian and I went to the tavern they were at to spy on them." My nerves may be causing an earthquake inside my bones, but my even tone reveals nothing.

"Spy on them?" Ailliard echoes. "Elowen, you are aware of the tensions between Vareveth and Imirath, yes? Do you even think?" My anxiety slowly morphs into irritation when patronization enters his tone.

"No, actually. I just sit places and look pretty." Finnian snorts and his shoulders shake in silent laughter. Ailliard opens his mouth to speak, but I hold my hand up to silence him. "It's *because* of the tensions that I wanted to find out why they're here."

His nostrils flare. "Did you?"

"Yes." I square my shoulders and straighten my spine. "I've made a deal with Commander Cayden Veles of Vareveth."

"A deal with a demon," Ailliard mutters, scrubbing his hands over his face before laying them flat on his desk. "We can still get out of this. You don't have to adhere to the terms."

"I will not be going back on my word." And I will not forsake my dragons by remaining within the borders when I have the chance to free them.

"Elowen, why can't you be content with what you have? Your ambition will get you killed. Make peace with your past and be done with it."

I clench my jaw. "You don't have to agree with my choices, but you will respect my decision."

"You didn't make a deal. You bartered away your soul."

The notion makes me laugh. "I bartered my soul for a blade many years ago, and I have no regrets."

"What are the terms?"

I take slight pity on him as his heel taps against the floor. He broke me out of my cell, swaddled my small frame in blankets, and rode into the Etril Forest. The freezing temperatures make it one of the most dangerous places on the continent. The abuse would've been unimaginable after the dragons burned my mother. Not because my father loved her, but because he failed to protect his queen in their castle. Ailliard never forgave Garrick for putting Isira in that position. He doesn't speak of her, but I know he loved his sister dearly.

"Vareveth will provide Aestilian with food. Commander Veles gave me an elixir that enables crop growth in rocky soil, and Vareveth will supply us through the winter."

"What do they get?" he asks tightly.

"I will travel to Vareveth with Commander Veles after signing a protection agreement prior to the formal alliance treaty. King Eagor believes my presence in Vareveth will convince other kingdoms to align with them, and I will remain in Vareveth throughout the war." My eyes cut to Finnian, and he subtly nods in encouragement.

Ailliard's eyes are glued to the wall next to us. My heart beats in tandem with his foot vigorously tapping against the floor. "There is no marriage clause?"

"No, uncle."

His eyes flash to mine again. "I do not want you involved with that man. Nobody knows where he comes from, and his reputation is ruthless."

"We're allies." Cayden's accomplishments have been whispered throughout the continent like legends you tell children to make them behave. On one occasion, before an ambush that a scout saw coming, he split a battalion of his soldiers, keeping one hidden in the forest and forcing Imirath to fight on two fronts. He turned a trap into a massacre. "But is it truly so incredulous to deem someone worthy because they rose in rank based on merit rather than their bloodline? He may be deceitful, but I'd rather share an enemy with a fiend I know. His depravity could be an asset."

Ailliard's lip curls in disgust. "You're better than this, Elowen. I've wanted you to give up the idea of revenge since you were a child."

I grip the sides of my chair so tightly my knuckles turn white. "Instead of chastising me for seeking revenge, perhaps you should lament over why I seek it."

The sound of a cane striking my skin echoes in my mind, the sound of chains rattling against the floor while my wrists were shackled, the sharp pangs of hunger that twisted my insides until I cried, the fresh sting of a slap delivered by a fully grown soldier to my seven-year-old face. My dragons shoved into tiny cages and carried away from me while I begged and fought until my nails bled, their pained shrieks that weren't yet roars still haunt me.

The humiliation.

The degradation.

The shame.

It all rushes back to me. I blink my eyes rapidly and drop my gaze to my lap. Finnian shifts in his chair and stretches his hand across the space between us, waiting for me to grasp it. But I can't. When those memories surface, finding comfort in physical touch is hard. I feel like my clothes are too tight. I feel like everything about me is wrong. Physical touch is something I had to learn to view in a positive light, and I still battle with it sometimes.

"We can organize more raids—" Ailliard tries to change the subject.

"We don't need more raids! We need a long-term solution." I cut him off, lifting my eyes after locking down the memories. "What happens when people here begin to have children and their children leave? What happens if someone sends a patrol into the Seren Mountains?" I slowly rise and place my hands on his desk. "What happens if someone learns how to navigate the mist? What happens when winter comes, and the snow is too thick to send out raids? What happens when my people start dying, and there's not a single fucking thing we can do? Do you want to bury their loved ones knowing that we could have done something to prevent it?" My blood is pumping in my ears by the time I finish.

"I just want to make sure you know what you're going up against. Your father is not a threat to be taken lightly." Ailliard sounds slightly remorseful, but his eyes are still lit with anger.

"Neither am I," I darkly state.

Finnian rises from his chair behind me. "I stand with Elowen in this decision. I'm going to Vareveth with her not only because she's my best friend, but she's also my queen. I'm aware your reaction comes from a place of caring, as did mine when she first told me, but I suggest you convey your feelings with more respect." Finnian places a hand on my shoulder, easing me away from the desk. "Take the day to cool off."

Finnian gently tugs on my shoulder, but I stay rooted in place like an old tree weathering a storm. "You can either stand against the tide or let it drag you under. I've made my decision, uncle; make yours."

Finnian guides me from the office and slams the door shut. We walk silently from the guardhouse to the field filled with targets painted on hay bales. I need to focus on something other than the emotions raging inside me, making me want to run and scream until my throat is raw. Finnian stands at the target next to me, nocking an arrow in his bow as I unsheathe a knife. The familiar weight of my blade is reassuring because this is a skill no one can take away.

Ailliard gave me my first knife on my eleventh birthday. That night, I vowed to myself, with only the stars as my witness, that I would never be helpless again. The memory of Garrick's guards beating me and demanding I break the bond threatens to resurface.

Never again.

My knife sails through the air and sinks into the center of the target. I drop my shaky hand to my thigh and pull the next free, squaring my shoulders and staring down the line toward the blade I just threw.

I don't remember much of the world before my imprisonment at the age of four and forgot what it felt like for the sun to warm your cheeks or to marvel at how tall trees can grow. The world is a magical place when you're not surrounded by those who corrupt the peace and solace.

My second knife lands an inch above the first.

My life has been dedicated to honing my skills in the hopes of freeing my dragons and taking my revenge. It has required grit and determination, but even when I was surrounded by a hurricane of chaos, my blades were the eye of the storm. I want to be exceptional or nothing, and it's a curse I bestowed upon myself, I suppose.

When I think about what I truly want, it's never a crown. It's my dragons. I made a deal with a demon, and I'd do it again, no matter what comes from it. There is no healing for me without freeing them, and I will never forsake them for safety.

Each day that passes is another sunset grinding a shard of my heart to dust, ready for the wind to carry it back to Imirath. My existence is haunted by my dragons. I'm destined to walk through a graveyard of hope.

The third knife lands an inch under the first.

I will survive this war just as I've survived everything else.

I throw the last knife, finishing off the perfect line I created. My hands have stopped shaking, my breathing is even, and I don't feel the need to scream even though I'm still upset.

From the corner of my eye, I see Finnian walking toward me. "Thank you for standing by me."

"I hate how he speaks to you when he's upset," Finnian says.

"I know," I mutter.

"It's not right." I glance at him, and he must see the mixed emotions in my eyes. "It's not," he reaffirms.

I nod, pressing my lips together while facing my target again. I inhale a steady breath. "Ailliard has a flaw in his logic."

"Which are you referring to?"

"The entire time, he kept worrying about Imirath coming for me." I observe the perfect line of knives. "But Imirath has no idea what's coming for them."

CHAPTER
SEVEN

F INNIAN LEFT A FEW HOURS AGO TO SPEND THE DAY WITH our blacksmith, Blade. It's not his true name but he's a man dedicated to his trade. Finnian was fifteen when he fell in love with the forge, around the same time I developed an interest in healing, and is an artist with steel. My twin dragon daggers were made by him, as was the only crown I own. It resembles a circlet of intertwined tree branches.

I look around at my dying garden and feel a pang of sadness knowing I won't be here for the next bloom. I'm sure Vareveth has gardens, much more extravagant than mine, but nothing that will bring me the same sense of peace. I initially took up gardening because I had to. I used any seeds I could get my hands on: berries, vegetables, and herbs. Sometimes I would even uproot plants and bring them back here.

Now I garden because I enjoy it. I still need the food I harvest, but I also grow flowers and other unsavory plants in the corner of the garden . . . hemlock, bloodroot, nightshade, and snakeroot, to name a few. I think it's ironic that poisonous plants often grow the prettiest flowers. Consistently underestimated by onlookers until they feel the deadly sting.

My head is tilted back on the cushioned chair when I hear footsteps approaching, not Finnian's. They wouldn't be as tentative. "Ailliard." I greet him without opening my eyes.

My anger is still ripe, but I've tucked it into a neat little box and can open it as I please. He speeds up slightly and claims the chair beside mine. Only members of the king's guard beat me, and Ailliard was a queen's guard. I don't remember seeing him in the throne room during interrogations, and we never bring up the past. Talking can't change what's been done. I'm sure he knew the extent of the torture, but I've never had the courage to ask.

"I—" He cuts himself off. I tilt my head forward and glance at him; a crease forms between his brows, and his lips press into a thin line. "I regret the way yesterday went."

I don't know what you're talking about. I think it went wonderfully dies on my tongue. I have two forms of defense other than fighting—sarcasm and humor.

"My fear overtook me, Elowen." He drums his fingers against the chair. "If it's all right with you, I would like to try again. To discuss it without lashing out."

"All right." This isn't a battle that needs to be prolonged.

He blows out a low breath. "Is the Commander of Vareveth blackmailing you in any way? Because if he is—"

"He's not," I interject. White-hot anger presses against the box before I rein it in. Ailliard forming an opinion of Cayden before they meet vexes me. Cayden vexes me as well, but we're allies.

"If any of you touch her, you die . . . and I promise to make it painful."

The finality and protectiveness in his tone cause goosebumps to rise on my arms. *No*, it must be the wind causing that. Cayden acted as an ally. Allies defend each other. It's like giving your neighbor some extra sugar. I shift in my seat, physically forcing his voice out of my mind.

"I just want to ensure you know what you're getting yourself into by leaving Aestilian. Your father will use all his power to get to you, and I highly doubt the words *safety* and *Veles* are synonymous."

"I've spent years learning how to defend myself, and I'll have an army at my back. I used to have only a few floors to protect me from

Garrick, and that didn't play in my favor," I state coldly. "I may not have all the answers, but I won't sit by and continue to do nothing."

"Elowen." Ailliard blanches. "You think this is nothing?" He spreads his hands wide, gesturing to the town beyond my house. "You've given people a home."

"It's not only me."

"No, but you're the crown."

I wave my hands through the air, brushing past this subject. "I won't wait for a move to be made on me, which it will, and lose my chance at an advantage. That's what Commander Veles offers me."

"How are you so sure a move will be made on us?" he asks without judgment, just curiosity.

"Power-hungry rulers don't just give up, they focus on the largest threat, and Garrick's largest threat is Vareveth. But if Vareveth loses the war and Imirath invades—who's to say his focus won't shift to me?"

"If Garrick invades Vareveth, he'll have many things to worry about."

I shake my head. "A ruler who doesn't think of every possibility won't have a crown for very long. Also, why should I wait for him to make a move when an opportunity has fallen into my lap?"

"We have the mist to hide us," Ailliard offers.

"You can't guarantee that the mist won't clear one day, and if we figured out how to navigate the mountains, so can someone else."

"You never were the patient type." I've been patient enough. "It's not that I don't support you, I simply want the best for you."

Only I can define what's best for me.

Right now, that's Vareveth.

"I'm tired of being a bystander in my own life," I admit as the tension eases between us. "Just because I outgrow something doesn't mean I love it any less. I love Aestilian, which is why I want to protect it. But I can't stay here forever, imagining what taking a chance on myself would have been like."

"I think I always knew this day would come, even if I didn't want to admit it to myself. You've always had this fire in you." Ailliard nods his head while stroking his beard. "It's why I taught you all the dances and protocol of court. There was always a *just in case* at the back of my mind."

"I do appreciate you teaching me all of those things." I offer him a small smile, and his shoulders loosen at the sight of it. It's normal for us to butt heads. He has a short fuse, and I light it on occasion.

"I never thought I would be going out into the world again." Ailliard participates in hunts and raids on occasion, but less so as the kingdom has grown.

"You don't have to come," I offer. "Finnian already said he'll accompany me, and Commander Veles is handpicking guards."

"I'm coming."

"What if you just ride to meet the battalion at the temple of the God of Earth?" Guilt from watching Ailliard visibly battle with his nerves makes me want to reach out to him, but I don't feel comfortable enough to do that.

"No," he states more definitively. "I brought you out of Imirath, and I'll be with you when you ride into Vareveth. I've watched you become the queen you are, and I'm not missing a moment more. Besides, you'll need more than Finnian to deal with the Vareveth advisors in the treaty negotiations. I've seen enough treaties to recognize hidden clauses."

I hadn't realized just how tight my shoulders were until they loosen. Ailliard has practically committed our ledgers to memory. I'll have to focus on the heist, which means spending more time with Cayden and less with King Eagor. It's good that Finnian won't be alone if I can't attend a meeting with him. He can handle himself, but I'd prefer him to have backup. This is new territory for Finnian and me, but Ailliard knows what it's like to be in a castle and deal with court politics.

"I won't lie; I'm relieved you're coming," I confess.

The wrinkles around his eyes deepen as he smiles. "You'll be even more relieved to know I acquired some fabric this morning and handed it off to the tailor."

"Really?" I shoot up from the chair, causing Ailliard to chuckle. I adore the way gowns flow and make me feel a different kind of power. Putting on a new, perfectly fitting dress feels like a breath of fresh air or the beginning of a new season.

"I only gave her enough fabric for one, but I've set aside some money for you and Finnian to shop when we get to Vareveth."

"What about you?" I inquire, my excitement halting for a moment. He waves his hand through the air while getting to his feet.

"You deserve to indulge, my dear." He outstretches his arms, and I walk into them. There are some moments where I would find more comfort in kind parting words than someone wrapping their arms around me.

"Thank you again." I've never had a royal wardrobe. I envision the gems, embroidery, and vibrant shades of fabric it entails.

"She still has your measurements, but stop by her shop tomorrow morning to make sure everything is to your liking," he says while walking toward the road. "I'm going to grab a pint to cope with time passing too quickly."

CHAPTER
EIGHT

POTS AND DISHES CLANG TOGETHER AS NYRINN TRIES TO find the serving dish she insists we use. The past four days have been a whirlwind of packing, organizing a group to escort me to the temple, and drafting a raid schedule and ration plan to ensure everyone will have enough food for the next few months. Part of me was too scared to dream that a day like this would come. It's an odd thing to fear, but they have power. Dreams can guide us out of our darkest moments, offering nothing more than the comfort of hope, but they also have the ability to break us.

Nyrinn caught me walking home last night and insisted I join her for breakfast. She's always so busy with healing people that I only planned on stopping by, but she pushed back the opening of her shop today. It's nice to spend time with her without blood smeared on our foreheads and up our arms. She taught me everything I know about healing and gave me helpful gardening tips when she could.

She and I painted her shutters bright yellow to frame her window beds, and the scent of lavender and chamomile lingers in the breeze whenever you pass. My favorite part is the several bouquets of dried herbs and flowers that hang from her ceiling. It creates the aura of an enchanted forest, like I'll catch a fairy flying between the petals.

Nyrinn flicks her short raven braid over her shoulder while setting a tray of pears and berries on the table, and a sweet scent mixes with rosemary. That and yarrow are the two herbs we use most, and the smell usually lingers on my hands for days, not that I mind.

"I don't know what I'll do without you here." She sighs while popping a berry in her mouth.

"You know I feel guilty." She doesn't accept anyone's assistance other than mine, and it fills up quickly in here most days.

"I'm teasing, but I imagine several others are succeeding in their attempts to make you feel that way." She looks me over with calculating eyes, and the pear juice turns sour in my mouth. "Idiots, the lot of them." One of the reasons I love talking to her is that she's unapologetic with her opinions and never fails to supply them.

"I think everyone got comfortable with the idea of me staying here forever," I say, not disagreeing with her.

"That's their own fault. You never chose to come here, but it's your choice to leave. I look forward to hearing of you making waves in the world." News of the alliance spread through Aestilian faster than a plague. Most people were excited about the guaranteed food supply, but I also caught a lingering sense of fear. The queen of Aestilian must leave Aestilian to keep it safe, it doesn't make sense, yet that's how it is.

"Who was it you met in the forest?" Nyrinn asks. "I've only heard bits and pieces."

My throat tightens at the mention of him. "The Commander of Vareveth, Cayden Veles." I take a sip of tea to relax. "Have you heard anything about him?"

"Not much." She purses her lips, emphasizing her Cupid's bow. Nyrinn is the best person to ask about any information I don't have. She comes off as harsh to some but transforms into something entirely different while healing. "We don't get many people from Vareveth, as you know. Most come from villages in the forests, Feynadra, or Urasos." She frowns while naming the last kingdom.

Magic is outlawed in some realms, including Vareveth once King Eagor ascended the throne upon the death of his mother. Some people think it invokes the gods' wrath if you use it by pretending to be a god. Nyrinn never used magic while healing, but that didn't matter. She was just too skilled for her village to believe otherwise. Even her former intended didn't say anything when they banished her. He went along with everyone else.

She told me his name when she was deep in her cups one night but made me swear not to hurt him. I didn't. But I did go to his house, stole several valuables, and traded them for new healing supplies and clothes for Nyrinn since she left all her supplies and clothes behind.

"It's fine; I was only curious," I say.

Recollection clears her features, and anticipation slides through me. "When I was stitching someone's head about a year ago, they were quite talkative. I kept inquiring for more information since I know it helps you. They said Commander Veles is . . . cold, ruthless, and reserved. He seems like the person whose bad side is the last place you want to be."

"Hm," I muse while drumming my fingers on the table. Those aren't the first words I would use to describe him: arrogant, cunning, *handsome*. Thank the gods the mug is back on the table, or else I would have spilled it. I want to smack myself when the last word flashes into my mind.

"Let's finish this outside." She doesn't wait for me to rise before slipping out the back door and is already stretched out on a chair with her golden-brown face upturned to the sun when I follow. The steady rush of the Syssa Falls draws my eyes to where I spend most of my summer mornings.

Finnian and I taught ourselves to swim by trial and error in that lake. One of us got in the water while the other stayed on dry land and held the rope tied around the swimmer's torso. If we went under too long, the person on land would use the rope to drag the swimmer to shore. Foolproof. It got the job done despite a few cases of severe rope burn.

"Don't trust their healers or court physicians," Nyrinn remarks while I sink onto a cushioned chair beside her. "I trained you better than any of them."

I laugh softly. "Do you honestly think I would let any of them give me a tonic? I don't even ask you."

"Fair point." She taps a finger against her cheek. "I wonder when you'll stop feeling guilty asking for things."

"When I stop having to ask for things."

She bends forward and reaches under her chair. "Good thing you didn't have to ask for *this*, then."

She tosses a dark leather satchel into my lap. My hands pause in the air, and I blink down at it. "I didn't get you anything."

"I didn't want you to. Go on, open it," she presses.

I run my fingers against the supple material, unlacing the string around the button and flipping the flap open. My jaw drops when I note several bundles of fresh herbs, even more dried herbs, new bandages, stitching needles, string, disinfectant, tonics, and salves. A strong sense of appreciation and gratitude weaves inside me, and her snort breaks me out of my shocked state.

"Nyrinn, how did you get all this? You should keep it."

"Absolutely not." She reaches her hand over and closes it around mine. "I called in a favor with one of the guards. They went out and got it for me two days ago." I can't restrain the broad smile that spreads across my face, but it falls slightly when I realize how much I'll miss her. I would take her with me if she wanted to leave Aestilian, but she has told me before that her shop gives her a sense of pride that nothing else could.

"Which guard?" I ask.

"They're all in my debt." The corner of her mouth tilts up, looking like a spider watching flies getting tangled in her web. "You should be calling in favors, too. They can be such babies when getting stitched up."

"Maybe I'll start when I get back." There's no missing the way her smile and eyes dull at my words.

She presses her lips together, suddenly looking serious. "Remember what I said about not trusting their healers. You know more than them."

I smooth my palms over my thighs. "I don't think I'll find trust in Vareveth."

She huffs. "That's a good mentality to have; keep it. I imagine all courts are the same—they smile at your face and stab you in the back."

"Well, at least I have new bandages." I knock my knee into hers, but her eyes have a glossy sheen when I look back at her face. "What's wrong?"

"You'll take care of yourself, right? The world"—she clears her throat—"it's not a kind place."

"I will, I always do," I assure her.

She blinks, and her vulnerability disappears just as quickly as it came. "No, you stick out your neck for everyone else and say you're fine until you're bleeding puddles on my floor—puddles I've had to cover with rugs."

"I'll be far away from your pretty floors." She reaches over and smacks the back of my head.

"I didn't train you just for you to bleed out in some foreign kingdom," she declares while getting to her feet. "You'll be departing soon."

I follow her inside and take one last look around to soak in the chipped paint, the tonics in glass vials on top of the fireplace, and the half-finished cups of tea. She halts her footsteps by the front door and slowly turns to face me.

"Never let anyone make you feel guilty for letting yourself choose how you want to live your life"—she blinks rapidly—"and give those bastards the hell they deserve." She reaches behind her to open the door, and I squeeze her hand, offering as much comfort as possible.

"I will." She vigorously wipes tears away from her cheeks, hardening her features again with much more effort than earlier. "For both of us," I promise.

The door shuts behind me, but I keep my eyes focused ahead. I don't want to see any more afflicted faces. If I look at them, I'll want to try to fix them. I'm sure everyone will be much happier when they see a cart filled with food rolling into Aestilian, and I keep that image burning in my mind as I enter my house. I don't think of anything else while packing my trunk. I only remove my satchel when it's time to arm myself.

I glance around my room, and a knot forms in my throat while I take in the horrendous flowers, rivers, moon, and stars I painted when I was bored. My eyes dance toward my reading chair and book wall with slightly fewer stacks because some stories are undoubtedly essential. My knuckles graze over the handles of my silver knives that line my thighs and waist, which always comfort me.

"You ready?" Finnian asks in a thick voice behind me. Inhaling a hard breath and lifting my chin, I turn to face him. He's wearing black leathers, a bow strapped across his chest, and a sword at his waist. His eyes are misty but filled with resolve.

"Always," I reply, shutting the door to my room. "You?"

"Absolutely," he answers.

I take in all the details of our home while making my way to the door. Our height chart, the playing cards on the coffee table, and the various blankets we covered ourselves in when we stayed awake all night. Beside each other on the wall hang the first knife I ever threw and the first arrow Finnian ever fired that hit the center of a target.

Turning away from everything, I whip the front door open and am greeted by cheers. The people of Aestilian line the road, clapping and hollering. Some even wave from the upper windows of shops along the main road. A drum sounds in the distance, and my heart beats in tandem with the loud booms. Finnian holds his arm out to me, and I loop mine through his.

He leans down to speak over the cheers, voice wavering in emotion. "You were the first face I saw when I woke up in Aestilian; let me be the last face you see before you leave."

The knot in my throat grows tighter when I remember Finnian first coming here. Ailliard rescued him after a clan dispute in his village led to a burned-down home and family that joined the ashes. He was little more than lanky limbs at the age of ten and fainted within minutes of arriving. He became my first friend after I stayed with him while he healed, but at age eleven I didn't possess skills aside from dabbing water onto his forehead. My home isn't the place we stand in front of; my home is standing beside me with his arm looped through mine.

"Together." I give his bicep a loving squeeze before he guides us through the center of the crowd.

For once in my life, I know I'm doing exactly what I need to do. I'm going exactly where I need to go. I can feel it in my soul. The wicked parts of me are not easily suppressed, and my blades call for payment in blood. Every corner of the world will say the lost princess has returned as a vengeful queen, and they won't be wrong. But I'm not only doing this for me. I'm doing this for the people who had their worth stripped away. The people who have only received hatred at the hand of someone who should have loved them. The people who have been shoved into darkness and clawed their way out with the sheer willpower to survive. Imirath wants me dead, but I still stand. Only now, I stand with knives drawn and a crown on my head.

I wave to my people, reaching my hand out to anyone I pass, and brand this memory into my brain. I keep my hand tight on Finnian's arm until we pass through the crowd. A few tears slip from my eyes when I mount my horse, but I wipe them away before anyone can see. My horse leads me into the mist, and I don't look back to Aestilian as the cheers fade behind me.

CHAPTER

NINE

―――――

A TWIG SNAPS, AND I JOLT AWAKE, KNIFE IN HAND. Finnian is beside me with an arrow nocked in his bow. Both of us immediately prepare for the threat, but my body sags and my hand falls in my lap as soon as my vision clears, registering the sight of Ailliard standing in front of us with his palms raised.

"Knock next time," Finnian grumbles before falling onto his back again. He drags me down with him, and the back of my head lands on his chest. It's where I spent the night. I jolted awake every time I dozed off, thinking bugs were crawling in my hair, ears, nose, and mouth. Eventually, he got tired of watching me flop around like a fish out of water and told me to lie on him.

"We're outside, Finnian," Ailliard points out.

"Knock on a tree," I suggest while rubbing the ache in my neck. Why am I constantly aching?

Ailliard cuts me a look that translates to *Really? Could you not join in for once?* "I was just coming to inform the both of you that we need to leave soon. Didn't realize you'd wake up ready to murder."

"That's our morning routine," Finnian says, his voice still thick with sleep.

"Wake up, coffee, stab someone, brush teeth," I add.

"Adorable." Ailliard turns on his heels to rejoin the group.

Finnian's groan vibrates the back of my head. "We don't have coffee."

"Maybe we could just die; at least then we'd be able to sleep," I grumble.

"That sounds more inviting than it should."

I slowly sit up again, squinting into the sunlight that bathes the forest. The sun is my enemy. I almost swat the rays poking between the trees before retracting my hands—no need to look as disturbed as I feel.

We left Aestilian under cover of darkness, taking an extra step to ensure it stays hidden. It's practically a death sentence to travel through the Terrwyn if you don't have your wits about you, especially at night. Fatigue weighed on everyone and after Jarek almost fell off his horse, we decided rest was the most sensible option. I'd hoped Ailliard would have brought one of the guards who helped me escape Imirath, but they're already taking on responsibilities in our absence. With the tasks divided up, it wasn't worth the risk.

The guards he selected are our best, but I take every opportunity to avoid Jarek. He's the type of person to tell you that you're wrong when you inform him of a mistake he made. With his wavy shoulder-length dark blond hair, gray eyes, and broad shoulders, he loves wielding his looks, not that they've ever worked on me. His personality probably made me immune. Dusting the dirt from my pants and re-doing my braid, I move to rejoin the group.

My skin prickles with surprise when the sharp sound of a shooting arrow infiltrates my senses. I drop to a squat, unsheathing two daggers as the arrow flies over my head.

"Attack!" a voice shouts behind a large boulder.

War cries fill the air, and at least thirty clan members hop over the rocks. The blood that stains their raggedy clothing hints toward them being one of the more violent clans. Wonderful. Who needs caffeine when someone is so graciously trying to kill you moments after waking up?

"Shoot straight," I say to Finnian.

"Throw true," he replies, finishing off our signature pre-battle exchange.

My guards rush to my side but don't bother getting in front of me. My pulse pounds in my ears, and my chest feels tight with the anticipation of battle. I whirl my knives in their direction while Finnian fires arrows, both of us charging side by side. We've taken down four before our groups clash.

I don't have the advantage of size, but I have the benefit of my mind. I've taken down people larger than me by timing my moves, scanning my opponent's footwork, and anticipating their moves before they make them.

The woman I'm charging raises her axe high, but I drop down, sliding in the leaves, and shove my knee into her shin. She falls forward, unable to protect her neck from my knife. Her warm blood coats my hand while I stand, readying myself for my next target. I unsheathe the sword at my hip and smirk when his eyes flash toward my blood-covered hand.

This is the kind of clan that killed Finnian's family. They travel through the Terrwyn and Sweven, burning villages in service to the gods, thinking the gods will find them superior if they kill the people that settled on godly land. No ruler can claim the reserved land, it's forbidden, and it's believed a curse will befall your bloodline if it's seized. Ordinary god-fearing citizens can make homes, but it can never be added to a kingdom. Aestilian is located on godly land, but I'm not above killing a god should they ever rejoin humanity and I do not fear their curses.

A cocky smile stretches across the man's cracked lips—so many have worn the same smile before taking their last breaths in my presence. The only thing I love about being underestimated is always proving people wrong.

"I don't want to hurt you, pretty." He licks his lips. "Why don't you put the sword down?"

I laugh and watch his cocky smile melt away. "Killing you is the only pleasure I'll take from you."

I block the first swipe of his sword; the metal clashes and vibrates my fingers. His eyes move before his sword does. Ramming my sword into his and knocking it to the side, I shoot my fist forward and pound it into his nose. If the skirmish weren't raging around us, I would have heard the crunch of bone. He flinches back, crimson blood leaking from his nostrils. He's unable to stop the tears that fall from his eyes.

"My gods don't like violent women." He spits blood in my direction, but it falls short of my boots.

"Well, they sound quite boring." He rushes forward in anger without anticipating how slippery his blood made the handle of his sword. I knock the weapon free from his hand and shove mine deep into his gut. "My blade is my god, and you can tell them I said that."

He crumples to the ground when I pull it free, and an ear-piercing shriek sounds through the area, followed by water splashing. Ten purple tentacles with venomous spikes shoot out of the small pond where our horses were drinking.

A vextree.

I've only heard of them but never encountered one.

The monster's long, sluglike body springs to the shore. Another high-pitched shriek emanates from its circular mouth—its entire face opens to display rows upon rows of teeth that travel far into its throat. The battle continues, but everyone constantly looks over their shoulder, waiting to see if the monster will move farther than the shoreline. Time stops when I see a flash of orange from the corner of my eye. A sharp stabbing sensation twists my gut as I realize it's Finnian being dragged across the ground by a tentacle wrapped around his calf.

"Finnian!" I shout, hating the helplessness that worms through me. So many people separate us, and I'm too far to throw knives. "FINNIAN!" I charge forward without a second thought.

I'm so caught up in my emotions that I don't notice the person rushing at me from the side. My feet pivot in their direction, and I attempt to raise my sword in time to block them, but I'm too late. They got the upper hand while my eyes were on Finnian. I brace myself for the impact, but it never comes because an arrow shoots from behind me, flying so close to my head that I'm certain the feathers brush against my ear. It sinks right between their eyes, cutting so deep into their skull that the arrow makes it halfway through before they fall to the ground.

Who was that? Only Finnian's aim is that good.

I turn in place, giving a slow, disbelieving shake of my head. My eyes blink rapidly, but the vision is real. Cayden Veles sits on top of his horse looking every inch the feared Commander of Vareveth the world knows him to be. Empty bow hanging in the air, his hand still drawn back from the arrow he fired *for me*. His eyes meet mine across the battlefield, blazing in anger. He shouts orders to his soldiers while charging forward, swinging his sword and never taking his eyes off me. Spinning on my heels, I rush toward the edge of the pond. Finnian fires arrows while the vextree continues to drag him toward the water.

"Elowen, stop!" Cayden shouts, but I keep pushing forward. There are too many people between us for him to catch up, and there's no way I'll let someone stand between Finnian and me.

"No!" I scream when the monster shoves Finnian under the surface. My fingers twist around the hilt of my knife while I push myself to move faster. A growl rattles in my chest when I reach the pond's edge, kick off the rocks along the shore, and sail through the air. The vextree notices me too late. I jam my knife into its throat, dragging it down as I slide toward the water. Thick black blood pours from the deep slit, burning my hands, but I keep going. Bringing my sword forward, I stab its belly, twisting and turning. I use it to hold myself up while I thrust my knife over and over again. Arrows fly into the monster's head and eyes now that I'm halfway down its body.

With one final mountain-shaking cry, the monster collapses into the water. I take my blades out and push off the front of the beast, falling into the murky water below. My boots fill with water as soon as the pond closes over me, but I kick off the pond floor and walk along the bottom until I breach the shore, sword and knife still in my burning hands.

The battle is on the cusp of finishing. Bodies litter the forest floor, but I zone in on pale fingers clawing their way through the thick mud.

Finnian is propelling himself forward with his head tilted to the side. I drop my weapons and sprint toward him.

No. No. No. No.

"Finnian!" I flip him onto his back. His eyes are glossy and fade in and out as he fights to stay awake. I shove my hands under his arms and drag him away from the pond. "Don't you dare shut your eyes!" I shriek. Fucking gods, my hands slip from his underarms. His soaked clothes make him heavier than usual. I lunge for him again, but an arm wraps around my waist, hauling me away. Another feral growl rumbles inside me, and I thrash against the hold. My captor groans when I elbow them hard enough that they can feel it through their armor.

"He's with me," Cayden says while coming into view, tucking his hands into Finnian's armpits and moving him farther up the shore with ease. I cease the punch I was about to deliver to the man's groin, and this time, he lets me out of his hold.

"I'll be right back." Without giving Cayden or the man a chance to protest, I sprint toward my horse and grab the satchel from my saddlebag. I feel Cayden's eyes on me but don't look anywhere other than Finnian as my knees sink into the mud beside him. A venomous spike juts out from his shin, and the skin around it bubbles and blisters as the venom seeps into him. I swallow the bile that shoots up my throat and cut off the pants below his knee.

"What do you need us to do?" Cayden asks.

"Hold him down." I plead with my eyes while reaching into my satchel, pulling out a tonic to stop the venom and a fresh roll of bandages.

"Ryder will hold his shoulders, and I'll take his ankles."

"Ellie." He weakly groans the childhood nickname he gave me. His blue eyes have a thick film over them, and I know he's fighting against the venom.

"Yes, it's me. I'm right here. I'm going to take care of you, Finny." I blink back my tears; now isn't the time to lose it. I place the leather strap of the satchel between his teeth. "Bite down whenever you need to."

Facing the wound again, I pull the spike from his leg. He thrashes against Cayden and Ryder's hold, but they keep him pinned to the ground with their combined strength. Placing my hands on the wound, I squeeze the venom from the hole left by the spike. Vextree venom clumps under the skin and moves toward the heart, so it's important to remove it before it can slip away from the surface and mobilize.

After squeezing a substantial amount from his leg, I sprinkle a few droplets of the tonic on his wound. Cayden tightens his hold so I can apply it more accurately. My lips press together to suppress the whimper threatening to escape when Finnian's pained screams meet my ears. He bites down on the leather, but it does little to muffle the proof of his suffering. I sneak a glance at his face, and a sob breaks free while I watch his head helplessly thrash side to side, teeth bared around the leather, while tears leave trails on his mud-splattered cheeks.

"I'm so sorry," I whisper.

"Look at me," Cayden states beside me, but I can't. I can't take my eyes off Finnian. I've bandaged him countless times, but he's never gotten this hurt. He's never had to be pinned down. I've never made him wail in agony. "Elowen, look at me." My eyes involuntarily meet his unnervingly emerald gaze, and our faces are inches apart once again. "You must continue. He can sleep off the pain when we return to the ruins, he's going to be fine."

"Okay." I nod, still in a trance, and grab a roll of bandages. "Okay," I repeat more definitively while wrapping the wound. The tonic must be working because he's already dozing off. Once the bandage is tied off, I place my hands flat against the mud. The cool texture feels good on my burned skin. My hands are covered in Finnian's blood, so I can't assess the damage yet, not that it makes a difference. The only thing I'm focusing on is taking several measured breaths to still my nerves.

"Thank you," I finally manage to say, lifting my head and meeting Cayden's stare. I swallow through my tight throat and face the person who was holding Finnian's shoulders. "Thank you both for doing that. I wouldn't have been able to hold him down."

"Yes, I'm quite relieved your lover is healed," Cayden dryly states.

The idea of Finnian and I together in that way is both laughable and disgusting. "I'd be lost without our passionate lovemaking."

A muscle in Cayden's jaw ticks. "Spare me the details, princess."

"You mean my scandalous relationship with the man I consider to be my brother and has never laid a hand on me in the past fourteen years? Yes, those details can get raunchy." Cayden clears his throat, and the man that held Finnian's shoulders roars with deep laughter. It's so contagious I find myself sharing in it. "I didn't know demons could experience emotions, but you look quite unsettled."

"I don't care enough to be unsettled."

"Jealous it is, then."

Cayden narrows his eyes. "Elowen, may I present my First General, Ryder Neredras."

My eyes scan over his features: dark umber skin, obsidian eyes, tight black, coiling curls cut close to his head, prominent cheekbones, and a wide nose. By the gods, is everyone in Vareveth good-looking? Is that a stipulation before you can gain entry?

Ryder stretches a hand toward me and lets it hover in the air between us. I reach for it but pause before I make contact with his skin, jerking back. "I'll take that handshake after I wash my hands."

"Deal."

"Also, I apologize for elbowing you in the stomach and for almost punching you . . . in your . . . you know." I trail off, feeling incredibly awkward. I would probably rub the back of my neck or fiddle with my necklace if my hands weren't filthy.

He breaks into a smile again, and my lips mimic his. "I can appreciate a good punch."

"You never apologized for punching me," Cayden remarks with a smirk. "In multiple places, on multiple occasions."

"That's because you deserved them." I smile sweetly.

"Oh yes, she's exactly how you described," Ryder comments. I don't miss the daggers Cayden's eyes shoot in his direction. The general raises his hands in surrender while getting to his feet.

Eager to change the subject to stop the burning in my cheeks that rivals my hands, I ask, "Why were you riding so close to here?"

"Hunting for food," Cayden replies. "Hopefully some other patrol was more successful, unless you're in the mood for vextree."

I grimace, causing the pair to chuckle. The battle has ceased around us, and everyone is regrouping. We should head out soon before someone or something is attracted to the scent of blood that lingers.

"I'm going to wash my hands," I say while walking away from our small group. The pair of them hoist Finnian and wrap an arm around each of their broad shoulders. It's a good thing they're all around the same height with Cayden being the tallest and Ryder being the shortest though by no means small.

I find a section of the pond that the vextree blood hasn't contaminated and bend down to wash my hands. The water increases the pain, but it'll only worsen if I don't clean the burns. I feel a set of eyes on my back the entire time, but nobody is looking at me when I turn around.

Ailliard jogs over, assessing me with his eyes to ensure I'm all right. I hide my hands behind my back; he doesn't need to worry over some irritated skin. "Those are the Vareveth soldiers we're supposed to be meeting?"

"Commander Veles and First General Neredras are helping Finnian to the horses. I haven't met any of the others yet."

"I'm glad Finnian will be all right, but you must be smarter about your decisions. You charged a fully grown vextree."

"I'm fully aware of what I did." I would have taken on an entire army of vextrees if they had Finnian. "Were any of the guards hurt?"

"Not fatally, but they could use your assistance."

I'm relieved to hear nobody died in the ambush. "We should send them home from here once I finish healing them. There's no sense in adding more time to their journey."

CHAPTER
TEN

It's dusk by the time we make it to the temple ruins, but bandaging my soldiers and bathing in a freezing river to get the grimy pond water off me took longer than expected. Jarek, the only Aestilian guard still with us, volunteered to ride with Finnian, which I'm sure he'll be *thrilled* about. He's still unconscious, and I'm not strong enough to keep him upright on a moving horse. Ailliard knows the mountains as well as I do, so he led the ride while Cayden and Ryder flanked me. Jarek will return home tomorrow morning when we begin the journey to Vareveth.

The ruins are just as I remember them. Pillars stretch high into the orange sky, but the roof caved in years ago, long before I was born. Some of it remains, creating an uneven border around the top of the temple. I slide off my horse and stretch my sore muscles. Cayden strides over to Jarek to help him get Finnian up the steps.

"He's quite light," Jarek says as he hooks Finnian's arm over his shoulder, and his tone makes me believe he's poking fun at Cayden and Ryder for sharing the load earlier.

Cayden slowly drags his eyes over Jarek, looking entirely unimpressed. "Agreed." He steps forward and hoists Finnian over his shoulder like he weighs little more than air. I raise a glove-covered hand to my mouth to stifle a giggle, but Ryder catches me and makes no effort to hide his, making Jarek turn red.

I grab Finnian's bedroll from the trunk strapped to the back of his horse and hurry after them with Jarek on my heels. Cayden strides through the temple, past a fire where several soldiers gather. I smile at anyone I pass, but my main concern is getting Finnian situated and signing the agreement papers.

"Here," Cayden says, halting in place. I lay out the bedroll and let him gently place Finnian on top of it. I lean down and dust some dirt off his cheeks. He's breathing evenly. The knot loosens in my chest at the proof of his body recovering. I'll change the bandages in a few hours in case any remaining venom leaks from the wound.

"Thank you, Jarek. You're dismissed," I state.

"Your Majesty." He bows before turning to find Ailliard.

I stand again and ask, "Are you surprised I kept my word?"

His scowl melts and his shoulders relax. "I would've hunted you down if you didn't."

"I won't deny that the thought of you appearing in Aestilian to beg isn't unwelcome." I tap my finger against my lips, and his eyes follow the movement. "Perhaps I shouldn't have come."

Mischief dances in his eyes as he takes a step closer, causing me to tilt my chin up. "My sweet affliction, I regret to inform you I don't beg."

Tension pumps into the air and tingles my palms, but I don't turn away. I refuse to be one of the many intimidated by him. "We'll see about that, soldier."

He arches a full, dark brow. "Will we, princess?"

Someone clears their throat beside us. "My apologies for the intrusion. Ailliard is reading over the agreement now, so if you'd like to follow me there or . . ." Ryder's voice trails off.

The heat between us cools as we follow Ryder to the other side of the temple. Ailliard stands behind a chunk of white stone that most likely belonged to the ceiling, and he looks up from the contract as I approach, confirming its acceptability with a subtle nod.

Cayden and I take his place, and I glance over the wording quickly, surprised it's the exact vows we stated in the forest without any alterations or embellished phrasing. He moves first, twirling the quill in his fingers before signing his name at the bottom of the page. My fingers tingle when they brush his, but I blame that on the venom burns beneath my gloves.

"I suppose it's time to find out how honorable your intentions are." I sign my name beneath his, and everyone around us claps as I place the quill back on the stone slab.

"Believe me, Elowen," he begins, drawing my attention away from the crowd, "my intentions are never honorable."

His strides away from me, and Ailliard steps forward with pride-laced eyes. "You should eat something."

"I didn't bring any food from home," I confess. I gave whatever I had to Nyrinn and the orphanage before I left.

"They're cooking deer. General Neredras informed me other patrols were successful this morning." I've been so preoccupied with everything else that my brain didn't register the scent of roasting meat. It makes my mouth water. "Come along."

I sit between Ailliard and Jarek on a log while one of Cayden's soldiers comes over to hand me some food, which I gratefully take. It's a tough piece of meat, but it's edible. The man seems kind; he tells me he'll set some aside for Finnian whenever he wakes up.

Jarek's thigh brushes against mine, making me jump slightly. The hair on the back of my neck stands up when I feel a set of eyes on me again. My gaze dances over the soldiers surrounding me, but everyone seems preoccupied with their dinner or talking to one another. A few people glance my way, but it's nothing noteworthy. I expect curious glances. It's not every day a princess essentially rises from the dead.

"I'm going to check on Finnian," I say.

"Would you like me to accompany you, my lady?" Jarek asks.

The last place I want to be is in a dark corner with him. "I'm fine, thank you."

Crouching beside Finnian again, I unravel the bandage around his leg and toss it to the side. The tonic is helping, but he'll need another round before I rewrap the wound. I get to my feet, sticking to the perimeter of the temple. The pieces of fallen ceiling make it easy to walk unnoticed. Technically I don't have to hide anymore, but I'm not in the mood to talk to anyone.

I don't even descend one step before hearing *him*. "Sneaking off again, little shadow?"

"Oh gods." I raise my hand to lightly smack my forehead while turning in place. "My apologies for not informing you of my plans to run away."

Cayden steps out of the darkness and cuts the distance between us. "Run if you wish, it'll provide me with some entertainment."

I roll my eyes. "Do I need traveling papers to retrieve my healing supplies?"

"The two of you are going to be an absolute pleasure to work with. I'll get it," Ryder grumbles before bounding down the steps.

The silence is heavy in his wake. Usually, I enjoy silence. I hate forcing conversations, but this unsettling energy between us makes me jumpy. Every second that ticks by feels like a minute. It feels like an hour has passed by the time Ryder gets back.

"Thank you." I take the satchel from him and sling the strap over my shoulder. He gives me a curt nod in response and sticks his hand out for the handshake I promised him. A searing pain shoots through me when his fingers close over mine. I yelp and jerk back. His obsidian eyes widen, and his brows draw together. Cayden spins me toward him, ripping one of my gloves off to reveal my red, blistering skin.

"You're injured," he growls through gritted teeth, emerald eyes blazing.

"It's just a few burns." I try to step away, but his hand stays firm on my elbow. "There's no need to worry."

"You're a healer and didn't think to bandage yourself? Is that why you've been wearing gloves this entire time?" He keeps his tone low. Nobody aside from Ryder can hear us, but his frustration is evident. Using his other hand, he removes my second glove to reveal equally mangled skin.

Make better decisions, Elowen. Ailliard's voice echoes in my mind, increasing my frustration. "I had my reasons."

"I'm sure," he scoffs.

"My injuries aren't fatal, and the gloves will keep the wounds clean." I yank myself out of his hold and take a step back. Truthfully, I don't want to waste medicine when I know my wounds will heal in time. The scowl still mars his face as his gaze travels over me. "Stop looking at me like that."

"Like what?"

"Like you're trying to figure me out."

I expect him to smirk or give a snide comment, but he doesn't. He stares at me a beat longer before turning toward Ryder and asks, "Can you bring me the medical bag?"

"I can use my medicine if the burns worsen," I say, hating how he can see right through me.

"No." Cayden shakes his head. "I shouldn't have spoken to you in that way. Besides, it's hard to heal your own hands."

I wonder if he's speaking from experience. Given his position, he most likely is. The pinch of sadness in my chest propels me forward, and I sit at the edge of the temple, dangling my feet over the side.

Cayden takes a seat beside me after Ryder gives him the supplies. He sits close, one leg over the edge and the other behind me. Reaching forward, he gently takes my wrists and places my hands on his thigh. Water burns my skin a few seconds later, and I intake a sharp breath while squeezing my eyes shut.

"I suppose I don't measure up to your healing skills," he lightly teases.

I huff out a strained laugh. "It's raw skin. Everything is going to hurt."

His frown deepens while he uncaps a tin of salve, dipping his fingers and coating them in a generous amount. My wrist tingles when he wraps his hand around it, rubbing soothing circles while gently spreading the salve. It burns initially, but the longer he rubs it in, the nicer it feels. He seems pleased when my shoulders loosen, his eyes tracking my reaction.

"What's our first step for the heist?" I ask, needing something to fill the silence.

"Kallistar."

"The Imirath prison surrounded by the sea?" I shake my head. "It's impregnable. It's said only one person has managed to pull it off *ever*."

"Improbability is a crutch used by those without the skills to navigate a challenge." He smirks. "Exactly how much information have you acquired through spying?"

"Not enough to tell me what we need from Kallistar."

"The key to the dragon chamber." My heart skips a beat, and I'm grateful he's done so much research before finding me. My response dies in my throat as he ties off the bandage, and his hard eyes glare down at the small pink scars on my wrists from where the shackles split my skin all those years ago. I hardly remember them anymore, but I force myself to look away as he begins working on my other hand. "We'll leave shortly after arriving in Vareveth."

I nod. I'll do anything for my dragons, including going back to the kingdom that haunts me. Each step I take is terrifying, but I won't relent. I try to pull my wrist out of his grasp when my hand starts shaking, but he tightens his hold.

"Can you do me a favor?" he asks.

"What?" I ask, feeling uneasy.

"Don't lock me in a cell in Kallistar."

I blink in surprise, then toss my head back and laugh. He looks up and stares at my smile like it perplexes him, but eventually a small one slides onto his lips and deepens two dimples in his cheeks. "I make no promises."

He sighs. "Why do I have a feeling you're going to be the bane of my existence?"

"Because it's a title I'll happily take."

He rolls his eyes while reaching for another roll of bandages, but it's halfhearted. "You looked uncomfortable earlier."

I scrunch my brows. "What do you mean?"

"By the fire." He looks up after tying it off, but absentmindedly continues rubbing circles on my wrist with his calloused fingers, warming my skin under his touch. I'm thankful the sky is dark because he would see my heated cheeks if it weren't. "You jumped."

So it was his eyes I felt on me. I wonder how long he was watching me. I mean, he is guarding me, so I suppose it's important he keeps an eye out. But I was surrounded by *his* soldiers. He should have known I was safe.

"It's just nerves," I mutter. It's not hard to believe, and it's not a total lie. There are no regrets about leaving Aestilian, but that doesn't mean I'll embrace the world with open arms.

"Right," he says, not sounding entirely convinced. His jaw clenches, and his eyes get that assessing gleam that they had before he started bandaging me. Each stroke of his thumb winds me so tight, to the point I feel like I'm going to combust. He clears his throat, dropping my hand. "I should get back to my post."

"Right," I say in a rush, practically jumping away from him and getting to my feet. "I should check on Finnian—thank you again for helping me with him today and for the bandages."

"No problem." He looks utterly unaffected.

I turn away but only take a few steps before spinning on my heels as he gets to his feet. "Do you want me to take a watch shift at some point?"

"No, go rest and watch Finnian." He strides toward me, and my hands tighten on my satchel. "Good night, angel," he says before bounding down the steps.

"Good night, demon," I whisper into the darkness after he's long gone.

CHAPTER
ELEVEN

T HE BRIEF TRUCE BETWEEN CAYDEN AND ME DISSOLVED quickly over the past four days. Between traveling, there has been endless bickering, which usually leaves one of us red-faced and the other smirking. At one point, I chased him with a knife before Finnian threw me over his shoulder and carried me away. I don't remember what prompted the knife chase, but it was fun. Cathartic. It's not like I could truthfully do anything with the blade.

Citizens of Vareveth saw our party getting closer to the capital, Verendus, and word must've traveled quickly because I can already hear the cheers of people crying out for their commander and the lost princess. My shaking hands tie off the flower crown made of bell-shaped purple starsnaps and some added greenery I've been working on. I don't want to dig through my trunks for my crown, but I also don't want a bare head for my first appearance post-exile. I wasn't planning on a grand entrance after traveling for almost a week.

Finnian watches me with narrowed eyes. "You sure you're okay with this?"

"Yes." I give him the same short answer I have the past five times he has asked that question. I'm not fine, I'm far from fine, but I must be fine. The thought of being surrounded by people is more intimidating than I thought it would be. My inhales are sharp and shallow, my stomach churns, and my palms tingle. It's not that I've never been in front of a crowd before—I've addressed the citizens of Aestilian more times than I can count—but the thought of being surrounded by people I don't know, people who could very likely be there to kill me, is daunting.

"You don't have to lie to me. I know you well enough." Finnian kicks off the tree and takes a few steps in my direction but never reaches to touch me. He knows it won't calm me right now. I don't want to stand still. I want to keep pacing.

"Have you decided to forgive me?"

"Fine." He holds up his hands in surrender. "I forgive you for not telling me you made a deal with two of the best-looking men I have ever seen. Other than myself, of course." My laugh sounds breathless, more like a gasp. Finnian's humorous demeanor, which usually appears effortlessly, is strained. "You definitely could have wiped the drool off my face, though."

"I was a little more focused on getting the venom out of your leg," I retort. Finnian was never actually mad at me. I'm also glad I didn't tell him anything about Cayden or Ryder because the look on Finnian's face when he first saw them was priceless. I had to push his chin up to close his mouth.

"A noble diversion." His smile fades. "Are you ready to leave?"

I dryly swallow, surveying the space around us. We're separated from the rest of the group by a rocky hill. I didn't want anyone seeing me like this, but Finnian doesn't count. Cayden had to send a letter to King Eagor once we heard the cheering, so we're taking a temporary break. His darkened eyes and deep glare were the only signs of his irritation.

"Mm-hmm." I make it a few steps before it feels like a hand has closed over my throat. My palms moisten. I dig my nails into my skin, but nothing can control the flare of anxiety coursing through me, conquering me.

"Elowen." Finnian's concerned voice surrounds me. My fingers close around two hilts while I sink to my knees and place my fists on the cool surface of the rocky hill. Sweat breaks out against my skin, but I feel incredibly cold. Shivers rack up and down my spine, making my teeth chatter together. My breathing is ragged, and black dots fill my vision. I pull on the collar of my leathers, which suddenly feels too tight. "Fucking gods, Elowen, look at me." Finnian drops to his knees beside me, but I don't look at him; I can't.

"What's going on?" Ailliard's voice drifts closer, followed by the crunch of leaves. But I keep my eyes on my knives to ground myself and take deep breaths to calm my nerves.

"The fucking parade! Who throws a parade for someone who spent the last fifteen years in hiding?" Finnian's tone rises in anger. I drop a knife and reach out to him, silently telling him to keep his voice down.

"It's what she signed up for," Ailliard hisses. "Elowen, be stronger. You can do this."

"She is strong," Finnian growls. "She can be strong and have anxiety. She's not made of stone."

"Finnian, it's okay," I rasp, desperately needing water. The tingling sensation still lingers in my palms, along with light-headedness, but I want to end their argument before it gets worse. "It *is* what I signed up for." I mutter a curse, getting to my feet and wiping the sweat from my brow. My body still shakes as I walk out from behind the hill, Finnian and Ailliard in tow. The latter whispers in my ear that I'll be fine before jogging over to his horse.

"I can find a back entrance," Finnian offers, uncapping a canteen for me.

"I have to do this." I take in several gulps of water before speaking again, "I don't want to be scared of living."

Leaves crunch behind me, but I don't have to turn to know who it is. I wrap my shaking hands around my torso and face Cayden, trying to appear unrattled. Even though I know it won't work. I've realized he seldom believes I'm fine when I say I am.

"I sent a letter with your proper titles so that Eagor will announce you as both princess and queen," Cayden states. The kind gesture catches me off guard. "My soldiers are lining the perimeter of the parade, and all attendees have temporarily forfeited their weapons. Ryder and I will flank you—"

"I'll be on one side of her," Finnian cuts in.

Cayden continues after I nod. "Finnian and I will flank you the entire ride."

I nod again, turning away from him and raising myself onto my horse. Finnian walks away once I'm settled, but Cayden remains, looking like he wishes to say something more. "Yes?"

We're learning how to read each other, and I know it irks him just as much as it unsettles me. We're two people who don't like anyone digging too deep, but he's met his match. If he wants to push me, I'll push him right back. His tongue pokes into the side of his cheek, eyes drifting over me.

"Looks good on you." He jerks his chin toward my flower crown before turning away, leaving me stunned and irritated.

The ride to Verendus is short, and the cheering crowd soon envelops us. Cayden's soldiers line the parade just as he promised. My horse's hooves patter against the cobblestone street as I give an effortlessly fake smile to the citizens. Various colored petals rain down, engulfing us in a sea of red, pink, purple, and yellow. It's hard to make out anything besides the petals, but I note vines creeping up several buildings along the main road.

Finnian soaks in the attention and seems to be smiling genuinely. It doesn't shock me when I look to my other side and find Cayden giving his signature glare. He must feel me looking at him because he quickly turns his head, and a smirk grows in place of his scowl. The scent of butter, cinnamon, and chocolate travels out of several bakeries, making my mouth water. Pastries have a special place in my heart—alongside dragons, knives, flowers, and books.

The petals clear, and in front of me stands a castle far more beautiful than anything my mind could have concocted. It's made of gray stone and sits atop a rocky hill resembling a small mountain. Vine-covered spires stretch high into the sky, and a deep blue lake set on the left side spills into a forest sitting at the foot of snowcapped mountains. A gushing waterfall pours into a river at the base of the hill that stretches through Verendus, and a stone bridge with gold embellishments sprawls from the main entrance, leading to a tall staircase bordered with emerald banners embroidered with golden trees.

King Eagor and Queen Valia Dasterian descend the steps, stopping on one of the platforms between flights while waving to their citizens. They look exactly how all monarchs are supposed to look: regal, untouchable, and rich. Matching gold and white capes drift behind them, and emerald crowns sit on their blond heads. Valia's hair is platinum and curled to perfection, whereas Eagor's is sandy and pushed back, with no strand out of place.

The crowd silences when their king raises his hand. "It is with my greatest pleasure that we welcome the lost princess of Imirath, Elowen Atarah. The queen of Aestilian, a nation she forged herself. We are honored to ally with such a resilient woman." The crowd cheers once again, drowning out Eagor's voice. I turn away from the monarchs and face the crowd, waving at them. Finnian raises his fingers to his lips and blows a high-pitched whistle that changes my smile from forced to genuine.

As inviting as this welcome is, I know sometimes the most beautiful things can be the most dangerous. It may seem like I'm looking at a rosebush, but I'm fully aware of the thorns that threaten to pierce my skin if I get too close or the vipers that will bite my ankles if I'm distracted. Everyone knows how you handle a snake should it threaten you: You cut off the head.

CHAPTER
TWELVE

EAGOR AND VALIA RETURN TO THE CASTLE BEFORE I HAVE the chance to meet them, but Cayden informs me of a banquet happening tonight. We bound up the steep steps, and my legs wobble by the time we make it to the entryway. The castle is enchanting . . . truly, everywhere I turn looks like an enchanted forest. Vines create a canopy above an elaborate fountain fashioned after the tree on the Dasterian banner, and floor-to-ceiling windows illuminate the room, sunlight dancing in the jeweled chandelier.

A servant leads me through the halls and up a tower. Each room we pass is more magnificent than the last. It's odd to think that this would all be normal to me if I had been properly raised in Imirath. She pulls a key from her pocket to unlock a set of double doors bordered in gold. "This is your suite, my lady. Your private bathing chamber has various soaps and linens, and I'll return in an hour to help you prepare for the banquet unless you need my assistance washing up."

"No, thank you. I'll see you in an hour," I say. She curtsies and tucks a dark red curl from her face before turning away.

A small gasp leaves my lips when I enter. If I thought the entryway was beautiful . . . it's nothing compared to this. Three tall windows set behind a dining table fashioned from tree roots stretch toward the peaked ceiling and face the snowy mountains beyond the castle. The sitting room is filled with cream furniture with gold floral embroidery and dark wood that complements the stone walls and fireplace.

I step through a door on the left and enter my private chambers. Lanterns and vases filled with lilacs border a four-poster bed with an emerald canopy drawn back. The dark wood floor is the same as in the sitting area, as is the stone that makes up the fireplace and walls, and I note that the sitting area before my hearth is a smaller version of the main room.

I push open two glass doors leading to a half-circle balcony and rush forward, pressing my hands into the banister and staring out to the forest and the crisp blue lake below. "It's gorgeous," I murmur.

"I'd argue my view is better." I snap my head to the side and, much to my dismay, find Cayden sitting on a chair with his boots propped up on a breakfast table. I have an identical table on mine. Our balconies are exactly the same—down to the shrubs, vine-covered columns, and stone carvings. "I'd love to get a closer look to reinforce my theory, though."

"The closer you get, the more inviting the jump looks." I gesture to the deathly drop to emphasize my point.

He places his hands on his railing—they span almost the entire width of it—and his mischievous gaze rakes over me. "Just trying to be neighborly."

"Neighborly?"

He spins away, walking through his glass doors, and I follow suit. I pull the door to my private chambers open to reveal an incredibly smug Cayden standing in a doorway on the opposite side of the suite. "Neighborly," he whispers.

He cuts the distance and shoves his hand onto my door before I can slam it in his face, stepping around me to enter my room. "This is a hilarious joke, but you can call it off now."

"It's for your protection." He crosses his arms over his chest and widens his feet like he's preparing for a fight.

"You're going to protect me from my nightmares?" I pout.

"Not my original plan, but if you feel the need to scream my name during the night, you may do so."

Oh gods, he makes me want to pull my hair out. He's like a walking supply of endless innuendos, smirks, and glares. "I'm not much of a screamer, and I doubt you'll turn me into one."

He takes several steps closer, my heart pounding every time his boots thump against the wood, and leans down to whisper, "We'll see about that, angel."

He graces me with his absence, and I slam the door to my bathing chamber shut. Ailliard is going to loathe this arrangement. White tile replaces the wooden floor, and a two-tier soap tray and oil rests beside a large clawfoot tub. I turn the handles and add some vanilla and lavender to the water. The tub is so deep that the water rises to my shoulders. I run my hands through my tangled hair and scrub every inch of myself with luxurious soap. My aches ease the longer I stay in the tub, and I add hot water whenever it chills.

"Your Majesty?" A soft knock on the door stirs me from my relaxed state. My fingers must look like raisins.

"I'll be out in a moment!" I quickly dry myself and slip into an ivory satin robe. The same redheaded maid stands by my vanity, setting out various makeup and hair products. She offers me a small smile and gestures for me to sit. "What's your name?"

"Hyacinth, my lady," she says shyly.

"It's nice to meet you." I smile at her through the mirror, wanting to ease her anxiety.

We fall into a comfortable silence while Hyacinth works on making me look like I've had a sound sleep within the past several days. She wraps my hair around some heated curlers that will help it dry quicker, then begins lining my eyes and plump lips before adding rouge to finish the fresh and light look.

"What would you like to wear tonight?" Hyacinth asks.

"Do you think my lavender gown is suitable for the occasion?" It's the newest addition to my collection.

"Yes," she says. "I think it's beautiful."

I slide the shimmering gown up my body and hold the bodice to my chest while Hyacinth tightens the ribbons of the corset. She runs her fingers through my curls and finishes the look with the crown Finnian made. When I stare at myself in the full-length mirror, soaking in every detail, I see a different version of myself. I see the princess I wasn't allowed to be, and the queen my people chose. There is no antidote for the poison of my past other than my future.

The gown hugs my slender frame and a slit travels up my thigh, revealing one of my dragon daggers. The handle depicts a dragon head, and an amethyst sits between the wings bordering the blade. Sheer trumpet sleeves stretch to the floor and gold floral embellishments grace the skirts and the bodice that amplifies my small curves. I slip my feet into a pair of heels as Hyacinth answers the sharp knock on my door.

"Good evening, Commander Veles," she says. Annoyance and anticipation tingle under my skin.

"Muse of my nightmares, you have returned." I sigh while straightening my dagger. "Are you here to escort me?"

Nothing but silence greets me.

I spin on my heels to find his darkened gaze roaming over me and his jaw is clenched so tight it must be painful. His cheekbones are so sharp I could hone a blade on them. A black leather tunic hugs his broad frame, and the gold buckles along the front match the rings adorning his long fingers. A sword hangs around his waist, and he looks . . . *No*.

He blinks and shakes his head as if he's coming out of a trance. "Did you say something?" He clears his raspy throat, but his deep voice has me imagining—*no!*

"I asked if you're here to escort me to the banquet."

He schools his wanting look with an unreadable, blank face. "This banquet and any other banquet, ball, or dinner." He must notice the confusion on my face because he tacks on, "You're stuck with me, princess."

"Don't you have a job to do? You're not a guard."

"I added you to my job description." He smirks while walking toward my door. "It now reads 'Cayden Veles—Commander of Vareveth and Defender of the Bane of His Existence.'"

I loop my hand through his extended arm and try to ignore the fresh scent of pine and spice that surrounds him. "So you have officially given me the title?"

"It was only ever yours to take."

"It's truly an honor." I grin. "I hardly recognize you when you look civilized."

"I can take my clothes off if it's too confusing for you."

I glare. He grins.

My skin prickles with anxiety, considering that every click of my heels on the tile brings me closer to the banquet. Ailliard and I had a conversation about Eagor and Valia before we crossed into Vareveth. I'll have to win them over if I want the alliance papers to be signed in a timely manner. Royals habitually push things off just to be vexing.

Cayden pauses when we get to a set of closed double doors. They're covered in green and gold detailing, just like the walls of the hall. "You ready?" he asks.

I raise my chin while staring down the doors before meeting his eyes, which are already on me. "I'm not bowing," I state.

"Good. I never do," he says, raising his fist to knock three times on the door before straightening himself out by my side.

"Have you ever bowed to anyone?"

"No."

A staff thumps against the floor, silencing whatever crowd has gathered on the opposite side of the door. My hand involuntarily tightens on Cayden's arm, but if he notices, he doesn't make it known.

"Commander Cayden Veles of Vareveth and Her Majesty Elowen Atarah, Queen of Aestilian and Princess of Imirath." The doors fly open as the cheers of the crowd rise to meet us. Cayden guides us forward, and into the den of vipers we descend.

Part II

THE ALLIANCE

CHAPTER

THIRTEEN

THE CHEERS INCREASE WITH EVERY STEP WE TAKE INTO the banquet hall. Several tables with intricate floral centerpieces are spread throughout the room, and an aisle in the center leads to one on a dais. Cayden gracefully helps me up the steps and escorts me toward King Eagor and Queen Valia, who stand at the front of the raised platform. They have coordinated their outfits to match Vareveth's signature green and gold. Eagor wears an emerald tunic with gold buttons, and Valia wears a modest gold gown with puffy sleeves and an equally full skirt. Her gray eyes flash toward my dagger, and her smile twitches disapprovingly before she recovers.

"King Eagor, Queen Valia, may I present Queen Elowen Atarah," Cayden says, introducing me.

"It's a pleasure to meet you." Eagor smiles.

I stretch my hand out, expecting him to shake it, but he brings it to his mouth, kissing my knuckles while keeping his green eyes on mine.

"You as well." I flash my practiced smile. "Your castle is lovely."

"It must be nice to be in a castle again. I assume Aestilian doesn't have one?" Valia asks with a broad smile on her face. My hand tightens on Cayden's arm at the subtle jab. Even if her tone is sweet, I can decipher an insult in disguise. Cayden cocks his head, but I open my mouth before he can say anything.

"Any home is a castle with a queen inside." I shrug, seeming unbothered.

"Very true," Valia replies. "I hope you enjoy the feast we've prepared."

"I'm sure you both worked very hard in the palace kitchens," Cayden dryly states before brushing past the pair as if they're no more than strangers and escorting us to our seats. He pulls my chair out and slides it in behind me. "Now, I have someone better for you to meet."

"That's not much competition," whispers a feminine voice beside me. The first thing I notice when I turn my head is a warm smile. She extends a hand in my direction, and I shake it. "Saskia Neredras. I'm the head of intelligence."

"Elowen." I know they just announced me, but it feels better to introduce myself to someone I'll be working with so closely. I note the similarities between her and Ryder—their eyes are the same obsidian color, but Saskia has something warm about her. Maybe it's her round cheeks that lift when she smiles. "Are you Ryder's sister?"

"I am. It's a pleasure to finally meet you." She leans forward to address Cayden, her long, midnight box braids falling over her shoulders. "And it's nice to see you home in one piece."

"It's nice to see you haven't died of boredom while Ryder and I were gone."

"The peace was a welcome change." She leans back in her chair, facing me again. "Even if it was short-lived."

"I can still hear you," Cayden mutters into his chalice.

Saskia ignores him. "I hope Valia wasn't too petty."

I glance in Valia's direction, but my eyes catch Finnian's in the chair beside hers. She chatters into his ear while he looks at me with pleading eyes. Ryder subtly rubs his temples like a headache is already forming. "Perhaps she'll warm over time," I say.

"Don't take it personally. She has a knack for jealousy," Saskia replies.

I visibly cringe but cover it up by taking a sip from my chalice. The wine is the perfect blend of sweet and tart.

"Do you like the wine, my lady?" Eagor inquires across the table.

I nod. "Is it made in your kingdom?"

"Indeed. We import it from the north," Valia cuts in. "Do you have wine in Aestilian?"

I place my chalice back on the table and meet the stare of a woman who seems to think we have nothing more than dirt and sticks. "We do."

She places her chin in her hand. "How interesting."

"Do you have a tavern there?" Eagor asks, seeming earnest. I flash my eyes to Ailliard, who gives me a subtle nod to proceed. I've never navigated a court before, and it's good to get a second opinion from someone who has.

"The tavern is one of our biggest buildings along the main road. The bartenders who own it make everything themselves. Their hard cider in the autumn is my favorite." It's a hot cinnamon–apple cider that warms you from the inside out. I go to the tavern almost every other day in the autumn to get a taste of it. Honestly, alcohol is the one thing we have in abundance, but alcohol and empty stomachs never mix well.

"It sounds established." Eagor runs a hand over his blond stubble. He even seems impressed. A tiny sliver of hope wraps around my heart; maybe getting the treaty settled won't be so hard.

Valia giggles loudly as servants carrying gold trays enter the room. "It's hard to imagine an established kingdom I've never seen."

Arguing on the first night isn't exactly the first impression I want to make. Everyone at the table can note the backhanded meaning of her statement.

"I've found that reading has expanded my imagination. Perhaps you should try it some time. I'm happy to supply you with a list of recommendations when I have a free moment," I say.

Her shoulders stiffen slightly. "How kind of you."

I return her fake smile before taking another sip of wine and leaning back in my chair. When wielded properly, words have the power to cut someone down with more pain and precision than any sword.

"Well played, princess," Cayden says.

Servers begin piling our plates with food: gravy-covered chicken, mashed potatoes, fresh vegetables, and bread with a glorious amount of butter. It's the type of meal I would dream about when all I had to eat that day was an apple. The last month of winter is always the hardest, especially when the frost stays longer than usual. By then, the snow is piled so high that patrols can't get out for raids or hunts, so we must make whatever food we have stretch for as long as we can.

I dip my chicken into the potatoes before bringing the fork to my mouth and fight to hold back a moan when the gravy dances along my taste buds. *This* is how food is supposed to taste. "I would kiss your chef if I saw them."

"You have a soft spot for chefs? Shall I don an apron over my armor?" Cayden asks.

"I'll only accept the pinkest and frilliest of aprons."

"You have my word."

"How long before we can start working?" I direct my question to them both, keeping my tone low. I glance over the table and am relieved to see Finnian and Ryder lost in their own conversation without Valia.

"What do you mean?" Saskia asks before taking a bite of bread.

"The alliance papers haven't been signed, so I wasn't sure if we must wait." Cayden told me that Saskia and Ryder believe I'm here to work closely with him in war preparations despite Eagor's plan to keep me close to the castle. But I'm not sure if they know about the heist yet.

Saskia waves a dismissive hand through the air. "They'll get signed when they get signed. I'm not a fan of waiting for someone to do their job, so I just do mine. They can catch up."

Oh, I *really* like her.

"Advisors take forever," Cayden mutters.

"Not a fan of authority?" I poke.

"I'm a fan of getting *around* authority."

"You're giving a great representation of Vareveth, Cayden," Saskia grumbles.

"I'm providing an accurate one."

"You're a commander. You're *the* symbol of authority here," I remind him.

"I never said I don't like having authority. I said I don't like people having authority over me." He takes a sip of wine. "While you're here you'll have the option of training with the army. I'd like to work on your footwork."

I narrow my eyes at him. "My footwork?"

"Someone's in trouble," Saskia sings into her chalice.

I pause my retort as servers clear the table and place a strawberry-and-cream-filled cake in front of us. I'm convinced this place is a food utopia. A piece of cake seems like such a trivial thing. It's accessible to so many people that they usually don't think anything of it, but I see my emotions reflected on Finnian's face. To us, it feels like a sunny day after months of rain. I eventually descend from my strawberry-scented cloud and remember I'm annoyed with Cayden.

"Do you not remember when I held a knife to your neck?"

"I actually think about it quite often, but if you want to remind me, you're free to do so." He licks some cream off his index finger, and I force my eyes away.

"I'll work on my footwork when you work on your personality." My tone is sweet despite the venom in my words. "Why are you grinning at me?"

"Everyone in the kingdom fears me, and yet you never miss an opportunity to insult me. I find it enthralling." His eyes scan my face. "I become more intrigued every second I spend in your presence."

"Your thought process is disturbing." His dimples deepen in his cheeks. I angle my body toward Saskia. "I'm electing to ignore you."

"That's mature," Cayden remarks.

"I respect her decision," Saskia says, unable to contain her laughter any longer. It's a light sound filled with mirth and merriment, and I find myself laughing along with her.

"Do you know any good dressmakers in town?" I ask while taking in the details of her dress. Dark purple skirts flow around her hips, and a metallic golden halter bodice covers her chest. It looks lovely on her. I won't be able to get by with the clothes I brought in my trunk for long.

"Plenty." She grins before biting into a strawberry. "I can take you tomorrow."

"You're sure you don't mind?"

She gives me an exaggerated eye roll, and a corner of her mouth lifts. "I've had nobody other than Cayden and Ryder to deal with the last few years. I'd be happy to go shopping with you."

CHAPTER
FOURTEEN

"I can't believe you brought your books with you," Finnian drawls, lying on one of the couches by my fireplace.

"Words are food for my soul," I reply after applying my lipstick. The curls Hyacinth created yesterday now fall in loose waves down my back. I need to learn how to use those curlers.

He props himself up on his elbows while giving me a no-nonsense glare. "Raunchy romance is your soul food?"

I toss one of the big pillows from my bed in his direction. "Don't judge my flavor palate."

His laughter is drowned out when it slams into his face. He doesn't bother moving it and stays sprawled under the fluff. The sun is shining today, so I can get away with wearing the light blue dress fashioned in the same silhouette as my gown from last night and tie a white cloak with lace detailing around my shoulders.

Finnian gets to his feet, straightening out his red shirt and brown leather vest before throwing on his quiver and bow and meeting me by the door. I slip my arm through his and approach the front of the castle where we're meeting Saskia. Finnian needs clothes, too, and I wouldn't want to explore a new kingdom without him. We pass through several extravagant rooms as we glide down the equally lavish halls and make it to the last step in the entryway when voices begin filtering through the exit.

"You hate dress shopping," Saskia says.

"I *love* it," Cayden retorts. He kept the doors to our separate chambers open last night, but I haven't seen him this morning. The only sign of life was a half-drunk cup of coffee on his desk while I snooped around his extremely impersonal room. Two guards are always stationed at the entrance, so it's not like he left me defenseless, even though I always sleep with a knife under my pillow.

"No. You and Ryder love getting drinks while I shop for dresses."

"Wait, are we not going to the tavern?" Ryder's confused voice joins the mix.

"I told you the plans last night," Cayden states in a tone that makes me believe he's pinching the bridge of his nose.

"I thought you were joking," Ryder groans. "Why are we spending the day doing this?"

"I think I know the reason," Saskia sings.

"Elowen!" Cayden cuts off their conversation and steps around Saskia when Finnian and I exit the castle. Saskia leans forward, her ivory gown flowing around her ankles, and whispers something to Ryder that causes them both to laugh before they slowly follow behind Cayden. He throws them a glare over his shoulder and stops before me.

"Saskia Neredras." She sticks out her hand to Finnian.

"Finnian Eira." His freckled hand grasps hers.

"You're coming shopping?" I quirk a brow at Cayden.

"I'm your guard."

I clutch my chest and widen my eyes. "Are the fabrics going to bite me?"

"If they do, I promise to rip them from your body. Can't have you getting hurt on my watch." He grasps my shoulders and ushers us toward the bridge.

I roll my eyes even though he can't see. The waterfall looks gorgeous in the sunlight, and I notice a bridge that rises over the peak of the falls. I turn away from the few gondolas gliding along the lake's surface as Verendus rises before me. It's much easier to absorb the details now that flower petals aren't flying through the air and crowds aren't lining the streets.

The shops along the main road are made of mixed gray stones and dark wood; some have vines creeping up the front and sides, but all have different-colored shutters and signs. Horses trot through along the cobblestones, people walk from shop to shop with baskets on their arms, and others wheel carts of fresh fruits and delicate fabric. Gowns and swords glimmer in the sunlight from the windows of their respective shops. We pass perfumeries, apothecaries, flower shops, and taverns. Droopy trees stand tall over the town, their trunks covered in the same moss that hugs some rocks along the road.

It's overwhelming. The group chatters around me, but I focus on taking in every little detail. I never thought I would walk down a street outside Aestilian where people could smile at me, knowing exactly who I am. I've hidden who I am for so long that sometimes I don't even feel like myself. Instead of being a ghost, I can be a person. People can know my name and remember my face after I leave a tavern or a shop. I've always wanted my dragons, but I never knew how badly I wanted the opportunity to exist out in the world.

The scent of vanilla, apples, and cinnamon draws my gaze and stops me dead in my tracks. A force slams into me from behind, and I only know it's Cayden when leather-covered arms wrap around me. I jump out of his hold as if his touch burns me—it may as well have. I still feel his chest pressing into me, even with the space between us. I'm unable to meet his eyes even though I feel them on me.

"Is something wrong?" Finnian asks, his eyes scanning the area, and a knowing smile slides onto his face. "She wants to go to the bakery."

"That's a good one!" Saskia exclaims and loops her arm through mine, practically dragging me over to the pink-trimmed door with a sign in the shape of a lemon. It fits the name well: *Lemon Drop Bakery.*

It's a tiny establishment, nestled between two larger shops. Our bakery in Aestilian is even smaller and usually only sells bread. Nothing too extravagant considering all the ingredients required to make one cake. I inhale the sugary scent deeply as Saskia and I walk over to the counter stacked high with honeybuns, fruit tarts, lemon drop cookies, jams in jars topped with pink linen and yellow ribbons, cream puffs, muffins, and more. Cakes with more tiers than I thought possible are displayed like prized possessions, and wicker baskets filled with bread line the wall, some even containing chocolate chunks.

An elderly man with flour on his cheek steps out from behind a curtain that I'm assuming leads to the kitchen. "Oh!" he exclaims. "I didn't hear the bell. What can I get for you all?"

Finnian, Saskia, and Ryder stand at the counter to discuss the vast options. Saskia isn't short, but she looks so while standing between them. I spin around and find Cayden leaning against the wall, lazily resting a hand on the hilt of his sword and tucking the other in the pocket of his black pants. The loose white shirt under his jacket is low cut, and the undone laces procure the same effortlessly striking look as his hair.

I walk toward him against my better judgment, stepping between the lace-covered tables with daisies at the center, and his eyes track me the entire way. "Not a fan of pastries?"

He shrugs. "I suppose not."

"Perhaps you should've had more birthday cake as a boy."

"Perhaps," he echoes, his lips tilting up in an expression that's not quite a smile before he dons neutrality again. But I saw the distant look, and it's one I know well. The broken and burdened have a language of their own, and only they can understand it.

"We can split one of my favorites if you'd like." His eyes flash back to me, and I feel so immensely stupid for offering something so childish. But a half smile graces his lips as he pushes off the wall, and I tilt my head up to watch him.

"Are you being sweet to me?"

It's apparent he finds being around people irksome, and if it weren't for me, I doubt he'd be ambling about the kingdom to shop. I swallow as I take in the scar carved into his cheek and the others exposed between the neckline of his shirt. "I know what it's like to be surrounded by people but feel out of place."

A few seconds tick by that feel like hours. I'm too much of a coward to hold his gaze, but a weight lifts off my chest when I feel his hand press into my back to escort me to the counter where Ryder is double-fisting vanilla custard tarts.

"Whatever the princess wants," Cayden says when the baker looks in his direction.

"One apple tart, please."

He blinks wide eyes between us and quickly wipes his flour-covered hands on his apron and bows. "It's an honor, Your Graces. My apologies, I didn't recognize you at first."

"That's all right." I smile to calm his nerves. "I only just arrived yesterday."

He gets to work, plucking a tart from a tray and cutting it in half before wrapping it in a white doily. I reach into my pocket to pull a few syndrils free when a large, calloused hand wraps around my wrist, and Cayden drops far more than necessary on the counter.

"I'll take that flower as well," Cayden says, jutting his chin toward a vase of irises, and tucks it behind my ear when the baker hands it over. "It matches your dress."

"Thank you." My voice is hardly a whisper, riddled with shock.

The cool air feels lovely on my burning cheeks when we step out. Finnian smirks around his honeybun when he spots the vibrant petals, but Cayden remains completely unbothered as he hands me half the tart. I watch him from the corner of my eye as his jaw flexes.

"Well?" I ask.

"I'm giving you a new title. Bane of My Existence." He licks his lips and taps his free hand against his jaw, appearing very contemplative. "And Pastry Advisor."

"You like it?" A smile breaks out across my face and the relief in my tone is evident.

The corner of his lips rises. "I do."

CHAPTER

FIFTEEN

SHOPPING WITH SASKIA IS LIKE A FEVER DREAM. FINNIAN picked out a few patterns he liked within the first hour we got here, but she won't let me off the hook that easily, not that I mind. Saskia has a keen eye for fashion and placed an order for some new winter attire.

"I promise just one last gown," she says with an excited smile while holding a swatch of fabric.

"You said that for the past five gowns." Ryder's annoyed tone drifts from the front of the shop where he and the others are camped out on couches.

"Leave if you wish. I'd prefer it." She places one hand on her hip, and the other points at a rack of clothes as if Ryder will materialize within the tulle he's hidden behind. "You'll practically live in sweaters when you come to the border, but you'll need the day gowns for political meetings and dinners. Ball gowns can be ordered as we need them."

"The border?" I ask.

"That's where the three of us spend most of our time. You'll be there soon enough." She hushes my next question by holding up a champagne-colored fabric in her hands. "This would look good on you."

I place my hand on the fabric, lowering it so I can see her face again. "How about I pay for the stuff we already sorted out and get the testy trio to the tavern?"

"Yes!" Finnian and Ryder shout in tandem, but Cayden's voice doesn't join the mix.

"What happened to solidarity?" Ryder asks in a hushed voice.

"I wasn't aware that the two of you rehearsed the response," Cayden fires back.

"So you *do* want to go to the tavern," Ryder remarks.

"Obviously, I want to go to the fucking tavern." Cayden's attempt at whispering fails.

"How I love having a woman around." Saskia sighs while throwing an arm around my shoulders and guiding me to the counter so I can settle my bill, but Cayden is already there, signing his name to a piece of paper.

"What are you doing?"

"Signing an order for all innocents to be slaughtered in the night," he responds without looking up.

I step forward and blanch at the number at the bottom of the receipt; perhaps I got too carried away. "You can't pay for this."

"Spend more if you want me to break a sweat, angel." He hands the order form to the owner and directs his next statement to her. "Please include gowns made from the fabrics Princess Elowen said were *too much* in the silhouettes she favors with cloaks, shoes, and gloves to match." He spins on his heels while I'm picking my jaw up from the floor, and Saskia pulls me forward. Ryder and Finnian are already rushing from the shop by the time I get my wits about me.

"There's no point in arguing," Saskia says. "Once his mind is made up there's no changing it."

"I don't want to be viewed as charity."

"Does he strike you as a charitable man?" She huffs a laugh. "He wouldn't have paid if he didn't want to."

I momentarily swallow my pride as we enter the Tipsy Troll and noise instantly pummels my senses. It's deafening, given the mixture of rowdy drunks and the usual tavern sounds.

"Take the ladies to a table while Finnian and I order drinks!" Ryder shouts above the noise.

Saskia keeps her hand laced through mine while I hold Cayden's arm. I suppose him being taller than most men has its advantages. Copper lanterns hang from ceiling beams, high enough so people don't hit their heads but low enough to illuminate the sea of tables of varying heights and sizes. Several patrons are playing or watching card games, placing bets on upcoming horse races and fights, but my favorite is the dancing taking place on the other side of the tavern. Couples intertwine, sway, and leap to a merry jig played by fiddles, drums, and pipes. There's an upper floor, but Cayden guides us toward a table nestled in a stone-covered corner framed by dark wood. As we pass, people throw smiles and bow in his and Saskia's direction.

"I can't believe it." I tilt my head so Cayden can hear me while I remove my cloak. "There are people here who actually like you."

"Funny." Cayden slides his leather jacket off before taking the chair beside mine. "I thought the same thing when you said goodbye to your guards."

"You have a natural talent for vexing me."

He pulls his sleeves up, exposing his muscular forearms and scars. "That's precisely why I reserve my worst qualities for you."

"You have good qualities?"

He smirks and says, "You'll see them one day."

Finnian and Ryder return to the table with a tray of twenty tiny glasses filled with whiskey. "We placed an order for other drinks that'll be brought over, but in the meantime . . ." Finnian waves his hands over the tray and plops down on my other side.

"The two of you aren't allowed to gauge how many shots to order," Saskia mutters, staring at the tray like it's about to bite her but grabbing a shot like the rest of us.

"We should toast," Finnian suggests while holding his shot in the air. He nudges me with his elbow. "Help me."

I search my brain, trying to come up with something as four sets of eyes settle on me. "To having a common enemy?"

"Fair point," Ryder acknowledges. "I'll drink to that."

"To wanting to murder the same people and not each other!" Finnian cheers as we clink our glasses and throw back the whiskey.

We're a really fucked-up group.

I think I like it.

We keep going until there are no shots left. I slam my fourth empty glass on the table, feeling delightfully giddy.

"That's my girl!" A broad smile covers Finnian's face as he takes in my warm cheeks. Alcohol goes straight to my head. I'm a lightweight, and he loves it. Downing four shots in a row probably wasn't the best decision, but bad decisions often lead to the best memories.

I cup my hands around my mouth and lean toward his ear to say, "We should get more."

He chuckles softly. "Cider first."

"What if I chase every shot with a sip of cider?"

"I can't encourage your bad ideas in front of the new people. Save them for later." I'm sure everyone else can hear our conversation judging by their snickers . . . maybe we weren't as quiet as I thought.

"Your drinks," says a male server while placing them around the table, giving Finnian a double take. I nudge him with my leg, and he nudges me right back. Finnian meets the server's eyes while taking a sip from his pint. Color rises on the server's tan cheeks. "Let me know if you need anything else," he mutters before scurrying toward the bar.

"I love bubbles," Saskia marvels while looking at the glass of cider in front of her.

"They're like friends inside your drink." I sigh.

"Exactly!" She claps her hands in front of her, causing Ryder to jump in his seat and Cayden to snicker again. "When do you go back to the border, Cayden?"

"Yes, normally you'd be there by now. I wonder what's different this time." Ryder leans back in his seat, easing one leg over the other while clutching his pint and taking a sip.

"Soon," Cayden replies shortly.

"When can I go?" I ask.

"When I'm sure it's safe," he answers.

He seems to be in a broody mood, so I don't push. He's fully aware I can take care of myself, and I'd rather not sprint headfirst toward the

Imirath army without being prepared. The other three have fallen into a conversation and—oh gods! What if one of them tells Finnian about the heist before I do? I forgot to ask Cayden if they know. My brain is too fuzzy to process all the damage that could cause. I bite my lip, and my hands tighten around my cool glass. The chilling sensation is helping me keep my nerves at bay.

Cayden dips his hand between us and pulls my chair closer to his before draping his arm across the back of it. "What's wrong?"

Perhaps it's the alcohol that makes my lips loose because I find myself inching closer to his ear, close enough for our thighs to press together. "Do they know . . ." I can't exactly talk about the heist in an open tavern. "Do they know what we're planning?"

I pull my face back so I can see him again. It takes a second for him to register my words, but he subtly shakes his head no. Relief floods through me like a dam breaking.

The music abruptly changes.

Finnian stands from his seat and bows while offering me a hand. "You owe me a dance, my lady."

"We'll talk later," Cayden says into my ear.

I place my hand in Finnian's, which is the only thing that keeps me steady while rushing to the dance floor. The alcohol in my body washes over me with a fresh wave of giddiness. He stands a few feet in front of me, hands clasped behind his back. The first note sounds; it's a sharp beat of a drum, and Finnian bows at the waist, outstretching his hand again. The second note sounds, and I curtsy. The third note sounds, and I place my hand in Finnian's. I twirl under his arm, his hand clasps around my waist, and we join the thrall of dancers.

"He hasn't taken his eyes off you," Finnian shouts over the music.

He doesn't have to say Cayden's name. There's nobody else he could be talking about. We left the conversation on an unfinished note. Maybe he's watching me because he's wondering if I'll tell Finnian right now.

"He's guarding me. It's part of his job," I reason.

Finnian snorts, spinning me again and resuming the steps. "He never complained once during dress shopping. He looked like he wanted to ram his head through a wall, but he never said a single thing."

We both stumble slightly, but it only adds to the joy building in my chest from a mixture of music, dancing, and cider. A smile beams on my face as Finnian lifts me in tandem with another sharp drumbeat. He places me back on my feet, and we follow the rest of the steps as best as our floundering feet allow us.

"Stop meddling!" I laugh. "We're allies, and I already told Ailliard nothing will happen."

"I know men, darling." I don't like the way his tone is changing. "When this dance is over, go to the bar. I give it five minutes before he's there."

"Finnian, you're being ridiculous. That proves nothing," I say as we finish the final steps.

"If it proves nothing, then do it. You have *nothing* to lose." We stop in place, and some people in the tavern clap while shouting their song requests. "I'll keep my eyes on you the whole time. I'm staying on for another dance." He treads backward and finds a man with long blond hair to dance with next.

I roll my eyes and fist my dress so I don't trip over the hem on my way to the bar or let it drag through anything unsanitary. My eyes spot an opening at the counter, and I slide into it, placing my elbows on the wooden surface while glancing at the different barrels of wine, cider, and ale behind it.

"Well, aren't you a beauty," a gruff voice next to me states. I was so preoccupied reading the names of all the places the barrels are imported from that I didn't realize someone had approached me. A man in black armor inches forward. His black beard is cut close to his face, and his dark eyes bore into me.

I don't offer a response, but that doesn't stop him from leaning farther into my personal space, stretching a hand toward my arm. I'm about to swat it away when someone cages me in their arms and pins his wrist to the bar.

"I was wondering what time you want to leave?" Cayden asks

calmly in my ear as if he's not making a grown man squirm beneath his firm grip. I spin in his arms and press my back into the bar so I can look at him. His tone may be calm, but he's far from it. That icy glare of his is on the man's face, and I have a feeling he's committing it to memory. "I'm going to assume you didn't see her stumble on her way over here," Cayden snarls before turning his intensity on me. "What did he say to you? I saw you stiffen."

"He said I was pretty."

"Damn understatement," he mutters. My breath catches in my throat, but he can't hear it over the roar of the tavern or his raging temper.

"C-Commander," the man whimpers.

"Leave," Cayden says, shoving the man back with enough force that he loses his footing. The man scrambles to his feet, slipping on spilled drinks, and hurries away. My eyes pop over to Finnian, and he flashes me one of the biggest smirks I've ever seen. I don't even think I was standing here for two minutes before Cayden came over.

"So, am I not allowed to speak to any men while I'm here?" Taunting him is far too inviting.

"I'm a man. Talk to me."

"I was about to hit him before you stole the show," I say, swaying between his arms.

The ice melts in his eyes as they follow my movements. "Would you have even been able to land the hit?"

"Want me to prove it, demon?"

His sneer has vanished, and I know I'm in dangerous territory because the only thought my alcohol-addled brain can manage is how handsome he looks. "I'm feeling like a gentleman. I'll give you the first shot."

"You're not a gentleman. You're insufferable," I say, more so to remind myself of who we are. Our goals matter more than drunken wants.

"Insufferable?" He quirks a brow, sliding his hands along the bar to lean closer to my face. "Have you wondered why you adore making yourself suffer? It's quite concerning, El."

"Don't call me that. You make it sound like we're friends."

His dimples deepen. "I think we're becoming *very* good friends."

"You're delusional," I breathlessly argue while fighting a smile.

"Oh yeah?"

I open my mouth to make another retort when a cold drink slides down the front of my gown. Cayden's glare is back in full force as he reaches toward the man responsible.

His eyes glance between Cayden and me. "I'm so sorry. I lost my balance."

"Calm down. It's nothing a bath can't fix." I reach for Cayden's outstretched hand and rein it back in, ignoring the weight of it in mine, and slowly push him away from the bar. His thin cotton shirt lets me feel the defined ridges of his muscles. "People will think we're more than allies if you continue acting like this."

"Let them think whatever they want. You and I have larger threats to concern ourselves with."

"It's not that simple." My people need this treaty signed before winter comes, and I don't want rumors about Cayden and me making me seem like an inept ruler. I must wear an impenetrable mask and never let anyone see through it. It's both my armor and my burden. "I appreciate your generosity in the shop, but—"

"I paid for Finnian as well." His heat is pinned on me now. "I brought you here. I paid for your attire. There's no ulterior meaning."

"Right." The flower he tucked behind my ear feels far too heavy, and the hand on his chest feels far too personal. I drop it away along with my eyes. "We should return to the castle."

Finnian has made his way back to the table, so I wave to the others and ignore the way Cayden is still looking at me like he wants to say something else. Our hands are covered in thorns, and every touch, no matter how innocent, draws more blood.

CHAPTER
SIXTEEN

"DO YOU STILL WANT TO TALK TONIGHT, OR DO YOU want to sleep off the whiskey and cider?" Cayden asks as we enter the suite, his tone back to being playful.

"We'll talk, but I'm taking a bath first because I smell like ale." My hand plucks at my drenched neckline. The walk back helped sober me up, and the five of us went down to the kitchens for some water and bread before retiring for the night.

"I'll grab some fresh linen and place it beside the tub, my lady." Hyacinth curtsies and exits the bathing chamber.

"Wait!" I call out, and she pops her head back in. "I took some extra chocolates from the kitchens for you and left them on my vanity."

"Thank you." She blinks slowly, and her cheeks flush as a shy smile graces her lips. "I'll be sure to enjoy them when I return."

I step out of my gown and sink into the bath, pouring another glass of water from the pitcher beside me and drinking half before setting it aside. My head doesn't feel as fuzzy as it did at the tavern, and I've had enough water that I won't be hungover tomorrow, which is a blessing. The door creaks open behind me, and I remember wanting to ask Hyacinth about the curlers.

"I was wondering if you could teach me ho—" My sentence is cut off when a pair of rough hands grips my shoulders and shoves me under the water. The tub is so deep that it doesn't take much to submerge me, and my legs aren't long enough to reach the end. I push against the bottom, fighting to breach the surface, but the person holding me down has incredible strength.

I choke on soapy water, and my chest burns from the lack of air in my lungs. I give up trying to shove myself above the water and attempt to pry their hands off. It's no use. Another pathetic choke escapes my lips—the bubbles rise, mocking me. I reach toward the side table and grip the crystal pitcher, slamming it over my assailant's head in a desperate attempt to free myself. Their hands move from my shoulders and latch on to my neck, squeezing hard. The light blurs above the water. I feel like I did in my cell all those years ago, looking out at the world through a sliver between stones. I can't die like this. Not when I'm so close to seeing my dragons again.

My hands pad against the bottom of the tub, and I curl my fingers around a shard of glass from the pitcher's handle. I plunge the glass into their wrist, and blood clouds the water around me. I pull it out and plunge it in again, cutting a vertical line down their arm. If I die, I'm taking my assailant with me. I'll give them a wound so deep that even their soul will wear it in the afterlife. They may think they found me powerless, but I'm never defenseless. I would've used my teeth if I had to. The blood grows thicker in the tub, obscuring my vision until a deep red cloud surrounds me.

The hands vanish from my body, and I haul myself forward, coughing water onto the floor while clinging to the porcelain like a lifeline. A pair of strong arms wrap around me, and my head is buried into a warm neck while I take in heavy gulps of air.

"Secure the fucking perimeter!" Cayden commands someone beyond the door.

"Is she hurt?" Ryder's rattled voice filters in.

"I have her. Go now!" he barks.

"Cayden," I wheeze.

"You're safe now, angel." He pulls me closer, and my chest presses into the side of the tub. "Elowen . . . the blood, is it yours?" His tone is frantic. One arm stays wrapped around me, holding me upright, but the other slides toward my head and gently pulls me from the crook of his neck. He cradles my face in his rough hand—the gentle touch is so opposite to the feel of him, all hard muscles, sharp lines, and glares. I didn't think Cayden could look like this . . . so distressed.

"It's not my blood," I manage through my raspy throat. His eyes flash toward my neck, and the way his nostrils flare leads me to believe bruises are already forming. My body starts to tremble as my brain catches up to the gravity of what just happened. Cayden must have slit his throat because a wide arc of blood drips down from the wall, and a man lies crumpled in a crimson puddle on the tile floor. "I'm fine. It's not my first encounter with an assassin."

He removes his hands from me, but not his gaze. His distress has morphed into rage and I'm thankful I'm not his enemy. Cayden's anger could end worlds and remake them. In all his chaos, there is calculation and contemplation. He's a fierce fighter, but his intelligence sets him apart from others. "That man didn't suffer enough, but I assure you anyone else involved in this plot will die a thousand deaths before I grant it."

I nod, droplets from my hair sending ripples in the bloody bath, still trying to wrap my mind around the fact that when I needed help, Cayden ran to me. Even if he only did it for my dragons and the war, he's here even after he knows I'm all right, kneeling on the glass-ridden floor.

"I'm going to lift you from the tub now," he says softly.

"I can stand." I shift my legs beneath me and glass shards I'm unable to see through the red water slide against the bottom.

"You'll cut your feet open." He reaches into the tub and lightly brushes his fingers over a spot to ensure there's no glass before holding his hands in front of me. "Guide my hands. I don't want to touch you anywhere you don't want me to. If you step on a piece of glass, I'll keep you steady or lift you before it cuts deep. My eyes will be on yours the entire time. Then, once you're stable, I can reach for the robe on the hook." He pauses momentarily, eyes flashing to the marks on my neck before meeting mine again. "Let me help you, El."

Vulnerability isn't an option for those who have licked kindness and humanity off knives, but our blades are pointed at the same enemy, and his eyes hold no judgment. He hears the words that I don't have to say. It's what pushes me to close my hands around his wrists and guide his hands to my hips. His face inches closer to mine, so close that our foreheads press together. His eyes dilate, and I hear his slight intake of breath when I wrap my arms around his neck.

"If your eyes wander, I'll cut them out myself." My breathless tone doesn't convey the gravity of my threat.

"They won't," he states in a low, gravelly tone. "Ready?"

"Mm-hmm." I don't trust my voice.

Slowly . . . *so slowly*, he tightens his hold and eases me to my feet. Our eyes remain locked, but I don't think I could look away if I tried. There's something mesmerizing about his gaze. His breathing deepens when I'm steady on my feet, and his hands linger until he's sure no glass pierces me under my full weight. Then, just as promised, he reaches to the side without ever taking his eyes off mine. He slides the ivory satin robe behind my shoulders, and his fingers brush down my arms while I fasten the sash.

"I'm still wearing my boots, so I'm going to carry you." His raspy voice sends a shock through my body and makes me want to press my legs together. How can he make me want to stab him one second and then feel like this? I don't even want to label exactly what this feeling is. I just know it's overwhelming, suffocating, and forbidden.

He steps back and hoists me in his arms, settling me against his chest. I take one last look at the corpse painting the tile in a portrait of his demise before Cayden carries me from my chambers.

CHAPTER
SEVENTEEN

CAYDEN SETS ME DOWN IN HIS BATHING CHAMBER AND turns the dials on the tub. "Use whatever you want. I'll grab you something to change into."

"Is this your usual suite?" I ask when he returns, setting some clothes on the counter.

"I don't have chambers in the castle. I prefer my own space." He shuts the door behind him, and I force the water to be loud enough to cancel out my thoughts, not that it entirely succeeds. I lather myself in Cayden-scented suds and wash the remaining blood from my skin. The clothes he brought in must be his because not only do the sleeves fall past my hands and the pants pool at my feet, but the scent of them is dangerously alluring.

Cayden is sitting on an emerald couch with a glass of whiskey when I enter, and his gaze lifts from the report he's reading, his smirk gliding against the rim as he takes a sip. "Perfect fit."

I sink onto the couch beside him and bunch the fabric up to flip him off. He leans forward to pour me a cup of tea from the tray he must have ordered while I was washing up. I mumble a thank-you and quickly down the cup, letting the soothing liquid coat my throat before pouring a second.

"How many assassins have tried to kill you?" His tone is quiet, but

I don't mistake it for calm. Cayden is the type of person to lock down his anger and weaponize it when needed.

I lick my lips and place the cup on the table to fuss with the sleeves that pool around my hands. There's no sense in avoiding it. "My father didn't know for sure if I was dead or alive, so it was only a few, and never within Aestilian borders. They stopped around the time I turned fifteen. Sometimes I itched for the fight, just to make me feel something." I stopped worrying about assassins years ago when I realized I could be as deadly as them. "That's not what I wanted to talk about."

The last thing I want to do is rehash my past with Cayden. Talking about it can't erase what happened to me. I want to move forward. Sometimes, when I don't talk about it, I feel I can ignore it, even if it's only temporary. Our bodies are maps of our pasts, but not every scar is physically marked along the journey. Those invisible scars can bleed like open wounds on bad days.

"Right." He clears his throat and closes his eyes briefly. When he opens them again, the quiet rage is filed away, hidden from the surface, and locked down for later use. "Shall we discuss when you were about to shove me onto the dance floor at the tavern?"

"I was going to shove you *away*."

His eyes dance with mischief. "Would you like me to twirl you around the room, princess?"

I reach for a pillow behind me and smack it into his face, muffling his laughter until I pull it back and continue my assault. He grips my wrists before I can hit him a fourth time and drags me back down beside him. "I told you I could land a hit, demon."

"I don't dance, but I'll make sure no pillows are around the next time I reject your advance." He doesn't remove his eyes from my smile and takes a sip of whiskey to sober himself.

"Let's talk before someone brings you a report," I say as I calm myself down. "The night we first met, I heard two people talking about you wanting me because of my dragons. If that wasn't Saskia and Ryder, who was it?"

"It was them," Cayden confirms. "Saskia was with us for the first leg of the journey. After a few days, she traveled back with a group of soldiers because she had a political meeting she couldn't miss. All they know is that I want you here because of your link to the dragons, but they've known me for years so I'm sure they have their suspicions. Did you find what you were looking for in the dragon book we stole?"

I flinch when he mentions the book, and I spy his fingers inching toward me before he thinks better of it and remains where he is. I'm sure his question has no malicious intent, but the chuckle that escapes me is anything but genuine while I reach for the whiskey in his hand and place my lips where his were. His gaze darkens, and it feels oddly intimate as I hand it back to him.

"You'll think me a fool," I whisper, staring at the floor.

"I won't," he responds quietly, the fire crackling beside us as he waits for me to continue. "Why did we steal the book, El?"

"Most dragon books contain fictional stories of quests and battles, and many are illustrated by famous artists all throughout Ravaryn. Sometimes I steal the books in hopes of finding a dragon illustration that resembles mine. I rarely leave Aestilian without Finnian and didn't want to waste the opportunity, considering he and I don't discuss the dragons. It's not vital to the heist, and I nearly threw it into a fire when I got to the last page. I didn't need you there, but you're annoyingly insistent." My chest feels tight, and I pour some whiskey into the teacup. "I search every corner of the world for a sign that my dragons are okay, but I've never found one. It was a hope of mine that Garrick invited an artist to a feast and let them sketch one. I'd recognize their scales anywhere."

He's quiet for a few moments, subtly shifting closer to me, and says, "Tell me about them."

I smile down at my teacup, but it's all wrong. Sometimes I feel as if I'll break under the weight of my memories. "Their scales are . . . captivating, especially when they're in the sun. There are two males, Sorin and Basilius. Sorin is emerald green with black-tipped wings and horns, and Basilius is pure lavender. Then there are the females: Venatrix, Calithea, and Delmira. Venatrix is crimson with pink and gold markings. Calithea is silver with white-tipped wings that look like snowflakes. Delmira is sky blue, like a perfect summer day, with yellow markings. Their eyes match their dominant colors: green, lavender, red, silver, and blue."

It's moments like this where I can feel every mile separating us. I'm filled to the brim with love for them, but it has nowhere to go and sits in my chest like grief. Sadness and pain are the price we pay for opening our hearts, but I'd rather die penniless than never know love.

"Elowen." The way Cayden says my name forces my gaze to his again. "I swear on all that I have and all that I've lost, you will see your dragons again."

I close my eyes, nodding as I force the storm raging inside me to pass, and inhale a sharp breath while standing up from the couch in search of something to occupy my mind. The desk piled high with maps looks like the perfect solution. "This is Kallistar Prison?"

I hate that he's looking at me with a calculating gaze, ready to decipher any statement I make and file it in his brain for future reference. His calculating expression is hardly different from his impassive expression; he probably doesn't even realize I can decipher it. The only difference is that his right brow is slightly higher than his left, and sometimes his lips pinch in the corner—but he never does either simultaneously.

"It is." He comes to stand beside me, his long fingers trailing over the map, capturing my attention far more than they should. "We'll have to wait for low tide before rowing there, or else we'll get shredded by the rocks."

I pause for a moment to erase that image from my mind. "I can use hunting down those involved in the assassination attempt as an excuse for my absence. We should leave tomorrow. Garrick is moving fast, so should we."

He tenses beside me, and the heat of his temper radiates off his body. "Anyone guilty won't live to see another sunrise."

I dryly swallow and fumble the maps on the desk, so unused to the protectiveness lacing his tone. "Just don't make a spectacle of killing the guilty parties. Let me tell Finnian about the heist in my own time, and he'll be suspicious if I disappear without a reason. We've been removed from the world for our entire friendship. I can't just throw everything at him and expect him to be fine."

Time moves slowly as I wait for him to respond, and I turn to face him. He looks ready to shoot me down, but something relents when he takes in my features, his eyes trailing down the bruises and where his clothes cover me. "Fine. We'll leave tomorrow."

I clear my throat. "You've started looking at maps of the castle as well?"

"Garrick is rigorous with security. His castle didn't earn the title 'the Impenetrable Fortress' for nothing. We need to find a way in that won't be under heavy guard."

I bite my lip while regarding several maps. I wasn't allowed in most parts of the castle, save the dungeon and throne room on occasion after my imprisonment, and I don't remember much of the layout. Even when I was allowed in the throne room, I was blindfolded while walking through the halls. I wonder if the seer who relayed the prophecy saw this, me, aligning myself with Imirath's enemy. One of the maps catches my eye, and I pluck it from the surface. It's a map of the eastern side of the castle that leads to the Etril Forest. It's where Ailliard and I fled from, but the exit we took is missing.

"Where did you get this?" I ask.

"Saskia drew it. She has spies in Imirath." His voice is close; he's peering over my shoulder. "I'll have to tell her about the heist soon."

"I know." It's good she has spies there; they'll have more knowledge than I do. I won't be able to offer much, but I can present this small piece of information. "There's an exit missing." I place the map on the desk again and grab a quill from an ink pot. "There"—I circle the spot on the map—"it leads to the dungeon."

Cayden's brows scrunch together while he drags a hand through his hair. "For what purpose?"

"To smuggle goods into the castle during sieges, but it hasn't been used in years. No guards were stationed there during my time in Imirath. It's so dark in the dungeon you can hardly see the door against the stone unless you're down there long enough for your eyes to adjust." Cayden stiffens beside me. I forgot I'm talking to someone who hangs on to every syllable that comes out of my mouth.

"I'll have Saskia investigate it in a few days." I'm thankful he doesn't pry further. "Now, on to the next matter of business. I think we should adopt the same plan as the prison and keep the dragon heist just the two of us."

"I agree," I respond without a moment's hesitation. I've already thought this through since the night Cayden and I met in the forest. I would never ask Finnian to accompany me into Imirath, I don't want him there, and I'm not dumb enough to think I can go alone. If Cayden betrays me, at least I'll be close enough to my dragons to burn him. "Just you and me."

"Just you and me," he echoes. A knock rattles the door against its hinges, and we straighten behind the desk. "Enter."

The door practically flies open and bangs into the wall.

Finnian surges forward, eyes on me. "Thank the gods." It's the only thing I hear before he latches his arms around me and lifts me off my feet in an embrace I feel throughout my entire body. He shoves his head into the crook of my neck, and a sob vibrates against my skin. The noise makes me feel like someone stabbed me through the heart. "Ryder told me you were fine, but I needed to see you."

"I'm fine, I promise," I murmur while running my fingers through his curls. His tears soak the collar of my shirt. "I would've found you, but I thought you were asleep."

"I heard the guards moving around, and then I saw Ryder in the hall. He told me someone tried to kill you," Finnian says while setting me on my feet and moving his hands to my shoulders as if he still needs to reassure himself that I'm here. "What happened to your neck?"

"I'll explain later." I reach up to wipe his cheeks. "We'll go over the report, and then we'll talk."

He lets out a shaky breath before nodding. He spins me on my heels and wraps his arms around my shoulders while placing his chin on top of my head. I stay locked in his arms while Ryder gets ready to give the report. Finnian is big on physical reassurance, so his need to hold me is something I expect.

"I'm going to say the worst part first," Ryder begins, a grimace contorting his face. "Garrick placed a bounty on your head, and it's high enough to make even the holiest person in Ravaryn contemplate murder." Finnian stiffens behind me, and Cayden tosses back the remainder of his whiskey. The tension in the room rises with the stakes of the game we're playing. It's something all of us expected, but not this quickly.

"How paternal of him to think I'm worth so much."

"I'd place a bounty on his head if it were worth it," Cayden states while strapping a sword around his waist.

"Why isn't it worth it?" Finnian asks, but I have a feeling I already know the answer.

"An assassin would be quick. Garrick deserves a slow, painful death," Cayden says with the same level of informality as someone ordering a pint.

"Not quick like drowning," I joke, but I'm met with two glares, and Finnian's arms tighten around me. "Okay, too soon. Noted."

"The assassin tonight was dressed like a servant, which is why the guards in front of the suite didn't suspect anything. I think he slipped in during the banquet and bided his time before making a move. The perimeter is secured, but we'll have to go into town to find more answers," Ryder finishes.

"We'll head there now," Cayden states, tossing on his leather jacket and a broadsword across his back. "I'm changing the guards by the door and ordering them not to let anyone into the room, no matter who they are. The previous guards will await a punishment I deem fit. I want to start with the man who spilled a drink on Elowen at the tavern."

Ryder purses his lips, waiting for Cayden to explain.

"He knew she would be in the bath when we returned." Cayden looks at me from across the room, scanning me from head to toe. He opens his mouth before closing it again, looking conflicted, almost like he doesn't want to leave my side. "If you need me, hand a letter off to a servant, and I'll come back."

Part of me wants to offer to go with him, but I need space to sort myself out. I let my eyes glance over him even though I know I should turn away now. "Be safe."

CHAPTER
EIGHTEEN

I DON'T REMEMBER WHEN FINNIAN AND I FELL ASLEEP, BUT I remember holding his hand while dozing off. We used to have sleepovers like that when we were younger, when one of us woke up screaming, but last night we climbed into bed right after Cayden and Ryder left because reality felt like a nightmare. He stayed in my room while I got ready for breakfast with Ailliard. It's early, and most people in the castle aren't awake, but I want to get to Ailliard before he hears about the assassin from someone else.

I bring the steaming cup of coffee to my lips and take a sip, glancing at Finnian over the rim. He still doesn't look fully present, and I hate the fact that I must leave him today. The advisor meetings commencing this week exclude the monarchs, and Saskia informed me they'll take hours, so I suppose we wouldn't be seeing much of each other anyway.

My limbs stiffen as the sound of boots against tile grows in volume. Drinking coffee probably isn't the best idea considering my nerves are bouncing off the walls, but nothing starts a morning off quite like self-destructive habits. Finnian bites his nails while pushing eggs around his plate; it's a nervous tic he's always had. The door creaks open, and Ailliard slips into the room.

"Morning." He looks the both of us over with curiosity and skepticism. Finnian is dressed for politics in a freshly pressed tunic, but

I'm in a new set of leathers, and Ailliard regards the two dragons burned above the diamond-shaped cutout on my chest distastefully. My attire is a mixture of deep purple fabric and harnesses on my thighs for knives, a waist belt with extra blades strapped along it, and buckles all made of dark brown leather with pants to match.

"Morning." I force my voice to stay even.

"How did you sleep?" Finnian asks, even though it's muffled by his hand.

"Fine." Ailliard draws the small word out as he takes a seat. "Someone tell me what's going on." Finnian's eyes flash to me. Is there even a right way to say this?

I place my cup back on its saucer. "An assassin made it into my chambers last night."

Ailliard's hands shoot forward to grip the edge of the table. "Do they not have guards outside your room?"

"They do, but the assassin dressed as a servant. General Neredras thinks he came in during the banquet," I state. Ailliard shakes his head while looking down at the table, disbelief coating his features, which soon morphs into anger.

"We should go home." He starts to get up from the table. "We'll leave today. We can cross the border before they realize we're gone." He needs to stop using running as a solution. My father knows I'm alive; it doesn't make sense for me to leave when the damage is done.

"Sit," I command, and he falls into his chair. "Take a breath. Commander Veles killed him before any real damage was done."

"What was Veles doing in your chambers?"

My hands tighten on the arms of my chair. "We're sharing a suite for my protection."

"That is entirely inappropriate," he snarls. "For the love of the gods, you're a princess! You assured me nothing was happening between you."

"Nothing *is* happening. We spend time together because we're allies, and he's the most skilled fighter in the entire kingdom."

He slams his hands against the table, rattling the dishes and making me flinch. "His skill matters little when he can't be trusted. You share the same blood as his enemy."

And yet he's never looked at me as my father's daughter. "I didn't arrange this meeting to discuss my living arrangements."

"Elowen, I told you I won't lose you like I lost your mother. Garrick is no threat to be taken lightly."

"Stop trying to derail me from the path I've chosen for myself." My temper rises with every word that falls from my lips. "You speak of my abuse as if it's a mere slight to be overlooked and never thought of again, but I'm the one who must live with it every day."

"This path is destructive," he says, trying to reason.

"Only if I lose."

"Have some sense, Elowen. An assassin got into your chambers!"

"I do not fear violence considering my life has been a series of survival." I get to my feet and toss my napkin on the table. The only reason I forced myself to stay alive, even after I left Imirath, was because of my dragons. They're still in the castle, and I will free them because life as a prisoner is no life at all.

"You may think I'm a monster, but I am the product of what was dealt to me." I shove my chair back, grab my satchel, and step toward the door. I don't want to be in here anymore. I want him to understand my choices, even if he disagrees. "I haven't mastered the art of turning away quite like you have."

How many nights did Ailliard fall asleep with a full belly on a feathered mattress while I screamed for someone to help? A god, a guard, my dragons, my own parents—it didn't matter. Finnian and Ailliard can't see the pained expression on my face while the memories surge into the forefront of my mind. The only thing that kept me alive all those years was feeling the bond in my chest, almost like my dragons were reaching out to me despite the walls separating us, telling me to hang on a bit longer.

"Elowen," Ailliard starts, sounding remorseful.

"No." My tone is final. He may have gotten me out of the castle, but he didn't save me. I saved myself. I fought every day, through every panic attack, through every nightmare, and through every person who tried to kill me because I realized I was worth fighting for.

The door slams shut behind me, and I walk aimlessly down the hall. Not caring where I end up, I just want to run. My boots slap against the tile. My lungs crave air, and my senses long to be outside with no walls confining me. I round the corner and collide with a hard chest. Hands reach out to steady me while I stumble back.

"Eager to see me?" Cayden's voice surrounds me.

"Excuse me," I mutter while slipping out of his hold and stepping around him. I'm not in the mood for his teasing.

I make it one step before he grabs my hand and spins me back around to face him. "What's wrong? What happened?"

"Nothing." I pull my hand from his hold again. I know he's mentally logging that I'm shying away from his touch. "We should leave now."

"Where were you running to?"

"Outside." I can't stop myself from pulling on my collar.

"There's an exit up ahead."

I follow his long strides and feel the pressure being lifted from my body when the sky is high above me and no walls surround me. My heart steadies as the cool breeze washes over my face. The black spots clear from my vision, and I can think properly again. My clothes no longer feel like a cage.

I turn my head to find Cayden glaring at me. "Why were you looking for me? I thought I had another hour before we left."

"You almost died last night. I was coming to check on your bruises before you caked all that on." He gestures to my neck.

"Did you expect me to waltz around with them on full display?"

"No, which is why I wanted to see you before you left your chambers." He crosses his arms over his chest. "You should wipe it off."

I bite my tongue and mirror his stance. The bruises were too tender for me to fully cover them. The sitting room was dimly lit, so Ailliard didn't notice them, but natural light exposes everything.

"I'll make sure to consult you on my brushstrokes next time I apply coverage." I'm glad to see we're back to normal. I press my hand against my sore neck and begin wiping the makeup off.

He sighs while taking a step forward. "Let me help you."

My body jolts when he makes contact with my skin. His throat muscles flex as his hand softly coils around the back of my neck. The gentleness of his touch will never fail to shock me.

"Tell me if I'm using too much pressure." His voice is low and soft. He covers his thumb with his black cloak and softly drags it down the column of my neck. The thumb at the base of my hair begins rubbing soothing circles that make me want to melt. I hate that he can affect me like this, and I hate that he's so close he can both see and feel my physical reaction to him. The only bonus is that I can also see his response to me—dilated pupils, parted lips, and the pulse in his neck beats just as rapidly as mine, if not more so. The wind carries a few dark brown curls across my face, which Cayden brushes away.

"Give me the name," he says, tone raspy. "All I need is a name, and I'll take care of it."

His fingers glide down my cheekbone, and I blame the chill that travels up my spine on me not wearing a cloak. I need him to take his hands off me, and yet . . . I can't bring myself to push him away. But then footsteps bounding down the hall pop our bubble. He slowly removes his hands, gliding his fingers against my skin like he's trying to savor the feel of me.

"Elowen!" Finnian's voice echoes against the stone. A second figure swiftly walks toward us, much farther back than Finnian. Not as tall, and more on the stocky side.

"I'll meet you in the suite. You should go," I mutter to Cayden, but he does the opposite by taking a step closer to me.

"He's an ass when he's upset," Finnian says once he gets close enough and hands me the cloak I forgot in the room. "Do you want to get out of the castle today? I'll blow off the meeting." I know this is his way of saying *If you need to find a place to scream, I'll find it with you.*

"Don't skip the meeting. I'm fine; I just needed some air." He doesn't look completely convinced, but he doesn't push me. It'll be good for him to have a normal day here, even if it's away from me. "I'll actually be tracking down those involved in the assassination attempt with Cayden the next few days."

Finnian eyes Cayden with suspicion. "You and Ryder didn't take care of that last night?"

Cayden's expression remains emotionless. "Not all of them. Those slippery little bastards are proving to be quite the challenge."

He smirks at my annoyance but doesn't have time to say anything further once Ailliard steps through the exit.

"Please, Elowen, let's talk," Ailliard pleads. Finnian's jaw clenches, but he doesn't say anything.

"You two should get to the meeting." My smile is forced; it's the one I use every day that nobody other than Finnian can see past. That is, until I met Cayden.

"It doesn't start for two hours." Ailliard takes another step forward. I want to melt into the earth. Cayden places his hand on my lower back, and I'm shocked that it comforts rather than unnerves me. Nevertheless, I lean into his hold, silently telling him it's okay to touch me, and his fingers begin trailing a line up and down my spine.

"Princess Elowen has promised her morning to me, and I imagine you'll be seeing very little of her the next few days," Cayden states. "Perhaps longer."

Ailliard's eyes roam over Cayden, and his face contorts into a distasteful grimace. My body subconsciously gravitates toward Cayden, wanting to protect him from Ailliard.

"You two seem to be spending a lot of time together," Ailliard observes.

"Yes. She's like my own personal plague—very hard to get rid of." Cayden's tone is humorous, but one glance at him, and I can tell he's riled.

"It doesn't seem like you wish to get rid of her considering you placed yourself in her private chambers," Ailliard sneers.

"Oh, I see. This is the part where you remind me of my station." Cayden drops his hand from my back and takes a step between Ailliard and me, staring him down like he wants to grind Ailliard into dust. His display of protectiveness ties my tongue, quite like it did mere hours ago. "Elowen is far more than a title, and I don't need you to remind me who she is."

"Elowen—" Ailliard flicks his eyes away from Cayden and tries again.

"Elowen is coming with me." Cayden cuts him off. "Do I make myself clear, or would you prefer me to write it down so you can comprehend it?"

"Ailliard, leave them. Commander Veles won't let any harm befall Elowen, of that I'm sure," Finnian says before leaning forward to hug me quickly. "Be safe." He turns his eyes to Cayden. "Don't make me into a liar."

Cayden nods, and Finnian escorts Ailliard into the castle. "Did you find the man who spilled the drink on me last night?" I ask.

"Yes. It didn't take much to make him talk." He takes the cloak from my hands and drapes it around my shoulders.

"So he was involved in the attempt?" My toes curl in my boots while he fastens the tie around my neck.

"The pair of them worked together. Nobody else was in on the plot," Cayden confirms. The bounty on my head is still there, but at least this assassination attempt is a closed case.

"Thank you for lying to Finnian. Will Ryder complicate the story since he was with you?"

He shakes his head. "I gave him an assignment to keep him at the border while we're gone."

"I'm also sorry about—"

He cuts me off and tilts my chin up with his finger. "You have nothing to be sorry for. We're starting our journey early." He points to the tree line.

"In a very dark forest with no horses?" I skeptically ask.

"The adventure lies *beyond* the forest," he answers. My eyes wander over his body. He's wearing black leathers with silver accents, accompanied by a broadsword on his back, two short swords at his waist, and throwing knives along his thighs.

"This feels a lot like the second time we met," I note as he grips my shoulders from behind and urges me forward.

He smirks down at me. "That was the start of our friendship."

CHAPTER
NINETEEN

"Are we close?" My legs ache from riding through rough terrain all day to avoid main roads. But I can't deny the sense of freedom that burst inside me when our horses sprinted through an open field with nothing but mountains surrounding us. The feeling that enraptured me in those moments was pure euphoria, which has misted over me sporadically in the past, but now I want a churning ocean that doesn't relent.

We tied our horses off on the outskirts of a Vareveth fishing village that looks far too pleasant to be near Imirath's highest-security prison. Livestock mosey around the sprawling hills behind weathered houses. Seashells and seagrass line the paths to their brightly painted doors, adorned with wreaths made of colored glass.

"Tired already?" Cayden retorts.

"Tired of your company."

"I can carry you the rest of the way, considering I got my practice in last night. Climb up, angel." He extends his arms, and I resist the urge to shove him. Not because I'm above it. But he probably wouldn't budge, and I don't want to listen to him ramble on and on about his strength.

"There was glass on the ground. That's not happening again."

He makes a noise as if to say *We'll see* as he shoves open the entrance to a boathouse swollen from the salty air. "This is an insult to the art of thievery," he mutters, glaring at the unlocked door like it personally offends him.

"Well, I suppose you can't lock that." I jut my chin toward the open wall covered by a simple net that leads to the sea. Water laps against a rectangular cutout in the floor bordered with railings for ease of boarding and disembarking.

He rolls his eyes. "If stealing had been this easy when I was younger, I would've eaten like a king every night."

"Agreed." I laugh. "Do you—" He cuts off my offer of assistance by gripping a boat, lifting it over his head, and placing it in the water like it weighs no more than a feather. I do my best to ignore the way his muscles strain against his sleeves, but I'm only human.

"If you're scared of the water you can sit on my lap," he says while grabbing two oars off the wall.

I drag my eyes from his biceps. "I'll take my chances with the monsters swimming below."

I decline the hand he offers and climb in, taking a seat on one of two benches. The sea sprays my face, but the cold helps keep my anxiety under control. Cayden throws his bag in before sitting across from me and rowing us into the night.

My breath catches in my throat when I spot Kallistar Prison shrouded in fog in the distance. It becomes so much larger than I imagined as Cayden continues rowing. The black rock rises like a mountain, and the ocean churning and crashing against it makes it look like a symbol of pure, impenetrable power. It's no wonder this is where the dragon key and the worst criminals in Imirath are kept. I doubt you'd be able to see it from the shore during a storm, erasing it from existence, just as I'm sure Garrick wants.

"There's a small cove where I'll be able to dock the boat. We'll climb from there."

"You speak as if you've been here before," I note and recall our earlier conversation while he bandaged my hands. "It was *you*! You were the person who made it inside, weren't you?"

The smile he gives me is wolfish. "Crime lords will pay a hefty sum when they find someone who can complete jobs deemed impossible. Members in their gangs died from failed attempts, and their desperation made my pockets heavy."

"You were an assassin?"

"Frightened of me yet, angel?"

I laugh at the idea. "You think I've never killed someone for money?" I remained anonymous for the jobs I sought out considering I was in hiding, but if I needed money, I wasn't morally righteous enough to overlook my skill with a blade. The criminals who hired me didn't care about who I was, only what I could do.

"I know you have," he says, and I regard him curiously. "The way you move through a room, little shadow. That kind of skill can't be taught, it's learned. Just like the way you fight."

His subtle praise stuns me to silence as he rows us closer to the prison, fitting us snugly in a small cove at the base of the mountain. The boat rocks lightly from the water filtering through the sharp rocks littered throughout the sea. Caves glow through the mountain, sporadically and unevenly.

"The prison is a labyrinth of tunnels, but I know how to navigate it. It was mentioned in one of the godly legends I read," Cayden says as he ties off the boat on a rock.

"Have you studied many of the legends?" I ask as he reaches back to help me onto the black sand beach. Tales of the gods are hard to come by. Most have been destroyed, and the stories still in existence are rarely complete.

"Enough to gain an advantage on my enemies."

I like his answer enough to give him another smile, but I'm cut off from saying anything further when my boot sinks into the sand and a sharp tugging sensation in my chest paralyzes me. I'd fall to my knees if Cayden didn't grip me by my elbows.

All traces of ease flee his expression. "El? What's wrong?"

I take in several steadying breaths to calm my racing heart. I feel *different*. It's like the ocean and sand are urging me to feel something, to remember. "It's the bond," I whisper.

"With your dragons?"

I step out of his hold and nod. "I haven't stepped foot in Imirath since I left. Being back here . . . it's unnerving. Anticipatory. I've never felt this before."

"You've never felt pain from the bond, but you do now?"

"I lived with the pain and emptiness for so long that I got used to it. But *this* is different. The emptiness is diminished. I feel like I'm being drawn somewhere." My eyes stray to the horizon, and I swear I can hear dragons roaring at the base of my skull.

Cayden's lips part as he scans my face. "Your eyes are flickering gold. You look . . ."

"What?"

He shakes his head, swallows, and turns away from me to mutter a word so low I don't hear it. Whatever it was, I can tell from his expression that he believes himself unworthy to view me in that way. When he speaks again, it's louder. "Will you be able to climb? I can carry you on my back."

"Tempting offer but entirely unnecessary." I pat his arm while taking two climbing picks from his bag.

He rolls his eyes and pulls a rope free, tying it around his waist before coming over to me and tying it around mine. His rich, masculine scent mingles with the salty air in an addictive way.

I turn away from him once the knot is secured and stare up at the mountain. I hope my dragons can sense me as I sense them. I hope they know I'll climb any mountain if it means getting back to them, freeing them. They will not suffer for much longer, but Imirath will suffer for the pain dealt to us. We will decimate their armies. We will make them get on their knees and bleed and beg.

I sink my pick into the rock and climb.

CHAPTER
TWENTY
———

THE WAVES DROWN OUT THE SOUND OF OUR HOOKS SINKing into the stone. Sweat trickles down the back of my neck as we ascend, and my muscles rival the burning in my chest. I try to breathe through it, but it keeps persisting. Cayden continues glancing my way, but I do my best to keep my expression focused and neutral.

"I'm going to get to the top and pull you the rest of the way," he says.

"Don't rush. The rocks are slippery from the dampness in the air." I pause to watch his conflicted expression. He's probably going back and forth in his head about staying beside me or rushing ahead to be my anchor. But eventually he relents, respecting my request.

My skills have never included brute strength. That combined with the sudden resurgence of my dragon bond pulsing in my chest makes this a difficult climb. But I've never been one to shy away from a challenge.

The jagged cliffside creates crevices for me to step, and I don't dare risk looking down. We're high enough now that a fall could either kill or paralyze us, leaving us to the mercy of the surf. It doesn't truly feel like I'm in Imirath considering I've never been here, but perhaps that's a small mercy to my anxiety.

"I'm going to make sure the cave is clear while you finish," Cayden says when he makes it to the top and swings himself onto a ledge, disappearing from view. I dig deep into myself to complete the climb as the wind rips the hair from my braid and obscures my vision. I sink the pick into the stone again and continue hefting myself up.

I think of my dragons.

I think of Finnian waiting for me in Vareveth.

I think of the life I could have if Cayden and I succeed tonight.

I don't want to be who I am. I want to be more. And I want to fight for myself.

I dig my pick into the stone ledge, but my wrist scrapes on a sharp edge and the bond flares so prominently in my chest that I cry out and my grip fails. Cayden slides to the edge before I fall and grips my bloodied wrist.

"I've got you," he grits out before tugging me up. I help him as much as I can by wedging my boots along the mountainside and pushing myself toward him. When he gets me high enough, he grips me around the waist and falls back with me on his chest. He abruptly flips us over while I'm still catching my breath, untying the rope around my waist to secure it on his belt. "Your death would be highly inconvenient for me, so if you could try a bit harder to not die it would be greatly appreciated."

He's off me in the next second, unsheathing his sword and offering me a hand up. I could be mature and pretend like I don't see it, but I smack it away after attaching the picks to my waist and climb to my feet instead, sharpening my knives against each other as I glare at him. The way he regards my features seems like he enjoys this.

"Where are the guards?" I whisper when we enter a suspiciously empty cave.

"They remain in the lower caves, but even if a prisoner were to escape, the current, rocks, or monsters would kill them before they got to shore. However, they patrol the halls throughout. Is the bond still acting up?" We halt before turning a corner, and he pricks the tip of his finger with a knife, letting a few drops fall to the stone floor.

The pressure in my chest has faded to a dull throb now that my blood isn't seeping into the stone, but I'll manage. "The magic here is having a strong effect on it. What exactly are you doing?"

"This is apparently where the God of Water kept his prisoners before the gods left us. The water in my blood will guide us to where we need to go. Not everyone knows the trick, and some people have died in the labyrinth while trying to find a way out."

At first, it doesn't look like much is happening, but the blood slides together after a few moments, creating a dark red dot. I try to remember what I know of the God of Water, but my memory is hazy, like I'm looking up at the sky from the bottom of a murky lake.

He presses a hand into my back and the droplet leads us down a torch-lined, winding path that splits off into two. I notice that there aren't any stairs, just a network of turns leading higher or lower throughout the prison. It all looks the same and would definitely be easy to get lost in. It's almost like it was designed to drive escaping prisoners mad.

Voices bounce off the walls when we step into an opening that juts off into three others. I move forward to swipe the blood droplet away to erase the evidence of our presence when I'm roughly grabbed from behind. I pivot and press my knife to my assailant's neck, halting the blade just before I pierce his flesh.

"You don't need to surprise me with knives, angel. I'll bleed for you if you ask nicely."

Drawing knives is a force of habit. He spins me again and presses my front into the stone, bracing his arms on either side of my head and getting maddeningly close. "I don't ask nicely when I dream of stabbing you."

"Do you wish to indulge me in what else you fantasize about me?"

I nudge my elbow into his stomach. "What in the hells are you doing?"

"Darkness is drawn to my cloak; it'll keep us hidden. We can't be found before we get to the key." He drops his voice to a whisper as the voices grow louder.

"But I thought—"

"Yes, magic is outlawed in Vareveth. Eagor's laws are adorable. I'm sure he recites them to Valia every night as a bedtime story. Now, stop fucking wiggling."

"You shoved me into a wall of stone. I'm uncomfortable."

"I don't care," he hisses, grabbing my hips to still them. But that's when I feel it . . . his hard length digging into me. The voices grow louder, as does the blood rushing through my ears. I try not to show a reaction, but I can tell he notes the way my breathing has changed when his shoulders stiffen after I shakily inhale.

His hands grip me harder.

My heart beats faster.

Maybe it's for the best we're in a place where we can't act on this, but teasing him is far too addictive, so I push my hips back onto his. He mutters a curse under his breath.

"Elowen," he warns.

"Perhaps I'm not the one doing the fantasizing, soldier," I murmur as the voices decrease in volume and blessedly turn down a different path.

He takes a small step back, enough to look down at me with dilated pupils. His voice is rough when he speaks. "I've never been called a fool, and denying your beauty would make me one."

I shake off the lingering feelings and we continue our hunt. The key must be kept in a separate section from the prisoners, and knowledge of its existence is most likely reserved for the higher-ranking guards. When I believe we can't go any higher, the cave narrows to a single pathway ending at a heavy metal door. A guard sits on the ground nearby, faintly snoring.

"I'll pick the lock. You take care of the guard," Cayden whispers, placing a velvet pouch in my hand. "Time to utilize your skills, little shadow."

I open it and dump a light blue shimmering powder into my palm. "You filthy criminal. You've been keeping a magical sedative secret from me this whole time. I wonder what your king would say."

"It'll be our secret."

"I'm going to keep some in case you vex me on the journey back. Your presence is tolerable when you keep your mouth shut."

Cayden glares, and I blow him a kiss while moving around him and keeping my steps as light as a feather as I approach the guard. He smacks his lips and grumbles when I lean down and blow the powder. It puffs around him like a cloud until it fades into the darkness as the spell takes hold.

"How long do we have?" I ask while Cayden removes two silver picks from his pocket and inserts them into the keyhole, unlocking the door in a matter of seconds.

"That'll last an hour and we'll be long gone before he wakes." He turns, taking in my wide eyes while holding the door to the chamber open for me. "Thievery is a skill mastered at the expense of morality."

I slide past him and enter. "And I suppose you're the master?"

"I'm the king."

A single stone pillar bathed in moonlight streaming through several barred windows resides at the center of the room. It pulses in time with my heart, and I feel it vibrating through my boots as we walk closer. But no key rests upon the surface; only an imprint chiseled into the stone remains. Cayden and I exchange a look, knowing this is more complex than an empty slab. We're at the top of a mountain riddled with blood magic.

I prick my finger, watching a bead form before letting it fall into the hollow imprint.

"Atarah blood of old and new, feed the mold for they wait for you."

I gasp. "Did you hear that?"

His brows furrow. "No, what are you talking about?"

I shake my head, taking his hand in mine to prick his finger as well. But when his blood falls . . . it seeps through the stone like it was never there, and yet mine remains. He shows no sign of the riddle being triggered by his blood.

"Fucking gods," he mutters, catching on to what this means. "Cut me again. Maybe it'll work on the second try."

"We must use Atarah blood to form the key, Cayden. They're my dragons, only my blood will free them." I turn away from the stone to meet his uneasy eyes. "The stone spoke into my mind."

"That's reassuring." I set the knives down to tug my sleeve up to my elbow, but Cayden grips my wrist. "Blood magic is tricky, Elowen."

"I know blood is sticky."

"Not the time."

"What other choice do we have?" I ask. He grits his teeth, and the frustration on his face for knowing there's no other option is evident. "Don't try to talk me out of this. You'll be wasting time, and considering we don't know the guard schedule, I suggest you let me bleed quickly."

I don't hesitate to grab my knife and stare at the stars glistening above the ocean, the same stars I used to count from the Imirath dungeon, the same stars I gazed upon in Aestilian while swearing I'd find a way back to my dragons, and slice my arm.

CHAPTER
TWENTY-ONE

THE MAGIC SEIZES ME SLOWLY, SOMETHING AKIN TO VINES creeping over my shoulders and dragging me down to the forest floor for a nap. All I see is darkness.

"Cayden?" I murmur, slurring like I've had too much to drink.

"I'm here," he responds, stepping behind me to keep me steady. "Gods, you're freezing."

The warmth of his chest keeps me tethered to the chamber, despite not being able to see it. Shadows swim behind my eyes like gossamer fabric flowing against the night sky. He rests his chin on my head and rubs his hand down my uninjured arm, holding me steady with his other. Flashes of green, lavender, yellow, blue, red, pink, gold, and silver shine through the shadows.

The colors of my heart.

The colors embedded into my soul.

"Dragons," I whisper. "My dragons."

"Elowen." He says my name with nothing short of reverence. "Your eyes are glowing again."

The shadows behind my eyes become green smoke. "Sorin."

The smoke clears in the center and I see Sorin's green-scaled sleeping face. My cheeks feel wet, and my heart sputters in my chest. His head is so much larger than the last time I saw him, and I wish the vision would let me see the rest of his body. I want to see his markings, his horns, his claws. I never want this to end.

"Venatrix." The smoke turns red, and I stare into Venatrix's red gaze and soak in her blood-red scales. "Venny, can you hear me?" She tilts her head to the side, and gold flecks appear in her eyes. "It's Elowen. I can see you."

The ground shakes under my boots but I can't pull myself from the vision, not when Venatrix huffs in acknowledgment. I can't let go of this one sliver of happiness.

The smoke changes to blue and I see Delmira. Flashes to lavender and I see Basilius. And finally becomes silver and I see Calithea.

The rumbling increases, and salty tears paint my lips. "I'm coming back for you. I promise. I'll see you so soon. Just hold on for me, please."

"The key is forged. It's time to let go," Cayden murmurs in my ear.

I grip the stone pillar with a shaky hand. "Sorin hasn't woken up yet. I haven't seen his eyes. He hasn't seen me."

"You'll see him soon, angel. I need you to let go now."

"I can't!" Basilius roars in distress. "Please don't make me leave them again."

But Cayden rips me away from the pillar, and my dragons are gone. I'm left with an emptiness deeper than the blackest part of the sea. The floor wasn't shaking, my body was and still is as sobs rack me. I don't realize I've collapsed until I try to stand, and the darkness surrounding me isn't from a vision but my face buried in Cayden's neck as tears slide down his skin. He rubs my back and pulls me close, trailing his fingers through my hair.

"We'll right this wrong, El." His voice is thick, rough. "You'll see your dragons again." He loosens his hold on me to tear off a piece of his shirt, but my knife is in my hand before he realizes what I'm doing. The blade doesn't even prick my skin before he wraps his arms around my wrists to restrain me.

"Just one more look, and then we can leave."

"No." His tone is final.

"I need to see Sorin's eyes."

"Elowen, that pillar is enchanted. Your father has sought multiple ways to keep you away from your dragons, and I don't doubt he'd create something like this with the intention of making you want to bleed out. If you were alone, you would've done just that."

"I won't bleed out." I struggle against his hold, doing my best to nick his hand just enough to unhand me. "Just one more second."

"El," he growls, pinning me to the wall and getting close enough to render my legs immobile. "Don't ask me to stand by while you hurt yourself. It's blood magic. It's not real."

"It was real! I saw them. They sensed me."

"I know, love. I know." His thumbs rub into my wrists where he pins them, careful to avoid my injury from the climb. "And you'll spend the rest of your life with them, which starts by getting out of this prison. I'm going to let go and bandage your arm. Can I trust you?"

I glance longingly at the pillar while letting his words sink in, swallowing the lump in my throat as I offer a resigned nod. It's just so hard to miss them, to long for them, and to have an image of them at my fingertips. But I know Cayden is right. I'd bleed out with hope in my heart and nothing else.

He continues speaking while wrapping my arm with more gentleness than I thought he was capable of. "Don't be angry at yourself, or me. Be angry at every single fucker that stands between you and your dragons. Turn your blades on them and reap their souls." His words awaken a fire in me. "Every time I step onto the battlefield, I tell myself it's one more kill before I make it to Garrick. His death has played out in my mind since I was a boy. Even when I had nothing, I knew your power existed. I knew I'd survive long enough to find the lost princess with a dragon bond and combine our forces."

I meet his eyes as he ties the knot on my arm, and he cups my face to dry my last tear.

"You will not die here. You will not be a prisoner to Imirath again.

I don't care if I must carry you out of here, but you decide how we leave this room."

I let his words stoke the fire within until it blazes through me, becoming the firestorm made flesh that the seer from Galakin prophesized all those years ago. It's time I turned my wrath on Imirath, unyielding, merciless vengeance. "I want Imirath blood."

"There she is." Cayden steps away from me, a smirk playing on his lips when he plucks the freshly forged key from the mold. My blood solidified into crimson metal, and it shimmers as Cayden twirls it around his finger before tucking it into his pocket. "You'll have it."

I keep the flames burning as we exit the chamber and pass the deeply snoring guard. I wonder what it's like to sleep that deeply, magically induced or not. Cayden pricks his finger again and we begin our journey through the winding caves to return to our boat. I'm slightly light-headed, but the fruit I left in my pack at the Vareveth fishing village will help. We're halfway down a long cavern when shadows dance along the wall. I whip my head behind us, but we won't be able to retreat without them hearing us run. Everything in here echoes.

"Looks like you'll be getting your wish for Imirath blood far sooner than I intended." Cayden chuckles, unsheathing two swords. It's comical how calm he is. A man completely in control of any fight he enters. I can't stop myself from softly laughing, despite what happened moments ago. Six guards escorting a prisoner round the bend and blink in confusion when they see us. I smile and wave while Cayden throws an arm around my shoulders. "Oh, thank the gods. Would you be so kind and point us in the right direction? We can't find the exit."

Their shocked faces increase my laughter, and I steady myself against Cayden as they unsheathe their weapons and charge us. The prisoner remains where he is, not that he'd get far with the shackles connecting his wrists and ankles. I take down one guard with a knife, spearing him through the eye before unsheathing my sword. The blade becomes an extension of me, and I move with it like the tide pushing and pulling against the rocks surrounding us. Cayden kills with the efficiency of a god going against a mortal army, barely breaking a sweat as he wields his twin swords, cutting down two.

Within the whirlwind of blades and blood, I hadn't realized I offered Cayden my back. It's a sign of trust I've only truly granted Finnian. I've been betrayed too many times to trust freely, but perhaps the alliance between the two of us doesn't have to stand on shaky ground. We're bound by sharing the same enemies, but this is the first moment where I'm happy to fight with him. Not because of his power but because I know no blade will pierce my back for as long as he stands.

I throw another knife from behind Cayden as he's about to kill the last guard, and he whips around to face me after. His lips spread in a devastating smile as blood drips down his cheeks, taking in my similar disposition.

"You're a vicious little thing," he says, pricking his finger to create another blood droplet to get us out of here.

I quirk a brow. "Scared?"

"Not in the slightest."

Our moment is broken when the prisoner picks up a sword from the ground and raises it at us. He looks as if he hasn't eaten or bathed in weeks, and it's impossible to see him as a threat considering his blade wobbles like a frail tree in a storm. I roll my eyes and retrieve my knives. We don't have time for this.

"I-I-I won't let you take me back out there," the prisoner stammers. Cayden and I exchange a look. If this man is more terrified of the world outside this prison, then he must've done something to earn his sentence and a six-guard escort while chained. "INTRUDERS! INTRUDERS!"

Cayden steps forward and swings his blade with enough force to behead him. The prisoner's body twitches as his head thumps on the ground. Silence hangs heavy between us, but it doesn't last long. Hundreds of footsteps echo throughout the mountain, rumbling the pebbles along the side of the cave. Cayden throws the prisoner over his shoulder and picks up the head before sprinting slightly behind, trusting me to follow the droplet to where we need to go. Hopefully Garrick thinks we infiltrated the prison to liberate a prisoner. It's not uncommon to break an inmate free from other prisons to face the wrath of a gang leader or someone else they've harmed.

We make it to the cave we entered through, and Cayden tosses the prisoner into the ocean. He stares down like he wishes he could command the sea to spit the man back out so he could torture him for jeopardizing our mission. The waves churn far more aggressively than they did when we arrived, completely swallowing the small beach we walked on. Our boat still floats but won't for long if we don't get down there in time.

Cayden slams his pick into the mountain and begins tying intricate knots to tether him to it. He steps toward me when he finishes and grips my shoulders. "How much do you trust me?"

I hate the timing of this question. "I trust you to not let me die."

"I can work with that." He reaches for me, wrapping both of my legs around his waist, and ties us together with the same knots he used on the pick. "Before you argue with me, know that this isn't up for discussion, princess. The tide is rising, and the guards are scurrying through this place like rats."

I tighten my arms around his neck when he dips over the side and begins our steady descent, keeping me secure between his arms as our hearts crash together. I've never feared heights, but once the cloud of thick fog surrounding the base of the prison obscures my vision, I bury my head in Cayden's neck and trust he'll finish the journey.

"Will you teach me how to use your lockpicks?" I ask, needing to distract myself.

His chuckle dances in the strands of my hair. "Corrupting you further is an invitation I'll never decline."

Cayden's boots splash in the surf when we make it to the bottom, and he unties the knots in one simple tug. "I'd like to learn that, too," I say.

"Deal."

I loosen my legs around him, but he tightens his arms, not letting me go until he deposits me in the rocking boat and pushes us out to sea. He notices my flushed cheeks as he rows us back to the Vareveth village where we left our horses and made camp in the forest.

"No point in us both getting our feet wet," he says.

"No ulterior meaning?" I ask, recalling his words from the tavern.

The grin he gives me is anything but innocent. "Never, angel."

CHAPTER
TWENTY-TWO

MY LAUGHTER HAUNTS ME LIKE A GHOST, AND EVERY-thing around me feels as if it's stuck in syrup, moving slowly. In Aestilian, I felt stagnant. But right now, I feel trapped in my own mind, slowly watching the castle crumble and windows shatter as I try to hold myself together.

The pain in my chest isn't from the bond, it's from loss. The theft of time. The fear of failure. The wind flows through the creaky trees toward Imirath, but I remain here, miles away from the creatures I saw so vividly it was like they were in front of me.

I have the overwhelming feeling of wanting to go home but not knowing where home is. A blanket is wrapped around my shoulders, snapping me out of my thoughts. I glance behind me, not realizing Cayden moved from his place by the fire.

"You're trembling." He runs his hands down my arms, and I do my best to keep my emotions contained, hating that I feel I'm on the verge of crying in front of him again.

"I'm sorry," I whisper, not really sure what exactly I'm apologizing for. Not being okay? Being too emotional?

His lips turn down in displeasure. "You've never apologized to me before today, so don't start now. Especially not over what you're feeling."

"I'll be better the next time I see the dragons. I can hold myself together. I was just shocked and unprepared." The words rush out of me in defense, though I'm not defending myself from anything other than the perception of weakness only I'm perceiving.

"I know you will," he says, taking a seat beside me again. He stokes the fire, and my eyes dance over how it pronounces his features. "But you don't need to right now." He looks at me, and my stomach tumbles. "I want to know what's going on up here." He gently taps his fingers on my head.

I shake my head, turning back to the flames. "Too much."

"I'll be the judge of that." He stokes the fire again, and sparks rise into the night sky. "Talk to me." He pauses for a moment before adding, "Please."

It's a small word but it holds the power to blanket the forest in silence other than the distant howls and crashing waves. Yet something about being here, away from the castle and prying eyes and expectations, façades and false laughter, has my lips feeling loose. I've often felt like I'm too intense for people, so keeping to myself has always been preferable. My thoughts are my own, but Cayden is looking at me as if they're made of air and he longs to fill his aching lungs.

"I've lived with guilt for so long I don't know who I am without it." I pull the blanket tighter around me. "When I was younger, I barely felt anything. I didn't even feel human. I had to tell myself to present an emotion so people didn't worry about me, and I just pretended I was fine so nobody would look too deeply and realize how much pain I was in. I felt like a statue someone carved, empty and smiling, because I could never have a moment of joy without thinking of how my dragons were suffering."

I feel like a kettle about to boil, and I press my lips together to stop myself from rambling. My fingers tug my pendant along the chain, and I try to dispel the tightness in my chest by breathing deeply.

"Keep talking, El," Cayden gently states, running a tentative hand down my back.

"I shouldn't be talking so much. I should be grateful for the life I have."

"Don't give me that bullshit." My eyes flash to his angry gaze.

"Don't belittle all you've endured for a perception of yourself that someone made you believe you need to be."

I swallow the lump in my throat and dig my nails into my palms, nodding when his hand strokes my spine again. "I was always told I'd never see my dragons again, and I was expected to accept it. But I never could, and seeing them tonight ripped open a wound that has never fully healed." I wipe the damn tears off my cheeks and continue. "I pretend like I'm not scared of anything, but I'm terrified. I can't fail my dragons again. I fought Ailliard when he took me out of Imirath so I could go back to them. I was ten years old, and I didn't care that going back meant punishment or death, because my dragons have always been everything to me. They're part of me, and I miss them . . . so much," I choke out.

I could never talk to Ailliard about my dragons without him reminding me they killed his sister. Nor Finnian without him listing off the reasons it was impossible, not out of malice, but out of fear for me.

Cayden tugs me closer, resting my legs over his and pressing my head below his chin. He's rigid at first, like he has no idea what he's doing and moved before he thought this through, but eventually he relaxes. His fingers thread through my hair, and my mind and body are so exhausted that I don't even try to fight the comfort. He's warm against the night, and steady in a way I need right now.

"I'm—"

"*Stop* apologizing." He threads his fingers through my hair again. "Each tear that falls from your eyes is another enemy that dies."

"I don't want you to think the person you aligned yourself with is unstable."

"You have nothing to prove to me. I sought you out." When I pull my head away from his chest, his glare is pointed at Imirath. "You're fierce and determined. You're brave, resilient, and lethal. You're a survivor, have seen the worst parts of human nature, and yet somehow never forgot how far one act of kindness can go. You're sweet and soft, too, even though you try to hide it." I feign a glare even though his words are bringing on a fresh wave of emotion, and his intensity cracks when he chuckles at my expression. "Surviving is a burden some days. I know what it is to live with guilt, how it eats away at you."

"I didn't realize you paid such close attention to me."

"What makes you think I've ever looked away?"

My heart flips in my chest. "Is there anyone I can help you get back to?"

He flicks his gaze back to the forest as his eyes take on a faraway glaze. "You can help me win this damn war once we free your dragons. That's all the closure I crave."

"We will." I nod, unable to tear my eyes away from his profile. "What did Garrick do to you?"

A rueful smile turns his lips, and he leans back against the tree, his bitter laughter floating up to the moon. Several seconds tick by and turn into minutes. Just when I come up with something to say to cut the tension between us, he relents and states with zero emotion, "My mother was executed on his order."

My eyes dance over the scar on his face and the lash marks peeking above his leathers. The markings of a hard life. "How old were you?"

"Eleven."

I take his hand in mine, and he looks down at it like comfort perplexes him. "Would it help you to talk about it?"

"The only thing that helps me is stepping on the battlefield," he says.

"Well, I'm here if you change your mind."

He looks at me again, and I feel if I were anyone else, he would snap at me. His eyes burn with anger, but it's not directed at me, and it doesn't scare me. He relents, nods. Even if he never takes me up on the offer, I'll never regret extending my friendship to someone who seems to understand loneliness and hopelessness as I do. Perhaps we're not only united in our capacity for anger and skill with blades, though the realization doesn't bring me any sense of comfort.

"Tell me something that makes you happy," I say. I don't want him to be lost in a past that is clearly painful.

"Happy?" The word is coated in disgust.

"Gods, I know you're a grump, but this is too much."

"Most people are infinitely irritating." He tosses a twig into the fire and sighs when he realizes I won't relent. "Money, whiskey, fighting."

I snicker and his eyes cut to mine, the anger slowly lessening. "I love reading. I stole books while I was living on the streets, but before that I used to reread the same three while growing up since they were all we had in the house. The words provided a refuge."

I understand him all too well. "May I borrow your favorite book?"

He nods, and his lips quirk. "You'll be disappointed in the lack of passionate romance, I'm afraid."

"Gods!" I cover my face with my hands. "Did Finnian tell you?"

"You're not the only one who likes to snoop, love."

"I had to make sure you weren't a murderer since we're living together," I huff. He blinks slowly and gestures to his weapons. "A murderer to me."

"And did you come to any conclusions from my soap tray and linens?"

"You smell nice and are very clean." I grin and prop my chin on my fists. He breaks into a fit of laughter and I can't help but join him.

"I like your smile . . . your laugh, too. You don't give me either easily." He runs a hand through his messy hair, and the waves flop back to where he brushed them off his forehead. They've curled more in the damp air. "Fess up, El."

"Baking." I nudge a rock with my boot. "Having something to do with my hands calms my mind. I love swimming in the summer and sunning myself on the rocks."

He taps his leg into mine. "Flour on your cheeks and blood under your nails, that's an endearing image."

I shove his arm, and he teeters to the side while chuckling, rubbing his shoulder when he rights himself. I furrow my brows. "Did I hurt you?"

"No." He drops his hand. "I broke my shoulder when I was a boy, and it still aches sometimes when I overuse it. Don't look at me like that. I'll carry you any damn day, it was the prisoner that did me in."

I tuck my hair behind my ears and move to a kneeling position before him. "What are you doing?"

"I'm a healer. I can try to ease the pain."

He catches my wrists before I have the chance to touch him, and I realize just how close our faces are. The way the dim light of the fire turns his eyes into sprawling spring meadows. The way his hair looks unrelentingly black. The stubble dotting his jaw that somehow grows around his scar. And lastly... I notice his lips that the gods must have spent extra time crafting.

Lips I have no business thinking of.

Lips I *can't* think of.

"You should go to sleep," he states in a gravelly voice, bringing my eyes up to his searing gaze. He looks at me like he wishes he knew how to look away but remains frozen in time. My heart pounds in my chest, and my fingers itch to touch him in a way I know I can't.

I can't. I can't. I can't.

But the voice in my head grows fainter the longer I look at him.

"I'm not tired," I whisper.

"El." His throat bobs, and hands tighten around my wrists. "I need you to walk away from me."

"Why?"

"Because I won't walk away from you, and I need you to be stronger than me."

The way his words make my blood rush isn't right. I can't feel these things. He's my ally. He can't be anything more.

I remove my wrists from his hold and stand. I can do this for him after what he did for me today. The blanket has been warmed by the fire, and I lie on my back to stare up at the stars. My eyelids grow heavy in the wake of today's events, but before sleep pulls me under, I whisper, "Thank you."

"For?"

"You're the only person brave enough to help me free my dragons." I know he's not doing it out of the kindness of his heart. There are stipulations to our arrangement. But his courage still counts for something.

He shrugs. "Achieving the impossible will give me something to gloat about when I'm in hell."

☩ ☩ ☩

By the time we make it back to the castle I'm practically dragging myself up the steps. All I want is a hot bath and a meal after riding through rain the past several hours. When I open the door to our chambers, I come face-to-face with Finnian, Ryder, and Saskia lounging on the couches in the sitting room. Cards are splayed out on the table like they've been waiting for quite some time.

Oh, sweet gods.

Cayden clasps my shoulders from behind and squeezes. "You're supposed to be at the border."

"I finished my assignment early, so I came back to give you my report, only to realize you weren't here," Ryder responds, throwing another card onto the table.

"My apologies for the sadness that must've caused you," Cayden responds.

"How was the assassin, Elowen?" Finnian asks.

"Great!" My voice is louder than usual.

He smirks. "Great?"

"He must've been a very charming corpse from the way you're smiling," Saskia says.

"Is anyone hungry? I'm hungry," I say, striding in the direction of my room.

"If the two of you want to spend time together, you don't have to lie," Ryder says, and I stumble over my feet, catching myself on the back of the couch.

Finnian laughs, placing another card on the table. "We all knew it was bound to happen eventually."

"Excuse me?"

Cayden glares at the whiskey bottle Ryder must've taken from his reserve. "How kind of you all to be so accepting over how we choose to spend our time."

"And where exactly did you spend your time?" Saskia asks. "The pair of you were gone before we even realized it."

"We rode to the coast," I say. It's not like we can lie and say we were in the city.

"The coast?" Saskia quirks a perfectly sculpted brow, and I sense I've said the wrong thing. "Interesting." Her eyes ping back and forth between Cayden and me, but Ryder and Finnian are too absorbed in their game to pick up on what's happening. "We'll have dinner after you bathe and catch up on treaty meetings."

CHAPTER
TWENTY-THREE

THE WHISPERS HAVE GOTTEN WORSE.

My palms prickle as I eye two female servants along the wall giggling to each other. Cayden has been at the border the past week, and our chain of correspondence has been a hot topic. I wonder if Hyacinth tells anyone I tuck the letters he sends me into a drawer rather than discard them with the rest of my mail.

At least it's impossible for the castle to know how the ink has smudged from rereading them before bed.

"The food supply sent to Aestilian before winter will have to be substantial considering how treacherous winter months are in the north," Ailliard says. The way he conducts himself in the alliance meetings makes me wonder why he was a guard and not an advisor.

"How large is the population?" Eagor asks. "We're a wealthy kingdom, but I must know if sending this much is necessary."

Ailliard looks to me to answer.

"Two thousand," I respond. It's less than that, but this means they'll have more than enough food and plenty to spare. Ailliard gives me a subtle nod of approval, but Eagor's calculating gaze remains fixated on me.

"May I inquire as to how many of your citizens were originally mine?"

"If you don't know who's missing, does it truly matter they're gone,

Your Grace?" Saskia interjects. She's seated on the Vareveth side but has been nothing short of an ally to Aestilian. "Forgive me if I overstep, but we should focus on what food to send to get them through winter and prioritize signing the treaty in a timely manner."

"I'm in agreement with Lady Saskia," Ailliard says. "Her Majesty and I will not disclose irrelevant information, and she has come here at a great risk to her safety."

Eagor gives a tight nod after several prolonged seconds. "I must apologize again for the altercation in your bathing chamber last week."

I give an even tighter smile. "I'd prefer to focus on my people than the past if that's all right with you."

He sighs, plucking some parchment off the long oak table lined with advisors. Saskia and Valia are the only women on their side, and I'm the only one on mine, sitting between Ailliard and Finnian.

One of my many grievances is how often women are left out of conversations when we're the ones who find logical solutions after a mess is made. So much time could be spared if more women were given the chance to participate from the beginning, rather than as a last resort.

"There will be a surplus of grains and oats, as well as other necessities. We'll supply livestock as well," Eagor says. "We'll be hosting a ball to showcase our alliance that Valia has begun planning."

Valia perks up at the mention of her name. It's the first time her husband has acknowledged her presence in this meeting. I can't help but pity her. She's been nothing but condescending since I've met her, but it's obvious her marriage was not a love match . . . it's not even friendship.

"The king, queen, and crown prince of Galakin have been invited. I sent their invitations with our exports this morning."

"They may not attend if there are storm surges as there often are this time of year," Eagor says as he stands up from the table, and the rest of us follow suit. "This meeting is adjourned. Ailliard, you and one of my advisors will meet with the keeper of livestock tomorrow to iron out the details."

"Yes, Your Majesty." Ailliard bows his head. "Thank you for your generosity."

Eagor smiles at the pair of us, but his eyes linger on me. I force my lips not to curl as his eyes dip to where my gown hugs my body. My people are more important than my pride and comfort. Nobody else notices. He knows how to be subtle about it, and I'm sure many would say I should be honored that a king looks at me in that way or that I'd never be worthy of his glance if I addressed his behavior.

Valia rounds the table and I step away from Ailliard and Finnian's conversation to greet her. Ailliard approached me the morning after Cayden and I got back to the castle to apologize, and we've been mending the wound left behind from the argument ever since.

"I wanted to let you know in advance that there will be several worthy suitors at the ball who are all eager to meet you." She smiles widely and clasps my hand. "I know you've grown quite close to Commander Veles, but a princess needs a man with a good family name."

I bite my tongue. "Commander Veles and I are allies."

She playfully rolls her eyes. "Don't worry, I won't tell Eagor."

"Queen Valia, I adore your gown." Saskia steps beside me and slides her arm through mine. "Forgive my intrusion, but Queen Elowen and I have plans this evening."

Valia's smile tightens, but she proceeds with the practiced grace of someone trained to be a queen since she was a child. "Enjoy your evening, ladies."

Saskia and I step into the hall and keep our pace swift and voices low, barely audible above our gowns swishing and heels clacking on the tile.

"Did Eagor say something to Cayden about our . . . situation?" I ask. "Is he in trouble?"

She shakes her head, keeping her face close to mine. "You must understand how threatening your existence is to the rulers of Vareveth. You have a link to five dragons and a claim to the Imirath throne, and you are unwed."

Ice slides through my veins when I think of Garrick and how my very existence was punished.

"The army reveres Cayden and are completely loyal to him. He's known to be one of the best swordsmen and strategists in Ravaryn history. He's both loved and feared, infamous and a mystery. Everyone knows to never underestimate how ruthless he is. They want you to wed someone they can control. Preferably a man of Vareveth nobility who wouldn't mind being Eagor's lapdog. If Galakin comes they'll most likely play their hand at a union between you and their prince."

"The rulers of Ravaryn must not be as powerful as they hope if they plot about how to control me." The walls of the castle suddenly feel too tight around me.

"Eagor ordered Cayden to stay away from you."

That statement shouldn't faze me. It shouldn't drape a heavy cloak over my shoulders. It shouldn't make me want to see him walk down the hallway with a familiar smirk playing on his lips.

"What did Cayden say?"

I open the door to my suite to avoid Saskia's observant gaze but nearly stumble over the rug. At the center of the table sits the most gorgeous bouquet I've ever seen. A crystal vase holds various flowers in shades of green, purple, white, blue, pink, and red—the colors of my dragons. The fresh scent of spring blooms around me as I walk closer and pluck Cayden's note off the table, dragging my finger over the crossed-sword seal.

"He said Eagor couldn't order him to do that." She runs a slender finger down one of the supple petals. "And then he laughed in the king's face."

CHAPTER
TWENTY-FOUR

"Your turn, Elowen." Ryder's voice pulls me out of my daydream and places me back into the bustling tavern in the village of Ladislava.

I lay my queen card on the table, overruling the soldier card Finnian threw down before me. The simple game is called Courts and can be played with up to five people all receiving seven cards from the deck placed in the center of the circle. Cards must be played in a strategic order to win with a king overtaking any queen, soldier, or jester. Failing to produce a card higher than the one placed before requires a player to draw one and skip a turn—which is exactly why Saskia is glaring at me.

But it's short-lived because Ryder plays his final king card, the game is over, and his pockets grow heavier with our syndrils. "Another round? It'll be on me."

"Not for me," Saskia says, eyeing my nearly untouched cider. "Would you like me to take you to some of my favorite shops? They'll be closing soon, and I'm bored of cards."

"I'd love that." Her insightfulness is both a blessing and a curse, but tonight it's the former.

"I'm not sure that's a good idea," Finnian says, eyeing the night sky through a window.

"Ladislava is safer than Verendus." Ryder begins shuffling the cards again. "But be back within the hour."

"I'll be fine, Finnian." I gesture down my knife-clad legs. "I have my consequence correctors if I run into trouble."

Ladislava resembles Verendus, set beyond the forest Cayden and I traveled through to get to Kallistar. It's where most of the army resides when they're not on the border, and it has a wide array of shops and restaurants. Most people walk around armed to the teeth while carrying baskets and cake boxes back to their homes, but there's the occasional gown in a sea of leathers.

Saskia slides her arm through mine, and we huddle together against the cold. Wind whips through the winding cobblestone roads bordered with autumn-enriched trees and quaint shops. The streets are nearly deserted given the late hour, but the scent of sugar from a day's worth of baking and herbal remedies lingers like a ghost in a graveyard.

The bell above the door to the tiny stone shop chimes when Saskia and I step through. The cold melts from my hands and I wrap my cloak tighter around me to keep from knocking herbs off the cramped shelves. It smells divine in here: flowers, spices, and something utterly peaceful.

"Lady Saskia, I was wondering when I'd see you again!" The tiny woman with long gray hair and warm eyes smiles from behind the counter. "And you brought a friend." The woman reaches for her glasses, but her face drops when recognition washes over her features. "Your Majesty," she says in a rush while shakily standing up from the stool, but I touch her arm before she can drop to a curtsy.

"There's no need for that." I smile, helping her back onto the stool.

"Can I help you find a blend you're looking for?" She nods, not looking fully convinced I won't execute her for not curtsying. "Commander Veles ordered one earlier this week, but he hasn't been by to pick it up."

Confusion cloaks Saskia's features, but she takes the light pink tin dotted with yellow flowers from the woman and tucks it into her bag. I quickly look away. It's obvious he intends to gift the tea to a woman.

The cider I drank must not have been good because my stomach starts burning with something I don't wish to identify.

"I'll just take my usual," Saskia says while placing several coins on the counter.

I mosey around while Saskia finishes her transaction and let her guide me back into the cold once she finishes. The back of my neck prickles. A sixth sense that's saved my life more times than I remember.

I shove Saskia behind a large oak tree when a sharp pain shoots through my shoulder. My legs wobble slightly, and I press my hand into the bark while ripping out a dart half filled with an inky blue liquid.

I break off the tip and hand it to Saskia. "Get to Finnian and Ryder. Tell them what's happening."

"I'm not leaving you."

"You're not armed and they're looking for me."

She wraps an arm around my shoulder, trying to get me to move. "You've been drugged. You can't fend them off alone."

I roll my neck and blink away the black spots dotting my vision, unsheathing two knives. "I've learned that one of the best weapons is being underestimated."

I've been fighting at a disadvantage nearly all my life. Odds stacked against me aren't scary, they're motivating. I've never been able to ignore the parts of me that crave blood on my blades, and tonight I want a red river flowing down the streets of Ladislava.

A shadowed figure stands on a nearby tree branch, huddling close to the trunk, while two assassins, a man and a woman, rush toward me. I throw a knife toward the shadow, but my aim is off, and my body is sluggish. They hit the cobblestones, but I know the throw didn't kill them. When a throw lands, I can feel it vibrating deep in the marrow of my bones.

Another knife finds its way into my hand like it never left, and I charge the masked man and woman on the ground. My adrenaline works against whatever drug is trying to slow me down. The man dodges my blade when I throw it directly at his head, but it wasn't meant to kill, merely to separate the two so I can fight them individually.

I draw a sword from my waist and use it to block the woman's swing. Her malice-filled eyes meet mine over our locked blades and I smirk, noting how hot her hatred burns for me. It'll make killing her all the more satisfying. I shove her back and cut my swords to the side, which she blocks and makes the mistake of positioning her blade lower than mine. Risking my balance and using my position, I kick her in the gut and revel in the way her skull smacks against a raised part of the uneven ground.

The man charges, and I have just enough time to pivot and block his blow before he shoves me back. Unlike the woman, I manage to stay upright and circle him.

"Are you feeling tired, princess?" the man goads.

I'm gravely aware of the drug coursing through my body with every second that ticks by, and I worry that Saskia was cut off by another assailant.

"Do you drug everyone before you fight?" I twirl the sword in my hand. "Many men suffer from performance issues, but I've heard with the right remedy—"

He growls and advances, but I don't trust my arm to block his blow, so I duck behind him and slice through a weak spot in his armor. I would've sliced his neck, but my arms feel like they're weighed down by stones. The woman comes at me, and I hear the faint sound of a bow nocking an arrow. I feign ignorance and use her anger to my advantage, blocking her sword and pulling her to my side as an arrow cuts through the air and pierces her neck. I pull a knife from my thigh and spin into my throw, using the extra momentum to concentrate on my aim and pierce the assassin on the ground between his eyes with a sickening crunch.

My muscles cry and my body urges me to collapse, but my mind keeps me fighting. It's always been my sharpest weapon. Before I had a blade, I had the determination to survive in spite of my circumstances. The top of my arm stings from a freshly cut gash, and my blood splatters on the stones below.

My vision blurs around the edges and the hilt of my blade is slippery with blood.

I will not die tonight, I promise myself.

The spin made me dizzier than I anticipated, and I teeter to the side under the weight of my sword. A crisp slap echoes against the shop-lined street, and my cheek blazes and my jaw throbs. The stones rush up to meet me and scrape my palms.

I push myself up halfway before he delivers a swift kick to my ribs. Using the momentum of the hit, I scramble to my feet as an arrow shoots from behind and sinks into his upper arm.

I could nearly cry with relief when I recognize the feathers.

For the first time tonight, fear flashes through his eyes before he bolts down the street, zigzagging out of Finnian's aim. I take a few steps in his direction before another wave of dizziness washes over me and my legs give out. A pair of hands grip me and hoist me up before my knees hit the road.

"Go get the commander." Ryder's snarl vibrates against my back. "Follow that man!"

"He'll worry too much," I protest, but a horse is already barreling toward the border.

"He's going to do a lot more than worry."

I'm ripped away from Ryder, and I close my eyes against the sudden movement. My entire body tingles like thousands of grains of sand are dusting across my skin. I hiss when Finnian grips my upper arm, and I hear his low curse when he notes the blood.

"The consequence correctors haven't failed me yet, Finny," I slur.

"I shouldn't have let you go. Fuck. *FUCK!*"

I open my eyes to stare into his panic-filled gaze. "It's not your fault. Don't blame yourself, please."

"I don't care how many soldiers it takes. I want every inch of Ladislava searched! Be on standby for further orders from Commander Veles, and I expect a report to the manor within the hour."

The vein in Ryder's temple is popping out as he gives orders to several soldiers on the street. "I also want to know where the fuck the soldiers on rotation are, and I want them brought forward."

I hadn't realized how much of a crowd Saskia acquired from the tavern. I do my best at feigning that I'm unaffected, but it probably makes me look worse, so I sink into Finnian while my eyes dart around the rooftops searching for another threat.

"Your Majesty, did you inflict any bodily wounds on him?" an older man with amber eyes and a Vareveth cloak asks, bowing his head when our gazes meet.

"I cut him on his back and Finnian shot an arrow through his arm."

He nods. "Move out, soldiers! You heard Her Majesty. Find the bastard and bring him to the commander."

Finnian hoists me in his arms and follows Ryder to some tied-off horses. He holds me so tight his fingers will probably leave marks once he puts me down, but I note the way his body has relaxed. I've always loved the way Finnian views the world, and I take on the role of protector to ensure that he never loses his optimistic gaze. Even now, drugged in his arms, I continue scanning the perimeter for threats because I'll always throw myself in front of Finnian, even if I know I'll lose.

"I've got her," Ryder says as Finnian sets me on his horse. "Follow me and keep alert." My eyes fall shut to stop myself from vomiting as Ryder urges the horse through the roads, keeping an arm around my waist.

"I shouldn't have been so careless," he says above the clattering hooves, his tone drenched in remorse and anger.

"Don't apologize; it makes me uncomfortable."

"Noted." He huffs a laugh in my ear. "Then how about I buy you a drink as a celebration for taking on three assassins while drugged?"

"Perfect," I mutter as I note the paint caked under his fingernails through my blurry vision. "You're a painter."

"I dabble. I'm not very good."

"Anyone who says that is usually lying." My stomach continues churning painfully. "Are we close?"

"Just up the road," he promises, yanking lightly on my braid before wrapping his arm around my waist again. "I'll hold your hair back if I have to, Atarah."

Thankfully that's not needed once the horse slows, and I get my bearings as Ryder guides us through an open set of iron gates with gold detailing and up a dirt path lined with dense trees. It's like I've entered another world when my vision clears, and a house set upon sprawling lands comes into view. A fountain with an open-mouthed dragon sits at the center of the entry circle. Ivy creeps along turrets adorned with stained-glass windows. My vision is still blurry and the full moon hangs above the house like its dark stones were made to be bathed in moonlight, but I spy the night sky, mountains, maybe even some flowers in the stained-glass windows.

Finnian hops off his horse and reaches for me. He takes me in his arms again and moves so quickly that I'm forced to shut my eyes against the blurring world around me.

CHAPTER
TWENTY-FIVE

Finnian places me down at the center of a room that's just as magnificent as the exterior of the home. It's hauntingly beautiful with the colorful glass windows depicting some of the designs I spotted from outside along with a stormy sea. Dark wood furniture covered in rich fabrics is littered throughout the space.

I spring forward when the backs of my thighs brush against the edge of the bed and scrub my hands over my face while I begin pacing the floor. If I sit down, I'll fall asleep and succumb to the sedative. I can't lose control of my body. I need to stay awake.

"Elowen." Saskia appears in front of me with a comforting smile and a thick navy blue sweater in hand. "I'm going to help you out of your clothes, and then I'll get a damp cloth for the blood."

"I can manage, but thank you." Saskia ignores my attempt at feigning that I'm unaffected and is already getting me out of my boots before working on my corset.

"I'll step out." Finnian kisses the top of my head before exiting the room. Saskia slips through a different door and the faint sound of running water follows. I remove my base layers and throw the sweater over my head. It's far too large on me but the comforting scent that follows makes me want to rip it off. This place is making me feel too at ease. I should be taking an ice bath or running the drug out of my system.

"Why don't you lie down?" Saskia gently offers once she finishes wiping the blood off my face and then taking care of my hands.

I shake my head. "I think I'll go for a walk. Where exactly am I?"

"You're in Cayden's private chambers. I don't want you to hit your head."

"I can't fall asleep. Not like this." Anxiety makes my throat tight, despite everything else about me feeling loose.

"You'll be okay," she promises.

I need to calm down. The lack of oxygen is only adding to my spotty vision. My legs wobble, but Saskia shoots her hands forward to steady me. I find my pacing pattern again. "I can wake up. I'm fine."

"Nothing will happen while you're asleep. I—" She cuts herself off when a loud bang rises from downstairs.

"She was *fucking drugged!*" Cayden's voice booms like thunder. "Did your brain crawl out of your ear and die or are you perpetually dense?"

"No," I whisper as the day comes rushing back to me. His footsteps bound up the stairs when he should be walking away from me. Sharing a suite in the castle as my guard is one thing, but I don't know what will happen between him and Eagor if he finds out I'm staying in his house. Vareveth is rampant with rumors of us. This will only add to it. Will that endanger the alliance?

My legs give out under the weight of everything on my shoulders, but strong arms wrap around me before I hit the ground and my face is shoved into a chest covered in black leather. I'd be able to recognize Cayden by the scent of his skin and the way his hands grip me like a lifeboat in a storm.

"You came," I whisper with relief I didn't realize I'd feel from his presence.

"I'll always come for you, angel." I missed the sound of his voice. I let myself have this moment in his arms, with his fingers weaving through my hair to pull me closer to his rapidly beating heart, before I shove away as panic settles in.

"You shouldn't be here, or maybe I shouldn't." Another wave of dizziness washes over me, and I force myself to begin pacing again. I'll force myself to be fine if I must.

"Why?" It's such a tiny, insignificant word, but the way he says it makes me feel like he'd love nothing more than to know the name of the person who put that thought in my mind.

"There are rumors about us," I settle on saying.

"If you have an issue with false gossip, then I humbly offer you my services to make it true." The hit I land to his chest feels more like a pat and sends another wave of dizziness washing over me. Cayden grabs my hands, but rather than stopping me, he treads backward. Saskia must have slipped from the room when he came in—there's no sign of her other than a turned-down bed. "What's going on in your head?"

"I can't lose control," I mumble. The knot in my throat tightens. I experience fear more than I'll ever admit, but it's never like this. This fear stems from fighting against the inevitable. "I'd rather face down an army than not have control over my own body."

"You're safe with me, always." Cayden gently slides his arms up and down my trembling frame. "Trust me like you did in the prison. I'm here and I'm not going anywhere. I don't care how long it takes, you have me."

This is the version of himself that Cayden will never show the world, and I'm greedy for it like a dragon guarding their trove in the stories I used to read. I know he guards me because he needs me to achieve his goals in the same way I need him, and maybe it's the sedative, but he's looking at me differently. It's like now that his eyes are on me, he can't even contemplate looking away.

"And if it takes me five days to wake up?"

He scoops me into his arms and gently places me on the bed. "Then some new rumors are bound to start."

I cover my eyes and release a groan that turns into a faint laugh as the feared Commander of Vareveth adjusts my pillows before sitting beside me. When he thinks I'm not looking at him, his face morphs through anger that burns so hot it radiates off him. It's an expression that I'd classify as a promise of death and makes me want to drag my finger down his scar. But my heavy hand lies motionless on the blanket, and Cayden is out of my reach in more ways than one.

He blinks away the expression when I shift in place, pulling him out of whatever darkness lives within him. "I like the flowers in your hair."

I blush, having forgotten I braided some of the purple flowers into the crown of my head and down my braid. "Thank you for them. They're beautiful."

"No thanks needed."

"I'm sorry for interrupting your schedule."

He huffs a laugh. "Your letters were the highlight of my days, and seeing you in person is incomparable."

My cheeks burn hotter. His letters were always the best part of my days, but I'll never tell him. My eyes slip shut for the final time, and I let myself trust someone that I know I shouldn't.

"Cayden?"

"Yes, El."

"I think I missed you."

I feel the bed shift, and something soft presses into my forehead. "I missed you more than I should have, love."

✣ ✣ ✣

Cool water laps against my body while I float in a lake. My dark brown hair fans out around me, and my satin night-slip clings to me. I let myself revel in this unfamiliar peace before opening my eyes.

The night sky stares down at me as bright stars make the inky black void shine. I push the water back and forth, gliding my hands through the silky surface. To the left is a mountain range; snowcapped mountains kiss the stars in ways I never could.

A loud voice booms from the sky just as I'm about to reach forward to grab a star. "Did you see who the fuck did this?"

Lightning litters the sky, and I shoot up in place, now wading in the water rather than floating. No, I realize, while staring into the sky, it's not lightning—the stars are falling.

"I'm going to find them and make them suffer in ways they never thought possible," the voice snarls again.

The stars splash into the lake around me and rain down on the shore. Some even ram into the mountains, making them shake. A mixture of snow and rocks tumbles down from the peaks and crashes into the lake. Fear spreads through my chest when enormous waves barrel toward me. My arms cut through the water while my feet swiftly paddle, but there's no outswimming the waves. They soon overtake me and sweep me under. Water burns my throat as I descend deeper into the endless pit below me. My hands keep clawing their way to the surface, but I feel like I'm swimming through thick syrup. I keep pushing and thrashing my limbs until I break the surface, gulping in large breaths.

"Elowen!" My head turns toward the shore; I hear someone calling my name through the waves, avalanche, and falling stars—it's as if the voice is right in front of me. "Elowen, *please.*"

The waves calm around me, and I feel something feather-light brush against my cheek and slide through my hair. I wrap my hand around something, leaning my head into the warm touch on my cheek. The voice along the shore is the same voice that made the stars fall, and the mountains shake, but now it's beckoning me to come closer.

It breaks through the chill the lake injected into my bones and embraces me like a blanket, reaching deep in my body and igniting something I've never felt. It's a feeling I don't know how to describe, but I want to feel it more.

I want to be near that voice. Something is tugging on the back of my mind, imploring me not to get closer because the voice is dangerous. I should swim away and hide in the mountains, but I can't ignore my desire.

The shore is even colder than the lake. My satin night-slip and hair are soaked; they stick to my cold body as the wind whips around me. A shadowed figure that looks like they're spun from the night sky approaches me, and wraps me in their arms just as green, lavender, silver, red, and blue streak across the sky. I watch, mesmerized, as five dragons appear. Not quite solid, more like a shimmering outline similar to the darkness that clings to me.

They twirl and tumble through the sky, their mighty wings stretching wide as they circle the lake. I reach toward the shimmering blue dragon that lands before me and am met with the solid texture of scales. "Delmira," I breathe.

Each dragon lands upon the shore of the lake; they look so real. The darkness moves with me, flowing behind me like a shadow while I walk between their towering frames, running my hand along their scales. Sorin nudges my calf with his snout. I turn back and his expression is almost . . . playful.

"Sorin." It's never felt so good to say a name. "Do you want attention?"

A humming noise rumbles in his throat when I walk closer, and he nudges my arm with his snout again. It's strange how he feels so real, and yet I can see through his body. I wrap my arms around his neck and yelp when he straightens up, taking me with him. The other four dragons take off into the skies, and a scream tears from my throat when Sorin flaps his mighty wings and joins them.

I soak in my dragons flying together like they own the skies. Sorin continues his path, holding me in a way that doesn't put too much strain on my arms. The bond tenderly throbs in my chest, and I note the slight gold glimmer on their scales.

This feeling is pure bliss.

And it's not real because I know I'm dreaming and yet it seems so familiar.

"I'm going to kill every single person who stands between us," I vow against his neck, not knowing how much time we have. "And once you're free, it'll be your turn to bathe Imirath in flames."

Sorin roars, mighty enough to shake the mountains and cause stars to flee across the sky. It's like he's also aware of our limited time and wants to keep us here forever.

In the skies with my dragons, I feel the sense of home and belonging that I've longed for. But I want Sorin to have full control of his body, to enjoy this moment without considering me, so I urge him to leave me on the shore. I press my forehead to his when he sets me on my feet, and he makes that same humming sound.

"Soon, sweetling," I whisper.

He nudges me one last time before joining the others again, and I'm left on the shore, unable to tear my eyes away as violent shivers rack my body. The darkness returns and offers me a shred of warmth.

"Demon?" I ask once the shivers subside.

"Yes, angel."

A name disappears as quickly as it came. Darkness wraps around me and settles me beneath a tree where I can watch my dragons and rest. Most people would run from darkness, but I can't shake the feeling that it's exactly where I need to be. It should be cold and uninviting, but this darkness is anything but that. My cheek presses into something warm while I wrap my arms around the figure beneath me.

"Don't go," I whisper. I stay here, perfectly content, while darkness intertwines with my hair and dances down my spine. I never want to leave the realm of dreams and dragons.

Another voice comes from over the mountains. "The reports . . . downstairs . . ."

"I don't want to leave her."

I tighten my hold. I don't want my darkness to leave me, either. A chuckle vibrates my cheek.

"It'll only take ten minutes." The feminine voice speaks again.

Much to my dismay, the darkness starts to shift. I curl my body toward the fleeting warmth, but it soon disappears. The only warmth that remains is a feather-light touch on my cheek. Tree roots wrap around my wrist when I try to reach forward. *Come back*, I want to say, but the words die in my throat.

"I should have assumed you'd be fussy." Something is placed next to me and I tug it closer, inhaling the familiar scent. "I'll be right back, beautiful. Don't go anywhere."

Loneliness wraps around my heart when my dragons are drowned out by the sun, their roars a distant sound that cracks my heart open. I yank my hand free of the tree roots that restrain me so I can follow them, but the light blinds me once I get to my feet.

CHAPTER
TWENTY-SIX

I'm thrust into the present like a crack of thunder waking me from a deep slumber. "Venatrix! Where's Venatrix? Where are my dragons?"

I try to move but my legs are tangled in blankets.

Finnian springs forward, hands gripping my shoulders. "Calm down, Ellie. You're safe in Cayden's house."

My heart pounds so rapidly in my chest I can feel it in the tips of my fingers. I stare into his concerned gaze while I catch my breath, some loose strands of hair falling into my face. A hazy fog surrounds my mind, but I swear I can still feel the sensation of scales against my palms. My arm no longer hurts, but there's a dull ache in my jaw from where the man hit me.

I clear the raspiness from my throat. "I'm in Cayden's room?"

Finnian nods. "He stayed with you the past three days, said he made a promise to you and looked like he'd bite my head off when I offered to switch."

"Three days!" I scramble out of bed. "Does Ailliard know?"

"Know that you were cuddled up in bed with the most feared commander in all of Ravaryn? Who he strongly disapproves of? No. He knows you're here, but I covered for you."

"Gods, this is a mess."

"Messes can be fun."

I drop my face into my hands and groan. "The alliance treaty hasn't been signed yet, and we need Vareveth's aid to survive. There is no room for feelings in my life."

"So you admit you care for him?"

"He's my ally." I walk toward where my clothes are neatly folded and begin putting them on to give myself something to do, not caring if Finnian sees my body. "His death would be highly inconvenient to me."

"Have you ever thought about how it's often the most brutal people who can be the gentlest? Maybe it's because they know how terrible the world is and will do anything to shield the ones they care about from it." Finnian rests his elbows on his knees and stares me down across the room once I finish getting dressed. "That's the kind of love you give me. Like you'd move mountains to make sure I'm safe. Now I'm going to ask you a question and I need the truth."

I nod, waiting for him to continue.

"Does the treaty with Vareveth include your dragons?"

I swallow, knowing this conversation was brewing like a storm creeping along the horizon. "My dragons are not mentioned in the treaty, but Cayden and I will be infiltrating the Imirath castle once it's signed to get them back. We broke into Kallistar Prison several days ago to forge the key to the chamber they're locked in."

He rakes his hands through his hair before tilting his head and sighing.

"Please don't ask me to rethink my plans."

"It's not that." He looks at me again. "You must know that the thought of losing you to all of this terrifies me. You became my family the day I woke up in Aestilian and saw you sitting beside my bed. You're the sister I prayed to the gods for after I lost mine in the fire."

He kneels before me as I attempt to blink the emotion from my eyes.

"I failed to protect you the other night, but I will not fail again. You have my bow and undying loyalty, always. I will help you get your dragons back in any way I can."

I drop to my knees and wrap my arms around him, burying my face in his neck as he pulls me closer. "I love you, brother."

I wipe the tears from his face and we smile through the pain that life has dealt us, the fears that stem through our trauma. But no matter what life has taken, it has also given. I don't know who I'd be without Finnian, and I thank the gods I'll never know.

"That's enough tears, darling. You can wash up before I take you downstairs where your knives and everyone is waiting." He points toward an open door. "I'll also tell Cayden to put a shirt on, so you don't turn into a strawberry."

✛ ✛ ✛

Finnian leads me through the halls of the enchanting home. Between the intricate carvings, stone fireplaces, lavish fabrics, staggering staircases, and windows as tall as trees, this place is magnificent. Cayden's private chambers are an entire wing reserved to himself.

Cayden has come a long way from having nothing.

We continue toward an open set of double doors at the end of a windowed hall leading to a singular tower with a peaked ceiling. Soft light bathes us as the sun sets behind the mountains, and my breath catches in my throat when we step into a library with more books than I've ever seen. This room is the perfect mixture of luxury and comfort, complete with leather and dark wood furniture covered in deep red fabric to match the various rugs. A fire roars in the hearth, whiskey sits on the table, and a grand black piano is situated before several windows overlooking a pond behind the house.

Saskia and Ryder greet me when I enter, the latter telling me he sharpened my knives while I was passed out, but Cayden sits quietly at the piano, watching me as if he's death donning a human form, quietly but constantly. I don't think I'd be able to look away from him if an army marched through the door, and my legs carry me toward him without my mind commanding them. His gaze is a contradiction that both paralyzes me and beckons me closer. Catching his eyes is a dangerous game I'm not supposed to be playing, but I can't seem to stop.

His hair is tousled like he dragged his hands through it one too many times, and dark circles shadow his bloodshot eyes. His long legs are spread wide, and he leans an elbow over the covered keys, but I don't mistake his leisurely posture for being relaxed; his eyes tell me he craves the blood of whoever tried to kill me.

"Angel," he greets me.

"Demon." My trance is broken when I round a highbacked chair and spy how many reports are scattered across the table. I can't even see the wood beneath. I surge forward to catch up on all I've missed, but hands wrap around my waist, lifting me away. "What the hells?"

Cayden ignores my protest and places me on the bench, leaning down to whisper in my ear, "You've been pressed up against me for three days. Now isn't the time to get shy, El."

I don't have time to think of a response before he grabs my knives from where Ryder must have laid them out on the piano and drops to his knees before me. My breathing gets shallow, and his eyes fall to my lips when I lick them and fill with more heat than I've ever seen.

"Your memory could get muddled if you read the reports. Tell me what happened while Saskia takes notes," he says, voice raspy as he slides one of my knives into my thigh holster and grips my hip with his other hand, pushing my shirt up slightly to run his thumb along my skin.

The desire coursing through me becomes impossible to ignore, so I close my eyes to filter through my memories. An impenetrable fog surrounds my thoughts, like the mist surrounding Aestilian. But the mist around Aestilian protects it; the mist in my brain hinders me.

I relay the evening to the best of my ability, pausing to work through the mess in my mind several times. But each time I pause, Cayden rubs my hip and slides another knife into my holster in silent encouragement. Saskia's pen continues scribbling as she sits on the couch with her, Ryder, and Finnian chiming in with important details I miss.

"Do you recall what the man looked like?" Cayden asks, sliding my final knife on the top of my leg, his fingers dangerously close to the apex of my thighs. I grip the bench and pull an image from the murky depths.

"He has a scar." I open my eyes and drag my finger across Cayden's forehead, letting it linger slightly longer than necessary as his throat constricts and his eyes bore into mine. "That's all I can help with, I'm afraid. I was more focused on killing them."

Cayden nods, squeezing my freshly armed thighs before standing and leaning against the piano behind me. I'm more relaxed after relaying my account, but the number of reports still bothers me. "How many people saw me when I was drugged?"

"It's tough to tell," Saskia says. "Every soldier in the tavern was ready to fight once I delivered the news, and more joined along the way."

I bite the inside of my cheek to keep myself from grimacing.

"You shouldn't be concerned with the perception of weakness." I turn my head toward Cayden's voice. "You fought off three assassins while drugged. If anyone calls you weak, then I'll drug them myself and send three assassins their way."

"I second that," Ryder states, but the tension between him and Cayden is palpable.

"I should meet with Ailliard to let him know I'm all right."

"I'll go with you," Saskia suggests, but she must note the uneasy expression I try to hide because she adds, "I'll be your excuse if you get too tired and wish to retire."

Her offer is temptation wrapped with a bow. Despite sleeping for three days, I'm not rested and not ready for a verbal sparring match. "You're sure?"

"We'll leave for the castle in a few moments." She gets to her feet and her simple blue gown flows behind her as she glides from the room. "You're my ally against my idiotic brothers, the least I can do is extend the same loyalty to you."

I laugh, and her smile widens. "I love this arrangement."

"Rude!" Ryder shouts before he and Finnian follow her from the room, informing us they're gathering their things, though I'm not sure how true that is considering Finnian has never been here.

The library is soon cloaked in thick silence that settles uncomfortably on my skin. I swing my legs over the bench and lean my arms against the closed piano. "Please don't be upset with Ryder because of me."

He bites the inside of his cheek and manages to look angrier. "If I didn't consider him my brother, he'd be dead."

"But he *is* your brother." I reach forward to grab his hand. "The mission is fine. Don't waste your energy."

He drops to his elbow to lean close to my face. "Why is it you don't believe you're worth my anger?"

I jerk back and lift the piano cover to give myself something to do with my hands, tapping some of the keys. He sighs, moving to stand behind me when he realizes I don't plan on answering. The back of my head settles against his shoulder and goosebumps rise on my arms when his large hands cover mine. He moves our hands together, playing a song so soft and light that it reminds me of a quiet morning.

There's nothing accidental about this connection. No other way to spin it than him wanting to touch me, and me not pulling away. I tell myself to pull my hands from under his, to not rest my head on him, to not let his scent intoxicate me. But my skin tingles and his proximity is clearly making me delusional.

"Thank you for staying with me," I whisper.

"I gave you my word." His voice dances with the strands of my hair.

"I know, but Finnian was here. You didn't need to be."

"What do you know about what I need?"

The way he says the words makes me turn my head. His fingers tighten around mine and the song turns darker when our gazes collide. I know he feels me shift on the bench, and he lowers his head in response. A shiver travels up my spine when his breath fans across my lips.

The song stops when his fingers slide through mine and hold tight.

He makes me feel like I'm teetering on the edge of a cliff, about to free-fall. My eyes slip shut but his wanting expression is burned into the darkness that awaits me. He releases one of my hands to cup my face, and a whimper catches in my throat when he brushes his thumb along my skin.

I tilt my head up, granting him the permission he was waiting for.

"Are you two coming?" Saskia shouts from down the hall.

I shoot forward and slam my hands ungraciously on the keys before rising from the bench and swiftly walking toward the door. Cayden strides lazily next to me with his hands tucked into his pockets, seeming completely unaffected. I open my mouth several times to say something, though I'm not exactly sure what.

"No need to get tongue-tied because you almost kissed me."

"It was a lapse of judgment on my part." He smirks when I glare at him. "I despise you still."

"Do you?" He snaps his fingers. "Tell me, love, do you often kiss people you loathe?"

"I don't know. Perhaps I'll go down to the tavern to test that theory."

"Condemn whoever you wish." He shrugs, placing a hand on my back to guide me toward the front door. "It'll provide me with some entertainment when I shoot them down."

CHAPTER
TWENTY-SEVEN

BACK AT THE CASTLE, MY EVENING BECAME UNEVENTFUL the moment Finnian and Saskia were pulled away to an advisor meeting. Time stands unnervingly still despite it being half past three o'clock in the morning. I'll dig a trench in the floor if I keep pacing, but Cayden hasn't returned and my anxiety beats through me like a war drum.

Cayden's tasks as Commander of Vareveth are shrouded in danger. He had to tie up loose ends at the border, but he said he'd come back. Ever since we've met, he's always shown up whenever he said he would; most of the time I feel like I can't escape his presence. But the quiet in the suite is deafening.

I can't stop envisioning him bleeding out in a ditch somewhere, knowing I possess the skills to both find and heal him. He's the only person I trust enough to pull off the dragon heist. Trusting him is beyond idiotic, and I can't do it fully, but we're united through our shared drive for vengeance. Assassins lurk around every corner, it seems, but I'm so tired of hiding and letting *what ifs* define my choices. If the world is threatened by me, then I'll give them a reason to be.

The only solace I find within the bitterness of needing him is that he needs me, too. We're two independent, power-hungry people stuck together in this loop of codependency. Freeing my dragons requires

Cayden to stay alive, and using those dragons in the war requires me to stay alive as well.

The door to his room is locked and deadbolted on both sides, but that doesn't stop me from strapping knives down my legs. People with a history of being locked in cages have a way of finding exit strategies no one else sees, which is why the guards at my door will remain blissfully unaware of the queen slipping through their fingers.

The night air engulfs me when I shove my balcony doors open. It's a deadly fall to the ground below, but I've jumped from rooftop to rooftop in search of information, money, or blood most of my life. Perhaps it'll teach Cayden a lesson on punctuality if I die.

I place the table and chair at the edge of my balcony for an additional boost and tuck the loose strands of hair behind my ears while staring down the gap. In my gut I know he would be here unless something important arose, and I won't sit in the castle like a docile princess waiting for him.

"Cayden Veles, if you're not bleeding then I'll make you bleed," I vow to the moon and stars before taking off in a sprint to outrun the logical side of my brain screaming at me to stop.

My boot hits the table with a loud clang before I thrust myself into the air. Wind whips at my face and through my cloak. I keep my eyes on Cayden's balcony as I propel closer, not entertaining the possibility of failure.

I land in a crouch and smirk over my shoulder, raising my middle finger and muttering a curse to gravity before pulling two small knives from my holster and picking the lock to his balcony doors. Not as efficient as Cayden's picks, but before long the door swings open and I'm met with the evidence of his absence.

I press my ear to the private door in Cayden's chambers to ensure that no guards will spot me when I step into the hall. It's the only other way to enter the suite and is mainly used by servants. I wrap my hand around the handle and cringe at the sound of the bolt retracting. The door softly shuts in my wake, and I keep my steps light and my head down. I've learned how to walk like a shadow over the years.

Darkness can't scare you when you're one of the monsters that lurk in it.

The damp earth cushions my jump when I slip through a window on the lowest level of the castle. This is the most entertainment I've had since Cayden and I infiltrated the prison. I toss rocks to get guards to turn away from me and quickly make my way toward the forest leading to Ladislava.

My throat burns as I sprint through the forest as if a netherwraith were gaining on me. Years spent in the Terrwyn have conditioned me to stay alert as I move swiftly. I've spent most of my life running from danger, and I'm now realizing that I relish a chase. I'm not out for a fight, but I wouldn't mind finding one along the way.

I creep quietly through Ladislava, scaling a building and hiding above unsuspecting soldiers with a broad smile on my face. The moon is the only witness to my secret mission, and I revel in my dalliance with danger.

I drop into an alleyway and slide myself onto a golden mare saddled and ready to be ridden. Saskia informed me of the pens in Ladislava that always have rested horses at the ready in case a soldier needs one for an emergency. I click my tongue and lead her through the trees, not trusting the main road, and jostle the reins after a few moments to signal a sprint.

Time passes quickly here, unspooling like a rogue ball of yarn being chased by a kitten. I know time is precious and that we should hold on to it while we can, but forsaking a life in favor of safety seems like a waste. When I greet the eternal darkness, I'll go there knowing I lived.

The mare gets spooked when a loud boom shakes the ground. I run my hand down her mane and whisper soothing words to calm her while continuing our journey at a slower pace. Curiosity and trepidation mingle within me, causing my heart to pound and my throat to tighten.

I slide down from the horse and keep my head down while walking into the camp, tying her off on a post close to the main road. More people than I anticipated are awake and roaming. I clasp the satchel strap between my clammy hands and weave through the rows until coming upon the largest black and green tent.

It calls to me like a sailor staring down land from a storm-throttled ship.

I raise my chin, not caring if anyone recognizes me now, which I'm sure they do given the surprised whispers. But I pay them little mind as I rip open the entrance without announcing myself and find Cayden *covered in blood.*

"Oh gods." My knees feel weak as I rush toward him. He glances at his whiskey before removing his reading glasses and slowly blinking at me. "You should be sitting down."

He stiffens when I roam my hands over his torso. The blood on the fabric dampens them, meddling with my search, so I slide them under his shirt and continue. When I speak again, my voice is much more frantic than I intend. "Where is the wound? Why isn't there a healer in here?"

His large hands frame my face and tilt my head up once his shock wears off. A mixture of worry and suspicion swims in his eyes, accompanied by something dark. "Why are you here? Are you all right?"

"You're bleeding!" I trail my fingers through the divots in his muscles and find *nothing*.

"It's not my blood."

"Wh-what?" Now it's my turn to blink slowly.

"It's. Not. My. Blood."

I abruptly shove away from him, wiping my bloodied hands on my pants in hopes of erasing the feeling of his skin from my memory. My frustration increases when it doesn't work. "Why didn't you tell me?"

"I liked feeling your hands on me." He smiles, but his eyes remain humorless. I throw my satchel at his face, but he catches it and places it on the desk. His eyes stalk me as I toss my cloak over a chair. "You shouldn't be here."

"Eagor ordered you to stay away, not me," I bite out, and his jaw clenches. "And it doesn't seem like you give any heed to that warning."

"It doesn't seem like you give any heed to several assassins making attempts on your life, considering you're roaming the streets like a commoner."

"I thought you were hurt!" I dig my nails into my palms to ground me. "If I could do *this* without you, I would. It would save me a headache."

"Likewise, princess," he scoffs. Ever since we met, we've pulled and pushed each other like the moon controls the tides, but tonight there's no pulling, only pushing.

"I can't stand you!" I suppress the urge to stab him when he gestures toward the several unoccupied seats in the room.

"Do you realize how close you're standing to Imirath right now?" The sound of his heavy boots coming closer fills the space between us. "You don't think that makes *me* worried?"

I refuse to let the way he stares down at me intimidate me.

"How about the thought of another assassin trying to kill you when absolutely nobody knew where you were tonight?"

I open my mouth to speak, but he stops me by lifting my chin with his finger.

"We can also discuss your brilliant idea of walking to a tea shop as if you're not the lost princess of Imirath with a link to five dragons." He walks forward when I step back, cornering me against his desk.

"If you're angry with me about that, then you should've said something earlier," I say.

"When?" Candlelight flutters across his face, illuminating the blood and anger. "You were drugged and scared, so I set my anger aside for you."

I flinch at his words. "Perhaps Eagor and Ailliard are right. Distance may do us some good. I want a different guard to stay in the suite with me."

"Elowen, so help me gods." He runs a hand through his hair, but the simple act holds my focus. "The only way another man is staying in that suite is if I'm dead, and even then, there will need to be some negotiation."

I wrap my hand around his wrist, matching his glare with equal venom. Dried blood is caked on every knuckle. I'm sure there's bruising beneath the mess. "You either tell me what happened or I'm walking out of this tent and finding out myself."

When he laughs, it's not with a smile but bared teeth. Papers crinkle beneath me when he abruptly reaches forward and lifts me onto the desk, standing between my parted legs and caging me with his body while I lean back on my arms.

"You're mine to protect, whether you like it or not."

"Likewise." He can handle my anger just as well as I can handle his, which is why even when his eyes shoot daggers in my direction, I know he'd throw a blade at anyone who wishes me harm. "You know just as well as I do that we're stuck together, which means I want to know where you are, if you're okay, if—"

"Watch your words, El. You're beginning to sound like you care about me."

"I care about my dragons."

He tilts my face toward him. "Then why did you drop your eyes to say that?"

Caring about him is a language I'm surrounded by but don't know how to speak. Meeting his gaze is like a dagger piercing my chest, and yet I can't stop. His eyes have claws that sink into my flesh and hold me hostage. My mind implores me to remember all the reasons why the way he's making me feel is forbidden, but he's so close, and all I can recall is how badly I wanted him to close the gap between us a few hours ago.

He leans closer to reach behind me and doesn't look away as he takes a sip of whiskey. "I found the assassin who ran." I absorb the news and release a shaky breath, digging my fingernails into his desk and waiting for him to continue. "It was one of my soldiers. They were working with assassins from Imirath and let them over the border. I suppose I lost track of time while educating my army on what happens if they even so much as think of harming you and betraying me."

I nod slowly while my stomach rolls at the mention of Imirath. "I suppose some of your soldiers will wish me dead for being the princess of Imirath."

His face doesn't change when he flatly states, "Then they will die."

If I didn't know him, I'd think he was calm, but his eyes give away the tight leash he has on his anger, ready to let go and weaponize it whenever he wishes. Sometimes I think his anger will burn him from the inside out.

I scan the dried blood on his cheeks, neck, forearms, and knuckles. My heartbeat increases as the silence stretches on and I come to a realization. He caresses my throat and slides his thumb over my pulse, looking eerily beautiful.

"You didn't come to the castle because you were torturing your soldier," I whisper.

"Finish the sentence."

I swallow. "For me."

"Good." He trails his thumb across my neck again, and his lips quirk when he feels the jump in my pulse. His face inches closer to mine, but I don't move, earning another stroke of his thumb. "Do you know what happens to traitors in Vareveth?"

"No," I answer steadily, despite feeling entirely unstable.

"A commander usually picks a soldier to fight in their stead, but I prefer to carry out my own sentences. The ceremony begins with the opportunity to physically fight the traitor without weapons or armor, and after that the commander can choose forms of torture and execution."

He looks down at me like he's waiting for me to push him away, but the thought of him fighting on my behalf to the point of busted knuckles caked in blood has the opposite effect on me. Maybe it's because I've never had anyone lose themselves through avenging me or going feral at the prospect of my pain.

"What did you do to him?" I feel like I can hardly get air into my lungs as I wait for his response. He monitors my reactions like a predator watching their prey from the bushes.

"He said several things about you that I refuse to repeat, so I cut out his tongue to continue the execution without his abhorrent babbling. Then I carved those words onto his back *very* slowly. I gathered my army for the demonstration. He was a friend to some, but I ensured he ended this night as an enemy to all."

He takes another sip of whiskey.

My words are trudging through mud in my mind. I have nothing to offer him other than silence.

"I apologize for not sending a letter to the castle, but I was waiting for the gallwings after I dumped him in the forest." I've never seen the creatures, but I've heard stories of the serpentlike beasts. The venom in their fangs makes your skin feel like it's on fire and slowly paralyzes you. "I managed to wait for their frenzy to pass and cut off his head to bring back to camp. There wasn't much of a job to finish, but I ensured that he felt excruciating pain until his very last blink."

"But a public execution on my behalf would mean . . ." I shake my head, unable to fathom it.

"I took a vow to protect you, Elowen. You have my loyalty, and now everyone else knows it, too." He slides his hand to the base of my skull.

"But Eagor—"

"Stop talking about Eagor," he bites out.

"My people need this treaty to survive."

"And they will." The intensity of his gaze keeps me pinned in place just as much as his body. "But I won't stand by for the sake of diplomacy. I will always hunt down anyone who harms you even if you're repulsed by me. I don't regret a single scream I stole from him; I savor them."

I can't fathom how he thinks I could be repulsed by his actions when I know I'd do the same if I were in his position. I can show Cayden the darkest parts of myself, the twisted parts I hide, and find comfort in knowing that the same darkness resides in him. He's never been my enemy. He's the first person to take on my enemy both with and for me.

I'll deal with the consequences when I hit the ground, but tonight I'm tired of walking a fine line. I turned away from him after we infiltrated the prison, but I'm not turning away now. I lick my lips while straightening my spine to get closer to him. His lips part, and a shudder travels through him when I cup his scarred cheek. Cayden won't take from me, so I want to give to him.

His hand shoots to my hip, holding me tight. "El?"

My lips are inches from his, and the pull is nearly more than I can bear. "Yes?"

"Careful, angel. You give a man a taste of salvation, and he might keep coming back for more." His arms are shaking from restraint.

"Is that what I am to you? Your salvation?" I whisper, brushing my lips against his.

"If you are to be my damnation, it's an end I'll happily meet."

He closes the gap between us, and our lips meet in a collision of pent-up passion. Everything else around me disappears from the world as if it never existed; the only thing that remains is him. My hands snake around his neck and weave through his hair, deepening our kiss. A moan slips from my lips when his tongue enters my mouth, and any leash he had on himself vanishes. He pulls my hips forward and presses his hardness into the pulsing spot between my legs that aches for him. I whimper at the new sensation, and he groans against my lips. Gods, that's the best sound I've ever heard.

I arch my back, wrap my legs around his waist, and am rewarded with another delicious, throaty groan from him. He kisses me like I'm the last woman in this world. His body fits perfectly with mine as he lays me back on the desk, and I roll my hips against his hardened length. I gasp into his mouth, and he takes the opportunity to kiss down my neck, biting and sucking as he pleases while rolling his hips into mine, echoing the same needy movements I'm giving him.

"Cayden," I moan as he sucks on a sensitive part of my neck. My fingers tighten in the strands of his hair, and my legs tighten around his waist.

He groans into my neck. "You're going to be the death of me."

Gods, it's true that the forbidden fruit tastes the sweetest. I've been kissed before but never like this. It's the kind of kiss I'd kill for. I remove my hands from his hair and trail them under his shirt to grip his muscular back.

"Say my name again," he demands, nibbling on my earlobe. But his name catches in my throat from the overwhelming combination of his lips, our bodies grinding together, and the weight of him on top of me. I'm so close to pushing off this desk and dragging him over to the bed. "I told you to say my name," he commands again, sliding his hands down to firmly grip my ass and press himself into me harder.

"Cayden," I gasp, writhing beneath him.

"Perfect." His teeth graze over the sensitive skin on my neck, and his fingers weave through my hair. "Did you enjoy the sight of me on my knees, angel?" I moan when he bites down and dig my nails into his back.

My back arches off the desk as he licks his way up to my mouth. He crashes his lips onto mine again, and I pull on his shoulders, wanting him even closer. He bends farther to comply as much as he can, given that the desk is too small for him to get on top of me. His hands feverishly roam over my body like a sinner grasping at redemption.

He'll always echo my intensity and urge me for more. He's a challenge, an ally, and a rival mixed together. I trace the raised scars on his back with my fingertips, and I'm rewarded with another groan. The feel of his bare skin makes me feel alive. I've never reacted to someone like this. It's addictive, and I can't stop myself from wanting more.

"Commander, I have—*Oh!*"

Reality crashes into me, penetrating the universe we briefly escaped into, and my body stiffens. Cayden doesn't break apart immediately; instead, he lingers above me for a few moments, brushing his swollen lips against mine. I swallow the whimper that rises in my throat and force myself not to roll my hips onto his again, no matter how much I want to. He wraps his arms around my torso and straightens me up with him.

"You can leave the envelope by the door." Cayden jerks his chin toward a small table with a letter tray on it. His hands move in languid strokes down my spine.

"Of course, sir." The servant bows his head before turning to place the letter on the tray. "Would you like me to assemble any of the generals to discuss the details?"

I glance toward Cayden and sense him saying yes before he does. His eyes are shadowed with the same exhaustion as this morning; he needs to sleep. I poke him in the back, and he glances down at me, quirking a brow before turning back toward the servant.

"We need a few moments," Cayden states.

"My apologies, Your Graces." The servant nervously tugs the bottom of his tunic while slipping from the tent.

Cayden removes one hand from my back and tilts my chin toward him, brushing his swollen lips over mine and smiling when he hears the small gasp it wrings from me.

"Are you okay?" he huskily mumbles, dropping his forehead to mine.

"We'll take the meeting in the morning. You need to sleep." I match his quiet tone even though we're alone. His eyes are lighter than before, and the sight of that eases something in me.

"I think we're going to take it now," he says, stroking the back of my head.

"You'll get used to being wrong eventually." He halfheartedly glares at me. "You found and killed the assassin, so whatever is in that envelope can wait until morning. We'll both benefit from space right now." What I don't say is that he looks far too tempting to fall into again, and I don't trust myself.

He slides his thumb over my swollen lips before removing his hands from me. "Don't look at me like you wish you could regret me."

"You know we can't do this." I gesture between the two of us, but I keep glancing at his lips. "What if your servant tells people he saw us . . ."

"Kissing? Nobody will believe it. You're too pretty for me." The dimples deepen on his cheeks when he notes my blush. "He won't say anything."

"How do you know?"

"Because I'll know who to kill." He pivots on his heels to inform the servant of his decision before striding toward his wardrobe and grabbing a sweater. "Do you need help with your corset?"

"Excuse me?" I nervously laugh as an image of him ripping off my corset flashes in my brain before I shove it away.

"You're sleeping here. I doubt you want to sleep in that."

I gesture to the small silver hooks that line the center when he hands me the sweater and say, "I can unhook this one from the front."

"My offer still stands." I try to glare but fail miserably. "You're staying in there," he says, pointing toward two pulled-back flaps leading to a dimly lit room. My hands tighten on the sweater as jealousy rises in me when I take in the second bedroom filled with womanly touches.

"I'll sleep on the couch," I mutter in a flat tone without turning to him. He can do whatever he wants with whoever he wants, but a selfish part of me doesn't want to know about it. He walks toward me, and his heat on my back makes me want to curl into him like a cat lying in a ray of sunlight.

"I've received many compliments on this room."

"I bet you have." I want to swim in a freezing river until my sanity returns.

"Saskia really thought the bedding was your taste, but I'll be happy to tell her she was wrong. Ryder might curse me for not going with the fabric he preferred."

I whirl around and nearly crash into his chest. "What are you saying?"

His eyes dance over my face in a way I'm becoming accustomed to. "It was always my intention to bring you here, Elowen. Granted, you showed up earlier than I planned, but I had my bedroom moved into my meeting room while I was gone. I take meetings in a separate tent now."

There's no exit in here, meaning if someone gets into the tent, they'll have to get through Cayden first. I look down at my boots, embarrassed and overwhelmed. "You didn't have to do that."

"I didn't do it for entirely selfless reasons." He reaches out to tilt my chin up. "Sweet dreams, angel."

CHAPTER
TWENTY-EIGHT

I DON'T KNOW WHAT I THOUGHT THE BORDER WOULD LOOK like . . . but it wasn't this. I expected something darker and drearier—wounded soldiers everywhere and unanswered cries for help on a never-ending loop. But it's fairly pleasant once you get over the fact that it's a war camp.

Cayden, who now walks beside me, explained that there are three lines within the camp. We're in the third line. The first is defense, the second is medical, and the last is supplies and residential. They even have taverns and markets back here—no permanent structures, just larger tents where soldiers can congregate.

"There's something I have to tell you." Cayden's words send anxiety shooting through me. I hate when people say that. It would be much less nerve-racking for them to just say it rather than add a buildup to their statement. "Saskia and Ryder know."

I stop in my tracks, and my mouth hangs open. "When did you tell them?"

"I let it slip when you were passed out." He grins at my expression. Cayden is too careful to let something slip; if he were a book you'd be lucky to get a glimpse at the prologue, but he hasn't inquired about my conversation with Finnian, so I won't prod into his familial affairs. "Saskia figured out what we were planning when we came back from the prison, and she and Ryder had a bet about who would reveal it first."

"Did they bet that you would?" The dimples deepening in his cheeks tell me everything I need to know. "Those bastards."

I'm ready to start my day now that I'm fed and caffeinated and continue the path toward our tent. The word *our* sounds too personal for our situation, but it's the word that fits.

"Not so fast, angel." Cayden's hand brushes against my elbow, causing me to jump slightly. He retracts the touch and gestures to the tent on his right. "This is where I take meetings now."

Another gathering to discuss another person who tried to kill me—a new tradition. I'm mesmerized by a fire blazing in a circular bronze pit at the center of the tent, considering that smoke should be wafting throughout the space.

"It's enchanted," Cayden states behind me. "There's one in your room."

I walk over to warm my hands and prove to myself that there truly is no smoke. "It's ingenious."

"It adjusts to the temperature in the air. If it's a cold night, the fire will adapt to keep your room warm." He takes a seat at the head of a long table, breaking the seal on a letter before opening his round reading glasses with his teeth, looking entirely too enticing. "However, you're always welcome in my bed if you're feeling particularly cold."

I pretend to be considering his offer by tapping my finger against my lips, drawing his eyes exactly where I want them. "I'd rather not tumble in the sheets with a criminal." He mercifully doesn't mention last night or my own crimes. "How many laws do you evade?"

"Any law that cuts into my investments or power, vexes me, or I deem irrelevant. Would you like a list?"

"Do you possess that much ink, or will you need to steal some?"

He snickers in response as Saskia enters the tent muttering greetings to the pair of us. "Ryder is escorting Finnian from the castle, so they'll be here shortly."

Their voices float away from me as their conversation continues; I'm too drawn to the flames to focus on anything else. The logs splinter as the fire dances for me. There's something moving in there, almost like a secret message as my bond tingles in my chest. Several sets of dragon wings flap and overlap as the fire flickers. Sweat gathers on my forehead, but I can't turn away from the colors of my dragons' eyes mingling with the mundane blaze.

I see their eyes.

They stare at me as if they can see into my soul.

A hand wraps around my wrist, pulling me away as I'm reaching toward them, and goosebumps dot my skin when my trance breaks. Blood rushes in my ears and I stare in disbelief at the ordinary fire. The ground feels unsteady beneath me.

"What did you see?" Saskia asks, arm around my shoulders while her hand remains on my wrist.

I force my gaze to her as Finnian and Ryder enter the tent with someone I don't recognize. He bows to Cayden before rounding the table and walking toward me.

"I saw my dragons' eyes," I whisper before licking my dry lips and summoning a smile when he kneels, taking my hand and pressing it to his forehead.

"Queen Elowen, may I present General Braxton of Vareveth," Ryder says while taking the seat at Cayden's left.

"Your Majesty," he says before standing. "It's an honor to make your acquaintance."

A memory rings in my brain. "You were in Ladislava after the attack." He was the man giving out orders as Finnian carried me away.

"Yes, my lady. I worked with General Neredras on tightening security."

I smile and nod as Saskia tugs on my arm and places me on Cayden's right while taking the seat beside me, across from Finnian. She readies a quill as Cayden's eyes drift over my face before he gestures for Braxton to begin.

"Commander Veles rooted out the final assassin last night, and with the added security to Ladislava, Verendus, and the border, I don't believe we'll have to worry about further attempts." He pauses, his eyes darting between Cayden and me nervously as he shifts in his seat.

"However, I don't understand how they could have managed all of this without having a spy placed here."

"In our ranks?" Saskia asks.

Finnian's fingers twitch on the table like he wishes to nock an arrow in his bow.

"No, a job like this would have to be taken on by someone undoubtedly loyal to Imirath," Cayden answers for him. "Someone to organize attempts while keeping a low profile to see the job through."

"My father trusts the soldiers in his personal guard most." I graze my fingers over my knives when I recall the years they tortured me. He could trust them to keep quiet. The idea that one of them is watching my every move makes my skin crawl. "I can provide details from what I remember, though they're most likely under an alias and I'm sure several guards have been changed out by now."

"Any information is useful," Saskia says before peppering Braxton with further questions.

The feeling in my chest becomes sharper, more persistent, and my eyes are drawn to the flames again. It's trying to tell me something, I feel it in my bones. I unclasp my pendant from around my neck and drop the moonstone on the table when the metal burns my palm.

Cayden leans his head closer to me, but his face is blurring. The only thing I see with clarity is the fire. "Are you all right?"

"I just need some air." But I'm too dizzy to stand.

"I'll escort you out," Finnian says, beginning to rise.

"I'll just be a moment." I push myself out of the chair with my eyes on the fire. Another image has formed—the amulet the priestess gifted me. I recall seeing it on Cayden's desk last night, and rip my wrist from his hold, rushing from the tent without a backward glance.

"Elowen!" he calls once I'm halfway across the path, and I know Finnian will be hot on his heels. They'll say the amulet is too high a risk, but I'm not letting us fail.

I quicken my pace as I enter the other tent and rip the amulet from his desk, gasping when it pulses in my hand like a heart. The metal is warm, inviting, tempting. A stark contrast to when I first held the necklace.

"Put that down." Cayden halts in place when I raise the amulet closer to my neck. Finnian, Ryder, and Saskia soon follow, all exchanging confused and worried glances.

"The priestess said this is essential to our mission," I say, trying to reason.

"*You* are essential!" he growls. "The link to your dragons doesn't depend on some cheap sorcery. The bond is in your soul."

"Put the necklace down, and we can figure this out together," Finnian says, taking a tentative step forward. If I blinked, I'd miss the way he and Cayden exchanged a brief glance.

"Some risks have to be worth it." I clasp the chain around my neck and feel myself falling through endless darkness before everything becomes silent.

Damp stone presses into me and seeps through my clothes. Two serpents slither around my arms in circular motions as golden flecks radiate off their bodies and flutter through the air around me. They illuminate the dark corner I'm in, but my fingers pass through their transparent bodies as heavy footsteps approach. I pull two knives from my holsters and jump forward to attack, but the guard doesn't even glance at me.

He walks *through* me.

The serpent glides around my palm while I stare down at it and realize I'm invisible. I'm nothing more than a puff of cold air in this damp, dark hall.

The snake on my right arm slithers forward, and I follow. The amulet obviously transported me here for a reason and I don't know how much time I have. I can't say I thought the amulet would have me following snakes down a corridor, but I suppose stranger things have happened in my life.

The snake turns a corner, but I halt as if my feet are cemented in the stone floor.

I'm in Imirath.

The amulet pulses on my neck, urging me forward, but suddenly I'm not the twenty-five-year-old staring into my old cell, I'm the six-year-old banging on the bars I'm locked behind.

My legs give out and I'm gasping for air. I dig my palms into my eyes and fight the onslaught of memories I keep locked away.

The gold flecks come alive within the cell, becoming a small girl and an oversized man. He picks the girl up by the neck, thrusting her shaking frame into the bars, and I swear I feel the pain at the back of my head.

"BREAK THE BOND!"

Gold flecks rain off her the more she shakes, but she knows this routine. She knows the guard will leave and she'll hold on to that bond in her chest to stay alive, not caring that it's a bleak existence because she's not only existing for herself. She endures because she has no other choice, but even if she did, she'll always choose to live despite all the pain.

"Never."

The man roars, throwing the child onto the ground as the flecks explode and fade away. My shoulder screams in phantom pain, and I hear the distant sound of chains sliding against the floor, feel the pangs of starvation, remember what it was like to crave sunlight and fresh air.

I dig my nails into my palms and stand on stiff legs. That little girl survived so she could become the woman I am today. I am more than the memories and past that plague me. I'm no longer the girl they locked up. I'm their ruination foretold by the prophecy. I'm the woman forged from the bars I melted in my mind and welded into blades.

I follow the snake when it glides forward and stride past my cell, never looking back. Darkness has befriended me in ways the light never could, and right now, I truly am nothing more than a shadow.

I am Elowen Atarah, and nobody will put me in a cage again—not my mind nor anything else.

I pass through walls and doors, walking freely through my prison.

I hardly remember the castle; most images in my mind have been distorted by fear. As the years passed, Garrick ordered me to be blindfolded when I had to appear in the throne room. I ignore the flashes of gold, purple, and red that make up the place that should have been my home. But I was escorted through the castle in shackles rather than roaming it in bows and dresses.

Crystals and candles hang from the ceiling of the ballroom. I dive behind a column out of instinct when I note several soldiers guarding a staircase, but I'm unsteady on my feet and the amulet tugs me forward. I hold my breath as I bound up the steps, not wanting to make a single noise. I know they can't see me, but walking in front of several enemy soldiers isn't exactly something one would do with ease—invisible or not. The steps split at the top, and the snake makes a sharp left. The amulet nearly chokes me as it swings, urging my body to follow.

We twist and turn through the guarded halls, and I sprint to get to the destination faster, worried the magic is running low. I'm pulled through an iron door and the pulsing and tugging ceases. I glance down at the amulet, afraid the magic is gone, but it slips from my fingers when a shadow swallows me.

A snout nudges me from behind and tears well in my eyes before I even turn. Venatrix's red eyes stare down at me in suspicion, and her scales flash to black. Each dragon possesses the ability to camouflage when they're scared or need to hunt.

She leans her head into my outstretched hand, but I realize she can't see me, only senses me. When she hums, a tear falls from my eye and splatters on the floor, which Calithea springs forward to sniff. She turns toward the other three dragons and roars.

Sorin sprints forward, smushing his face against Venatrix's and taking her place in my hand. She snaps at him, and he snaps back. They look as if they're about to wage war on each other before I reach forward to run my hands down their scales. Their pupils dilate and their fangs retreat.

When I turn to pet Delmira, I'm met with a heavy chain. My

blood chills and boils all at once when I drag my eyes between each dragon, noting the collars around their necks and shackles on their ankles. I hadn't realized when I first saw them, too overwhelmed by their presence.

Unadulterated rage pours through me like lava, and I long for the day I'll paint the world with the blood of those responsible for this. As if the dragons can sense the change in my mood, they begin stomping their feet and roaring so loud it shakes the chamber.

This is the song of war.

Perhaps I could've let go of my anger if the torture were only directed at me, but I will never forgive Garrick for harming my dragons and locking them away. Nor will I forgive the army of soldiers that stands between us. Garrick may wear a crown, but dragon fire can melt gold. His title and flesh will be erased from this world while we remain.

"Give me more time." The amulet begins pulsing again, and I try to rip it off but there's an invisible barrier surrounding it. Basilius is about to reach my hand, his purple eyes full of hope and longing, when a gold barrier surrounds me, and our cries mingle together.

CHAPTER
TWENTY-NINE

My body jolts forward like I've awoken from a nightmare. The amulet is ripped off my neck and thrown across the room. My vision is peppery, and my heart beats like I ran to Imirath and back. Cayden's arms are wrapped around me as he kneels beside me, and I rest my head against his chest, unable to stay upright.

"I saw them," I whisper, staring at the amulet. My mind can't fully grasp what just happened.

"Who exactly did you see?" Saskia asks softly, kneeling on my other side along with Ryder.

"My dragons," I tentatively say, forcing the words to pierce my veil of confusion. Everything rushes at me like an avalanche: the dungeon, the dragons, *the chains.* I press a hand to my chest expecting to feel shards from where my heart was ripped out, but the hollowness is locked away. "The amulet took me to the Imirath castle."

"You're positive?" Finnian gasps.

I shakily push away from Cayden. "Did I say anything while I was in the vision?"

"No," Saskia says. "Cayden tried to take the amulet off you, but when it burned his hands, we concluded it may harm you if we disturbed whatever magic it was forged from."

"Your eyes turning gold was the only sign of life." Cayden's words are emphasized by his glare. An apology is on the tip of my tongue, but he shakes his head as if sensing it.

"Even so, you can speak freely in here. We have runes set in place for privacy," Ryder informs me.

"Runes!" I shriek while scrambling to my feet.

"You saw runes?" Saskia asks.

"Yes, the snakes led me there."

"Of course," Ryder mumbles. "I love those trusty snakes."

"They were friendly, slightly pushy, though."

"I shall behead them on your behalf," Cayden mutters.

"Stop talking! They might hear you."

Cayden and Ryder exchange a brief glance before slowly nodding.

I grab a quill and paper from the desk and begin to draw. I've never been an artist, but I think it looks okay. Saskia leans over my shoulder to check what I've created. "I saw them branded into the dragons' door before I passed through it."

She holds the paper closer to her. "These are a mixture of silencing and strength runes, most likely to reinforce the door."

"The blood key will get us through the door despite the runes," Cayden says, silencing my worries before they can fully form. "Can you re-create the path you took?"

Saskia walks over to a trunk in the corner and pulls out several maps after I nod, carrying them over to the dining table to cross-reference. The details flow from me with ease. My despair can't do anything for us in this moment, but my memory can. Ryder and Finnian jot down every word while Saskia and Cayden hover over the maps, pointing and dragging their fingers along the drawings.

The tent falls into quiet murmurs once I finish. Finnian and Ryder compare notes before handing them off to Cayden and Saskia. In this moment, it feels like we're a team, but I'm drowning. I try to share in the electric energy coursing through the discussion, but all I can think about are my dragons. My eyes grow misty when I think of Basilius nudging empty air in hopes of finding me. Their wails are echoes in my soul, but I don't want to escape their pain while they're shackled to it.

"This is brilliant, Elowen!" Saskia smiles at me, and I do my best to return one. "I've been piecing a route through the castle based on spy reports, but this is what we've been missing. Will you be able to plan a route from the back gate to the dragon chamber? I feel that may be your best option."

"The back gate?" I slowly ask, and Finnian shifts uncomfortably.

"It will give you the most coverage, and I'll know the guard rotations in time for the heist."

She looks at me expectantly, and I hate to be the one to crush her hope. "I can't create a route from anywhere other than the dungeon." Finnian knows this, but it doesn't stop him from ducking his head. Understanding and remorse wash over Saskia's and Ryder's features, and Cayden looks like he's cursed with all the wrath in Ravaryn.

"I'll draw up some maps and go over them with you tonight if you'd like," Saskia offers. I'm thankful she moved on quickly. Sympathy is one of the reasons I don't disclose much about my life in Imirath.

"That's perfect." I pluck my necklace from Cayden's fingers when he holds it out to me and ignore the gaze that sees right through my smile. "The amulet drained me, so I'll be in my room until I'm needed."

I close my eyes and sigh once I'm alone, trying to dispel some emotions while I put my necklace on and fiddle with the pendant. I've gotten myself through all these years, I can get myself through a few more weeks.

Just because I'm cracked doesn't mean I'm broken.

My room is a mixture of soft and dramatic tones, flowers and darkness. It's as if Cayden stepped into my mind and didn't miss a single detail. White lace is canopied over the four-poster bed covered by a sage-green comforter embroidered with gold flowers. Pillows with equally beautiful detailing line the couches and chairs of the seating area, and at the center is a fresh bouquet of starsnaps and books stacked around the vase.

I smile when I imagine Cayden frowning at fabric samples and smother my giggles with my hands when I pull a stack of colorful books toward me and note that they are all romances. Knowing him,

I'm sure he found me the raunchiest novels. The other stack consists of gardening books, a few on herbal healing remedies, and several titles on dragons.

A tea cart in the corner is topped with a delicately painted set of porcelain, and the yellow and pink tin Saskia picked up from the shop in Ladislava. I crack the lid open and inhale the sweet scent of lavender and chamomile that soothes anxiety.

I spin at the center of the room, reveling in the first place in this world that's felt like me. Cayden shouldn't be the one to gift me this, and yet he is. It makes me wonder at all the details that have spilled from my lips, or have been revealed by my eyes, and remained insignificant and invisible to anyone but him.

I sink onto a couch that feels more like a cloud and prop a pink clothbound book on my lap. Words have given me wings when I've needed an escape. Books breathe life into the mundane and have brightened the darkest of days for me with merely some pretty prose and hope. Some of my favorite nights were when my candlestick melted and dawn chased away the night while I was lost in a maze of words and wonder.

I'm deep within the pages of a tale about star-crossed lovers when Cayden opens the curtain separating our rooms and leans against the post, crossing his exposed forearms littered with red and white scars and hooking one boot over the other. "Do you want to talk about what you saw?"

I tuck a pressed flower between the pages and close my book. Sometimes I feel like I've kept things bottled inside me for so long that I don't know how to take off the lid. "May I bandage your knuckles?" Now that the dried blood is washed off, it's easy to see how mangled and bruised they are. I should've done it last night, but touching him in even the most innocent way could've led to something more. "I need to do something with my hands," I add when he glances down at them.

He kicks off the post and grabs my healing supplies, placing the satchel beside me and taking a seat on the table, resting his arms on his knees. I tug his hands forward and place them on my lap while I dig for the gauze and ointment. I've always found peace in healing others because I don't have the first clue on how to heal myself. I pop the tin open, and the beloved scent of rosemary hits me as I dip my fingers in. He *destroyed* his knuckles . . . for me, and the burns on his palms only add to the carnage. The thought makes me glance up at him, but my eyes linger. Cayden is so handsome, it's impossible to look away.

"They're in chains." I continue lightly spreading the ointment. "I assumed they would be, but it was different to see it for myself. They were put in cages when my father separated us, but I always prayed they were given free rein in a tall chamber. I've been filled with a fool's hope, and the vision at the prison didn't show anything but their faces so I didn't see the shackles then."

He sighs. "You're not a fool to have hope."

I shake my head, brushing off his comfort. "I wish we could leave today, but I have too many people relying on me to sign this treaty and it's . . ."

"Suffocating?"

I nod. Sometimes I wish Ailliard had named himself king so I could focus on my dragons, but I think that's exactly why he made me queen. Bestowing that responsibility on me forced me to split my attention.

"You're going to sign the treaty by the end of the week," he says with certainty.

"The alliance ball isn't until the end of the month, and that's when Eagor—"

"I'll move it up."

"But the invitations have already been sent."

"Elowen." He squeezes my hand when I tie off the bandage. "Why are you arguing with me?"

"I don't want to be let down, and I think it's my default when it comes to you." I shrug. "Do you have that kind of pull in court?"

"Well, if they refuse, I'll start torching their precious manors until they agree." He sounds like he's speaking from experience; he probably is. I continue working on his other hand with shaky fingers, trying my best to quell the anticipation surging through me. Basilius's tortured cry rings in my ears again, and my heart thumps in my chest. Cayden tilts my face to his when I finish tying off the second bandage. "You *will* sign the treaty in five days."

"You truly mean that?" My voice is so thin he could snap it in half with an ounce of doubt.

"I do."

I throw my arms around him before sense catches up to me, and he stiffens when our bodies collide. It's a quick embrace, one that I don't let his mind register before I pull away and kiss his scarred cheek. The confusion in his eyes has me pressing my lips together to keep from laughing. "Thank you."

"Right." He clears his throat. "You can repay me by telling me how you snuck out of the castle."

"I seduced my guards." He growls a curse while unsheathing his sword and standing from the table. "I'm joking, demon." He halts in place, already halfway to the door, but remains tense and prepped for an execution. "I jumped across my balcony to yours."

He drops his head and groans while sheathing his blade. "So the consequence of poor communication is you jumping off a balcony?"

"I jumped *across* a balcony."

"If I weren't so annoyed with you, I'd actually be impressed." He turns back to me and moves too quickly for me to stop him. "Excellent choice of literature, love."

"Give it back!" I spring from the couch and toss a pillow, but it doesn't faze him.

"What part were you up to? I recall this one being particularly sinful."

"Was she blushing when you walked in there?" Finnian shouts from the other room.

"No."

"Then she wasn't reading anything raunchy or romantic. She always blushes, squeals, or kicks her feet," Finnian says. When did those two become so damn chummy?

"Finnian is an idiot," I huff.

"I suppose it wouldn't hurt to test his theory." Cayden holds the book out of my reach while flipping through the pages. He shoves my legs away when I try to hook them around his waist to gain leverage.

"I'm not above biting you!"

"Don't tease me with empty promises, angel," he purrs. I pull on his face, trying to divert his eyes away from the lusty paragraph he managed to find in record time and continues reading aloud. "What an interesting position the author has described! Do you want to try it? I think we could make it work."

"I would sacrifice my firstborn child to be in an alliance with absolutely anyone else." I jump onto his back and the book is nearly in my grasp, but still too far. For the love of the gods, I wish he had normal-sized limbs. I alter my technique and cover his eyes with my hands.

"But I just got to my favorite part." His laughter vibrates my stomach. "She refers to herself as a cream-filled pastry. I bought you this one because you love pastries!"

Finnian howls from the other room, and I slide down Cayden's back. He turns to face me, and I begin pushing him into his room after grabbing the book and tossing it on the couch.

"I read them all so we could discuss our favorite bits together," he manages to say through his boisterous laughter, glancing toward his bed. "If you want to get under my sheets, you only have to ask nicely."

"Absolutely not," I respond, hating the fluttering feeling in my chest when I look at his damn dimples. His laughter is hoarse, deep, and rich; it's like the sound must make its way through rusty pipes after years of neglect. I've seen many expressions on him, but there's something so beautiful about catching a genuine smile from someone who rarely deals them out. Happiness is my favorite thing he's ever worn.

It doesn't hit me until later that night that Cayden was the person to make my burden feel lighter, and to make me laugh when hopelessness surrounded me.

CHAPTER

THIRTY

M Y IVORY GOWN RIPPLES AROUND ME LIKE A RIVER and shimmers like a fresh snowfall. I've never worn anything so beautiful, nor could I imagine such a dress myself. The bodice is embroidered with green, yellow, purple, and pink flowers that trail down my skirts to frame each side of the high slit. Moonstone beads drape over my upper arms to create the illusion of sleeves, and the crown resting on my head consists of two gold dragons biting another moonstone at the center. Voluminous dark curls reach my lower back, and Hyacinth lined my eyes with a skillful hand, making them stand out like dying embers in a hearth.

"The king and queen of Galakin were in Urasos when the date of the ball changed and hastily traveled to make it in time," Ailliard informs me as he escorts me to the ballroom. "You'll be seated at a table with them, Commander Veles, King Eagor, and Queen Valia."

"Is there anything about them I should be aware of?"

"Well," he begins, looking slightly uncomfortable. "The prince of Galakin is unwed and about two years older than you. They won't say anything official, but a potential union might be mentioned. It would be an excellent match considering you can't stay here without a permanent position, and that would put a great deal of distance between you and Imirath."

"Oh," I say, remembering Saskia's forewarning. A prince to go along with all the other suitors Valia mentioned. "Yes, I suppose you're right."

"But tonight isn't about that. Tonight is about you." He wraps his hands around the tops of my arms. "There will be several lords of Vareveth fighting to dance with you, but nobody deserves to revel in tonight more than you. You're not a queen because you were born into it. You're a queen because you lead with your heart but wield your intelligence like the sharpest blade." He leans forward to kiss my forehead. "I'm so proud of you, my dear. I don't say it nearly as much as I should."

I offer him a watery smile. "Thank you for your guidance throughout the years."

"It was all you." Ailliard steps back and looks at me as I imagine a father would. "I want to get to my seat before you enter, but remember that no man who plans on fighting for your hand tonight deserves you."

I watch him go, but what I really want is to ask him if he thinks one particular man might. I know what he'll say, and I know how it'll make me feel, so I tuck my words into a corner of my mind to save them for another day.

Braxton steps forward to knock on a set of double doors enriched with golden swirls and crystal knobs. Every detail in this castle is like a fairy tale brought to life. There's beauty at every turn and a regal energy surging through the halls and towers.

Three loud thumps vibrate the floor, and the chatter dies down. I smooth my hands down the front of my dress and square my shoulders after tossing my hair behind them.

Breathe.

"Esteemed guests of King Eagor Dasterian and Queen Valia Dasterian. It is with the utmost honor that I present to you Her Majesty Queen Elowen Atarah of Aestilian, Princess of Imirath, the Dragon Queen!"

I glide into golden light as strings are plucked and keys are played to produce an angelic melody. The ballroom itself bewitches me. Thick green vines creep up the walls and drape across the ceiling, some hang down, and all are dotted with small white and purple flowers. There's even a tree at the center of the dance floor adorned with golden lanterns. The trunk stretches high, and the branches sprawl like a spider's legs.

Tables have been created by twisted tree roots, and the guests who crowd the room blur together like a sea of rich jewels. A sharp whistle cuts through the thunderous applause and my eyes find Ryder. His curls are perfectly sculpted, much like the midnight-blue tunic that hugs his frame. Saskia stands beside him with her braids piled high on her head and her crimson velvet gown making her look entirely stunning. Finnian is seated with them as well, and Ryder pats his back while he gets emotional *again*. The white and sage tailored suit he wears makes his ginger hair stand out like the first rays of sun over snowcapped mountains.

Eagor waits for me at the bottom of the steps, and he graciously takes my hand before guiding my arm through his. It's hard to believe a few months ago all of Ravaryn thought I was dead, and now I'm here, gliding through a ballroom with a crown on my head and a king on my arm. He leads me to a raised gazebo made of more twisting roots and vines. The candles cast a warm glow throughout the private space, illuminating the set of unfamiliar faces waiting for me.

"Queen Elowen, may I present Queen Cordelia Ilaria and King Erix Ilaria of Galakin," Eagor says while gesturing between the pair.

"It's so lovely to see you again." Cordelia steps forward. Her dress is the shade of a sunflower, complementing her deep brown skin and auburn hair. She smiles at me like she found a trinket she wants to take home.

Erix reaches forward and brings my hand to his lips. He shares the same skin tone and outfit color as his wife, but his eyes are brown, and his hair is gray. "The girl who hatched dragons from eggs that were no more than stones passed down in my family for centuries. It's a day I'll never forget."

"I can't thank you enough for bringing them to me." The mention of my dragons is welcome, as are the people who gifted me the eggs.

The music abruptly ends, signaling us to take our seats. Fire licks at the back of my neck, and anticipation buzzes like a bee in my palms when I meet Cayden's gaze. He leans against one of the posts with his hands tucked into the pockets of an impeccably tailored black suit with gold embellishments. He looks more like a dark prince than a commander, ready to whisk me away to his realm of terror and tragedy but never let either touch me. I'm practically floating through a dream as I walk toward him knowing that approaching him, to anyone else, would be a nightmare.

"You look . . ." His husky tone makes my toes curl. "*Beautiful* is too mundane a word."

"You gifted me this gown," I say. My original was green and gold as an ode to Vareveth. I thought there was a mistake when I opened the dress box, until I realized each detail was plucked and polished solely for me, down to the heels with straps that climb up my legs like vines. "You designed it."

He shakes his head. "Must have been someone else."

"You're the only one I speak of my dragons with. Nobody else close to me would know what these colors mean."

His fingers slide across the beads before brushing down my arm and pressing into my back, guiding me to the table and pushing my chair in behind me. Goosebumps rise on my arms when he leans close to say, "I do not believe your beauty needs any embellishment, nor do I believe anything can compare to it, but that dress would have paled in comparison to you."

His smile deepens when he takes in my flushed disposition. "The original was also beautiful."

"I agree." No matter how hard I bite my lip, I can't fight the smile that now sits on my face in plain sight for him. His eyes dance along my features as they often do, taking in every detail. "But it never would have measured up to you."

Erix dives into a tale from his travels while a creamy pumpkin bisque is placed in front of us. I bring the spoon to my mouth, and a mixture of cinnamon and nutmeg creates a delicious burst of flavors on my tongue. Cordelia whispers the fallacies of her husband's story in my ear, such as the sea monster he slayed while crossing the Dolent Sea was really a whale he named and mentions often. When I accidentally brush my fingers against Cayden's under the table, neither of us pulls away.

"My son, Prince Zale, would've loved to come to the ball if the date hadn't been changed," Cordelia says as servants clear the plates. "He was looking forward to meeting you."

"I'm sorry to have missed him," I reply.

"We would love for you to come to Galakin one day." I pull my fingers away from Cayden when she fully turns toward me. "You may even find you like our continent better than Erebos. It's much warmer."

"Is your court seer still there?"

Her face drops. "She is. You must know she never intended for King Garrick—"

"My father's choices are his alone," I cut off her unnecessary apology and offer a small smile. "My dragons are a blessing, not a burden."

The room falls silent when Eagor stands and extends his glass in the air. "Queen Valia and I thank you all for attending this celebration given the short notice, and offer a special thanks to King Erix and Queen Cordelia of Galakin. Vareveth has suffered for too long at the hands of Imirath, but new alliances have arisen from the strife." Eagor turns away from the crowd and raises his glass to me. "Queen Elowen, we toast to new beginnings with you. To the Dragon Queen!"

"To the Dragon Queen!" echoes the crowd. Couples filter onto the dance floor once the toast ends. Cayden stiffens beside me and takes a long drink of wine from his chalice, which somehow looks small in his hand.

"Queen Elowen, will you give both me and our alliance the honor of your first dance?" Eagor circles the table and extends his hand to me.

The thought of being close to him sets me on edge, but I place my hand in his and bury my discomfort as we glide into the crowd. Eagor rests his hand on my lower back, and I rest mine on his shoulder as the dance begins. He leads me through the steps I've practiced since I was a young girl stepping on Ailliard's toes.

"I hope you're enjoying your time in Vareveth thus far," Eagor says above the music.

"It's lovely," I answer as he places his hands on my hips to briefly lift me when the music calls for it. The assassination attempts aside, there have been good parts.

We sidestep before he dips me. "Did you know there was a chance we would be married if you had never left Imirath?" My smile gets tighter. Every part of me is urging myself to put distance between us. "My mother and your father only brushed upon negotiations, but those ceased after you disappeared." The soldiers who came to my cell would poke fun at the peace offers Garrick received. He's a tyrant with no moral compass.

"Thank the gods," I mutter.

"Sorry, what was that?"

"I said that's very odd," I say above the music. "It's a good thing it didn't work out, because now you have Valia."

He spins me in tandem with other couples, but his hand is lower on my back than when we first started dancing. "She and I are a marriage of convenience, not love. We both have other . . . arrangements."

Gods, I feel trapped. The only thing I can do is smile and finish the dance. I can't make an enemy of him minutes before the stroke of his quill will determine the difference between my people surviving or starving. I can suffer for them a bit longer.

"There's a very expensive brothel close to the castle. Sometimes royals or people of means go there for a night to forget who they are and escape servants' prying eyes." It's a miracle I keep the sneer off my face when his thumb begins to stroke my hand. "The atmosphere is reason enough to go and meet someone in a private room."

"Why are you telling me this?"

Don't start shaking; just keep smiling.
Don't start shaking; just keep smiling.
Don't start shaking; just keep smiling.

"You've lived hidden away for your adult years. I'm unsure of how much experience you've had, and I want to make sure you go to the right place to seek it." The instruments play a shrill note, and he takes the opportunity to press his fingers into the center of my back, hard enough to feel them through the thick material of my corset. "You're a very beautiful woman, Elowen."

"You don't need to fret over my life experience. I've had plenty." Anger, disgust, and malice boil in me. "In fact, do you know how I punish untoward advances?" My smile keeps him intrigued. "I end the offender and make it look like a disappearance. If the princess bonded to five dragons can become a ghost, I suppose anyone can."

He flinches and falters the final steps of our dance. Doors at the opposite end of the ballroom open and trumpets flare, signaling that it's time to sign the treaty.

I smile sweetly at him. "Shall we, Your Majesty?"

"Of course," he mutters while extending his arm to me. Let this be the last time Eagor Dasterian looks at me as anything more than a political ally.

Cayden is already signing the treaty when we enter, and I detach myself from Eagor the moment the doors shut to do the same. An immeasurable weight I didn't realize the magnitude of rises off my shoulders with each stroke of my quill. My people won't starve, and I can finally focus on my dragons. I stare into the blazing fire in hopes of catching a glimpse of their eyes or feeling the bond pull at my heartstrings, but neither occurs.

Eagor hardly has a chance to rest the quill on the desk before Cayden grips his tunic and shoves him into the nearest wall, rattling the frames. "Unhand me!"

"You told me to stay away from her? Now this is me telling you to do the same and there will be *severe* consequences if you don't heed my warning."

"I'm your king!"

"I don't give a fuck if you're a god. If I see you reach another hand toward her, I will happily cut it off." Cayden's voice is laced with lethality. It's dark and cold, just like one would imagine death to sound.

"We were dancing," Eagor growls.

"You and I both know you overstepped, and unless you want a rumor started about the precious powder you love to snort, I suggest you remember who you're dealing with."

Eagor pales, and his mouth parts in horror. He looks at Cayden like he's a demon before his eyes dart toward the door. "The treaty is signed; therefore it's my time to return to my guests."

"Good boy." Cayden pats his cheek before shoving him in that direction. Eagor stumbles and rights his crown before slipping from the room.

"What just happened?" I ask breathlessly.

Cayden turns in my direction and cuts the distance between us, pressing my back into the wall before I have a chance to process what's happening. He dips his head close to mine but doesn't kiss me. Our hearts beat as one, and his eyes are burning and almost unhinged.

"Cayden," I gasp. He drops his head and trails his lips down my neck, biting and sucking on the soft spot below my ear. "W-we can't. Not here."

"I don't care," he groans against my neck, pressing closer and pulling another moan from me. He hitches my leg around his waist, and his hand tightens over the dragon dagger on my thigh. "Gods, I love this."

I thread my fingers through his hair as he whispers compliments against my skin and touches me like he can't fathom taking his hands off. All the reasons we should pull apart are silenced when his lips glide against me. He treats me like a cherished secret he'll keep to the grave.

He moves up my neck and rests his forehead against mine, keeping me close without taking this further than we have. He seems content to just stay there, looking at me. We're dancing on the edge of a cliff without caution.

"You got your treaty," he states in a gravelly tone.

"Yes, you're shackled to me for the foreseeable future." My voice is shaky even to my own ears.

"You already had me." He drops my leg and takes my hand, abruptly pulling me off the wall. "We're going to dance."

"How sweet of you to *ask*." I hurry my steps to keep up with his long strides. "You told me you don't dance."

"I make no apologies for wanting the kingdom to know you're mine for the night." He smiles at me, and the soft candlelight graces his face like a lover's caress, making him look innocently sinful.

Truthfully, I don't want to dance with suitors or suffer the liberties of their bold hands. I tell myself that's why I'm curtsying to Cayden on the dance floor when he bows. Butterflies swarm in my stomach when he pulls me close, and we move into the proper position. The way people are staring at us in a mixture of disbelief, jealousy, and curiosity makes me wonder if it's truly so rare for Cayden to dance. He notes my rising anxiety due to the attention we've drawn and tilts my chin back to him.

"It's just you and me, angel. You keep those pretty eyes on me," he whispers close to my lips, giving me the urge to close the gap despite the prying eyes.

Cayden whisks me into the fray of tulle and measured steps. He leads me as he does his army, definitive and steadfast, moving with measured grace. He's not the type of person to flow, he's the type to command the tide. I spin between his arms and press my back into his chest as we continue the steps. The dance feels enriched by the old magic deep within the roots beneath our feet. I allow myself to fall into the cloud of clandestine touches.

We're closer than what's deemed appropriate, and I'm sure Queen Cordelia's watchful gaze has noticed, but I can't bring myself to care. I don't need a prince to validate my power or place in this world.

Cayden's breath fans against my collarbone, and I lean my head back to rest against his shoulder. He glides our intertwined hands across my stomach, and they feel like they were made to do exactly this. He lifts me off the ground when the music builds to a crescendo, and it feels like the harpist is plucking the strings of my heart. We feel like a melody long forgotten plucked from a shelf, dusted, and placed before a musician to remind the world of our tale.

My arms wrap around his neck as he glides me down his body at a sinfully languid pace. Our breaths mingle in our own private universe amid the chaos. The invisible ropes tied around our wrists have twisted through the dance, but perhaps things must knot before they snap.

Stars dance in his eyes as he looks down at me. "Dance with me again."

"Will you ever ask me properly?"

"Why would I offer you an escape route?"

"It's polite."

He makes a face like the notion of pleasantry disgusts him. "I don't want you getting confused about what I am."

The next song begins, and I don't step away. I know we're being watched, but I want to be selfish. "What are you?"

"A monster, but for you, never to you."

A smile plucks at my lips. "I might get too tired to walk out of here if you keep me dancing all night."

"Then I'll carry you."

"Even if I step on your toes?"

"Always."

He whisks me away into a new dance. His hold never falters the entire night, and he always pulls me close to him after spinning me away, molding our bodies together as stars mold constellations in the sky. He twirls me until the only person in the ballroom I can see is him.

CHAPTER
THIRTY-ONE

Steam rises from my cup as I lounge on my bed in the castle, flipping through one of the dragon books I brought back from the border. I had a dream about baking tarts for them after reading that apparently, they adore fruit. The guilt I feel for leaving them has amplified throughout this morning, as has the pain of their absence. I hid it well while having breakfast with Queen Cordelia, who spent most of the time complaining about the cold. She and Erix begin their journey back to Galakin tomorrow, wanting to get home to their kingdom and their *handsome* son whom she *subtly* fit into our conversation before a sea storm surges.

Footsteps pad through the suite, but I don't have to see Cayden to know it's him. His presence sends a shocking current through me.

"I have something to show you," he says while leaning against one of my bedposts, and I groan in response. "I told you not to finish off the last bottle of wine."

Saskia, Ryder, and Finnian left the ball with us, and we spent the night gorging on wine and slurring jokes until the sun rose. Saskia collapsed beside me in bed after we ran barefoot through the gardens while the others chased us.

"But it was made from strawberries," I mutter, swinging my legs off the bed. My emerald gown embellished with gold trails behind me as I walk toward a pair of satin slippers. The thought of wearing heels today is unfathomable, but I donned the gown to trick my mind into feeling better. The sheer, loose sleeves flow like a breeze, and the intricate detailing on the bodice and skirts reminds me of drooping branches on a willow tree.

"Yes, you informed me several times while threatening me with a knife as I tried to take it from you." I press my fingers into my forehead and groan again. "I found it endearing."

He speaks like he's looking back on a fond memory. He's deranged. "Did you find it endearing the first time I held a knife to your neck?"

He licks his lips, and my traitorous eyes fall to them when he speaks. "I felt something entirely different the first time."

Our shoes slap against stone as he leads me from the tower, down spiraling staircases and through a maze of decadent halls. I'm slightly dizzy by the time we reach an exit and slide my arm through his as we step outside. Cayden points toward a series of wagons and a woman with a scroll listing off directions to servants. Crates filled with vegetables, fruits, meats, grains, oats, and spices line the grass. I remember watching delivery crates being carried into taverns and shops while on missions knowing I wouldn't be able to bring all that food home with me. It feels like a storm that has shrouded me for years has finally passed and daylight caresses my face.

Aestilian will live on. The parents and caretakers won't have to forgo eating in favor of their children. Nyrinn's hands won't shake while she stitches someone. The guards who monitor the border will be sharp and clearheaded, and none will risk their lives trekking through snow to bring back scraps.

A shiver runs through me when I recall the harshest winter in Aestilian. I spent most of my time wading through snow and sliding down icy peaks after dark. Sleep couldn't find me if it had a map, and Finnian was deathly frail. I stole and killed for what we needed to survive, but he's never forgiven me for giving him my rations. He caught on to my lie when I fainted in our yard and monitored my meager meals like a hawk afterward.

"I received word of your people crossing the border. The letter was dated a few days ago, so they'll be here soon," Cayden says.

I clear the emotion from my throat. "My spies have been waiting for news of the treaty being signed. They probably rode day and night to get here so quickly."

"You work fast, little shadow." He leads me back into the castle and I rub my hands together to warm them. "I have a proposition for you."

"Do tell," I say, fisting my dress to begin our ascent.

"Your soldiers will have less of a chance at being attacked or robbed if I send several Vareveth soldiers with them. They won't travel fast with that many wagons."

I bite my lip, contemplating his offer. "Will you choose the soldiers yourself?"

"Yes. I won't include anyone unless I can personally vouch for them."

It's a generous proposal, but the recent assassination attempt has me treading cautiously. "They can cross the Fintan with my soldiers, but I'm wary of revealing the exact location of Aestilian. We both know that not everyone in your army welcomes me here." He opens his mouth to argue. "Even with your threats."

He clenches his jaw and glares. "After the recent execution, no one would dare, but I respect your wishes and will give the order."

I'm aware of the impression he must have left on his army, and the gossip about Cayden's brutality and mercilessness has been incessant. Eyes often linger on us while ladies hide their mouths behind their fans to whisper tales of the demon commander and the lost dragon princess.

Finnian spots us from down the hall and hurries our way. "The soldiers are here. Ailliard sent me to find you."

"That's sooner than expected." It's a relief, truthfully. I want to tidy up my loose ends and get back to Imirath.

We follow Finnian to the main hall where I first entered the castle, and the trickling water of the fountain is an afterthought to Ailliard's booming laughter. I'm more anxious than I should be, but it feels like

I'm meeting a new person despite knowing I'm the one who has metamorphized. I'm stronger and surer of myself and my future, and I can't pretend that I could go back to the way things were.

We walk down the steps to greet Nessa, Lycus, and Jarek. Nessa steps over to embrace me with Lycus at her side while Jarek continues conversing with Ailliard. I quickly step away and slide my arm through Cayden's, not wanting Jarek or Lycus to extend the same greeting Nessa did.

"Nessa and Lycus are two of the guards that escaped Imirath with me. This is Commander Veles of Vareveth," I say, gesturing to each.

Nessa grins, causing her deep-set eyes to crinkle in the corners while stretching a hand in his direction. "It's a pleasure to meet you, Commander. I've heard stories of your victories for quite some time."

Cayden extends the same pleasantries before asking, "You get news of Vareveth in Aestilian?"

"Only because we could never keep Elowen inside the borders no matter how much we tried."

"How was the journey?" I ask, quickly changing the subject.

"Uneventful. You look well, my lady," Lycus answers. He's always been a man of few words and plenty of formality. "The elixir worked wonderfully, sir. We managed to store a decent amount of food before the first frost came."

Cayden nods. "How long will you be staying? I'll alert the servants to ready some rooms."

"Only for the remainder of the day. We want to get the food back as soon as possible and would prefer our presence stay unnoticed by King Garrick," Nessa answers.

"I suppose it's for the best," I respond. "Commander Veles will be taking me on a tour of several Vareveth cities now that the treaty is signed."

"That sounds lovely." Nessa beams, glancing down at our joined arms. I don't know if she'd be smiling as much if she knew the true reason for our fabricated alibi. Ailliard threw a fit but eventually relented when I convinced him I need the exposure to the world.

"Nessa! Lycus! I remembered what I wished to tell you," Ailliard calls to his friends, and they bow before excusing themselves.

Cayden tilts his head in my direction when they're out of earshot. "What tales have you heard of me, angel?"

I shrug. "They must not have been that remarkable because I can't seem to recall."

We face forward as Jarek approaches and Cayden's lip curls. "Why are his pants so tight?"

I cough to cover up my laughter, but Cayden's expression remains frigid. "Would it kill you to smile?"

"Yes," he replies.

"You smile at me."

"You're different."

"Your Majesty." Jarek greets me and presses a kiss to my knuckles.

I barely repress the urge to wipe my hand on my skirts when he releases me. "It's nice to see you again, Jarek."

"I didn't think you'd volunteer for the journey given how vital your presence is in Aestilian," Finnian says, appearing at my side. It's like I'm pressed between two guard dogs.

Jarek clearly doesn't note Finnian's sarcasm as he replies, "A journey for my queen could never be considered a waste."

"Right, then," Cayden says, stepping in front of Jarek and blocking him out while glancing at his gold pocket watch. He's certainly not jealous, more so bored and disgusted. Finnian snickers at Cayden's lack of manners. "I'll be late if I don't leave now."

"Where are you going?"

"To steal sweets from children." He grins at my eye roll. "I have a meeting to discuss our person of interest that you're more than welcome to attend."

The mastermind behind my assassination attempts weighs heavily on my thoughts, but I can't leave my citizens when they've traveled all this way. There's nothing I want to do more than ponder theories and scour the streets before we leave. "Can we discuss it later?"

He nods, taking my hand and bringing it to his lips. "I look forward to it, love. I'll see you in our suite."

Servants descend the steps to show everyone to their rooms, and Finnian and I take it as a sign to slip from the castle. We walk down several stone staircases leading to the wagons.

"Well, the battle of the bulges was proper morning entertainment," Finnian says.

"Gods, Finnian," I groan, and yet I can't stop myself from laughing.

"Cayden won, if you were wondering. But I swear if we waited a few moments longer Jarek would've challenged him to a duel."

"I'm not listening!" I cover my ears and sprint toward the wagons when we reach the grass. My laughter makes my sprint sloppy, but he never catches me. It's easy for him to do so considering how much longer his legs are, but even when he hit his growth spurt, he always let me win. "We're no longer friends!"

"Fat chance, Ellie!"

☩ ☩ ☩

I'm exhausted by the time Ailliard and I finalize the distribution schedule for the rations, and I happily take the tea Nessa hands me.

"How's your little Moriko doing?" I ask. She and her wife adopted a five-year-old from the orphanage. Moriko is a short little thing with more curls than body and is an absolute sweetheart once she's comfortable.

"She's good." An easy smile filled with love spreads across her face. "Esme's been knitting sweaters for her to wear this winter, and she keeps the flower crown you made beside her bed. She must've picked up a mischievous streak because she's hiding around the house like you two did when you were younger."

A soft knock taps on the door, and I rise to answer it as Finnian laughs softly behind me, probably getting the same flashbacks of our childhood as I am.

"A letter from Commander Veles, Your Majesty." The servant

bows at the waist before turning down the hall. I quickly break the seal to unfold the letter.

Elowen,

I've concluded that the assassin is in Verendus. Ryder and I are heading there for further investigation. The group of soldiers that will cross the Fintan with your team are assembled and waiting by the wagons.

   I'll see you soon, angel,

Cayden

Verendus is the most populated area, meaning that the assassin is hiding in plain sight. I press my lips together and filter through all the new theories in my mind.

"The castle is much bigger, but it's not the best place to hide," Finnian says.

"No, too many people are watching you in a castle," Nessa agrees.

Realization slams into me like a gust of wind as Eagor's words clank through my mind.

The brothel.

People go there to escape. Nobody would question an unfamiliar face in a brothel because they're there for *something new.*

I grab my stomach and suck in a sharp breath. Two sets of concerned eyes flash over to me. "Oh no, is it your monthly?" Nessa asks.

I nod and force a pained expression to cross my features. "Would you mind if we said goodbye now? Finnian, it's just as bad as it was before we left Aestilian."

"Oh, darling, I'll walk you back to your room. You don't mind, right, Nessa?" Thank the gods he picks up on my excuse.

"Of course not," Nessa says, embracing Finnian. "We'll be leaving soon anyway."

Nessa embraces me, and I do my best to pretend I'm relaxing into it, but nothing about me is at ease right now. "Take care of yourself, my lady. I'll give Nyrinn your reply as soon as I get back."

I smile. "Have a safe journey, Nessa."

"Come on, darling." Finnian places a hand on my back. "Let's get you to bed."

We slowly walk to the door but burst into a sprint once we enter the hall. Finnian doesn't question what's happening as we practically throw ourselves down the stairs. The trust we've built over the years goes hand in hand with knowing when to follow.

I don't speak until we exit the castle and continue running toward the stables. "I know where the mastermind is."

"What? How? Where?"

"Brothel." I force the word out. "There's an expensive one close to the castle, and places like that are notorious for gossip. If Eagor goes there, then we can assume Cayden and I are spoken of considering he doesn't approve."

"Fucking gods," Finnian curses.

"Cayden and Ryder are already on their way to Verendus, and we need to catch up with them," I say. The stables smell of damp hay and apples. Finnian slides onto a freshly saddled horse and extends his hand to me as Braxton rounds the corner.

"Your Majesty." He suspiciously glances at us. "Did you get Commander Veles's letter?"

I could kiss his cheeks for appearing at the perfect time. "I did. Do you know exactly where he went?"

"Are you in trouble?" He grasps the hilt of his blade.

"I'm not, I swear it. I just need you to tell me where he went."

"He and General Neredras are starting their search at Chalice of the Gods, it's a tavern along the main road. Leave immediately, they make quick work of whatever they do."

"Bless you, Braxton!" I exclaim, climbing onto the horse and wrapping my hands around the saddle horn as Finnian takes off. The steep, hilly forest he leads us through is nothing compared to the Seren Mountains mixed with mist. "Find Cayden and leave me at the brothel."

"That's a terrible idea." He pulls on the reins and veers to the right.

"It'll look too perfect if we arrive together."

"What's your plan?"

His question would normally fill me with embarrassment, but I'm too energized to give a damn. "I need him to pretend we went there looking to escape the castle considering how many rumors are spread about us. If we manage to pull it off, the mastermind will reveal themself while we're *distracted*."

I know it's a solid plan when he curses under his breath and guides the horse onto the main road. "You're sure you want to be bait for an assassin?"

"I'm sure I want their blood spilled by the end of the night, and I'll do whatever it takes to achieve it." I squeeze his hands. I'll use every weapon in my arsenal to best those who have wronged me, including seduction. "I trust you to find him. Trust me to stay alive while you do."

The Golden Rose lives up to its name. Golden and white roses creep up the brothel, covering it, emphasizing its ambience of escapism and otherworldliness. Sensual music descends into the street to lure in the curious souls passing by. The thick glass windows obscure what's happening inside but don't entirely hide it.

I slide down from the horse and make my way up the path, my excitement and trepidation growing with every footfall. The memory of Cayden's hands on my body resurfaces, and the shiver that crawls up my spine has nothing to do with the breeze.

CHAPTER
THIRTY-TWO

THE SENSUAL MUSIC GROWS WHEN I PUSH THE DOOR open, as do my nerves, but not enough to make me regret my decision. Breathy moans filter into the foyer, and a woman in a gold satin gown sits behind a desk adorned with two lanterns encrusted in rubies.

The woman slowly stands and bows. "Your Majesty, I hoped you'd come to the Golden Rose one day."

"I've heard wonderful things." I smile graciously before donning a demure façade. "I'm expecting someone."

She takes a long drag from her pipe before blowing smoke through puckered lips. "May I ask for their name so I can escort them when they arrive?"

"Commander Veles." Saying his name brings me more comfort than it should.

A knowing smile spreads across her red lips. "The rumors around court say he's very enchanted by you, my lady. I'm grateful for your patronage."

Her gown trails behind her as she leads me through the foyer and a shimmering set of curtains. Several candles are placed upon gold tables, dripping wax and filling the room with floral scents. Drapery gives the illusion of privacy without fully gifting it. The various couples and parties in here don't grasp my attention because my mind is solely focused on how Cayden's lips feel on my skin.

"Your private chamber is equipped with everything you need, but if you wish for other comforts just let me or one of my workers know," she says while leading me down an equally lavish hall, plucking a key from the ring on her belt, and unlocking the door before handing it to me. "There's a selection of fresh outfits in the closet of varying sizes and colors. Will you need help getting out of your gown, my lady?"

"I can manage. Thank you for your hospitality," I respond. She curtsies before shutting the door and retreating. I press my forehead into the wood as the pulsing between my legs becomes incessant. Gods, I need to get hold of myself before Cayden gets here.

There are more modest pieces within the wardrobe, but I disregard them. I want to bring the man who kneels for no one to his knees. The scrap of red lace can't be considered panties, and the matching two-piece leaves little to the imagination. Thin gold chains hug my thighs, peeking between the high double slit of the floor-length skirt that sits low on my waist. Every sensitive part of my body is rubbed by the delicate lace. More chains hang down my shoulders and torso, attached to the tiny corset. My dark curls fall down my back, and I place the final piece of the outfit around my head: a gold circlet with a ruby at the center of my forehead.

The door opens and slams behind me, followed by a string of muttered curses and prayers for strength. I slide my hands down the delicate fabric of my skirt before turning and reveling in Cayden's tortured expression. He looks at me like he can't tell if he loves my outfit or wants to burn it. His knuckles are white from how fiercely he's gripping the handle.

His eyes drink me in like a dehydrated man who has found a lake after trekking through a desert for months. "Do I need to kill someone?"

My blood pumps so fiercely I can hardly hear him. "Nobody touched me."

"But did they see you before I had the privilege?" he asks, not dispelling the roughness in his tone. We're separated by a few feet, but it feels like miles. He looks like something that crawled out of a dark dream with his leathers, scars, and weapons. "You're an evil woman and a blessing all at once."

"Evil?" I question. "Well, I'm sure there are plenty of other men who would love—"

He pushes off the door and wraps my legs around his waist before pressing me into the embroidered bedding. His pupils have dominated his eyes, the same way he dominates me in this position. I bite my lip to keep myself from moaning when his bulge presses into me.

"Their blood will be on your hands." He rests his arm beside my head and presses the other into my back, arching it and pressing me fully into him. "I'm not a good man, Elowen. Never overestimate my compassion or underestimate my brutality."

I reach forward to toy with the waves curling at the nape of his neck. "You don't scare me."

"That's because my nature is flawed when it comes to you." He presses his lips to my neck and groans when I tighten my legs around him. I've never felt this kind of pull to anyone; it's intoxicating. "I'm greedy for the sight of you and starved for the taste of you."

He helps me shove his jacket off and returns his hands to my body once it hits the floor, pressing his forehead to mine after kissing up my neck. Our labored breaths mingle together as I speak. "Lie to me, touch me, do whatever you must to make it look like we're here for pleasure and nothing else. Make me believe you."

"When this night is over nobody in the kingdom will doubt how much I want you." His lips brush over mine. "I have a condition." My response becomes a moan when he shifts his hips. "Seal the deal with a kiss in here first. I told you I'm starved. You can't put a feast in front of me and tell me to take it slow."

I tilt my head up, and his exhale fans against my cheek as if he was holding his breath until I kissed him. His hand tightens in my hair, and he devours me. This is nothing like our first kiss; this is urgent and feverish. This is hands that can't grab enough rather than a thorough exploration. He doesn't seek permission; he dominates me with every stroke of his tongue. His lips and hips move against mine, amplifying my passion and demanding that I give more of myself.

My frustrated growl vibrates against his lips when I shove his shirt up and it keeps falling back in place. He chuckles, using one hand at the back of his neck to remove it after he separates our lips. My eyes dance over every inch of his torso, mesmerized beyond words. I knew he'd be muscular, but seeing him and imagining him are entirely different entities. He's built like a god. Broad shoulders, bulging biceps, and finely carved muscles wherever I look, all littered with a mixture of red, pink, and white scars from years spent as an assassin and soldier. He has a tattoo of the five phases of the moon on the left side of his torso along with a smattering of stars trailing down his ribs.

"Don't look at me like that," he commands, voice thick with lust.

"Why?" I rasp.

"Because we'll never leave this room." He weaves his fingers through my hair again to bring me to a sitting position. "Are you going to be all right without your knives?"

"I don't have much of a choice. If we're here for pleasure only, why would I remain armed?"

"They don't know our bedroom tastes." He detaches himself from me and walks toward my pile of blades, adding four to his thigh holsters and leaving his sword belt on. My gaze snags on the long lash scars stretching from his neck to his waist, and the pink lines make my vision turn red.

"Did you kill them?" Anger burns hot under my skin, and I know I'll kill them myself if he hasn't.

"Slowly." He turns back to me and presses his lips to my forehead. A wave of desire washes over me at the sight of our knives mingling together.

The dark aura encompassing the brothel makes me want to stay here for a while, letting the shadows mask my lustful acts. Everyone cranes their necks in our direction as Cayden leads me through the main room slowly, like he wants each person in here to see us together. I wonder if the mastermind has spotted me yet, and if they think me showing up here is too good to be true.

Cayden chooses a love seat beneath a sheer gold canopy with a tray of candles to offer us extra light. My heart pounds when he places his hands on the back of my thighs and trails his long fingers along the chains covering my stomach before replacing them with his mouth. He makes me feel like a living flame, and he's the oxygen feeding me.

His grip becomes assertive, and he yanks me forward to straddle him, looking up at me with the same soul-devouring expression he gave me when he first saw me wearing this. I hover above him, not wanting him to feel the pounding between my legs. This is a mission, it's supposed to be an act, but my body's reaction to him is undeniable.

"Are you sure this is all right?"

"No," he answers, and my cheeks heat in embarrassment. He places both hands on my hips, yanking me down to straddle him fully with no space left between us. "*This* is perfect."

His hard bulge presses into my soaked core, and he slides his fingers along my spine, causing me to arch into him. He wraps his lips around my nipple, visible through the fabric, and my head falls back in a moan. I place my hands on his shoulders and sway my hips to the beats of the song.

"That's it, angel," he groans. "Don't give them a show, give it to me."

I pull his hair to lift his face and cover his lips with mine. Our kiss is slow and sensual, the kind you share when you know you'll have more. It makes me want to peel his clothes off slowly and put my lips on every inch of his skin. I continue rocking our hips together and explore his body with my fingers, savoring the feel of his skin and adoring his reaction to me. When the kiss ends, I press my forehead to his and open my eyes, finding his already open and gazing at me. But it doesn't last long before they close again, and he leans forward to give me a chaste kiss that feels remarkably intimate.

He leans us back, locking his arms around my waist while I rest my head on his shoulder. He continues gliding his fingers up and down my spine in long, relaxing strokes. We must look like a regularly intimate couple to anyone else. I nuzzle into him before sitting up, even though being held by him feels right. Our bodies may have stopped moving, but the tension hasn't eased. The longer he looks at me, the more it builds. It's like we charge each other simply by touching.

His hands travel from my back to my thighs, and I shudder when he inches closer to my soaked panties. I narrow my eyes when he smirks, offering me his best version of an innocent expression that's far too mischievous. He pulls me close and bites the sensitive spot he knows renders me mindless. I snake my hands around his neck, and he leans me back, sliding his hands to my ass to keep me grinding. The music and our moans grow louder as sparks fly behind my eyelids. The possessive hold he has on me tells everyone here that I'm his, and trying to pull me away would be a feat equivalent to ripping apart the castle stone by stone with bare hands.

"Do you think—" He cuts me off by biting my neck again, and the pleasure is too much to speak through. "Don't be a prick." My curse is a breathless whisper.

"What did you call me?" There's a dangerous undertone to his question, and he pulls his head from my neck to look me in the eyes.

"Pri—ah!" He presses his fingers into the soaked lace between my thighs.

"Call me names again and I'll bend you over in front of this entire room." My thighs tighten around him, but he didn't dissuade me from cursing him, he made me want to call him every curse I know. Wickedness shines in his eyes, knowing I'd love that. "What did you want to ask me, angel?"

I glide my hands across his torso, getting lost in the stars and scars. I want to know more about *him*. Not the demon commander. Cayden Veles is becoming my favorite mystery to uncover.

"Angel?"

"Right." I clear my throat. "Do you think our performance is believable?"

His fingers slide through my hair, tugging at the roots. "If you want more, all you have to do is ask."

My hair fans across the cushions when he tosses me to the side and climbs on top of me. The couch is hardly large enough to fit his frame, but he makes it work. His tongue presses into my stomach and he licks his way to my breasts and finishes his path on my neck. My body squirms beneath him, desperate for friction, but he pins my hips down. He shoves two fingers into my mouth when I whine. No man has ever looked at me with the unwavering want he does; he looks at me like he needs me.

"Suck," he commands.

I wrap my lips around his fingers, swirling my tongue and bobbing my head slightly, wanting him to imagine what I'd do to his cock. His eyes darken and he drops his hips, finally rewarding me with his hard length. My arousal builds and builds, unrestrained, and I moan around his fingers.

He replaces them with his lips, and his groan sends a shock to my core. He grants me sharper thrusts and I dig my nails into his back. My head is dizzy and drunk on him, and I want him so badly it hurts.

"You're being so good for me, Elowen."

I love his praise. I want more.

He trails kisses down my stomach until my wish has been granted, and he's on his knees before me. The man who bows and kneels for no king or god doesn't hesitate to do so for me. I prop my head against the loveseat to watch what he's doing.

"Cayden." I can't manage more than his name when he tosses my legs over his shoulders, leaving love bites along my thigh.

"Your reactions are addictive." He tosses the center panel of fabric to the side and buries his face between my thighs. My head rolls against the back of the seat, and I slap my hand over my mouth to suppress a scream. "So fucking perfect." He nibbles on my panties, sending shocks throughout my body. I thread my fingers through his hair, and he moans between my thighs. "There's nothing more that I want to do than slide these panties to the side, but the first time I taste you won't be for anyone else, it'll be because you crave what I can give you as much as I crave to give it to you."

He continues teasing me, licking, sucking, and biting. Giving extra time and care to the places on me that make my legs shake. I'm a trembling mess by the time he kisses his way back up. He keeps me pinned below him, and I have no gods-damned idea how we're supposed to move on after this. But if he's going to torture me with his tongue, I'll do the same to him. I won't be the only one leaving this brothel with tormented priorities.

"Sit," I command, and he obeys. He pulls me onto his lap before I can slip from the couch, but I hold my hand over his lips when he tries to kiss me again, and I giggle at his annoyed expression and frustrated groan.

My lips skim his neck, and he shudders beneath me. I kiss my way down, stilling on the spots that make him moan, running my tongue over them, biting and sucking. He presses my head closer to him when I do, wanting me to mark him. I continue my pursuit, kissing between his pecs, along his tattoo, across several scars, and down his abs until the love bites stretch from his neck to his waist. He stares at them with pride as he cups my jaw and I slide down to my knees. I've never knelt for a man before, but Cayden makes me feel empowered by the way he truly views me as his salvation and damnation in human form.

I look up at him through my lashes. "Do you like the sight of me on my knees, demon?"

"Elowen." His tone is rough and heavy. I trail my hands up his thighs and palm his bulge through his loose pants, undoing the laces with my teeth to give him more room. "*Fucking gods.*" His eyes roll back in his head when I run my tongue along his torso and continue palming him. My thighs clench together when he shudders, and I note the tip of his cock protruding above his pants. He's just as aroused as I am. I angle my head so I'm able to lick the tip.

"Fuck, El." His hands fly to my hair and keep me there. I rest my cheek against his stomach and continue pleasuring him. I'd remove his pants and wrap my mouth around him if we had discussed public sex, but I'm happy to watch the most powerful man in Ravaryn writhe and pant from my touch.

His fingers tighten, and he forces my head up, smashing his mouth onto mine. It's carnal and filled with need. He bites my bottom lip, and I'm so irrevocably lost. I'm yanked off the floor and carted away, but I don't care where he's taking me, all I care about is his touch.

A lock clicks in place and my back is shoved into the door. Cayden's kisses take on a new level of ferocity now that we're alone. His hips slam into mine, he bites my neck again, and I can't stop myself from nearly screaming. I'm close to finishing from all the teasing.

"Please let me touch you," he groans against my neck. "I need to touch you, El. Let me take care of you."

Sweet gods, his begging will be my undoing.

His fingers press into the spot where I need him so damn badly. I can't speak through the relief it gives me.

"I need your words, beautiful. Tell me if this is okay."

"Please don't stop," I whimper.

"Thank the fucking gods."

He carries me over to the couch by the fireplace and pushes two fingers inside me after sliding my panties to the side. I shove my head into his neck and moan loudly. My body trembles while he strokes his fingers at a slow, torturous rhythm.

"You're so wet," he practically moans. "Is this all for me?" I keep my head buried in his neck. He drives his fingers deeper. "Answer me."

"Yes!"

I don't know how he affects me so much.

I want to hate how he affects me this powerfully.

His kisses consume me, his fingers overrule me, and all I can feel is him. My body feels like it's on fire, and he stokes the flames with every stroke.

"Ride my fingers like you would ride my cock," he mumbles against my lips.

"Fantasizing about me?" I palm him again and he presses his forehead into mine. "Perhaps I'll turn you into a screamer."

He darkly chuckles and traps my wrists, halting his fingers inside me. "When I fuck you, Elowen, it won't be in some seedy brothel. It's going to be somewhere I can make you come so many times your throat will be hoarse from screaming my name." His fingers begin to slowly move again. "I'm going to fuck the idea of me only being your ally right out of your pretty little mind."

I grow wetter at his words and the power he exudes. His breaths have turned shallow, and he looks like he regrets denying me and wants to pin me down and take me right here.

He swallows and locks his jaw. "Be a good girl and ride my fingers."

I rock my hips, rolling them slowly, wanting to feel his fingers press against every nerve possible while obeying his command. We continue this until he can't hold back any longer and drills them into me. I'm nearly sobbing from how overwhelming the sensation is. I can't breathe.

He presses his sweaty forehead into mine again, keeping his crazed gaze locked on me. "You can comfort yourself by saying tonight is a mission, but we both know you're not going to give me something fake. There's nobody around but you're still on my lap. Moan my name because my fingers are fucking you exactly how you want them."

I try to say his name, but I'm cut off by the sheer magnitude of what he's doing to me.

"You're such a beautiful mess, love." He licks his lips. "One day my tongue will replace my fingers, then my cock will replace my tongue. You'd like that, wouldn't you? You want me to fuck you until all you can think about is how you find religion when you're alone with me."

"Cayden," I moan, digging my nails into his back, unable to answer his questions and too sure of myself to deny the truth they hold. He rubs my clit and I bury my head in his neck to muffle some of the sounds coming out of me. Even his scent drives me further to the edge. He yanks my hair and forces me to look at him while my pleasure is driven to its peak. I scream his name as he wrings every ounce of pleasure possible.

I'm a mess of whimpers and moans as I cling to him for dear life. He releases my hair and slides his hand down my back in long, soothing strokes, kissing my hair and massaging the roots. He slides his fingers out of me, bringing them to his mouth to suck them clean, and his eyes roll back in his head.

"I want to do something for you."

"Believe me, you just did," he says, continuing his massage with both hands. "Your pleasure is my pleasure." He takes my face in his hands, noting my unease at the thought of leaving him unsatisfied, giving me a series of soft, sweet kisses until I'm smiling against him.

"I suppose the mission was unsuccessful," I mutter, picking at the lace on my skirt.

"It wasn't." My head shoots up. "I could see the light dancing under the door, and I heard someone get slammed into the wall. It's why I didn't take you over to the bed."

I lean closer and smirk when his eyes flash to my breasts. "Is that the only reason?"

"You and your communication," he mutters, and sets me on shaky legs. "There are holding cells under every building along the main road. Ryder will have taken them there for questioning, and we'll head down after getting dressed."

CHAPTER

THIRTY-THREE

My gown flutters from the icy chill rising from the dark cellar beneath the brothel, and the rickety steps look like they're about to fall apart. Knives line my legs no matter what I wear, and something as simple as a gown won't tamper with my bloodlust.

"He's restrained," Ryder says from the bottom of the steps.

I give my eyes a few moments to adjust to the dim light provided by a few torches lining the stone walls. The air down here is damp and reeks of mold. It's obvious nobody comes down here from the layers of dust cloaking every surface. A man stands with his head bowed, and dark cascading hair obscures his features. His wrists are chained by two shackles attached to ceiling beams.

"How do you wish to proceed?" Cayden asks.

"His room will need to be searched and his partners questioned." Lips always get loose during pillow talk.

"I'll start with the room," Finnian says. That's probably for the best. Finnian has never judged me for reveling in revenge, but that doesn't mean he enjoys watching the ways I lose myself in my methods. Something in my brain shifted after knowing the cruelty of this world long before I should have.

"Knock on the door when you're done so I can help with the questioning," Ryder says.

I turn toward the man once Finnian shuts the door. Chains rattle as he shifts in place, slowly lifting his head. I've seen this pair of soulless eyes before. "Princess Elowen, how lovely to see you again."

Robick's voice is one that's haunted me for years. As Garrick's most trusted guard, he took the beatings further than most and looked forward to our sessions. Craved them. Beating me was the best part of his day. Cayden and Ryder stiffen and exchange a glance above my head.

I have the overwhelming urge to throw my body in a bucket of acid to rid my skin of the memory of his hands. He might appear handsome to someone other than me, with his sapphire eyes and a strong jaw. But abusers learn to weaponize their charm. You can't always detect them as someone detects poison in a drink.

"Robick." I dip my hands into the slit of my dress and pluck two knives from my thigh, twirling them as I step forward. "I must confess I prefer you to be the one in chains."

Cayden and Ryder unsheathe their swords, and Robick laughs while glancing between them. "I will not betray my king when I know death is inevitable."

"You will beg for death long before it embraces you," Cayden states.

"The infamous Commander Veles," Robick drawls. "I could tell by the scar."

My fist collides with his nose, and his head flies back from the force. An idea sparks in my mind and I sheathe my knives for later use, wrapping my hands around a broom in the corner as the sound of a cane breaking my ribs plays in my mind as clear as if Robick were hitting me right now. I break off the bristled end and turn back to him.

"I see that the memories of our time together stuck with you." I do my best to ignore his taunts and focus on this opportunity. "Do you remember how you begged?"

I deliver a swift hit to his ribs with the splintered side of the broom, and his cry is one of the sweetest sounds I've had the privilege of hearing. I pull back and deliver several more until his ribs snap.

"Hit me all you wish. I won't tell you anything," he rasps.

"Hitting you is for my enjoyment." I laugh, delivering another hit and noting the bloodstained splinters with delight. "Torturing you is for information."

I swing it into his stomach before discarding the pole and circling to the front of his slumped frame. Blood drips from his lip when I roughly lift his chin, forcing him to look at me with the eyes that used to light up when he first drew blood during a session. I dreaded his presence above all others, and had feared him for so long, but no more.

He slumps when I drop his chin and glance toward the hooks on the ground that the chains are threaded through. "I need the chains lowered and the table brought to me."

Robick's breathing becomes heavier, shakier.

"Which is his sword hand?" Cayden asks.

"His right."

Cayden places the table where I need it, and he and Ryder resume their original positions behind me. The pair of them look ready to pummel Robick into the earth, but a hint of sadness graces Ryder's features. Cayden's anger consumes him and transforms him into the demon whispered about throughout Ravaryn. The demon his enemies have nightmares of in their next lives. No form of salvation or reincarnation will be enough to escape Cayden Veles.

"You both have my permission to wait by the steps."

"We're staying," Cayden says, and Ryder nods.

I unsheathe my knife again and the familiar weight brings me comfort. When my nightmares made my throat raw from screaming, I thought of a moment like this. I gathered all the broken shards of myself, even when it felt like all the pieces couldn't fit in my hands, and forged a sword sharp enough to slay any enemy. I found solace in vengeance. Violence made me into a monster, but dedication made me lethal.

"How many dragons do I have?" The table creaks when I pin Robick's hand to it. "Don't want to talk?" I glide my knife down his cheek, and he grunts when I press it hard enough to draw blood. "We can count together."

His body shakes as he fights to keep any noises of pain and fear trapped behind his tight lips. But he can't stop the guttural scream from echoing around us when I slice off his thumb and flick it to the side. Blood gushes from the gash and coats the table.

"That was for Venatrix," I say above his screams.

I cut off the second finger, ignoring his pain. "For Sorin."

Third finger. "For Calithea."

Fourth finger. "For Basilius."

Fifth finger. "For Delmira."

I kick the table to the side once I finish and grasp his face, smearing blood onto his lips and tightening my grip when he tries to recoil. "Are you working with anyone here?"

I squeeze the fresh gashes that ooze blood like a waterfall.

"NO!" he wails. "Not even criminals will take a job after that sadistic bastard executed his own fucking soldier."

No sign of a lie lingers on his face. His blood drips down my face and soaks my gown, but I have no urge to wipe it away.

"Where is the key to the dragons' chains kept?"

"You can't open them with a key." He gives me a delirious, pain-drenched smile and glances at my neck. "The object to unlock them was stolen."

"The amulet," I state. The amulet must call to the chains, forged from the same magic. I wish the priestess spoke truths rather than riddles so I could make sense of how she knew to take it.

Disbelief blankets his features before he recovers, baring his teeth like a rabid dog. "You will die in this war and be put down like the bitch you are."

My eyes flick to the shackles on his wrists, staring down the man who helped take everything from me. "A death with a blade in my hands is far more enticing than a death in chains."

"King Garrick was smart to lock you up."

"And a fool for never finding me in exile."

"He tried to save you from that prophecy," he snarls.

"Save *me*?" I raise my brows. "Forgive me for not recognizing his generosity sooner. I suppose I should also give thanks for his dedication to preserving my virtue by forbidding you from taking the torture down the route you wished in hopes of selling me to a kingdom once my bond was broken."

Although I was a prisoner, I was still a princess. He needed me to be an asset to the kingdom if the time came for an advantageous marriage.

Cayden's sword clatters on the ground as he slips between Robick and me, landing a punch so severe the chains strain against the bolts on the ceiling. "You sick bastard!" he shouts, wrapping a hand around Robick's throat and continuing the assault. Robick cries and thrashes but can't escape Cayden's grip. Ryder pulls Cayden back before he can snap Robick's neck without realizing.

"Not yet," he snarls, trying and failing to keep Cayden restrained.

"Not yet." I echo Ryder's words when Cayden is about to lunge for Robick again. He halts, dragging his gaze to mine and looking at me with eyes that would implore someone to end themself before he gets hold of them. He hesitates but nods, and Ryder releases him when he's sure Cayden won't pounce.

"I may have spent years in chains, but make no mistake when I tell you that you will die in them," I state, turning back to Robick. He's gasping like a fish out of water, with blood covering most of his skin. "In fact, I'd like to take this moment and thank you for a lesson you taught me."

I never begged for myself when he beat me; I begged for my dragons. I pleaded for them to be set free. I'd take the beatings until I died if it meant they didn't have to suffer, and I'd sacrifice myself to save them. Even when I was battered to the point I couldn't move, I could still feel my dragons. That bond kept me tethered to this world when death seemed much more inviting than living.

"You taught me that desperation is the greatest leverage." I round his body and direct my next statement to Cayden and Ryder. "Did you know that the guards and soldiers of Imirath have a series of numbers sewn into their shirts?"

Robick thrashes against the chains, splashing more blood in the process, but can't escape the knife I bring to the fabric. I'm careful to keep it as clean as possible while tucking it into my bodice. "It helps their bodies be identified if they die on the field or on a mission, and their families will be contacted."

"Leave my family out of this," he chokes.

"Allow me to bestow a lesson upon you, Robick. Don't teach someone the ways of torture and expect them to forget the origin of their pain."

"I'll tell you anything about your dragons. I know how to forge the key to unlock the chamber!"

"As do I."

"Leave my family out of this. I beg you."

"I've made many men beg; your performance is subpar." I tsk. "We know everything we need. You have no leverage here. You're powerless."

"PLEASE, PRINCESS!"

I laugh at his poor attempts. "You care for your family, and yet you had no qualms about spending your time in a brothel. I'm going to burn the cloak of morality you hide behind. Perhaps I'll begin by informing them how you stripped me bare on occasion." Shame bubbles in my throat, but watching him suffer under the weight of his own actions is worth it. I step forward again to cut the clothes off his body, wanting him to feel just as humiliated and small as I did.

Garrick's orders didn't stop him from threatening me with the methods he wished to use, nor did it stop him from running his hands over me. Which is exactly why I step forward and castrate him. Avenging myself and any others he may have touched without consent. He sobs and screams, bleeds and pleads to the gods. But his prayers are useless because the only gods present are myself and my blades.

I've seen him grovel and made him bleed, but now I want to *watch* him bleed. My fighting skills are aim, stealth, and scheming. I don't land the hardest punches, but Cayden can make him suffer the beatings I did at his hands.

"Your turn, demon."

Cayden erupts in a wave of violence and ferocity. Feral growls slip from his lips as blood splatters his face and coats his hands. He lands punch after punch, fisting Robick's hair to bring him back into the line of fire.

"Please," Robick slurs. "Please, please, please."

"I'm going to make you wish you were dead long before Elowen ends you," Cayden snarls. Robick collapses in the puddles of blood when Cayden releases the chains from the hooks on the floor. We watch Robick stumble to his feet, swaying when he finally gets there and he sloppily limps toward me.

Cayden locks his arm around his neck before he takes three steps. Robick claws against the tight hold, smearing Cayden with more blood. "You can die with the knowledge that no matter what you did to Elowen, she won."

Cayden releases his hold and throws Robick into the blood again, and he glares at me when he flips over, gasping for breath.

"Don't fucking look at her." Cayden's voice drips in poison as he drops to his knees, pinning Robick's body between his thighs. He unsheathes my knife from his thigh, slashing Robick's eyes, causing his body to contort in pain as his cries amplify. Cayden forces Robick's mouth open, and he screeches when blood pours from him like a fountain. The tongue is tossed aside, and Cayden tips Robick's head up, drowning Robick in his own blood as it slides up his nostrils and pools in his mouth. He's a coughing, sputtering mess. Robick has lost all fight in him by the time he's yanked forward, spitting his blood at Cayden, coating his face and hair.

If wrath were personified, it would look like this version of Cayden.

He drags Robick back to where he was initially standing and chains him into a kneeling position. He's broken and on the brink of death. Blood sloshes under my slippers and drenches the hem of my gown. I take time committing this version of Robick to memory. This is the face that will replace the original in some of my darkest memories and nightmares.

"You deserve to have your torture dragged out for days," I begin, squatting in front of him. "But I'm going to be busy bringing Garrick and Imirath to their gods-damned knees after I free my dragons."

He sobs before I slide my blade clean across his throat and his blood sprays my face for the final time. I feel like I'm frozen in time. *He's dead*, I tell myself.

He's dead.

He's dead.

It becomes a chant in my mind, but doubt continues creeping in. I sink my knife into his heart before pulling it out and get ready to strike again, but a hand clasps my wrist. Another hand gently turns my head away from Robick, and I stare into the eyes of the one person who I think understands me in this moment. Being understood and accepted is one of the greatest forms of intimacy. He doesn't shy away from my darkness; he walks toward it and kneels with me in the blood we've spilled.

"I'm here for whatever you need." I can't form words, so I hang on to his reassuring expression and calm voice. His hand on my face is keeping me from disappearing into my past. "But he's dead, El."

"He's dead," I echo in a hoarse voice, and my knife clatters on the ground when it slips from my fingers.

"You got your revenge." He speaks softly, but there's nothing weak in his tone.

"I wish he took the memories with him." I wonder what it would be like to glide through the world instead of braving it every time I left my home.

"I know," he murmurs. "But if you allow me, I'll find a way to help you carry them when they get too heavy."

"Remembering everything makes me feel sick. Sometimes I don't know how to live with all the pain." I recall the lash marks on his back. "How do you?"

"I use the memories as armor and ammunition. Nobody wins

harder than someone who once lost everything. Don't let them take more from you." He picks up my knife and holds it out to me. "You're so much braver than you believe, and stronger than you feel in this moment."

I sheathe it on my thigh, taking breaths until my heart stops galloping in my chest. He's giving me the choice of how I end this night, but I don't want to spend another moment in the presence of Robick. *He's dead.*

"I want to leave," I firmly state. Cayden nods, helping me to my feet while I glance where Ryder watches us in fascination. "I'm sorry you had to see this."

I don't want him thinking less of me. I've found happiness in the moments spent with the five of us, and I don't want to lose it so soon.

"Never apologize for a kill you deserved to take. I would have done the same." A dark grimace contorts his face, and his deep brown eyes meet mine in earnest. "I'm going to find Finnian so we can handle the questioning and leave as soon as possible."

Cayden presses a hand into my back and ushers me up the steps. "We can wash up before you leave if you wish."

When we step into the light, proof of the cruelty we're capable of is written in crimson against our skin. Even after we wash it off, it will forever linger. Having any part of Robick on me disgusts me, but I want to send a message.

"I want to ride to the border like this," I say, sliding my hand into his. He makes me feel like I don't have to face every threat alone because he'll be right here—unjudging, understanding, and just as bloody as me. "I want my enemies to know what fate awaits them if they make an attempt on my life. Ravaryn is threatened by my existence, but I won't hide any longer."

"I rather enjoy it when you threaten me." Something comes alive in me when he slides his fingers down my face like I'm the most delicate thing he's ever held. "Your enemies are my enemies, El. Never doubt that."

Part III
———

THE HEIST

CHAPTER
THIRTY-FOUR

"What route did you take when you left Imirath?" Saskia asks, staring down several maps.

My mind conjures the icy, treacherous path we took. "We went through the mountains."

Her eyes widen in shock. "Hardly anyone survives a trek through the Etril."

"That's precisely why we took it."

The Seren Mountains stretch along the eastern side of Erebos, but the Etril Forest resides between Imirath and Vareveth. Beasts lurk within their icy peaks, and conditions alone are a risk to anyone seeking shelter.

"There are caves Cayden and I can seek shelter in on the first night. They're far enough from the border, but close enough to reach before nightfall." Ailliard would've taken me there if Garrick didn't know of their existence. It's a religious site for the Goddess of Life, so ceremonies are held there on occasion.

Saskia snaps her fingers in recognition. "Perfect. There are no holidays coming up, so they should be deserted. The most difficult part will be crossing the border."

"Yes, remaining hidden and infiltrating the castle will be nothing." I laugh under my breath and pinch my tired eyes. "Did anyone fill you in on the information we obtained last night?"

Her head shoots up. "You went on a mission? Where?"

The tent entrance opens and Cayden, Ryder, and Finnian stroll through. My nerves shoot up when Cayden stares at me with such intensity that my knees feel weak. Most people layer themselves in armor before a battle, but Cayden's outfit is made of durable black leather with silver armored accents. At least he's armed to the teeth with knives, a sword on his back, and double axes on his belt.

"Morning, ladies." Ryder greets us, standing beside Saskia and glancing over the map.

"Why didn't you tell me you went on a mission last night? Elowen was about to go over the details," Saskia says. I look anywhere other than Cayden, who now stands at the edge of the desk. My cheeks heat further when Ryder smiles. "Where were you?"

I lick my dry lips. "The Golden Rose, but that's beside the—"

"What in the hells were you doing at a brothel?" Saskia cuts me off, and I let out an awkward laugh while pressing my hand to my burning neck and resisting the urge to crawl under a table.

"Elowen thought of a plan to catch the mastermind behind the assassination attempts, and we helped her follow it through," Cayden informs her with ease.

"I would've helped if you'd sent word," Saskia grumbles.

"Honestly, Sas, I've never seen Cayden quite so . . ." Ryder waves his hand in front of his face, trying to pluck the perfect word from thin air. "*Dedicated* to a mission."

"I'm also dedicated to silencing those whose voices irritate me," Cayden responds.

"The pair of you can finish this later." Saskia's eyes flash between them. "Elowen, what did you discover?"

Bless her thirst for knowledge. "He wasn't able to hire new assassins, he was working alone, and I can use the amulet to unlock the dragons' chains. I believe they're forged from the same magic."

Saskia's smile grows the more I speak. I think knowledge and intelligence sustain her more than food and water. "Brilliant! Did you manage to get his name?"

"Robick." The mood in the tent gets darker. "Garrick's head guard."

"I would've stayed if I'd known it was *him*. You should've told me to stay." Finnian turns a sickly shade of green, and his hand shoots forward to grip the desk. "Tell me you made him suffer."

"I did."

"Well, whatever you did, he still deserved worse," Finnian adds. "I'll shoot in the archers' line with your permission."

"Permission granted," Cayden responds.

The archers' line is behind the charge, so my chest doesn't tighten with worry like it would if he were *in* the battle. But neither of us has seen a battle of this magnitude so I ask, "You're sure?"

"Killing more soldiers gives you a better chance when you cross the border." He rises to his full height and turns to me, affectionately squeezing my arms. I have no right to persuade him to stay other than selfish reasons. "Are you all right?"

"Of course." I grab his face to bring him down to my height and kiss his cheek. "Shoot straight, bloodthirsty archer."

"I'll find you as soon as it's over," he says before leaving the tent.

"I follow Imirath's battle techniques, changes in rank, and weaponry developments, so I'll ride down with Finnian," Saskia says while shoving a few pens into her pocket, and she glances between Cayden and Ryder again. "Be careful."

"We always are," Ryder responds.

"That's not comforting," she groans before exiting.

"Her lack of faith is refreshing," Ryder says. "Are you ready?"

Cayden nods. "And consistent."

The pair of them turn to leave the tent, but I grab Cayden's hand before he can follow Ryder. He turns to me and his confusion melts when he notes my fear.

"I'll be fine," he says. "We can't get to the dragons if we can't find a weak spot in their lines."

"Then I'm coming with you." I try to pull my hand from his and step toward the exit, but he keeps them joined and pulls, pressing my back to his chest, and wraps an arm around me.

"You've never been in a battle like this."

"I'll learn by experience," I argue.

"I promise I'll train you when we get back from Imirath, but they'll target you as soon as you're recognized on the field, and I won't be able to focus unless I know you're safe." I hate how calm he's remaining while I'm submerged in panic.

"That sounds like your problem, so let me figure out mine." I struggle against his hold to no avail. "If you wanted a docile queen, then you should've made a deal with someone else."

"Yes, you are my problem." His chuckle vibrates my back. "But I'd never waste my time on someone lesser than you."

I shove his arm away from my waist and spin to face him. It's easier to do this when he's not pressed against me. "I can't just stay here while you're all off fighting."

"Let's compromise." He sighs, scanning my face as he often does. "Would you like to be a healer in one of the medical tents? It'll keep you occupied."

It's not the battle, but at least I'll be useful. I nod once before walking past him and toward his horse. The battle is starting soon so I don't want to waste time tracking one down. The second line is far, but within sight, and Cayden slows the horse once we breach it. There are no clear paths; it's a tactic used to slow a possible invasion. I don't know where we're going, but I assume the grimmer it gets, the closer we get. We stop in front of one of the largest tents I've ever seen and slide down from the horse.

"This is where I leave you," he says.

"Don't get yourself killed." My lighthearted attempt fails when my voice shakes.

He frames my face in his hands and stares at me with absolute certainty, stroking my cheekbones with his thumbs. "I swear to you, I'm coming back. I'll never make you a promise I can't keep."

A deep battle horn cuts through the air and several drumbeats follow, cutting me off from saying anything. His eyes dance over my face again, and I realize mine do the same to him, watching as he treads backward to his horse, only looking away to swing himself up.

"If you feel left out, I'll find someone for you to stab later," he calls out over his shoulder.

I cross my arms over my chest. "I'd like to stab you."

His grin widens. "I love it when you sweet-talk me."

A surplus of wounded soldiers trickle into the tent once the battle begins. I quickly lose myself in stitching and bandaging. Healing has always made me feel useful and gives me a sense of reward once a task is done and someone is taken care of. I like knowing I have the ability to care for someone, to nurse them. Cries of the wounded increase as time goes on, as does the scent of sweat and blood.

At least two hundred cots are set up throughout the space, all equally distanced and equipped with medical and sanitization supplies on an attached shelf below. I occasionally must weave between soldiers lingering by bedsides, holding conversations or a wounded soldier's hand. The healers keep their work quick and precise and are all dressed in black. I catch the occasional curious glance at my green shirt, brown waist corset, and pants tucked into boots, but it fades when I'm recognized.

My eyes dance between cots, looking for the people I care about, and my heart stops when I spy a familiar set of braids tumbling over the side of one. Saskia's face is scrunched up in pain when I reach her, and blood leaks from a gash on her arm. I search for signs of Finnian as I approach but find none.

"Hi, Sas," I say. Her eyes snap open and the relief that washes over her at the sight of me squeezes my heart.

"El," she breathes. "Finnian wasn't in the hit. I was at the tail end of it." Thank the gods. I shake out my hands and stay focused on my task, picking through the supplies under the cot. Thankfully nothing is stuck in her wound, so I grab the antiseptic and splash it onto some cotton.

"This is going to sting a bit," I warn, and dab her gash as lightly as possible. Her body jolts on the table, and I offer her my free hand.

"Fucking gods," she seethes, and squeezes it so hard I feel like it'll break. She sucks in a sharp breath and slowly blows it through parted lips, relaxing slightly.

I sanitize the needle and loop thread through the top, grabbing a clean rag to dab the blood away. The wet rag thumps when I toss it next to her and begin sewing her wound shut. I dab as needed while issuing the first set of stitches and turn the needle to sew up the wound.

"Do you have pain anywhere else?" I ask.

"No, just my arm." I'm glad her voice has stopped trembling. "Thank you for helping me."

"You don't have to thank me," I reply, never taking my eyes off her stitches.

"How are you, truly?" she asks quietly. "After seeing that man again."

"I'm okay." I pause briefly, feeling her eyes on me. But it's not to pick me apart, it's the concern of a friend. "Cayden helped me."

"Torture is one of his specialties."

"He helped me after the torture," I quietly say. He found me trying to scrub the blood from under my nails, panicking and shaking on the floor from the feeling of a piece of Robick lingering on me. It was too much to handle, so he handled it for me by gently cleaning the blood from both my and his nails and making me a cup of lavender and chamomile tea. "He stayed with me."

"*Tell me if my hands on you are too much. I'm happy to just sit beside you,*" he'd said. But I asked him to stay, and he held me until sleep granted me reprieve. He kissed my forehead before slipping out of bed to start his day, and I pretended I was still asleep. Too much a coward to face him right away.

"He's a good man, even if he doesn't believe it," she says as I finish off her stitches, and I can't help but agree.

"How are you feeling now?" I ask.

"Better." I wish I had a tonic to ease her pain, but I'm sure she has one in her tent. I reach down and embrace her as best as I can, and she raises her good arm to hold me.

"Can I get a hug next?" I straighten up and rush toward Finnian, throwing my arms around his neck as his chuckle vibrates my cheek. "Before you start poking around, I'm not injured."

I step back to scan him, wanting to make sure he truly is unscathed. A fraction of my nerves eases by his presence, but I won't be completely calm until Cayden and Ryder make it back.

"Forgive me for worrying about you." I reach up to ruffle his hair that's been flattened by a helmet. "Can you get Saskia some water?"

"Of course," he replies before brushing past me in search of water.

I move on to the cot beside Saskia's and offer a smile to a man with a gash on his leg, finding the same supplies I used previously and stitching him up. After I finish him, I make my way to the following person, repeating the pattern until I've lost count of how many people I've bandaged. My fingers have gone numb, and blood is caked under my nails and splattered across my arms.

I finish stitching a woman and glance toward the entrance again. It's the ritual I do whenever I finish. I'll have whiplash if Cayden doesn't show up soon. Even the slightest bit of movement by the entrance makes me pause and look up midstitch.

"Thank you, Queen Elowen," the woman says as I wipe her blood from my hands. I smile at her as she swings her legs over the side and leans against another soldier to help her hobble away.

My eyes stay glued to the opening, but Cayden never appears. Countless soldiers enter and exit, but they're never him. I toss the bloody rag onto the table once my hands are clean, and all the reasons he may never walk into this tent plague me. "Where are you?"

"Who's the lucky man capturing your attention?"

I spin toward the voice, and relief pummels into me. Cayden's wavy hair is flattened, and he's streaked with a mixture of blood and dirt. Even postbattle, he's still handsome enough to captivate me. He pushes off the cot he was leaning against and comes closer, caging me in his arms.

I grip the cot behind me and wonder how long he was watching me. "You don't know him."

"No?" He gives me a sadistic smile, dimples and all. "I'd love to introduce myself."

"Was the charge successful?" I ask, pressing my lips together to hide a smile. If he notices people are watching, he pays them no mind. I know we should be careful despite the treaty being signed, but I've never been a fan of rules, and breaking them with him is so damn tempting.

He nods. "We'll leave in a few hours."

My smile breaks free. The danger is an afterthought because I'm going to see my dragons again. "Sit on the table, I'll wrap your shoulder before we leave." I cut him off when he opens his mouth to protest. "Now isn't the time to be prideful. Shirt off and sit down."

"I'm not being prideful," he grumbles, removing the sword from his back and revealing his torso dotted in love bites that he happily shows off. "I'm still breathing and getting bossed around by someone half my size; life has never been better."

CHAPTER
THIRTY-FIVE

WE BATHE, PACK, AND PREP FOR THE NEXT FEW HOURS. Go over details of the castle, memorize our route and our meetup points if we get separated. The lump in my throat grows every time Cayden pulls out his pocket watch; the gold chain dangling on his leg taunts me.

The air feels thin no matter how deeply I breathe, and I busy myself securing the straps on the purple and brown set of leathers I wore while infiltrating Kallistar. A sword is strapped on my back and waist, and knives hang from my thick corset belt and line my legs.

"You should eat something," Cayden says while I stir some sweet syrup into the coffee I poured. My nerves don't need the extra jolt, but I'll thank myself while sprinting to the caves.

I turn to where he's sharpening his swords on the couch, clad in the same black set of leathers he wore when we first met. "I'd rather not sprint with a full stomach."

"Will you be able to fly home once you free the dragons?" Ryder asks.

I flinch without meaning to. "They may not trust me enough for that yet."

"It's not necessarily about trust," Saskia says. "I found this ancient text about a bond between a rider and their dragon. Supposedly, that kind of bond can never be broken, only dulled by time, but you'll always find your way back to it. The bond is . . . inevitable. There are ways to help you renew it, but you won't be able to do it until you're out of enemy territory."

I offer a tight nod in response. I've had visions of the dragons, but I don't know how they'll react to me when they truly see me. I don't know if they'll be relieved, elated, or enraged. The prophecy foretold the tale of a girl and five dragons with a bond not even time or distance could break, but bonds can always be rejected, and prophecies aren't always true.

I trace the column of my throat, recalling how I screamed until it turned raw and thrashed against Ailliard, begging him to take me back to them. I wonder if they sensed it. I wonder what it was like for them to experience our dulled bond and not know where I was.

I was Imirath's princess, but I'm now its ruin. I'll free my dragons and burn Garrick's reign to the ground for all the pain he's caused. But deep down, I know I'll let my dragons go if they don't wish to be with me. Perhaps they'll come back in time, but I won't free them from one prison only to force them into another. I love them enough to want what's best for them.

Cayden glances at his watch again. "It's time."

I nod, tying my brown cloak around my neck and throwing my satchel over my shoulder. The tension in the tent is nearly suffocating. We all know the dangers of this mission, but I don't focus on the fall, I focus on the possibility of the flight.

"I'll ride to the border with you and take the horses back," Ryder says, but Finnian and Saskia get to their feet as well, all wearing expressions that mingle with helplessness. I'd feel the same way if I were in their positions.

The five of us ride to a covering of trees beside the camp. They're so dense that hardly any moonlight trickles through the branches. We remain silent, leading the horses over trickling streams, fallen trees, and humongous roots popping up from the earth like spider legs.

Cayden holds up a hand, signaling us to stop. It's eerily quiet in the forest, making it easy to hear Finnian's choppy breaths as he dismounts beside me. He embraces me the moment my boots hit the dirt, and I breathe in his scent. Finnian looks like autumn but smells like summer. Being wrapped up in the arms of the person who became my family when I felt entirely alone is one of my favorite feelings.

"You didn't forget to take your tonic this month, right? You tend to forget to take care of yourself when you're overwhelmed. You won't be able to have the tea that helps your cramps while you're in Imirath, and sometimes your hands shake from the pain so your aim will be off."

"I took my tonic," I gently say to quiet his rambling. "I'll be back before you know it."

"Tomorrow is ideal." I pull away from him to wipe the tears off his freckle-filled cheeks, but he must notice the anticipation on my features because his arms fall away from me and he asks, "What is it?"

"You're my brother in every way that counts." My eyes have already begun to burn. "There's a letter in the top drawer—"

"No."

"It's merely precaution."

"Elowen, no." He rakes his hands through his hair, looking like he wants to scream. "I can't think about losing you."

"I'm coming back to you. I always do. But I need to make sure you're taken care of in case something happens." I speak calmly, doing my best to comfort the first person who ever made me laugh. The first person to show me what it is to live. We've never needed blood to be siblings, and I know the bond we've created is something I'll carry with me into the afterlife or the next life, whenever the time comes.

"I love you, Ellie." He presses his lips to my forehead. "So much. Don't force me to learn what it is to live without you."

"You won't have to." He learned to live without his family once, and I won't let him go through that again. I'll do whatever it takes to get back to him.

Saskia clings to Cayden and I know he's trying his best to comfort her, but the awkward way he's patting her head breaks some tension within our group. She doesn't pull herself away until she hears us approach, and she flings herself at me, tightly wrapping her arms around my neck. "I'll see you when you come home. I refuse to tolerate a different outcome."

I squeeze her tight. "Start planning where to shop for our winter wardrobes."

She gives me a watery laugh in response.

"I'll be seeing you, Atarah," Ryder says as I release Saskia. "Don't let him die out there."

"Her rogue knives will probably take me out before Imirath does," Cayden says, glancing at his watch again. "You should head back."

Ryder looks like he wants to argue but nods. He and Cayden clasp hands and slap each other on their shoulders. "I'll see you soon, brother."

We're cloaked in eerie silence once they're gone. My cloak flutters around my ankles, almost like nature is trying to persuade us to stay out of Imirath. We still have a few hours before the sun rises, but we need to get past their lines and deep enough into Imirath by the time it does.

"It's just you and me, angel," he says.

"I'm still trying to figure out if that's for better or worse."

"Do let me know once you discover your answer."

He doesn't have to ask me if I'm ready before beginning our journey; we've both been ready for years. We creep through the forest like the Lord and Lady of Death and Vengeance tracking down which souls they'd like to take next. My bond pleasantly hums in my chest once we've gotten a decent way into enemy territory, and I caress it in my mind, trying to send comfort down the solid strands.

We spy Imirath soldiers coming our way and keep to the shadows as we wait for them to pass. I'll always love the night, not only for the moon and stars but for the comfort and safety that darkness has always provided. They're completely unaware of our presence as they stride past, their swords sheathed at their waists.

Torchlight bleeds through the trees like sunlight through stained-glass windows as we get closer to their camp. We sink deeper into the forest, but it's not enough coverage. Soldiers are everywhere.

"Stay here," Cayden whispers.

I wrap my hand around his wrist before he can leave the shelter of the rocky hill. "Are you deranged?"

"Depends on who you ask," he replies, checking his watch again. "We don't have much time. I'll be back before you have the chance to miss me, love."

He disappears after that. I don't even hear his footsteps. It's like he blended into the night as nothing more than a shadow. Thank the gods I never had to face him as an assassin. Seconds turn into minutes, and there's still no sign of him when I climb to the top of the hill and peer over it. There's a dispute somewhere in the distance and I can't tell if it's a mere skirmish or a true fight, but I'm not staying here wondering.

Ailliard took me away from my dragons, and Imirath kept us apart; I'm not letting Imirath do the same to Cayden and me. I'd rather throw myself into danger with him than be safe without him. He's my ally, and we're in this together until the end.

My anxiety is so high that every breath I take makes me cringe. My fear of Imirath is paralyzing, but I don't let it affect the fluidity of my movement. I keep to the trees, jumping between the trunks before the patrols notice me.

An arm wraps around my waist midjump and a hand covers my mouth. I elbow the person in the stomach and flip the knife in my hand, aiming backward at their head, but the hand around my waist moves to my wrist.

"Again with the knives, El. You know I adore them, but now really isn't a good time." Cayden throws me over his shoulder and carries me behind a boulder cleaved in two.

"I could've killed you!" I snap quietly when he sets me on my feet.

"What a lovely way to go." He presses his back into the stone and pulls me close.

"What are—" He turns my head into his chest to cover my ear and mouth, muffling my scream when a series of explosions shakes the ground. We're far enough away that dirt doesn't rain down on us, and the flames won't reach us, but all the soldiers in close proximity rush toward the scene, not knowing that the true source is pressed against me.

"Just like hounds flocking to fresh meat," he says.

We rush out of our hiding spot, sliding down the hill I climbed to find him, and run toward a cliff with a shallow stream below. The soldiers continue shouting orders to put the flames out while we slip out of sight, splashing in the muddy bank when we land. We push through, making it onto the solid forest floor, and run between twisted trees with roots so tall we occasionally walk under them like archways and bushes dotted with ruby red berries. Crystal streams flow throughout the terrain with mist cloaking it like a blanket.

The sun chases away the night, and we don't speak as we push forward, occasionally having to stop and hide when a patrol rides through. I hold on to the knowledge that every step I take into Imirath is another step closer to my dragons. They keep me grounded. I want to live the kind of life that makes me long for the next morning and the little moments.

I feel a weight lift off my shoulders when we make it to the caves. Two waterfalls cascade down the moss-covered rocks, and ice frames the pool under them like a portrait painted by nature's faultless hand. We drink our canteens to the last drop and refill them in the falls before carefully climbing up to the caves behind them. Light purple starsnaps border the entrance.

I toss my satchel to the ground and quickly follow it, thankful for the moss in here to provide some comfort while we rest. Cayden takes the spot across from me, mirroring my position and leaning his back against the wall.

"Did you plant those explosives during the battle?" I ask.

He nods. "I needed to be close in case the timer didn't work."

"You're clever."

"I'm going to ignore your surprise and choose to take your statement as a compliment," he says before biting into an apple. "Eat something. You didn't eat before we left, and I'd prefer to not have to carry you the entire way to the castle. Might earn a few unnecessary stares."

I roll my eyes, digging in my bag for some cheese. Sometimes I forget how much he pays attention to me, it's like I deprive him when I deprive myself. We eat in silence, listening to the falls and accepting the momentary peace. He gets to his feet when we finish, untying his cloak and laying it on the ground.

"What are you doing?"

He looks at me expectantly. "You're freezing and we can't build a fire."

"I'll be all right." *Last night was different,* I tell myself. *It was a friend helping a friend.* But I know friends don't look at each other the way he looks at me. When his eyes are on me, it's like he craves my presence.

"Would you rather be all right or comfortable?" He sits on top of the cloak and pats the spot next to him, and his warmth is tempting. The caves are beautiful, but the dampness is killing me. I untie my cloak and crawl over to him without meeting his eyes while he tucks an arm under his head and wraps my cloak around us. I press my cold face in his neck while his hands slide along my back and through my hair before bringing one of my hands to his mouth to warm it, kissing my knuckles when he's done.

"I've always loved the sound of water," he says. "It's calming yet powerful. It's like listening to the sound of life after being surrounded by never-ending death."

"Is that why your house has a pond?"

"It's one of only a few places my mind quiets."

My eyes slide shut as his warmth, scent, and touches soothe me. "Where else does it?"

He chuckles, arm tightening around me ever so slightly. "Maybe I'll tell you one day, angel."

"Wake me up in a few hours so I can take second watch," I sleepily mumble.

I never thought I'd be able to sleep in Imirath considering it's the place where my darkest nightmares were born. But here, in Cayden's arms, I can imagine I'm somewhere far from here. With every gentle stroke on my spine, he transports me like no amulet ever could. It doesn't feel like I'm in Imirath; all I'm surrounded by is Cayden.

CHAPTER
THIRTY-SIX

―――

A SQUEEZE ON MY ARM TRIES TO WAKE ME, BUT I SWAT IT away, trying to snuggle into the intoxicating warmth that makes me dream of forests, rivers, and moonlight cloaking a lush garden. But a chuckle is what has my eyes popping open, because Cayden is hovering above me with a finger pressed to the cocky grin on his lips.

I don't have time to be embarrassed because that's when I hear it:

Crack.

Crack, crack, crack.

Cayden helps me up and unsheathes his sword while I pull two knives from my holsters, concealing ourselves in the back of the cave. There's no way we can leave without being spotted.

"I'll throw a knife if they come to the opening," I say.

He nods. "It doesn't sound like there's more than four."

A bird whistle chirps through the air, the pitch slowly getting higher as it goes on. Cayden stills, becoming even more alert. He pushes off the wall when the whistle is repeated.

"Ryder," he growls, stalking to the entrance of the cave, and raises his voice loud enough for the approaching party to hear. "Elowen, we're so lucky to have been blessed with not one, but three daft children."

I rush beside him, peering down the cliffside at three all-too-familiar figures cloaked by the sun's golden rays. I mutter a string of curses, knowing I should've taken more precaution against Finnian disobeying orders. Cayden must be thinking the same about Ryder and Saskia. Hells, we would've followed them if the roles were reversed, but that doesn't mean I support their damn decision.

The trio trade anxious glances and fumble their words when they finish their climb into the cave, trying to convince us with logic that's been reduced to flailing limbs and half-thought-out sentences. Ryder waves his arms so much he looks like a rogue vextree trying to take flight.

Cayden speaks above them. "I'll separate you like prisoners if you can't manage a single decipherable sentence."

Saskia steps forward, squaring her shoulders. "We had every intention of remaining in Vareveth as discussed, but I couldn't stop myself from imagining the dangers of this mission. All the possible scenarios the pair of you could get caught in."

"I was already arming myself by the time Sas voiced her concerns," Ryder says.

"And you?" I ask Finnian, whose eyes have remained fixated on me this whole time.

He takes a step forward. "Reading your letter."

I let out a disbelieving laugh, barren of humor. "I named you my heir should I die in the very place you're standing in!"

"You would've followed me" is all he replies.

"And you would've followed us," Ryder says, staring Cayden down. "You used to trail me on missions *you* trained me for."

"You also used to guard me whenever I left our living quarters," Saskia adds.

"You were a rich prick who hopped around like a frog that decided to be an assassin," Cayden says to Ryder. "And you had no interest in carrying a blade," he says to Saskia.

"Unnecessary," Ryder groans. "Take as many jabs as you want, but you know damn well you'd never allow me to walk into enemy territory without you. You stood with me when odds were stacked against us, and we fought our way out."

Cayden rakes his hands through his hair, knowing he doesn't have an argument for that. Anything he replies would be hypocritical or a lie.

"You can't expect me to love you for half my life and be happy to see you here," I say to Finnian.

He steps forward again, close enough to squeeze my shoulders. "And you can't expect me to watch you leave."

None of them display an ounce of regret for crossing the border, which they must have managed while the soldiers continued taking care of the explosion. We practically left a trail for them to follow like stags running from a hunting party. I hate that my anger fades the more I listen, the more I note the desperation on their faces and the relief that they found us. I don't think love is always about letting someone walk away; sometimes it's about chasing after them to the ends of the earth, even if the journey is treacherous.

A strange feeling settles in my chest, a sense of belonging. Nestled in a damp cave in the one kingdom where everyone wants me dead, I've never felt safer. I'd be honored to fight beside everyone in this cave, but I can't pick their battles for them. We're a group created by aligned goals, but I never realized how important who I achieved those goals with became to me.

I sigh, closing my eyes. "Damn it."

"Don't you dare give in," Cayden mutters. "You glared at me for five days after I kicked a dog *in your dream.*"

"It was a cute dog." I nudge him in the side, smiling while he stares down at me with an incredulous look.

He throws his head back and groans. "I'm assuming everyone thinks you've tagged along on our tour of Vareveth?"

"Yes," Saskia answers.

"Right, then." Cayden pinches the bridge of his nose. "No more talking about feelings, it's giving me a headache, and I'm too tired for this shit. Ryder, you better have brought enough food because you ate all mine last mission."

Finnian and Saskia throw their arms around me while Cayden and Ryder delve into bickering. It's darker in the cave than it should be, and I immediately detach myself and whip toward Cayden. "You never woke me up!"

He shrugs. "You reveal a lot of things in your sleep. It was entertaining."

"I don't talk in my sleep."

"Well . . ." Finnian trails off when I glare at him.

"You said my name quite a few times," Cayden adds.

I cross my arms. "You are the most vexing person I've ever met. I must've been dreaming of the day I'll never see you again."

"And yet I'm still on your mind, love."

Darkness soon greets the forest like a lover returning home after a long day as I keep watch. Its embrace is gentle yet consuming, with only tiny forest creatures disturbing the peace. Everyone sleeps peacefully aside from Cayden, who wakes up every ten minutes. He's so on edge, it's like his mind rebels against the vulnerability that sleep bares him to.

Saskia is the first to sit up, and the others soon follow. Not gracefully, might I add. Ryder gets tangled in his cloak when Finnian groans, thinking a bear infiltrated the cave. Cayden made us laugh until our stomachs hurt while he imitated Ryder, who pouted while eating some bread, telling us we're going to hell.

Moonlight has drawn the forest a blue bath, granting us just enough light to navigate. We continue staying off main roads while we can, taking care to avoid making too much noise. Eventually, the forest becomes a blur. I don't think of anything other than keeping my footing. Dampness seeps into the air around us as we near the Emer River. It's the longest river on the continent—stretching from the Seren Mountains to the Dolent Sea. Legend says that the Goddess of Souls lived in the Etril Forest before the gods left us and sent mortals to cry their tears of sorrow into the Emer.

Every human is broken somehow, whether for love or life, because we feel everything. We're not like the gods. No matter how much we try to detach ourselves from emotions, they still grip us in their clutches. It's why the river is so vast; every soul has something to mourn.

The moon glides away, and the stars disappear as the sun chisels cracks in the darkness. The Emer becomes louder; what was a faint hum is now a roaring current. I'm thankful when Cayden holds his hand up, and I press my hands into a trunk, bowing my head to catch my breath.

"A group of soldiers are up ahead. Their horses' saddles bear the Atarah trident and crown sigil," he whispers. "Seven are sleeping and one is on watch."

"Thank the gods," I huff, earning strange looks from Finnian, Saskia, and Ryder. "I'm not running the entirety of our journey."

"You're going to kill sleeping men because you want their horses?" Finnian asks slowly.

"It's not like they're going to need them," Cayden says.

"The two of you . . ." Ryder trails off. "What's the plan?"

Finnian nocks an arrow in his bow. "I'll take out the one on watch before we reveal our position."

"Stay back so you can pick off any if they try to ride away," Cayden says, unsheathing a sword and an axe.

We peer through the bushes as Finnian silently creeps through the woods for a higher vantage point and a better shot at the watchman. The arrow flies, piercing the man through the neck, but the pots he falls into clatter loud enough to startle the sleeping party.

"Didn't mean for that to happen!" Finnian shouts, and I run into battle laughing.

Cayden throws his axe, the force of it throwing a soldier backward when it sinks into his skull, and I take out another with a knife before they reach us. Saskia stays behind to monitor the battle with Finnian, finding openings to shoot soldiers down without endangering us.

"Down, Ryder!" I shout, throwing my knife at someone approaching his back while Finnian takes out the soldier running toward a horse.

The three of us flow like a breeze, making quick work of the small skirmish as if we've fought together for years. We aid each other when we can and trust each other when we can't. My hands are speckled with blood by the time I take on my last soldier, spinning around his swing and stabbing him in the back of his neck. He falls to the ground, gurgling on his blood, and soon joins his fellow patrol in the afterlife.

I sheathe my sword as Finnian and Saskia join us, sending leaves and rocks tumbling down the hill. Cayden plants his boot on the soldier's chest and pulls the axe from his head, and I begin collecting my knives.

"I found something!" Saskia exclaims, holding up a letter she found while picking through pockets. "We can use this to get across the Emer."

"How so?" Finnian asks. "We don't resemble this patrol."

"It's a general order to get back to Zinambra for a masquerade ball. It's not addressed to anyone, which means it was most likely given to several soldiers on the border."

There's a small crack in the woods behind us, and we fall silent while reaching for weapons again. But it's nothing. Probably a small animal searching for food.

"We'll speak more when we get into the city. Let's just focus on getting across the Emer," I say.

The horses and bridge access will cut our travel time immensely. None of the soldiers are in Imirath armor; they're all wearing casual leathers and tunics, much like us. Ryder takes whatever money he finds off them and we climb onto the horses, taking the remaining three with us so we can plant them somewhere easy to find and wash the blood off us. Leaving them would haunt me more than murdering sleeping men.

We ride the short distance to the crossing, and my anxiety grows each second. The reins become slippery with sweat as the forest clears, and a curved stone bridge looms over the river dotted with moss-covered rocks that create miniature waterfalls. I might admire it if we weren't getting in line to converse with two Imirath soldiers on guard, or if it weren't for the twenty littered throughout the crossing filtering through carriages and carts. Cayden takes out a black mask and hooks it over his ears.

The line splits when we're halfway across and I ride beside Cayden, who hands the letter to the soldier. He quickly reads it over, eyes flicking between the pair of us but lingering on me. "You're coming from the border?"

"Yes," Cayden answers. I force myself to keep my smile pleasant, unbothered, calm.

"What is the name of the general who gave you this letter?"

"General Davian," Cayden answers again, saving me from babbling like a fool for information I don't know.

The soldier's irritated glare falls on Cayden. "Who are you to speak for this woman?"

"Her husband," he answers without hesitation. My hands tighten and butterflies erupt in my stomach from that one damn word, but I blame it on the situation.

"I see." His suspicion continues to grow. "Remove your mask."

"Sir, please. Is that truly necessary?" I ask, faintly hearing Ryder reach for his sword behind me.

"We have strict orders from the king." Time slows as Cayden reaches for his mask. If Robick knew of his scar, surely others will too.

"He's sick! Riddled with fever." I sharply sniffle. "I'm not a soldier, I'm a healer. I followed my husband to the border to be close to him, but his sickness has gone beyond my capabilities." I summon tears and a wavering tone. "We're to see a healer in Zinambra while the rest of our party attends the festivities. Please, sir, I don't want the gods to take him from me so soon."

"You're covered in knives."

"Merely a precaution to ward off thieves on the road." I subtly kick Cayden's shin, and he leans to the side, groaning before turning it into a coughing fit that has the soldier stepping back.

A fraction of sympathy mingles with self-preservation. "The mask stays on for the rest of your journey. I wish you the best of luck."

He lets us pass, and I continue my tears while Cayden chokes, only stopping when we're a decent distance away. I glance at him from the corner of my eye as he slips his mask off and dive into a fit of laughter, in which everyone soon follows.

"You little snake," Finnian says, riding up next to me.

"Very moving performance," Ryder adds. "Nearly brought me to tears, too."

CHAPTER
THIRTY-SEVEN

WE MAKE IT TO THE CAPITAL OF IMIRATH AFTER DARK, the city of Zinambra. We're nestled on a dock attached to the inn that Finnian stepped into a few moments ago. Several isles make up the city, with canals jutting between them. Water pushes and pulls under the dark, weathered wood as boats with fishing nets hanging off the sides slowly float by, dodging small pieces of ice. The smoke lingering around chimneys is a mocking contrast to the breaths that puff from my lips.

Finnian ends my suffering by waving us toward the front door, fiery curls dancing in the wind. "Almost everywhere is full due to the ball, but they have an attic room we can take."

"So long as there's a bath and a bed, I'm happy," Saskia replies, entering the inn made of the same weathered, gray wood as the dock.

The cold slowly melts off me once we enter. The inn doubles as a tavern, as most do, and the smell of a hearty winter stew hangs heavily in the air. I keep my head down, not wanting to risk making eye contact with the wrong person, and follow Finnian's footsteps to a narrow staircase.

The ceiling is warped and slanted, causing three out of the five of us to hunch over as we climb several levels, not stopping until the steps lead to a singular door. Finnian bounds up and slides his fingers on top of the doorframe to retrieve a key, puffing dust into the air in the process. It creaks as he pushes it open, and our view of the canal through three large windows is breathtaking.

Lanterns hang from the tips of boats gliding under bridges carrying people buried in furs to take in the sights. It's darker here than in Vareveth, both in architecture and feeling. The buildings have sharp silhouettes and steep steps leading to the water. Some restaurants reside on their own private islands speckled throughout the city. People walk arm in arm down narrow streets, some wearing freshly painted masks and others shouting about the decadent gowns made of velvet and silk that'll catch the eye of any suitor at the ball.

The room is equipped with plush furs and blankets strewn about, but anything is better than sleeping outside again. It's clean, warm, and safe enough. I dive onto the furs and wrap myself in a thick blanket after untying my cloak. It's a fight to keep my eyes open while I watch everyone settle in.

"Move farther away," Saskia hisses. "If you kick me in your sleep, I'll throw you in the canal."

Cayden chokes on a laugh when Ryder's mouth drops open, but he soon recovers and glares at his sister. "Seeing your face would give me nightmares, anyway."

The Neredras siblings would die for each other, but gods, they don't miss an opportunity to bicker.

"Let's make a plan," she says, looking to Cayden.

"People are most likely making wagers on invitations to the ball, so we'll need to hit a gambling den."

"We're gambling?" Ryder perks up.

"I don't place a bet unless I know the outcome. We're stealing them," Cayden says.

"We'll also need attire for the ball," I add.

"Gods, we sound like a gang." Finnian laughs.

"Don't think of it as stealing." I smile at him. "Think of it as redefining ownership."

"Deviant," he replies. "We need to decide on roles for infiltrating the castle. Walking up to the front door, masks or not, when nobody knows us is a risk."

"That's why we're stealing castle guard uniforms tonight as well," I say, immediately grasping everyone's attention. "You three are going to enter the castle through the dungeon and break into the office of the captain of the guard to forge an order for all the guards in the east tower to attend an emergency meeting in the west wing. Once that's complete, one of you will come to the ball to give Cayden and me a signal."

"And after that?" Ryder asks.

"You'll leave the castle and begin the journey back to Vareveth," Cayden answers.

"But how will you find us?"

I sink my nails into my palms. "The dragons are . . . unpredictable. They might follow me right away, or it may take them time to accept the bond once they're freed." *They might kill you for leaving them. Your mind could've tricked you into believing they still love you.* "We'll do what we must to flee and survive, but the path we take will most likely be forced upon us through circumstances."

"Forge travel papers while you're in the captain's office. You can steal a boat and travel down the Emer. It's the perfect cover because of the ball," Cayden adds. I offer him an appreciative smile before he fixes his hard eyes back on the group, daring anyone to challenge us.

Finnian's and Ryder's jaws are locked, and Saskia twiddles with her tied-back braids. "I despise that this is our best option," she whispers.

✣ ✣ ✣

The gambling den vibrates my feet, and I can already smell the pipe smoke pouring from the open windows. I grip the edge of the roof and drop myself to a ledge before climbing onto a thick wooden rafter, hardly dodging a cobweb, and coating my fingers in dust. If I weren't wearing a mask, I'd probably give my position away by delving into a coughing fit. Dark purple drapes hang like a star from the pointed ceiling, matching the tables below. Coins clatter to the ground, fights break out, and people kiss their precious winnings with tears streaking down their faces as I weave through the rafters like a spider, spinning a web of thievery and deception.

I do what I've done for most of my life, wait and observe, taking in the details most people think nobody notices. The man plucking a card from his pocket to rig the game in his favor. The woman swiping a man's wallet off the bar while he's mesmerized by her smile. The pair who exit a coat closet looking far more ruffled than when they first entered.

A man claps his hands and hollers obnoxiously, making a show of waving around two stiff pieces of paper trimmed in silver. I can see the fancy swooping script detailing the invitations to the ball from here. Gods, some people make it too easy. It's like they're begging to be robbed.

I turn back to the window when I've seen enough, hopping along the beams and doing my best not to plummet and break my neck. Cayden grips my wrists once I'm out and hauls me up. "Hear anything interesting, little shadow?"

I pause when he recites the first words he ever spoke to me and stare up at his face illuminated by moonlight, much like it was in the forest when we made the deal. But we've changed since then, whether we like it or not. He's always looked at me with intensity. I've always known he'd pull me from fire if I was in danger and torch those who'd harmed me once I was safe. He'd haul me through a battlefield, through worlds, or steal me from a god to accomplish his goals. But there's a softness in his eyes now, a familiarity. It terrifies me just as much as it exhilarates me.

"There's a man who won two invitations coming out soon," I say.

He nods, and we lean over the edge to watch the front door. Cayden whistles when I point him out, and Ryder kicks off the wall to trail him. We hop from roof to roof, the scent of smoked fish and meats mingling with the salty, damp air. In all my nightmares of Imirath, I never imagined there to be so much . . . life. It feels like I've been lied to, but I know I haven't. I don't know how to describe this feeling. I could've been one of these people ambling through the streets in fine gowns or taking boat rides through floating gardens, but I'm a common thief in place of a princess. Part of me mourns for what could've been, while knowing I'd never sacrifice what I have now.

We hop down when Finnian and Saskia cut the man off at the end of a deserted street. He stops in his tracks and raises his shaking hands. "I don't want any trouble."

Ryder jams the hilt of his sword into his head, and we watch as he collapses onto the road. The worst he'll have when he wakes is a headache as he laments the loss of the two invitations Saskia leans down to pluck from his coat pocket.

"We should put him in the stables," I say, pointing toward an open stall.

"Your kindness knows no bounds," Cayden says, hauling the man into his arms. I may have helped rob the man, but I have *some* compassion. Cayden tosses him into the hay with the same amount of care someone exercises when discarding rancid meat.

"I saw a tavern a few roads over. There should be some guards still in uniform," Ryder says. "We should get started since we need three and can't steal them from a shop."

"Two," Cayden responds.

Ryder scrunches his brows. "Three."

"I killed a guard while you were all resting and stashed the uniform in an empty barrel beside the inn."

"We're supposed to be doing this *together*." Ryder sounds extremely offended despite being told we have one less thing to do.

"My apologies for not napping with you. I know skin-to-skin contact is very important for babes and their mothers." Cayden leans against a post and begins cutting an apple he plucks from a barrel, holding his knife to my lips to offer me a piece. He dusts his fingers against my cheek when I take it, so quickly it feels like a hallucination.

"No." Ryder pulls me away from his side, wrapping his arm around my shoulders while Cayden watches us, lazily chewing on the apple. He must be used to Ryder's dramatics by now. "You're sitting the next guard out, and she's with us."

I gulp the apple down when Ryder smiles at me, already knowing I won't like what he has planned.

CHAPTER
THIRTY-EIGHT

"This is the best you could come up with?"

I was correct.

I hate the plan.

"This plan is foolproof," Ryder argues, and Finnian adamantly nods behind him.

I glance at Saskia for some assistance, but she shrugs, looks me up and down, and says, "You know I hate to agree with them, but you look amazing. Cayden might have a heart attack, but it's all in good fun."

I roll my eyes. "Why can't any of you do this?"

"Because you, my darling, demonstrated your acting capabilities when we crossed the bridge," Finnian adds.

"Your support is truly admirable." I flick his hands off my shoulders. The cold is biting into my exposed skin and I'm tired of arguing. I just want to get this over with. "Enjoy the show."

"Channel that night at the brothel, sunshine," Ryder jests as I shove the door to the tavern open.

"I'm going to channel my knife in your eye socket, Neredras." I blow him a kiss.

I turn away from the three of them grinning like children in a sweet shop and focus on the mission. If I'm going to do this, there's no way in hells I'm failing. *It's for the dragons,* I remind myself as I glide toward the barkeep, resting my elbows along the dark wood and offering a sweet smile when he appears. I've charmed many men into getting what I want, and this is no different.

"What can I get you, love?" he asks, drying a pint glass with a rag and trailing his eyes across my plunging neckline.

"Honey whiskey, please."

I flick my curls over my shoulder while he fixes my drink, subtly dragging my eyes over the crowd and landing on the guard who's already looking my way while sitting in a black leather booth beneath a drooping fishing net. He's admiring my gold gown that leaves little to the imagination, between the intricate cutouts along my torso and the thin fabric that shimmers in the dim light. I offer him a coy smile when he finds my face again and turn forward as if I'm nervous he caught me.

"For you, my lady," says the barkeep, placing my drink in front of me with a mock bow. His flirty demeanor makes my smile briefly authentic. I take a small sip of the liquid courage as a shadow cloaks me and an arm covered in purple fabric with a trident spearing a crown sewn into the cuff rests against the bar.

"Is it safe to assume you're here for the ball?" His voice is smooth, confident.

"Why do you ask?"

"I'm wondering if I'll be lucky enough for our paths to cross twice."

I bite the inside of my cheek to refrain from cringing, the demure smile remaining on my lips. "And who says they're crossing tonight?"

"I pray the gods they do." He laughs and steps a bit closer. "What's your name?"

"Faye."

"Would you like to sit down, Faye?"

No. "Yes, that would be lovely . . ."

"Evrin."

I grab my whiskey and slide my arm through the one he extends as the door to the tavern opens. Goosebumps speckle my skin, but it has nothing to do with the icy wind that filters in. I feel his presence, it's like a sixth sense. When I peek a glance at Cayden, his glare is zoned in on where my hand rests on Evrin's arm. I've seen him angry, but this is different. He knows how to control his anger, but unpredictability and bloodlust pump off him. Ryder looks both elated and terrified when Cayden cranes his neck.

"Bad luck for him. You're with me, beautiful," Evrin says, pulling me away.

"Something like that."

I try to tell myself this is a good reminder for where we stand with each other. Cayden is with me for my dragons and I'm with him for his army, but it's getting harder to remember that by the minute, especially when I hear him shove Ryder into the wall, knowing that if it were anyone else, they'd be dead. We're not supposed to be together, not supposed to feel the things we do, and it's exasperating. Sometimes it feels like nothing can keep me away from him, that we're destined to be drawn together, but the reality of our situation hurts me more than I want him to know.

Finnian manages to break them apart and forces Cayden onto a stool. He orders a whiskey, downs it like a shot, and never takes his eyes off me as his glass is refilled. I'd be lying if I said I didn't love how much power I have over him, how tortured he looks knowing this is his punishment for going out on his own in enemy territory. Thinking of what they would do to him if he was caught makes me want to prolong his misery. A task off our list is a relief, but the risk he took was unnecessary and irresponsible.

He keeps his hood up, and the shadows cloaking his face make me feel like I'm toying with death itself.

I smirk.

He grinds his jaw.

"Do you know him?" Evrin asks.

I bring my whiskey to my lips, making sure Cayden notes my drink of choice. "No. He's not the type of man I usually acquaint myself with."

Cayden sneers at me, and it sends a chill up my spine. I return my focus to Evrin, trailing my fingers across his shoulders while subtly inching back. No matter how much I want Cayden to wallow, I despise getting close to this man. Part of me wants to stab him and be done with all this bother and fuss. I laugh when I must, making sure he believes I'm enraptured by his humor. My eyes light up as he talks about his promotions within the castle, and I make sure to blush when he covers my tab and orders another whiskey for me.

I tip my head back, subtly pushing my breasts up and sweeping the curls off my neck. A stool scrapes across the floor but I pay it no mind, envisioning my dragons to get through this last bit. I'm tired of the arm around my shoulders that makes me want to scrub my skin and the thigh pressing into mine that feels so damn wrong.

"Are you warm?" Evrin asks.

"Terribly," I huff, pouting my lips. "Would you like to step outside with me?"

His smirk makes my skin crawl, and he helps me to my feet, pressing a hand far lower than appropriate. "I'd love to."

My fingers graze the hilt of my dagger as he opens the door and leads us down the steps, nearly shoving me to the alley beside the tavern and tucking us behind some barrels in the darkest corner possible. "Gods, I've wanted to do this since I saw you."

I spin on my heels, but a pair of hands wrap around Evrin's head and quickly twist until a sharp crack echoes throughout the small space. He collapses, revealing Cayden with that damn hood still up.

"I was going to kill him," I say, but my argument is breathless.

"Of that I have no doubt." He steps over him like a puddle, coming so close I can smell the essence of his masculine scent. "But I wanted the honor of snapping his neck myself. Would've prolonged it if I could get blood on the uniform."

"He hardly touched me."

"Oh, love." He chuckles. "Even if a man even *hardly* touches you, it'll be the last thing he does in this life. I told you not to make me into a better man than I am. For you, Elowen, I'll become the worst version of myself."

"Don't say things like that." I fist my dress to stop myself from touching him. "This was just a mission. We needed a guard uniform, and I did what I had to do."

"As did I."

"I'm not yours, Cayden. I *can't* be yours." My voice is as thin as a frozen lake on the first days of spring. "I know the lines have been blurred—"

"That line has been decimated long before you realized."

"We're allies. We work together. Your king forbids—"

He growls, backing me up against the tavern and placing his hands on either side of my head, forcing me to look up at him. "Why do you believe I would let anything keep me from you? I've searched for you since I was a boy, when the whole world thought you were dead, when it seemed hopeless—I searched for you."

My heart speeds up at his confession. "F-for my power."

"Don't be a fool, Elowen." He shakes his head, wrapping one hand around my chin. "We've become deeper than power. You've driven me to madness. You haunt me while I sleep and you're there when I wake. Your presence is agonizing and yet I'll beg for the pain if it means I can have a moment with you."

"You're not being fair!" I shove my hands into his chest, but he doesn't move. "This is cruel, Cayden."

He runs his fingers through my hair, his eyes softening a fraction. "Careful, angel. Your glare doesn't sting as much as it usually does."

I glance at his mouth. "It stings you?"

"Deeply." He drops his face closer to mine. "Your fire captivates me."

"You make yourself into a target."

"Perhaps." He slides his thumb over my lips. "But that doesn't change the fact that you are the sweetest curse bestowed upon me."

My breathing becomes shallow, and he shoves his knee between my legs when I try to press my thighs together. I subtly shift my hips, but he catches on right away and presses into me harder. I drop my head to his chest and whimper, and when his hands drop to my hips to grind me onto his leg, I don't stop him.

He murmurs my name into my hair, pinning me to the wall with one hand and teasing the slit of my dress with the other. Knowing how well he takes care of my needs has my head spinning at the possibility. "I want to bury my head between your legs before his corpse gets cold. Maybe his soul will linger to watch how I take care of my woman."

He dips his hand between my legs, sliding beneath my panties and swirling a finger on my clit. I grip his biceps and choke on a moan when he glides it inside me, pumping a few times before pulling it out and licking it clean, groaning and lifting me as he does. He places me on a barrel and pushes my dress up my thighs.

"I never wanted him to touch me." I don't know why I say it, but when I think of Cayden doubting me, it hurts.

"I know, love," he softly states. "But you want me to touch you?"

"Yes."

He pulls my panties down my legs and tucks them into his pocket. "Lean back and keep these pretty thighs open for me."

My body is stiff with adrenaline and the pleasure I've been denying myself, and I squirm when he bares me to the cold air while sinking to his knees. He yanks my hips forward and throws my legs over his shoulders. "So perfect, in every damn way."

The first lick sends a full-body tremor through me, and I thread my fingers through his hair while my head rolls against the wall. He licks as if I've starved him of his favorite meal, and he's worried he'll never get another taste. He savors me, devours me, and dips his fingers inside to slowly pump my pleasure. He's taking his time, not rushing or caring that we're in enemy territory.

Noises of pleasure fly freely from my lips, and I do my best to keep quiet, but it's so hard when it seems like he knows exactly where I need him. "Not a day has gone by that I haven't thought about what you would taste like when I bury my head between your thighs."

His tongue twists and flicks, and my back arches off the wall. I'm a panting, pleading mess, just as he wants me. He groans against me when I roll my hips onto his face, so greedy for him I can't think straight.

"You," he pants, "are so fucking sweet."

He yanks on my thighs, pulling me farther off the barrel and pushing me wider. His mouth closes around my clit and he sucks, having to reach up to cover my mouth and muffle my scream and the noise of protest that follows when he pulls his mouth off me.

"You know I love your noises, angel, but I need you to keep them down a bit because if someone comes looking, I'll have to stop to kill them, and neither of us wants that."

"I'm sorry," I pant when he pulls his hand away.

He shakes his head. "I've never been obsessed with anything." He presses a finger onto my clit, and I swear I see stars. "But this." His tongue dips low, teasing my entrance. "You." He begins placing sloppy kisses on me again and I'm so close to surrendering to all he's doing to me. "I'm a fucking goner."

He adds a third finger, curling them to reach exactly where my sweet spots are. "Cayden, I . . . I'm—"

His hand shoots up again to muffle my screams as my hips spasm, and he continues licking me through my wave of pleasure. It's earth-shattering and all encompassing.

He kisses up my body once he's done, replacing his hand with his lips and snaking his tongue into my mouth. It's sweet and slow, and I know he doesn't expect anything from me, but that's precisely why I grab hold of his shoulders and shove him into the wall behind us. Our kisses become heated, and I reach for his belt.

"Elowen, if you so much as graze my cock with your finger, I'm going to bend you over a barrel." A tortured growl claws from his lips when I don't stop unfastening the clasps. "The first time I fuck you isn't going to be somewhere I have to stifle your screams and don't have time to memorize every place you love to be touched."

I hand him his sword once I get his belt off and slide my hands up his chest, wrapping my arms around his shoulders to murmur against his lips, "Is your control slipping, soldier?" He lets out a shuddering breath. "Are you worried you won't be able to handle me?"

He fists the fabric around my hips, eyes blazing hot. "I think I'm the only man who can handle whatever you throw at him and happily take it."

"Prove it." I palm him over his pants and suck on his bottom lip. His eyes roll back in his head before he slips them shut, and I slide kisses down his neck. The way he shivers against me is invigorating. "Do you want my mouth?"

"Fuck," he rasps. "Yes."

"Hmm." I slowly undo the laces holding his pants up and stroke his length when it springs free. "Did it make you murderous when you saw me with that guard? Did it torture you when you thought about his hands on—"

"You little tease." He tightly fists my hair and pulls my face to his again. "Get on your knees like a good girl and open your mouth."

He keeps his hand in my hair while I sink in front of him; the cold stone bites into my skin but adds to the essence of depravity. He's far larger than anyone I've been with, but I don't grant him the satisfaction of telling him. I dart my tongue out, lightly dusting it from base to tip, and wrapping my lips around the head before popping it out.

I want to make a mess of him. The man who's always in control. I want to be his undoing. He stares down at me like he'd cut off his sword hand if I asked.

I continue fisting him while tracing my tongue along the veins on his shaft before taking him in my mouth. He covers his face with his hand, tilting it back against the tavern and letting out a series of curses through gritted teeth. Hollowing my cheeks, I quicken my pace, bobbing my head, wanting to earn more moans from him.

"That's it, love. You look so beautiful on your knees."

His reaction to me has me pressing my thighs together despite my core still throbbing from what he did to me mere moments ago. The awe in his eyes while he looks down at me has me pushing forward, taking more of him until I'm gagging.

"Fucking gods, woman." I dig my nails into his hips, urging him to thrust into me. "Too perfect."

I moan around his cock when his grip in my hair gets tighter and his thrusts get sloppy. My lips tighten around him, and my hand pumps at the rhythm I've learned he loves. It's not long before he's groaning my name and spilling down my throat, and I work him until he leans back against the wall, panting and cursing. He lifts me off the ground and places me on the barrel, rubbing my knees after he tucks himself back into his pants. I rest against his chest, and he massages the roots of my hair while placing his cheek on my head. He unties his cloak and wraps it around my bare shoulders, running his hands along my arms to warm me.

We don't move for a few moments, listening to the water in the canal lapping against the buildings and catching our breath. He kisses my hair a few times before tilting my chin up and placing a tender one on my lips. I don't care that there's nothing to blame this moment on other than our own wants. I'm in Imirath. We're going to free my dragons. I'm too tired to analyze why I can't want him and can only revel in having him right now.

"I didn't know I had a soul until you stole it from me," he says. I laugh in response, kissing him again as he lifts me from the barrel and sets me on my feet. "Where the hells did you find the dress and heels?"

"Saskia nabbed them from a showgirl's bag when she wasn't looking, but I want to get my leathers from her before heading back to the inn." Walking around in this dress is sure to earn too much unwanted attention. "I got a guard uniform, though!"

"And seven years off my life." He leans down to kiss me again, but I'm abruptly shoved behind him when someone whistles at the mouth of the alley.

"Well, don't you look adorably disheveled," Ryder says, stopping beside the corpse. "*Gods*, how depraved are you two?"

I roll my eyes. "All we did was argue."

"That's foreplay for us." Cayden leans down to whisper it, and I pinch his arm.

"Whatever you say." Ryder crouches beside the guard to remove the purple tunic and black polished boots. "Lipstick always ends up on my neck after an argument, too."

CHAPTER
THIRTY-NINE

SASKIA WAVES A RASPBERRY-JAM-FILLED PASTRY IN FRONT OF my face to revive me, but not even caffeine can get the job done at this point. It doesn't stop me from opening my mouth and taking a generous bite when she places it between my teeth. When we get back to Vareveth, I'm sleeping for a week. Every little creak at the inn woke me, too anxious to be caught by Imirath in my sleep.

"Better?" Saskia asks.

I open my mouth for a second bite, savoring the bit of vanilla syrup that melts on my tongue. "Yes."

The bell above the door of the teahouse chimes, and I sit up in time to spy Finnian walking to our table. I long for coffee, but Imirath doesn't trade with Galakin so rose tea is how I'm starting my day. It tastes like a bottle of perfume. "There's a dress shop on the isle beside ours, and I spotted some inventory stored near the back entrance."

"It's best if fewer people see our faces today," I reply, finishing off my cup. I'd like to avoid any castle guards concerned over the whereabouts of Evrin . . . unless they're in the mood to fish. I shove the remainder of the pastry into my mouth and follow Saskia to the door.

Merchants have tents set up in the crowded streets, shouting about their wares. I weave through tables, women's wide skirts, and fire pits. A light dusting of snow crunches under my boots as we cross the bridge made of stone, lined with torches every few feet. My stomach sours when I realize they're made to look like dragons blowing fire . . . and even more so when I glance down the canal and realize they're the same on every bridge.

I flip the hood on my cloak up to hide my scowl, which doesn't resolve until we make it to the dress shop and I have a task to focus on. I'll have no trouble finding a fine gown, judging by the satin curtains in the windows and the gold candelabras framing the door with a stained-glass peony at the center. We rest against the building adjacent to the shop to subtly monitor the back door but realize it's not used very often.

"Why did someone open it when you were here earlier?" I ask.

"A delivery. I would've taken one of the dresses off the wagon but they were packed up so I couldn't see the sizes."

I pull the lockpicks Cayden gifted me from my holster and kick off the wall. No wagons are near, so it's best to do this while we have an open window. "Finnian, keep watch. Give us a signal if trouble approaches."

Saskia and I cross the road, keeping our heads huddled close as if we're battling the cold and not plotting a robbery. She stands behind me, subtly spreading her cloak to cover me as I place the picks in the keyhole, listening to Cayden's voice relay the instructions in my mind, larger one on the bottom and use the smaller one to retract the bolt. I slowly turn the handle and peek through the crack to ensure that nobody is on the other side. It's an office, but it's vacant and has two racks of dresses, which is all that matters.

We seal ourselves inside and Saskia patters over to the window to keep an eye on Finnian. The styles here match the architecture of the kingdom: decadent and dramatic. In Vareveth, the gowns are made of material that flows around you like you're always caught in a spring breeze, with long lace sleeves and delicate embroidery. Imirath is skirts upon skirts with no slits, higher square necklines, and elaborate prints. They're beautiful in their own way, but not for me. It's how I feel about this kingdom in general.

I pick through the rack, settling on a sky-blue gown with pearls sewn into the billowing skirts and the bodice with long sleeves that loop over my middle finger. Forgoing a box, I find a bag with pink bows on it to fold the dress into, which is a feat considering the amount of fabric.

"Fucking gods," I mutter as a voice from down the hall grows louder and footsteps approach.

"Nobody's in the alley. Time to go." Saskia yanks the door open and shuts it a second shy of the owner entering her office, but I don't want to loiter because she's bound to notice the missing gown soon. Finnian strides past without looking at me and effortlessly transfers the bag to his hand on route to the inn.

Saskia and I glide away from the shop, joining the never-ending street market again, but we clearly don't blend in as well as I hope because an authoritative voice shouts an order behind me. "You! Stop right there." Everyone around us backs away, making a straight path for the castle guard I vaguely remember from the tavern.

"Find a mask for me and get to Finnian. I'll meet you both back at the inn," I mutter to Saskia, releasing her arm and striding forward.

"It's too dangerous," she hisses.

I smile over my shoulder. "That's the best part."

A second guard joins the pursuit, both of them scowling and unsheathing their swords. Clearly they already find me guilty. I am guilty, but a morsel of decorum would be appreciated. "Gentlemen, may I ask why you're approaching me?"

"A man went missing last night. You wouldn't happen to know anything about that, would you?"

"Men are like carriages. If you miss one, then you just get on the next. Eventually they all start to blend together, so you'll have to be more specific."

His lip curls under his full mustache. "His name is Evrin."

"Was."

Two of my knives find a home in their throats, and I spring forward to retrieve them as the crowd screams and a few ladies faint. I hop onto a table and run through the market by leaping from surface to surface. Trinkets clatter to the floor, fake jewels are crushed under my boots, and scarves fly behind me like feathers in the wind. The crowd is too thick to weave through them properly, and I find Saskia struggling with a guard hot on her heels.

Without thinking of the repercussions, I reach down and toss a bottle of rum into a fire pit, sending scalding flames into the canopy above this section of the market. The fire travels quickly. All attention is on me, but at least it's off Saskia. I narrowly dodge an arrow as I jump down from the last table, frantically looking for the best escape route, but the streets here are so small and narrow that it's like trying to chase a bumblebee through a maze.

"Stop right there! By order of the crown!" a guard shouts, barreling toward me. Gods, if only he knew the irony of that statement. I'm seconds away from throwing another knife, mourning the loss of it because I know I won't have time to retrieve it, when someone behind me takes the guard down with one of their own.

"What happened to all that stealth, little shadow?"

"Your presence must've contaminated me." I smile, running toward Cayden and Ryder while several guards trail us. We weave through side streets that thankfully don't have tables but are still so damn congested that we spend more time pushing through people than we do running. The only mercy is that the guards suffer the same fate as us. "Where's the third uniform?"

"Stashed it at the inn so we didn't draw attention by carrying it around," Ryder pants. "But *now* they're going to want us for murder!"

"They already had an inkling from Evrin!"

"You remember his name?" Cayden deadpans.

"Not the time," I growl.

We cut a corner, losing the guards momentarily and running along a canal. We can't run to the inn and give away our only safe place within the kingdom. Our options are lessening by the minute. Orders are being shouted down every street in our vicinity, and an image of the dungeon pops into my mind before I burn it and let the ashes flow away as I sprint.

Cayden leads us down the steps to the canal, looking around before climbing onto a sleek black boat and untying the knot that attaches it to the dock. Ryder shoves a fur hat onto his head, and I wrap myself in a blanket to cover my hair and leathers. Cayden dons the maroon cloak most likely left behind by the owner and pushes off, rowing us under the bridge with an army of guards in search of us.

We float beneath, using the stone pillars to hide us until it's safe to move. I wrap the blanket tighter around me. Now that we're not moving and sitting above water so cold that ice coats parts of the bridge, it's impossible to not feel the damp chill seeping into my bones.

Cayden is the first to speak. "I personally find it admirable to be wanted in a kingdom as a thief, murderer, and princess."

"Only you would view that as an accomplishment," Ryder grumbles.

✦ ✦ ✦

Fifty, fifty-one, fifty-two . . .

I gaze up at the same sky I did as a child locked in the dungeon, count the same stars, but feel as if I'm a different person entirely. Maybe it's a coping mechanism, but when I think of my younger self, it's like I'm looking *at* myself. My mind is a mirror, and I despise the reflection.

Moonlight dances across the canal, performing for a kingdom that doesn't deserve it. My fingers have gone numb from where they grip the edge of the roof, but though the cold can prick my skin with thousands of individual stingers, it still can't numb me. I did my best to reassure my dragons, knowing the bond was active from the way my eyes glowed in the reflection of my knife, wanting to offer them a sense of comfort. But once I let go of our connection to let them rest, too many emotions assaulted me at once.

Anger. Despair. Loneliness. Longing. Helplessness.

I'd contemplate jumping if I was sitting up this high when I was younger, but I survived because my love for the dragons and the hope of building a life for myself burned brighter than all of Imirath. But the flame gets low sometimes, and ripping myself from the shackles of my mind isn't easy.

The window creaks open and someone sits beside me, their boots dangling with mine.

"You should be resting," I say.

"I could smell the wood burning from inside." Cayden taps his finger against my head. "El?"

"Mm-hmm."

"Look away from it." His voice is gentle.

"I can't." My eyes are glued to the black jagged rocks that look more like a fortress than a castle, and the white statues of dragons bordering the path to the main entrance. I take in a shuddering breath and only slip my eyes shut when they start to burn again. "Did you see the dragon torches? Or the dragon banners gracing the main road?"

I see him nod in the corner of my eye. "I tore some down when I could."

"Thank you," I murmur, nudging his shin with my boot. But the golden flare he shot through me quickly fades, and I'm surrounded by darkness again, surrounded by Imirath. I feel trapped like I did when the amulet showed me my cell. Being here . . . it feels like I can't breathe. The jagged edges of the castle pierce my soul, ripping out the stitches I sewed after I left.

He slides his hand beneath my hair and rubs his fingers into the top of my neck. "Don't retreat into your mind unless you're taking me there with you."

A broken laugh crackles in my chest. It's hollow and forged in the realization that Cayden Veles is under my skin and in my mind, and I don't want to get him out. I let him lean me back until we're facing the moon and stars, two things that have always brought me comfort.

"You love the night," he says.

"I do." Several moments of silence pass, but his patience is admirable. Too many memories are consuming me; maybe that's why some spill out. "I used to count the stars, still do, but it started when I was locked in the dungeon. There was a small sliver in the stone, just enough to see through if you closed one eye. It gave me something to focus on other than the pain."

There's not much he can say to that. Part of me feels guilty for putting him in this position. I'm about to apologize when he responds, "I used to count raindrops." He clears his throat, tilting his head to look at me. "When I lived on the streets it distracted me from my hunger, and sometimes I'd use it to focus on something other than my thoughts. Pain, as well."

"Is that why you love water?" I ask. He nods.

"Is that why you wear moonstone every day?" he asks. I nod. "Will you tell me why you came out here, or do you need silence?"

I sigh, counting the stars for comfort and becoming more aware of the rushing water below. "I'm scared." Admitting that is harder than sharing why I love night. "I'm scared to see the dragons again. I'm scared for you. I'm scared I'm leading everyone into a trap."

"The only time a person can truly be brave is when they remain standing as fear tries to cut them down."

"You don't seem like someone who experiences fear."

"I'm numb to most"—he shifts so he can stare down at me, and twirls one of my curls on his finger—"but I fear certain things. Mostly hypotheticals."

"I used to fear that a vextree would crawl up the pipes in my bathing chamber and drag me down."

He barks a laugh. "You are a wildfire I have no intention of smothering, and I knew we would end up here from the second we struck the deal. I'll always believe in you, even when you don't know how."

"Do you believe the dragons will still want me?"

"I find it hard to imagine a reality where you could be unwanted."

I offer him a watery smile as he drags a knuckle down my cheek. I'm greedy for this side of him that he doesn't show the world. "There's a chance we'll be recognized tomorrow. If that happens, and we get separated, I need you to promise to leave me. Flee the castle and win this war. I'll be a bigger target than you."

He rips himself off me and drags a hand down his face. "I don't take orders from you, princess, and I will not offer you lies under the guise of comfort."

"Please," I croak.

"I will find a way to defy death itself to keep you here. We have a deal." He abruptly turns, grasps my chin, and brings our faces close. "Do you remember what I said about the promises I make to you?"

"You'll never make me one you can't keep."

"I'll never leave you behind. It's you and me until the end—whatever end that may be. If you're to die with a blade in your hand, then I'm to die by your side with a sword in mine." He says the words like a curse, as if he hates the way they taste but can't stop, damned by some higher power to spill his thoughts.

The path we're navigating is both treacherous and reckless, and the forest surrounding us is filled with poison berries, cliffs that can send us plummeting to our deaths, and creatures only nightmares can conjure. There's no map or compass to guide us, but we don't stop walking. I keep my hand laced though his as we walk through darkness illuminated only by the moon and stars, with the faint sound of water as our only companion.

"I hate how stubborn you are," I say, resting my forehead against his. "And I hate how you always know what to say."

He tucks a curl behind my ear. "What else do you hate about me?"

I could take this opportunity to hide how I feel behind a joke, but he deserves more than that. Which is why I separate us enough to lean over and kiss his scarred cheek to whisper against his skin, "I hate that you've made it impossible for me to hate you."

His soft chuckle fans across my lips. "Then I consider myself a lucky man."

CHAPTER

FORTY

"C AN YOU STOP STARING AT EVERYONE LIKE YOU WANT TO kill them?" I jab Cayden hard enough to feel it under the two layers of clothing. Half of his face is covered, but his glare *still* manages to draw attention.

"And what if I do want to kill everyone here?"

I look up at him, letting a smile spread across my lips. "Then I'd tell you to wait a few hours and I'll help."

Ice is replaced by fire when his eyes rake over me, and my heart flips in my chest. "You are the most exquisite creature I've ever met."

His words ignite something in me, and I can't help but reciprocate the sentiment. The silver and black doublet he wears and matching mask that tilts up like horns pump a darkly enchanting aura into the air. Being in his presence is like getting lost in a land of wonder and danger, and I never want to be found.

The field before the castle is filled with a series of tents encompassing a show of riches for guests to marvel at. We enter the final tent, the signal for Finnian, Saskia, and Ryder to head off toward the dungeon. No goodbyes were exchanged, opting for a simple *"Don't die"* as we left the inn and took our parting glances.

Thus far we've walked through tents filled with cakes that looked too pretty to eat—I swear one had pink butterflies that moved between layers. We've seen enormous jewels, fountains of sparkling wine, tapestries embroidered with legends of the gods, and hand-painted masks available for anyone who forgot theirs. But I have no need for them; Saskia managed to find a white mask that shimmers like starlight and resembles two wings fanning away from my face. She also took the time to weave matching pearls into my hair after pinning the front pieces back.

The air in the final tent is damp, and a wave of color washes over me, stealing the breath from my lungs when the scent of spring engulfs me. It's as if we've walked into a rainbow sea. Everywhere I turn in this greenhouse has bright and beautiful flowers; some have bloomed in shades I've never seen. Vines littered with candles and light pink flowers drape from the ceiling, and I reach up to drag my finger down a silky petal. I've always adored the way they feel between my fingertips.

But it's a distraction, nothing more. That's made apparent when we reach the end and are engulfed by the night air again. Anxiety pricks my skin like thousands of needles, and I lock my eyes on the obsidian east tower. Just a bit longer and that's where I'll be. Failure isn't an option. The pathway leading up to the castle is made of the same white stone as the bridges in Zinambra, a path cloaked in purity to hide the corruption as we approach.

My nerves engage in a battle with bloodlust, surging through me like a cavalry charge. I'm submerged in my past, drowning in it. Vines shoot from the shadowy depths, wrapping around my ankles to pull me under. This castle is a prison, a cage, it's the root of my nightmares. I want to leave here as quickly as possible.

"Stop worrying about me," I say, feeling Cayden's eyes on me.

"Worrying about you has become second nature." I squeeze his bicep as we continue walking. "I'll make sure you get what you want, no matter how bloody or godless."

"You sound sure of yourself. Have you forgotten that Garrick isn't a small threat?" As much as I loathe to admit it, Garrick rules with an iron fist.

"Nothing easy is worth doing," he replies, cutting himself off briefly to hand our invitations to the awaiting servant. Thank the gods for these masks. We glide past the guards standing beside the entrance, none of them aware they're letting the lost princess and the enemy commander inside their hallowed halls. "Garrick is a tyrant. He has influence but he's not as strategic as he believes. Power is chaos if you don't know how to wield it."

"You speak as if you're a servant to power."

"Power kneels to me, love." His dark chuckle dances along my neck. "You wish to reduce this place to ash or rip it apart stone by stone? Done. I'll be right there with you."

I absorb the decadent décor and obnoxious displays of wealth as we slowly make our way to the ballroom. Dark portraits of the Seren Mountains and Imirath's victories decorate the walls painted with tiny gold dragons. *My dragons.* Garrick has never called himself the dragon king, but it certainly seems that's how he wishes to be perceived.

I tear my eyes away. "I wish to show the world the claws I grew when they clipped my wings."

All the injustices I suffered will be answered with justice, but they will stand trial in my court. I'd never consider myself forgiving when it comes to righting wrongs. I don't mistake myself for being morally pristine or righteous by any means, but the world turned away as I suffered. Perhaps one day I'll be able to put my blades down, but it certainly won't be in the near future.

Silver and gold ribbons rain down from the ceiling and are wrapped around the pillars throughout the ballroom. Cayden and I find a modicum of privacy beside one after accepting wine from an eager servant. Several castle guards are present, but none are the impostors I'm looking for. We pass the time by people-watching mostly in silence; occasionally I make up an elaborate story about some couples and partygoers. Cayden rolls his eyes and mutters about my dramatics, and yet he's the one who begins pointing people out and asking for more.

"Is there a table we can set these on?" I ask, gesturing to the chalice in my hand as a woman in a dark purple gown with a high gold collar glides down the steps with a rolled-up scroll.

But a servant cuts in before Cayden has the chance to reply. "Is the wine not to your liking, miss?"

Cayden takes a step closer, placing his hand on my back while I sigh and smile. "It's too much to my liking, unfortunately." I drag his hand to my front to cover my belly. "I won't be having it for quite some time."

"Congratulations to you both!" She takes my goblet and adds it to her tray. "Would you care for a different drink, sir?"

He shakes his head, managing to give some semblance of a kind smile. "I'm refraining from drinking in solidarity with my wife." That damn word makes me shiver like I'm an abandoned temple braving a windstorm.

"That's lovely." A smile spreads across her face as she glances between us. "I hope you enjoy your evening."

I relax against him once the servant is out of sight. Just a bit more performing and we'll be free. The urge to sprint to the dragon chamber is overwhelming.

"Tell me how your evening is, *wife?*" He tightens his arm around my waist, pulling me closer.

"That depends on if you'll dance with me to pass the time, *husband.*"

"That can be arranged, though I thoroughly enjoyed another dance we shared. If you recall, you were on my lap and in far less clothing." Images of the brothel flash in my mind, and a fierce blush creeps along my skin as I try to squirm away. "Don't be bashful. That's how we made Elowen II."

"Shut your mouth," I huff, giving up the fight and relaxing against him again as his laughter vibrates against my back.

The woman finishes her descent, stopping on the midway platform and raising her voice above the chatter. "Esteemed guests of King Garrick Atarah, we wish to welcome you to Imirath's masquerade ball! Tonight is a celebration like no other and marks the beginning of a prosperous friendship." The crowd begins to cheer, and I wrap my hand around Cayden's wrist. "Lords and ladies, please welcome our fierce leader, the head of our armies, the protector of the kingdom, the true and only claimant to the throne of Imirath—King Garrick Atarah!"

Noise is drowned out when I see him again, and Cayden's arm keeps me from falling. But it's not fear rushing through me, it's shock. I thought seeing him would be worse than seeing the castle ... but he's merely a man, not the monster with claws my mind remembers. Any man can be killed, even a king. Some people view monarchs as invincible, but all humans bleed the same. Garrick's long black hair has streaks of gray, and when he removes his mask to address the crowd, his gaze isn't even menacing. It almost makes me want to laugh.

He never remarried after my mother was burned to death, but I note his mannerisms. He's always scared; perhaps he fears the day that the ghost of me will come back to haunt him. But I wait in the shadows to strike, and when I do, I'll sink my fangs so deep into his veins that no healer will be able to stop the venom.

"Have you ever wanted the Imirath throne?" Cayden asks.

"No. I could never live here," I answer without any hesitation or regret. "Though I suppose I should start thinking about where I'll go after the war."

"Why must you go anywhere?"

"I don't have a permanent place in Vareveth. Galakin seems interesting, I suppose." I need a long-term solution for my people. Eagor won't continue sending food once the war is over, and I've changed too much to happily return to Aestilian. The world is too vast for me to stay hidden in a tiny corner. There's far too much liberation once I let go of my shame for existing.

Cayden stiffens behind me. "Do you want a permanent place?"

"I—" I crane my neck to look at him, but his eyes remain on Garrick. "I haven't thought about it."

I shake off my thoughts, burying them in a place where even I won't find them. Garrick raises his hand to quiet the crowd, stepping forward to speak. Thank the gods for my mask because there's no hiding the suspicion marring my features. He hasn't taken his throne on the platform, and it seems he's preparing to make an announcement.

Garrick's voice booms throughout the ballroom like thunder. "Lords and ladies, before I properly thank you for traveling to Zinambra to attend these festivities, I'd like to introduce the reason we're gathered in celebration. It is with the utmost pleasure that I announce Queen Aveline and King Fallon Lilura of Thirwen!"

Another round of cheers begins as the rulers join us, both adorned by silver attire tailored in Imirath's liking. They're a magical kingdom, same as Galakin. Imirath hasn't outlawed magic, but it's not as woven into the culture, which is part of the reason they hate having Vareveth on their border. Before Eagor took the throne, magic was rampant in his kingdom; now it's only found by those who know where to seek it. Cayden clearly does, and I'll get the information out of him one day.

I've always found it strange how people seek to judge what they don't know rather than taking the time to appreciate new things. I wonder how different the world would be if people ceased thinking the unknown is a threat. People remain ignorant when they don't open their minds to new teachings. They remain frozen in time like a statue while everything progresses around them.

"You suspected this, didn't you?" I ask.

"Who do you think arranged for the rulers of Galakin to attend the alliance ball?"

"Clever."

He sighs. "I still don't understand why that surprises you."

Guards flank Garrick and the rulers of Thirwen as they make their way to the dais and the chords for the first dance are played. A blur of tulle and velvet rushes into position, eager to perform for their king. Cayden slips his hand into mine, tugging me toward the festivities and bowing when I curtsy. He sweeps me into motion and leads me through the dance made of three circles; the middle one moves in the opposite direction of the other two. We pivot and glide until the dance ends and Cayden dips me low, keeping us in this position for an extended beat of time.

"You hate dancing," I whisper.

He gives me a half smile. "You're my only exception."

"You're secretly kind," I say as he straightens us up, brushing the pearl-laced curls behind my shoulders and lightly caressing my neck.

"I despise seeing you in the arms of another man and wish death upon each and every one, not caring if they're good people." His dimples deepen. "Better?"

I roll my eyes, turning away before he can see my smile. All eyes are on Garrick, who has his goblet extended to toast the evening.

"The kingdom of Imirath is honored to align with the kingdom of Thirwen, though it deeply saddens me to express why this alliance is needed." He makes a show of placing his hand over where his heart *should* be. "Princess Elowen Atarah, my lost daughter, has come out of hiding years after murdering your queen to align with our enemy! She has spilled Atarah blood and will die for going against it."

I'm right here, Father.

Put a blade in your hands and I'll show you just how well I can spill Atarah blood.

"With the aid of Thirwen, we will find a way to break her bond to the dragons. The dragon princess, the demon commander, and the puppet king will be nothing but a memory."

I glare up at him, imagining all the ways a man can be killed.

Garrick raises his goblet. "To the alliance!"

"To the alliance!" the crown echoes. People drink deeply and couples on the dance floor cling to their partners as their cheers bounce against the walls and windows. Garrick gestures for a second dance to begin and asks Queen Aveline for her hand.

"Ryder is here," Cayden whispers.

Thank the gods. I loop my arm through his and he leads me off the dance floor to where Ryder is playing the part of an Imirath guard perfectly. My adrenaline surges with every footfall I take away from Garrick and closer to my dragons.

This is it.

It's the moment I've waited fifteen years for.

"So clumsy," Cayden chastises, setting me down on the cushioned bench Ryder stands beside. He kneels before me and takes my boot-clad ankle in his hand. "Guard, would you mind looking at my wife's ankle? She seems to have sprained it while dancing."

Ryder moves from his spot and kneels beside Cayden, speaking quickly and quietly, "We arranged the meeting successfully and forged the travel papers. I don't know how much time you have before the guards catch on, so get to the first stairwell through this archway—your swords and axes are stashed there."

"Is everyone all right?" I ask.

Ryder nods. "Finnian and Saskia are securing a boat and we'll be heading home right away." His eyes snag on Cayden, and the anguish he feels knowing he must leave him behind is apparent. "Don't be an idiot."

"Likewise, brother," Cayden responds.

"I still owe you a drink, sunshine. You can't die with debts, it's a bad look for the soul." Ryder's eyes find mine. "Go get those damn dragons."

CHAPTER
FORTY-ONE

———

THE STAIRWELL IS CLEARLY ONLY USED BY GUARDS AND servants, given the lack of décor. We rip our masks off and toss them aside, beginning to do the same with our attire.

"I need you to untie my corset."

"If you wish for me to ravish you, you should've spoken earlier." He doesn't waste time untying it, he rips it in half. "Fucking gods," he mutters as footsteps quickly approach the top of the steps. I try to filter through the skirts surrounding my legs for a knife considering I have both mine and Cayden's, but there's so much damn fabric.

Cayden yanks me up, grasps my corset to keep it from falling, and backs me into the wall. "It's showtime, princess."

He slams his lips onto mine, and I shriek in surprise, hardly recovering by the time the door at the top of the steps creaks open. I give in to the madness of his plan, kissing him back and lacing my fingers through his hair. He slides his tongue into my mouth and shoves his knee between my parted legs when the familiar throbbing sensation arises.

"Get off each other. I don't have time for this." The guard quickly descends.

Cayden hikes my leg up, and a moan slips from my lips as I feel him slide a knife out of my holster. He strokes a thumb over my thigh, and I practically taste his praise.

"Do I have to pry you two off each other?" the guard asks, his voice right next to us.

But he doesn't get the chance to touch us before Cayden flips the knife behind his back to transfer it to his other hand and stabs the guard's throat without removing his lips from mine. He only pulls back when the guard hits the floor and then rips his doublet off to expose his leathers. I slide my arms through the sleeves of mine and don my weapons once I'm situated while Cayden plucks his knives from my legs.

We take the steps two at a time and slip through the door once we know the path is clear. I glance around to get my bearings, conjuring the memory of the snakes leading me through the castle. Our pace is swift, we only halt to peek around corners, but it seems all guards in the east tower haven't figured out that the order was forged.

My skin heats, but it's not from running or nerves. It tickles the back of my mind like a talon brushing against it, and the bond in my chest comes alive. I let it guide me without caution, and it's not long before Cayden peeks around the final corner.

"Six guards stand at the chamber entrance. We'll charge them together but take the first opportunity to get inside. I'll follow you after I've killed them all." He pulls the key and amulet out of his pocket and places them in my palm. The darkness that lurks within me rises to the surface at the prospect of killing. "Bloodthirsty angel."

"You adore it."

"More than I should. Take the one on the left." He pulls a knife from his thigh and rounds the corner with a lazy, swaggered strut. We throw our blades together and kill two instantly. The blood of the one Cayden killed sprays the man beside him.

"You're guarding something of mine," I state as they rush forward, and Cayden draws a second sword. "I've returned for them."

The merriment of the ball drowns out the sound of clashing steel. The decision to leave Garrick behind is easy. My dragons matter more than him, and they always will. Together we'll become the spitting image of Garrick's nightmares.

Cayden slices through a guard like warm butter, spilling guts onto the polished floor. I drag my sword from belly to chin and kick the guard backward before his blood shoots me in the face. Instead, it rains down on me like mist.

"Go!" Cayden barks, fighting the last two guards.

"You're sure?"

"You're forgetting something, angel," Cayden begins while stabbing one of the guards in the leg. "I enjoy this." A bloodstained smile spreads across his face, and the guard in front of him flinches before Cayden unleashes himself. I rush forward, jamming the key into the hole and shoving the now red, glowing door open. It falls shut behind me, and I'm encompassed in darkness.

A low, rumbling growl echoes throughout the chamber, and a mixture of agony and longing punctures my heart. I've dreamed about that sound. Sometimes I swore I heard it while I was in Aestilian, haunted by these beautiful creatures.

My eyes slowly adjust, and I'm met with a pair of glowing green eyes.

"Sorin," I breathe. My heart shatters and mends all at once. He tilts his head as he regards me.

The only light comes from moonlight pooling through several windows facing the Seren Mountains. They've been chained and forced to gaze upon skies they couldn't touch. How in the hells is an amulet going to unlock the shackles around their necks and ankles?

I raise my hands as I step forward, wanting to show them I mean no harm. All I want to do is throw my arms around them, and I don't realize I'm crying until I taste salt. The chamber is vast, and made of black volcanic rock, but a dragon is limitless. They're born to rule the skies, not be confined to a chamber.

It reeks of dragon droppings and rancid meat from leftover carcasses that haven't been removed. The only small mercy is the pool of running water for them to drink from. They track my breath and steps; all vibrant irises are glued to me, but their scales remain black.

Venatrix growls when I reach for my pocket, her red eyes blazing like a fire.

"I'll never hurt you." My voice is surprisingly calm despite my tears and nerves. "I'm going to get you out of here."

Venatrix ceases growling, and I pull the amulet free, holding it up to the moonlight and causing the dragons to shriek in unison. I drop to my knees from the sheer magnitude of the volume. They fight and struggle against their chains, scratching their claws on the ground to get closer. The amulet begins burning my palm, and in my soul I know it's not meant for me, just as it wasn't meant for Cayden when it burned him.

I toss it into the space between the five of them, and together, they breathe fire, illuminating the chamber and causing my already tearful eyes to water further. I can't believe this is real. It feels as if I'll wake up at any moment and be miles away again. I'm mesmerized by the way their flames dance together, and even more so by their wings that I'm now able to see.

The last time we were together, they were tiny enough to perch on my shoulders, and now they're magnificent beasts larger than I ever imagined. I've missed so much . . . it's time I'll never get back. Memories that will never be made. I shove my sadness aside as best as I can and focus on the task at hand.

Sparks drift up from the flames and band together, forming red sparkling streaks that wrap around their chains. The more fire they blow, the stronger the streaks become. I choke on the smoke flooding through the room, and just when I think I can't take it anymore, the shackles snap and clatter on the ground. They toss their heads back, roaring in their own ways. The sound is heartbreaking and breathtaking.

They deserve so much better from this world, and I'm going to make sure they get it.

I find my footing, but the dragons whirl on me in an instant. I stand my ground, unsure of what to do next. They keep their wings tucked close as they circle me, their black, scaled bodies blending effortlessly. Panic rises in me. There's a new set of eyes everywhere I turn. A crack echoes through the chamber as a brutal hit rattles my ribs. I double over, falling to my knees as a tail slithers away.

I get over the initial shock and rise.

If this is what they need, I'll take it.

Another tail hits the other side of my ribs, but I grit my teeth and stand my ground. If they wanted to kill me, I'd be dead within seconds.

"I tried to come back for you."

A tail connects with my left thigh and is accompanied by a shriek that makes my ears ring.

"I never wanted to leave you."

The smoke from the fire makes my throat feel raw and scratchy, but I don't move. I deserve their anger, their pain, and the hits they've dealt me. For so long, I hated myself for being unable to get back to them. Kingdoms, armies, and assassins stood between us, and I tried to face the world alone, to take it all on for them, but I failed so many times. Every plan I concocted had too many flaws from my lack of knowledge.

The visions fooled me, or perhaps I was naïve to believe they might hold the same love for me as I do for them.

Another tail collides with the right side of my ribs, and I crumple again. I stay down for a few moments and settle on kneeling.

"I'm so sorry," I whisper, my voice breaking on the last word. "But you can't hate me more than I hate myself."

My body throbs and every breath I inhale feels like someone is stabbing me. My head is dizzy from the smoke and pain, and I have the overwhelming urge to lie down. I long to reach out to them, but their hitting has ceased, and I don't want to spark their anger again.

Their heads inch closer, hovering above me, and their scales briefly flash to vibrant colors before reverting to black again. It happens a few more times as they look at me, almost like they don't believe I'm real. Sorin nudges my boot with his nose and sniffs up my leg.

There's a sharp bang behind me, and I get to my feet as Calithea lets out another deafening roar. I reach up to cover my ears, but Delmira notices my quick movement and swipes her tail under me. The back of my head slams into the stone floor, and the spots in my vision worsen as I sit up again.

"ELOWEN!" Cayden shouts my name as if he's cursing every inch that separates us. My senses are dulled, but I turn my head in time to see him barreling toward me, throwing his body over mine as an arrow whizzes over him, so close that it brushes a few strands of his hair. He softens my fall by placing his hand behind my head, and a blazing fire flows over us like a river. I try to shove Cayden off me, urging him to stay against the wall and away from the dragons, but he shoves my face into his neck and tightens his hold.

"I told you it's you and me, angel," he says. I try to speak through my scratchy throat, but all I manage to do is cough. My body is weak from the lack of oxygen, and the more I fight, the tighter he presses me into him. "I suppose they realized the meeting was a setup." His sharp jaw is clenched, and he looks toward the door with nothing short of a cold, unyielding promise of death as blood trickles from a cut under his eye and flames continue flowing.

The guards keep pushing forward, running into the chamber despite all logic. They act as Garrick's obedient dogs, willingly running into the fire. Orders are shouted beyond the door, and soon the castle will be surrounded. Cayden briefly climbs off me and pulls something from his pocket and covers me again as a loud boom shakes the chamber and stones fly around us. The wall of windows shatters into smithereens. Once it's over, he gets to his feet, grabs my hands, and pulls me up.

"We'll have to run into the Seren Mountains and trek through Etril Forest," Cayden says.

"That's better than getting captured."

No Imirath soldiers are stationed in the mountains, considering it's practically a death wish to live there, especially in these months. My stomach swarms with butterflies as we drop to the ground and the dragons take to the skies.

We land in a snow pile and take off into the forest as wind whips down from the icy peaks. "Have you been carrying a bomb this entire time?"

Cayden smiles. "I don't recommend going on a mission without one on hand."

My steps falter when a booming roar echoes behind us, and flames shoot toward the tower the dragons escaped from. Another two sink their talons into the already gaping hole and rip it further apart. I feel a pull in my chest that travels its way up to my mind, but I don't have time to analyze it before the ground begins rumbling. We whip forward and resume sprinting. The more I run, the stronger the pull grows.

I see a pair of green eyes when I blink.

I shut them again.

Green eyes.

Again.

Green eyes.

The rumbling grows, and I know the guards are gaining on us. An arrow slices through the air and jams into the tree trunk next to my head.

"*Fire.*" A smoky whisper forms when I force my mind to tug on the bond.

"*Fire.*" The thought gets louder.

"That's the princess! Don't let her get away!" someone shouts behind us. Cayden and I cut through a narrow set of trees while another set of arrows is shot our way. They bounce off thick trunks, skimming my bruised leg and the top of Cayden's shoulder.

"Keep going," I tell Cayden, but I slow my steps, turning to face the army as they charge.

The bond lives within me. My link to them is strong enough to withstand magic, time, exile, and torture. I can do the bond ceremony, but I don't need it to forge what the dragons and I share.

"Elowen, I will throw you over my damn shoulder," Cayden growls.

"Trust me."

Cayden curses, shoving me behind him as he draws his sword, prepared to take on a cavalry charge for me. The bond is beating in my chest like a war drum. The lost dragon princess has returned, and I want them all to see exactly who I am.

"Sorin!" I shout, stepping in front of Cayden. "Burn them all."

He's there in an instant, decimating the battalion in mere seconds. The scent of burning flesh wafts through the forest, and soldiers cloaked in flames run screaming in all directions until they collapse. Sorin lands within the fire, roaring mere inches from my face as he steps out and approaches me. My hair is blown back as I stare into his mouth lined with fangs, but I don't step back. To the world, perhaps they'll always be monsters, but I see his soul shining through his eyes.

His emerald scales are on full display now that he's in his element, and he quietly regards me. Not as he did in the chamber; there's no malice in his eyes now.

He's ethereal.

He's hot from the flames, but I extend my hand, bowing my head as I wait for him to make the next move. A whimper rumbles deep in his throat as he presses his snout to my palm, and the sound of contentment that follows is like music to my ears.

I look up into his eyes. The color I searched for in every forest. "I've missed you, my sweet boy."

He leans closer, pressing his forehead to mine, flapping his wings and stomping his feet. The bond is no longer pulling me anywhere; it's content. It feels like lying in the grass after a battle, soaking in the sun and peace. I laugh at how playful Sorin quickly became, but I know he wishes to spread his wings.

"Fly all night, sweetling." I step back to soak him in again. "Find me in the morning."

He screeches once more, nudging my bruised leg softly as I drag my hand down his scales before he takes off into the night, joined by four other vibrantly colored dragons dancing in the stars. With the flames at my back, I turn to find Cayden staring at me with parted lips . . . looking at me as if he's seen a goddess.

CHAPTER

FORTY-TWO

THE ONLY THING PROPELLING MY BRUISED, ACHING BODY through the icy forest is determination. I'll need at least two pots of tea to stop the icy, burning sensation in my throat, and a scalding bath to bring back the feeling in my toes. At this altitude, we're able to reach the Emer much quicker than we did on our journey into Imirath, but that does little to comfort me when haunting, beastly howls penetrate the otherwise silent forest.

We pause, and I bring my hands to my mouth to attempt to warm them. "I can try to summon the dragons again."

"It's best if we don't reveal our position. If they sent beasts after us, it means they lost the trail." Cayden steps closer to rub my arms, offering me some warmth from the friction. The beasts will be able to track our blood leaking from injuries. "We'll have to cross the Emer, but the bridges up here are in no condition to bear weight."

It could be a death sentence, especially once we enter the Etril. But we have no other option, and we always knew the journey back to Vareveth would come with limited options. Our lives have been built through hard decisions, never having the option of comfort or coddling. "I'd rather die fighting than waiting for the choice to be made for me," I say.

We begin running again, increasing our pace when the howls get louder. My bruises and severe temperatures are an agonizing combination, but at least I know my ribs aren't broken. The trees start to clear as a wide river looms before us, separating us and the eerie Etril. My breath flies away from me like a startled bird when the icy spray dots my cheeks.

"Don't let go," Cayden commands, taking his first step into the river and cursing through gritted teeth. I do the same and choke on a whimper.

He hops down the steep dropoff and the water rises to his chest, meaning it'll reach my shoulders if not higher. His shaking hands wrap around my waist, but rather than helping me down, he sets me on his right shoulder and begins trudging through the frigid water.

"Hold on." He tightens his arm around my legs. "That's an order, princess."

I do as he says, grasping the hilt of the sword strapped across his back, and finally admit to myself that there's a chip carved in the shape of his name within the walls I've built around myself. Something about him makes me feel alive, and like I've found the place I've been searching for without prematurely knowing my destination.

A reflection of a white, furry beast in the water catches my eye, and I turn my head to watch it sniff along the trees where we just were. It's as tall as a horse and far deadlier judging by the fangs hanging out of its mouth that drip venom and the unnerving milky-white pupils that make it look possessed.

"Cayden, put me down," I whisper, but either he can't hear me over the river, or he refuses. "We need to hide from a beast."

The beast will see us if we exit the river, and this entire trek will have been for nothing. I won't let him die for the sake of protecting me from the cold, and jam my foot into his chest. The sudden pain throws him off kilter and the icy water surrounds me. I choke beneath the surface, swallowing a mouthful as I try to wake my frozen reflexes. The water pierces my body with thousands of little needles, slicing every inch and driving me to madness.

"Fucking gods, woman. Are you suicidal?" he seethes, wrapping my body around his and shoving my face into his neck.

"H-h-hide."

He changes our position, offering the current his back and finding shelter behind a cluster of rocks. Our bodies tremble together, his more so now that we're immobile and both soaked.

"I was going to get you across to give you a lead." Even through his anger, there's tenderness and desperation. "Your head is wounded. The cold will amplify any dizziness you have."

"A lead?" My voice trembles. "To where?"

"Give me those pretty eyes, El." He runs a hand down my back and doesn't speak again until he's sure I understand him. "There's a village north of here. Keep running and don't look back."

I shake my head, tightening my hold around his neck. "Don't ask me to do something you wouldn't."

"I'll find you, always." His icy hand cups my cheek. "You have to keep going. Never let the flames that make you who you are burn out. You have your dragons, but all of this is empty for me without you."

I've told myself that he was a distraction for so many months, but distractions aren't supposed to keep me awake at night, wondering if he's okay. I'm not supposed to want to get lost in a distraction.

"I'm fighting with you or I'm fleeing with you, but I'm not leaving you." I press my forehead against his. "Throw a knife as far as you can to distract the beast, and we'll get to that village together."

I unwrap myself from him and find my footing on the rocky riverbed as the water rises above my shoulders. He removes a knife from his thigh, glaring at me in disbelief, like he both hates and adores the fact that I refuse to abandon him. He doesn't speak again and throws the knife, knowing that any further argument will prolong our time in the water. He laces his fingers through mine, and we wade out of the river as quickly as possible. My leg, head, and ribs throb, but I don't let it stop me from taking off into the Etril Forest.

"How far is the village?" I ask through chattering teeth, doing my best not to keel over.

"About five miles."

I don't stop to ask him how he knows of this mysterious village and prioritize getting there. If it were mapped, Ailliard would've taken me there when we fled Imirath. I rely on Cayden to lead me through the forest, especially when trees start blurring. It's no wonder why hardly anyone settles here or why it's rumored to be where the Goddess of Souls lived. The trees are in nearly perfect rows, and there are no signs of life, just the bitter wind whistling through the tallest trees I've ever seen.

A wave of dizziness hits me, and I stop to catch my balance by resting my hand on a trunk, not noticing the low-hanging branch that scrapes my wounded leg until it's too late. I close my eyes, doing my best to fend off the wobbly world.

"What's wrong, love?" Cayden murmurs, dropping to his knees before me, his fingers gently checking on my cut.

"Just a bit dizzy like we expected." I force my eyes open, letting out a surprised yelp when he scoops me into his arms and begins running again. "I can run. I'm better now."

"Body heat will help until we can get you into a bath," he replies. I snuggle closer, knowing I'd lose this battle just as he lost the battle in the river, and let him carry me the rest of the way through the forest.

We return to silence as he runs, and his heartbeat lulls me to a half-asleep state that I only resurface from when I hear a horse chuffing as we cross into the village. It's dilapidated and run-down. Warm light streams from small houses made of stone with thatched roofs, and other homes look as if they're uninhabitable. Snow dusts the village like powdered sugar on cakes, falling down from the sky where dragon silhouettes blend into the darkness. Cayden travels up the vacant dirt road, hard eyes fixated on the inn.

"How do you know about this place?"

"It's where I was born." His discomfort is visible and goes deeper than the cold. He hesitates but sets me down before we enter, and my knees weaken at the sudden blast of warmth. Tables and barstools are filled with people sipping from tankards and smoking pipes. Cayden catches the eye of the man behind the counter who tosses a towel over his burly shoulder and nods in our direction. "Go stand by the fire. I won't be long."

I step to the hearth and raise my shaking hands in front of me, trying not to crumple to get as close to the flames as possible. Heat trickles into my soaked boots and returns some feeling to my toes.

"I can keep you warm, darling," chimes a male voice from one of the tables. His friends slap him on the back and stare at him as if he hung the stars in the sky.

My lip curls. This is the second to last thing I want to deal with right now, the first being Imirath soldiers. "I don't think I could get past your stench."

"I do like them feisty." He gets to his feet while his friends watch in anticipation. I narrow my eyes and square my shoulders, ready to pelt him with another insult, but a pair of hands snake around my waist.

"As do I," Cayden states, staring the man down over my head. "Was he bothering you?"

"It was all in good fun." The man begins to back down.

"Is she laughing?" Cayden asks. "Make another pass at her again, and the last thing you'll see is a knife flying straight between your eyes. You should know I adore her violent streak and don't mind cleaning up her messes."

Cayden doesn't wait for a response before tugging my body away from the fire, up some steps, and into our room. It's simple and charming without much fuss or flair and only one bed that I force my eyes away from. The sound of splashing water comes from the bathing chamber as a servant prepares the bath Cayden must've ordered, and I stride toward the freshly lit fire. I begin undoing the clasps and ties on my leathers and nearly moan when the pressure is relieved from my bruises. Cayden does the same, taking it a step further, and removes his undershirt.

Gods, how the hells am I going to sleep beside him when he looks like that, and we don't have a change of clothes. My mind wonders what it will feel like to have his muscular frame pressed against me as I untie my boots, but the fluttering in my belly is soon replaced by irritation when the servant exits the washroom and gazes at Cayden with hearts in her eyes. I get to my feet and angle my body in front of his, and he doesn't hide his smile as he caresses my hips.

She tears her eyes away and shuffles to the door, muttering, "I'm off for the night and nobody else is here to heat more water. The pitcher on the counter is filled for morning washings."

"You're first, demon," I say.

"Not a chance. I'll throw you in the tub if I must, and I won't be gentle."

"I don't want you to be." My breathing catches in my throat when I notice how he pauses while undoing the laces on his boots. "I'll get in if you get in with me."

He looks up at me, and I wonder if he's recalling the other occasions he's knelt for me. "You're sure?"

I'm burning for him despite the cold. "Yes."

CHAPTER
FORTY-THREE

STEAM HAS NEVER LOOKED SO ENDEARING, AND I QUICKLY submerge myself in the tub before moving forward for Cayden to slip in behind me. The water rises to the brim with his added presence but looking behind me is daunting, so I focus on removing the pins and pearls Saskia wove into my hair.

"May I offer you my assistance?" he asks when he notes my struggle.

I sigh. "Saskia was quite thorough."

He begins gently removing pearls, running his fingers through my strands to undo several knots. "I love your hair." He sounds ... shy. "It doesn't matter how you wear it."

I adopt some of his timidity. "Do you have a favorite style I've done?"

He slides a finger down my spine, earning a shiver from me. "When you braid the top half, weave flowers into it, and leave a few curls to frame your face. You're always beautiful but ..." He trails off, laughing softly, and I can picture his dimples deepening as he shakes his head. "May I wash it for you?"

I nod, not trusting my voice. His fingers begin massaging my scalp before coating my hair in a light, clean scented soap. He takes care, ridding it of knots without pulling too hard, and it's strange knowing that these are the same hands he's split open multiple times on my behalf. My arms loosen around me the more I relax, reveling in being cared for like I never have. But his fingers stop, and his legs stiffen on either side of me. Without looking down, I slide my hand across my torso, sucking in a sharp breath when I press a bruise.

Cayden wraps a soapy hand around my wrist. "What happened?"

The warmth I felt with Sorin flees me, and all I'm left with is shame. Cayden tilts my head back and gently rinses my hair while I find my words. "The dragons weren't happy when they saw me. They regarded me as if I were an illusion and tried to prove I was real, but—" I clear my constricted throat and fidget with my pendant. "May I wash your hair now?"

"You don't have to," he replies. "But you can if you wish."

I look over my shoulder while kneeling between his legs, forgetting how to breathe for a moment. I've seen his chest many times, but I doubt I'll ever become accustomed to his beauty. The pink, white, and red scars that stand out against his olive skin, and the stars on his ribs that stretch above the surface. He runs his hands over my sides once I'm settled, and stares at me as if there's no other person he wants in front of him . . . like no other person exists aside from me.

His chest rises and falls unevenly as he takes me in, tongue slowly dragging across his lips as his eyes linger on my chest. "Beautiful," he murmurs, more to himself than me. "You are the embodiment of beauty."

He rises off the edge of the tub so I can wash his hair without spilling water on the floor. His hard length pokes me in the stomach, and I bite my lip to stop a moan from slipping out, but he cradles the side of my face, gently using his thumb to ease my lip from between my teeth. His breath warms my lips while his hand on my thigh warms everything I'm made of. I place a hand on his chest and drag some water over the cut on his bicep and under his eye.

"Talk to me, love." The tenderness in his tone heightens my reaction to him.

"The dragons calmed down once they realized I wasn't an illusion," I begin, tilting his chin up to run some water over his hair. I could spend hours playing with the soft, wavy strands. His eyes slide shut, and I wonder if anyone else has taken care of him, selfishly hoping I'm the first. "But their method of verification was hitting me with their tails."

His eyes shoot open, all traces of peace lost as he scrutinizes the dark purple spots.

"Please, don't judge them for this. They've been in so much agony. This is a small price to pay." Tears leak from my eyes, and I quickly wipe them away. "I know you'll disagree, so you don't have to say anything, but I deserve this pain."

"No, El. *No.*" He sighs, leaning forward to press his head to my stomach, still stroking his hands along my sides. The bruise on my right stretches from my breast to my belly button, and the left is about half the size. He gently pulls me down, settling me between his legs again, and leans forward to kiss my tears. "You don't deserve this pain."

"Gods." I force a laugh. "I'm sorry for getting like this again."

"Listen to me." He pulls back and frames my face. "Enduring pain doesn't mean you deserve it."

"Sometimes I just feel so guilty . . ." I lick my salty lips. "For surviving."

"I understand." He reaches beneath the water to grab my hand, placing it on his scarred cheek. "But they're free, and no longer just surviving. They're reclaiming the skies."

I smile, turning to the foggy window, feeling lighter with the knowledge that my dragons are flying somewhere close. "Exactly how long did you search for me?"

"I've looked for you anywhere I ended up in the world for as long as I can remember." He runs a hand through his wet hair before gliding it down my arm. "I saw you once when I was a boy, at the last summer solstice festival you attended before the imprisonment."

My jaw drops. "We met when we were children?"

"Gods, no. I was nothing more than a commoner. I broke my wrist falling off a roof trying to get a better look at you. You were there in your purple gown with dragons perched on your arms, feeding them honeybuns, in your own world with them, and I wanted to be part of it." He laughs, and the sound of his happiness warms the dark parts of me in rays of golden light. "I even forced my mother to teach me the recipe for the blueberry cake she made on my birthday so I could bribe you to be my friend."

I lean closer, trailing my hands through his wet waves as I imagine a younger version of him standing on a stool with flour on his cheeks and blueberries on his fingers. "Well, I probably would've liked you much more if you brought a cake to the forest instead of tying me to a tree."

"No, you wouldn't. I nearly burned our house down trying to make it." He rests his hand on my hip again. "Angel, you are the sickness of my thoughts and I have no intention of finding the cure."

"But everyone thought I was a ghost," I state in disbelief.

"I never said you were easy to find." His knuckle caresses my cheek. "You've been a light through my darkest times. Granted, as I got older your power was a big incentive, and I had no intention of falling for you, but now I know you, and you're . . . everything. Sometimes I look at you and I think I'm dreaming but I know that's impossible because you're more than I ever imagined."

His words make my heart throb, and I wish I knew how to describe this feeling, but I've never experienced this. He takes me to a place that no one else can, and I love who I am when I'm there. I press my lips to the top of his scar and slowly work my way down, savoring the feel of his skin on my lips. His heart beats rapidly beneath my palms, and he laces his fingers through my hair, keeping me close when I finish. "You're a good man, Cayden Veles. Far better than most, even if you don't believe it."

"Don't say that," he whispers.

"Why?"

His eyes are laced with longing, but his next words cause my nerves to rise like the tide. "I followed you to Aestilian."

"*No.* You didn't. I didn't hear you. I would've . . ." I sit up, covering my chest with my hair. "I would've heard you tracking me. I don't understand."

"I was the highest-paid assassin in Vareveth for my ability to move silently." His voice is even, gentle. "I didn't reveal the location to a soul, and nobody knows I was there."

Nothing but the droplets falling from my hair fill the silence, and once I note the lack of remorse, I say, "You don't regret it."

"I can't," he confesses. "I lost you after that festival, and I refused to make the same mistake again. You have always been the only person I believed was worth taking a chance on. If you slipped into the shadows after I finally found you again, *that* would've been my greatest regret."

All this time, I thought nobody cared when I disappeared. Even the assassins were infrequent and stopped several years ago. I believed my existence to be as insignificant as a single snowflake falling to the earth, never to be thought of once it melts. But throughout Cayden's whole life, no matter what changed, I've remained in his mind.

"If nobody knows you followed me, why did you tell me?" The words come out as a hoarse whisper.

"You've ruined me in this life, the next, and any that follow." Those full lips curl into an almost-smile, and his jaw clenches anxiously as his emerald gaze watches me intently. "I'm irrevocably lost in you, and it's the only place I want to be. I'll hurt anyone for you, including myself." He leans forward to kiss my cheek and grips the side of the tub when he pulls back. "I know this is a lot, and you must be overwhelmed. I'll give you some time."

I wrap my hand around his wrist before he has the chance to leave. "I don't want time." We've suffered enough. I'd take him to Aestilian tomorrow if we had time. I would've done the same thing if I were in his position, and he would sooner deny himself happiness than keep this information from me. "I want you, the man who faced the impossible and never gave up on me."

I grab his shoulders and cover his lips with mine. He remains frozen but melts once I slide my fingers through his hair and frame his hips with my legs. He kisses me slowly, and I feel it in every inch of my body. He lights every nerve on fire and renders me mindless. My core aches for him as I squirm in his lap, desperate for friction, and grind my hips onto his.

Perhaps we've always been inevitable.

The kiss becomes more urgent. Sensing my need without breaking the kiss, he rises from the tub with my legs wrapped around his waist. I tighten my arms and press myself into his chest, reveling in how it feels to have him pressed against me with no barriers. He lays me on the bed and removes his lips from mine to trail them down my neck, pausing on the sensitive spots he knows I love. I arch my back and lock my ankles around his torso to draw him closer, but he doesn't move.

"Need to taste you again." He flips us over and settles beneath me. "Take your throne, princess." I try to move back to ride him, but he halts me with a hand on my hips. "Sit on my face."

"Y-your face?" I stutter. "Will you be able to breathe?"

"Breathing isn't my top priority at the moment." He yanks me up his body, tightens his grip on my waist, and brings me to his mouth. I suppress a scream of relief, but he pulls my hand away and pins it at my side. "I didn't say hover," he growls. "I said *sit*."

My thighs spread around his head, and he groans his approval, stroking me reverently. His eyes roll back in his head at the taste of me, and I grip the headboard to keep myself upright. I writhe on him, unable to keep my cries of pleasure quiet as he gives me exactly what I need and more. My thighs shake aggressively, and he rocks my hips back and forth, amplifying my pleasure further.

"That's it, gorgeous," he groans when I begin moving my hips as he directed. He palms my breasts and my head falls back as I moan his name. I want to surrender myself to him and never forsake this pleasure. "I'm not fucking you until you come on my tongue."

He quickens his pace, sensing I'm close. He wraps his lips around my clit, sucks, and the scream I let out has me worried someone will check on us. Instead of relenting, he continues torturing me until I let go of any restraint, grinding on his face and chasing the high only he has ever given me. I fall apart, calling out his name as he sends me into oblivion and only flips us over when he's sure I've finished.

His dark chuckle dances across my skin as he kisses up my thighs, the bruises on my torso, my neck, and *finally* my lips. There's no trace of cockiness in his gaze when he pulls back, just pure desire and tenderness. I raise a shaky hand to his cheek, and he leans into it, tilting his head to kiss my palm.

"Is this still okay, beautiful?"

I lean up to kiss him, whispering, "Yes."

He settles his hips between my legs and presses his forehead to mine. "I've never been a religious man, but I will worship you in ways the gods will envy."

He teases my entrance, dragging his cock up and down as I dig my nails into his shoulders to pull him closer, tired of the torturous teasing. I suck in a sharp breath when he begins entering me, needing time to adjust to his size. He groans and fists the sheets beside my head, pressing his lips to mine when I whimper.

"Don't stop," I plead against him.

He slowly rocks his hips into mine. "We'll make it fit. I've got you, angel, just relax."

The pain slowly melts to pleasure, and I'm soon a moaning mess beneath him. He grinds deeper the wetter he makes me, muttering curses and praises as he pulls out to brush his cock against my clit before sliding in again. I begin moving my hips against his, wanting to give him as much pleasure as he's giving me. His thrusts become harder, faster, and I wrap my legs around his waist to fit him deeper.

"Harder," I moan, knowing he's still holding back, scared to hurt me.

But he complies, and I swear I see stars falling from the ceiling. "You want me to fuck you like this, beautiful?" He rises to his knees, lifting my hips and drilling into me. "I want an answer when I ask a question, El. Now tell me—am I fulfilling those fantasies you have at night when I hear you moaning my name into your pillow?"

I gasp, but I'm too lost in pleasure to feel an ounce of embarrassment. "You heard that?"

"Stroked my cock to it." He smirks. "Did you imagine taking all of me like the greedy queen you are?"

"Yes," I moan, letting my pleasure heighten with the image of him fisting himself to me. "I hated you for making me crave you."

"Such a dirty princess." He abruptly pulls out and flips me onto my stomach. "I should've lifted your hips and gave you what you were begging for."

I can't count how many nights my desire for him kept me awake, tossing and turning until I took care of the throbbing between my thighs. The urge to cross the suite and climb into his bed was overwhelming, and I don't think I'll ever be able to stop myself now that I know he's better than anything I imagined.

I arch my back for him, rest my cheek against the mattress, and spread my legs wide with my hips in the air. He strokes his cock a few times, soaking me in with his heated gaze. "So good to me, love." I don't let the mattress muffle my moans when he enters me again, and the headboard bangs into the wall from his sharp thrusts. He palms my ass and reaches forward to thread his fingers through the roots of my hair to haul me back against his chest.

"Gods!" I cry out as he reaches between my thighs and rubs me.

"The gods aren't in the bedroom. I am. You scream my name or nothing. No god or man will ever fuck you like I can." His tone is unhinged, ravenous, and he moans deeply when I tighten around him. I press my hand into his cheek and bring his lips to mine.

"You're the only one I want," I confess. He drops his head, teeth and tongue skimming my neck before he flips me over again to yank me up by my thighs, sits back on his knees, and thrusts up, keeping me in his lap as he moves my body on his shaft. White spots dance in my vision from the added friction.

"You have me," he pants, driving deeper. His mouth finds my sweet spot again as I tighten around him and my pleasure peaks. I drag my nails down his back, and it sends him over the edge. Our lips collide but it's hardly a kiss. He sits back on his ankles and presses his sweaty forehead to my shoulder. "Fuck," he murmurs.

I laugh. "Fuck, indeed."

He sets me down on the bed, searching my eyes to make sure I'm all right as he pulls out. A lazy smile spreads across my lips before I kiss him again, humming as he relaxes in my hold.

"Get under the covers while I hang your clothes in front of the fire," he says before turning away. I make a noise of protest and try to hold him to me, but he softly chuckles and reaches around to remove my hands from his neck, kissing both my palms.

My eyelids are heavy by the time he joins me and props his head on his hand. "I'm never letting you out of my sight."

"You're not supposed to say that like a warning," I sigh as he leans down to kiss my neck.

"It feels like a threat." The confusion on his face makes me laugh. "I don't understand this feeling."

"Calm down, demon. It's new for me, too."

"It's sickening, but I don't want it to stop," he mutters as he lies beside me, dragging me onto his chest and wrapping his arms around me like he's worried someone will steal me from him while he sleeps.

I press my lips to the scars and stars that litter his skin as he plays with my hair. It's strange to feel so wholly content, and it's hard to believe I'm not dreaming. I sit up, kissing the scar on his cheek again, my eyes flashing between it and his eyes. "Will you tell me more about how you got this?"

His hands twitch before resuming their movements. "What would you like to know?"

I press my lips together but don't drop his gaze. "Was Garrick responsible?" He keeps weaving his fingers through my hair but doesn't respond. Rain patters against the shutters, and the log crackles in the fire, but the silence encroaches me with guilt. "I shouldn't have asked."

"It's all right," he says gently. "You're asking me questions I've never answered, so it's just taking me a moment to find the right words."

He sighs deeply, running his hands along my back. "My parents were in hiding, but my mother went into Imirath on occasion to see her friends. Sometimes she'd take me with her." He clears his throat, and I continue trailing my fingers on his chest. "A guard must've recognized her while she was chasing me through the market, because Imirath soldiers came to our house that night."

He climbs out of bed and wraps a blanket around his waist before reaching for my hand and leading me toward a window. I throw a blanket around my shoulders and lean into him as his arms circle my waist.

"I use the term *house* lightly, but it was a home when my father wasn't there." He points to what looks like the remnants of a shack by the tree line. "They carved my cheek open after I killed a soldier . . . told me to use it as a reminder to know when to stop fighting." I spin in his arms and rest my hand on his cheek. He flinches before relaxing into my palm. I recall our conversation after infiltrating Kallistar . . . he was only eleven. "I apologize for the lack of eloquence, it's just that being back here is . . . I've never spoken about that day."

"We have time, Cayden," I say, and he leans down to kiss my head. "Were you able to give her a funeral?"

"No, I—" He shakes his head. "I'm sure the villagers built her a pyre, but I wasn't here to see it."

"Would you like one?" I ask, forcing myself to not question where he went after that tragic day. His confusion fades as his eyes flick to the tree line again, and he nods.

"Are you sure you don't want to look around first? I'll go with you."

"There's nothing left for me here. The Imirath soldiers torched it, but clearly it wasn't entirely successful, and looters would have taken anything that remained."

I turn toward the window, watching my eyes glow gold in the reflection while calling upon Venatrix. I'm not able to see her through the storm and the darkness, but her fire is there in seconds, burning what's left of Cayden's childhood home while he holds me. We remain silent, and I trail my fingers over his forearms, resting my cheek against his bicep until he spins me around, framing my face with his hands.

"We're both burdened by our pasts, my scars just aren't as visible," I murmur. "And I'm so thankful you survived."

"Every part of you, every scar, both visible and invisible, is utterly beautiful to me."

"I can plant something there for her in the spring if you'd like to come back," I offer.

"Grow a garden at my home instead," he says. "She wouldn't want to be remembered in a place like this, and flowers make you happy. Staying away from you has proven to be quite difficult to me, and I have no intention of going to bed without you."

My cheeks redden. "I'll have to get some tools."

"Done." He brushes his lips over mine. "I'll find a way to gift you the stars if you wish for them. You can have anything you want, love."

He kisses me, and the only thing I can focus on is twining our bodies together again. It's slow and heady and tender. He caresses my thighs and whispers sweet nothings against my skin. I've never felt quite so cherished, and I find myself silently praying that the moon is kind and grants us a few extra moments before dawn.

CHAPTER
FORTY-FOUR

A GUST OF WIND RATTLES THE SHUTTERS, STIRRING ME from sleep. I reach out, expecting Cayden to be there, but I'm met with nothing but a cold and empty space. I glance toward the fireplace, where a crackling fresh log pours heat into the room, but his clothes are gone.

"Cayden?" I call out, hating how vulnerable I feel when I don't get a reply, and sip some water to aid my raw throat. Footsteps bound up the steps, and I ignore the pain in my ribs as I grab a knife off the bedside table. The door creaks open, and Cayden quirks a brow as he takes in my crazed state.

"Was the sex that bad?" He kicks the door shut and sets the breakfast tray on the table, throws two cloaks over a chair, and sets a burlap sack on the ground. Clearly, he's been busy . . .

"Terrible. Absolutely horrendous."

"Is that so?" He licks his lips while cradling my face. His proximity eases my nerves and ignites something wanton in me.

I reach out to grab his belt loop, pulling him closer. "Yes."

He tilts my chin higher and lowers his lips to mine. I press my thighs together as his tongue dips into my mouth, stroking and teasing me. Butterflies erupt low in my belly, and I sink into his hold just as he pulls his mouth from mine and smiles down at me in accomplishment.

"Always a demon." I glare at him. "What's in the bag?"

"Apples, angel." He grins, hoisting me in his arms and placing me on his lap, waving a cup of coffee with a dash of sweet syrup in front of my face. "We have plans after breakfast."

✢ ✢ ✢

We exit the inn after Cayden settles the bill, and he gestures to a pair of horses tied off by the entrance.

"By the gods, is Cayden Veles, esteemed Commander of Vareveth, stealing horses?" I swing myself into a saddle and grasp the reins. "One night with me and you're already corrupting your pristine morals."

He glances over his shoulder and winks. "My soul is only yours to corrupt, love."

He leads us toward the tree line behind the inn, not glancing back at the remains of his childhood home as we leave the village. I hope he found a sense of closure in the flames. Living with loss is akin to having a poorly stitched wound that never goes away and bleeds when you least expect it. Lush evergreens stand tall in the forest as we leave the Etril behind, and I veer left with Cayden, utterly astonished by the view.

White, rocky mountains span before me, making me feel like a tiny speck in the world in comparison to their grandness. The snow-covered cliff Cayden brought me to comes to a peak before a steep dropoff, overlooking the bluest lake I've ever seen. I inhale a deep breath, firmly believing that simply being in nature can feed the soul.

"Call upon the dragons," Cayden says, dropping the bag of apples at my feet. "You mentioned that one of your books said they like fruit, so I nabbed this in the stable."

"No honeybuns?"

"Not this time, love."

Giddiness parades through me and I squeal as I jump into his unexpecting arms. He stumbles back before recovering, wrapping me up, and chuckling. "Thank you," I say, kissing his cheek.

I kneel in the snow, but I don't do anything before a shadow rises in front of the cliff like steam from a kettle. Calithea's silver gaze is on me while she perches on the edge and nudges the bag of apples with her snout, stomping her feet in excitement and sending snow tumbling below. Staring up at her, I get a flash of how tiny she used to be and shove down the sadness stemming from all the years missed.

"Not yet, sweet girl." I hoist the bag in my arms, but her forked tongue springs out to steal a rogue apple from the ground. "Calithea!"

She swallows it whole before diving off the cliff, angling her white-tipped wings to spin in the air while calling to the others. They appear in an instant, their vibrant scales even more beautiful against the wintery backdrop. Venatrix's pink and gold markings along her back glitter in the sun like she was always meant to embrace it.

Delmira is the second to land in front of me, and I slide a hand down her sky-blue scales. Her markings are sunflower-colored swirls on her chest and down her ankles. She circles me, launching herself above my head when I toss an apple in the air.

My heart slowly mends in their presence, and the bond strengthens in my chest like a blacksmith is welding us back together. Our souls are forged from the same flames; nothing can unweave me from them. It's one thing to dream of dragons, and another to watch them dance. Sorin is pure emerald with black-tipped wings and horns, twirling with Basilius, the only dragon without a single marking. He's entirely lavender.

I throw an apple as far as possible, watching them zip through the air, hot on Venatrix's tail as she catches it. I clap my hands, cheering for her as she corkscrews higher than the others. Cayden chuckles behind me, sitting against a tree as he watches the show. Sorin catches the second apple and presses his forehead against Venatrix's, his emerald eyes coated in a cocky victory.

I make sure Delmira, Calithea, and Basilius get plenty while the pair continue waging a war filled with shoves and chuffs. Once they catch on to the fact that their pettiness is cutting into their treats, they call a ceasefire and swoop back into the game. We continue until the bag is empty, but they continue twirling and gliding, diving into the lake before springing into the air again with eels hanging from their mouths. Well . . . not Sorin, he yelps when Venatrix tosses one at his face and presses his forehead against mine while he pouts.

I didn't think it was possible for a dragon's face to reflect so many emotions.

I try my luck at climbing onto his back, but he shies away. A little needle prods at my heart when I catch the uncertainty in his gaze, but I offer him a reassuring smile and slide my hand down his neck. I'll fly when they're ready, but I'm happy to take a seat beside Cayden and rest my head on his shoulder while we watch them.

"If anyone could turn lethal, fire-breathing beasts into oversized dogs, it's you," he mutters.

"You adore it." I poke him in the side. "Taming beasts is my specialty."

He rolls his eyes, not missing my hidden meaning, and dryly states, "My adoration for you increases daily."

I flinch when Basilius kicks Calithea in the head, but she quickly recovers and smacks him with her tail. "Do you think the others are all right?" I ask quietly.

"I do." He squeezes my thigh reassuringly. "Imirath's focus will remain on us, and they're traveling in the opposite direction with travel papers. Finnian and Ryder are probably driving Saskia mad by now."

I laugh nervously. "I suppose you're right, but we should leave now to have ample daylight while we ride."

"As you wish, love."

We dust the snow from our pants and climb onto the horses again as the dragons fly overhead, always in my sight. I adore how clingy they're being. On the rare occasion the trees clear around us, a dragon will fly beside me, glancing at me from the corner of their eye. I'm eager to take them to a place that feels like home, wanting to cherish every moment with these sweet beasts.

CHAPTER
FORTY-FIVE

I'M SO EXHAUSTED I COULD FALL OFF MY HORSE. WE HAVEN'T stopped riding, wanting to get out of enemy territory and back to our friends as soon as possible. Granted, the dragons would kill anyone who threatens us, and they'd make resting much easier, but every time I close my eyes, I think of all the possible dangers Finnian, Saskia, and Ryder could've run into.

The silver lining has been learning more about the dragons, such as their love for burying their heads in snowbanks and secretly dipping into ponds to scare me by popping out. They also love it when I stand beneath them. Sometimes they'll bend down to rest their chin on my head and hide me from the world with their wings.

News of the heist will have reached Vareveth by now, and I haven't thought about what I'll say to Ailliard when I see him. I understand his reluctance toward them considering they killed my mother, even if it was self-defense. A cornered animal can't be blamed for snapping, especially when they were so young. Anyone who deals in magic knows that the consequences can be deadly, and my father should've realized that before he tried to break my bond.

The horses propel us forward, and my heart pounds in my chest as I note the sounds of the Vareveth camp: chattering soldiers and clattering steel. We cut through the mountains, so we were able to cross the border without having to concern ourselves with Imirath soldiers.

Tent peaks loom between the forest brush, and I urge my horse to quicken her pace.

The dragons dip down from the clouds in a perfect triangular formation led by Basilius, and their roars are the only things loud enough to overpower the cheering soldiers who sprint out of tents to get a look at them. We break into the crowd, slowing our horses so we don't trample anyone, and I immediately spy Saskia jumping and clapping with tears sliding down her face as she watches us.

Chants begin streaming down the border, all centering on Cayden, the dragons, and me. People tip their awe-filled eyes to the sky, unable to believe what they're seeing. Some have even fainted facedown in the dirt. Finnian exits a tent behind the crowd and makes a beeline toward me. The relief that overtakes me is enough to throw me from my horse.

Finnian's grin is contagious, and he scoops me into his arms, hoisting me in the air. His hollering is muffled by my chest, and I tilt my head back to cheer along with everyone else. As if they're trying to speak with me, the dragons join, and the laughter that spills out of me is pure happiness. Pain knocks against my ribs, but no amount of discomfort can overpower this moment.

I ruffle Finnian's curls as he sets me down, so immensely thankful that he's alive. He's a loss my soul can't bear. Saskia has her arms wrapped around Cayden's neck, and his lips are quirked in a way that leads me to believe he's saying something sarcastic. Which she confirms by smacking the back of his head as Ryder spills out of a tent, nearly falling on his face when Venatrix lands beside him.

Saskia rushes toward me with her arms outstretched, and I wrap myself around her once we meet in the middle. "I'm so happy to see you," I say.

"Gods, I missed you."

"I missed you, too, Sas."

She guides us to where Ryder has his arm wrapped around Cayden's shoulders with his fist in the air, cheering along to the dragon chant. The last knot of worry unties itself, and my knees almost buckle. All ten of us, we made it. I can't stop the onslaught of emotion when more tears pour from Saskia's eyes, and I lose myself in the bliss of this moment.

We enter the tent Finnian and Ryder came out of and throw ourselves around a dining table. It's clear they haven't slept either, but it appears they've been here long enough to wash up and change their clothes. "How did you know to come to the edge of the border?" I ask. I thought we wouldn't see them until we reached the section closer to the castle.

"We saw the dragons escape the castle when we were sailing down the canal. We knew you'd either be dead or forced to flee from the tower, and there was only one route you could've taken," Saskia says with a grim smile.

"But you'll be pleased to know that our generous King Eagor has planned a celebration dinner tomorrow evening," Ryder mutters.

Cayden groans and falls back against his chair, and I can't say I'm much happier than him. I'd prefer a night at the tavern, or a day of sleep. I slump in my chair but spring forward when my corset presses into a bruise.

"Do you want me to loosen the ties?" Cayden asks.

I nod, offering him my back and facing an all-too-invested Finnian, who drums his fingers against his lips. When the corset sits comfortably around me, Cayden pulls my chair closer to his and skims his hands along my sides.

"I called it!" Ryder exclaims, pointing a finger at Saskia.

"Reward is sweet," Finnian says, performing a dance in his seat that makes him look like he has to relieve himself. Saskia leans forward, resting her elbows on the table while she rubs her temples.

Cayden sighs. "You know, I'd like to take a tonic to forget the things you do."

"Did—" I wave my hands between the three of them, working my way to a conclusion. "Did you three have a bet about us sleeping together?"

"You can't be mad considering it happened," Finnian reasons.

"Everybody wins," Ryder adds.

"You and I get money." Finnian gestures between himself and Ryder. "You two had sex." He gestures between Cayden and me before turning to Saskia again. "Well, you lose money, but you can relish the fact you won't have to watch them eye-fuck each other from across the room anymore."

"How eloquently put, Finnian," Cayden dryly states.

I narrow my eyes. "Perhaps he should consider becoming a poet."

"I'm too sleep-deprived to deal with you all at once," Saskia mutters, but the mirth in her eyes betrays her words.

I slip from the table in need of a bath as Finnian and Cayden announce they'll bring back food for us. The steaming water caresses my sore muscles, and hunger is the only thing that motivates me to move. If I could eat in this tub, I'd never leave. I smile to myself when I spy my favorite soaps and oils on the tray and lather myself until my skin turns pink. Cayden mentioned he has tents stationed down the border, and I suppose each is stocked with things to bring me comfort given they're unopened. After the room he designed for me in his usual tent, I shouldn't be surprised.

I don the emerald sweater and black cotton pants that I've come to favor over the past few weeks that Saskia must've grabbed before coming here. Cayden's clothes are too comfortable to resist. I scrunch the remaining water from my hair and am carried back to the table by the savory scent of herb-encrusted meats, seasoned vegetables, and buttery potatoes.

Cayden piles a plate high, sets it in front of me when I take the seat beside him, and rests his arm along my chair, occasionally rubbing my back. I've learned he can't keep his hands off me for too long.

"What happened in the dragon chamber?" Ryder asks. "I'm assuming it went well considering five beasts are currently circling this tent."

"Well . . . yes and no. The bruises on my torso and leg are from the dragons," I reply after taking a sip of cider. "But Sorin burned some soldiers for me. He's the green one."

"She's being modest," Cayden cuts in. "She decimated a battalion in seconds." I smile fondly at the memory and send a loving stroke down the bond to Sorin.

Ryder whistles. "Remind me not to get on your bad side."

"Did they claw apart the castle once you got the chains off?" Finnian asks.

"Cayden blew it up," I answer.

Saskia groans. "You take far too much interest in explosives."

Cayden fists his pint, smirking. "I'm a firm believer in widening my skill set to be as lethal as possible."

A sea of laughter encompasses us, and I relax in the presence of friends. Each person in this tent has changed me in some way, welcomed me into their lives without question, and didn't merely open locked doors with me. They helped me decimate the doors and burn them to smithereens. We walked toward danger together and came back stronger.

I have my dragons and a place where I don't feel I need to dilute myself. Being around people who truly accept you feels like pure magic.

My eyelids grow heavy, and fatigue ends the day before I'm ready. We'll return to the castle tomorrow, but none of us are ready for the ride to Verendus. There are four additions to the main tent, one being a spare bedroom that Finnian now occupies, which leaves me with . . .

Cayden kisses my knuckles. "The room on the left, angel."

"Not so fast, sunshine." Ryder draws the attention of the room. "Thin." He points at me. "Walls." He points at Cayden.

"The next time you have a thought, let it ruminate in your head for ten seconds before speaking," Cayden says.

"Thin walls!" Ryder repeats.

"Jealousy isn't a good look on you, darling."

Ryder glares over his ale before shoving Cayden's shoulder. Gods, the two of them bicker like an old married couple. Yet all it takes is one look between them to know they'd do anything for each other.

Finnian stands from his chair and throws his arm around my

shoulders to lead me toward Cayden's room. "I get her while you bathe, Veles. She's my girl first."

I'm too tired to add anything so I laugh softly and lean farther into Finnian's body. I'll always be his girl. I dive onto the bed and cocoon myself in comfort as Finnian stretches out beside me above the blankets. We lie on our sides to face each other, and I can't count how many times we fell asleep like this when our nightmares woke us. We were two tortured children and the only shelter we had from the world was each other.

"You okay?" I whisper.

"Just soaking it in." A knot forms between his brows. "I was terrified I'd never see you again."

"I know the feeling." I lace my fingers through his, so utterly grateful he's unscathed. "And yet you weren't scared enough to resist gambling over my *activities*."

He smiles wide, laughing softly. "I'll buy you a treat with my earnings."

"I want another one of those raspberry pastries I had in Imirath."

"Fine."

"You very well could have lost money," I grumble.

"Oh, Ellie." He sighs like he's about to tell me the fairies that leave presents for us on the winter solstice are a myth. "That man can't keep his eyes off you and looks for you even when you're not in a room. But when he does find you . . . it's like he's always seeing you for the first time."

My heart flips in my chest. "You've become quite perceptive."

"I'm in charge of looking out for your best interests."

I laugh, snuggling deeper into the blankets. "Well, no one will ever be good enough for you, Finny. So when you find someone you're interested in, he better be man enough to withstand me. I'll make good on my inevitable threats if he hurts you."

"Likewise, and I'd expect nothing less from you." He leans over to kiss my forehead. "Good night, darling."

"I love you," I mumble before fully losing my battle with sleep.

I'm welcomed into the magic of the night as my dreams vividly perform behind my eyelids. My dragons are here, almost like they refuse to lose me to anything, even sleep, now that we're reunited. I soar with them and swirl around the clouds, hopping between their backs to fly on each. But a gentle pressure on my forehead wakes me before I can touch a star.

"Go back to sleep, angel. It's just me," Cayden whispers, placing another kiss to my forehead.

I dig my palms into my eyes and blink a few times to get my bearings. My sweater rests just below my breasts, and Cayden rubs white cotton bandages between his hands. He sits beside me with wet hair and pants hanging low on his hips, and it makes my toes curl beneath the covers. Even more so when he begins wrapping the bandages around my torso, his fingers skimming the underside of my breasts as he arches my back for me.

A sigh leaves my lips when the bandages heat up. "Gods, this is magical." My spine goes rigid in an instant. "Are these truly magical?"

He smirks at me as he ties them off and leans down to kiss above the waistband on my pants. I press my lips together to stifle a moan, and he hooks his fingers to slide them down my legs and toss them to the ground. He takes a second roll and bends my leg to wrap it around my thigh.

"This isn't fair. I want to know where all the magic is hidden." His smirk turns into a grin. "I'll stab you if you say something vulgar."

"Princess Elowen, your mind is far too depraved." He lies down and wraps his arms around me. "I was merely recalling the moment you said you'd never get in bed with a criminal."

"I do it for the thrill, I suppose. The world won't believe the Commander of Vareveth has a soft side."

"People will write ballads about the irony. The commander has a soft spot for the queen who held a knife to his neck." He kisses the spot between my brows that creases once my smile fades and props himself on his elbow. "What's wrong?"

I swallow my nerves and take a deep breath. "Will Eagor be a problem . . . for us?"

He slides his hand up my torso to rest it on my cheek, dragging his thumb over my cheekbone. "I will not let him, or anyone, keep me from you."

He lowers his head to give me a slow and sweet kiss, filled with comfort and reassurance. I don't want to relinquish my hold on him but know I should. It makes me want to bundle up in blankets and only do this for a whole day. I slide my fingers through his hair to pull him closer, and sigh into his mouth.

"Thin walls!" Ryder shouts from the room beside us. Cayden groans and drops his head to my neck.

"How did you even hear that?" Finnian's voice joins the swarm.

"I. Hear. Everything."

"Stop talking," Saskia hisses.

"If we were fucking, you would all know," Cayden says, and I punch him in the arm. "I didn't specify you're the reason."

I huff and turn away from him, so he doesn't see my blush, but he kisses my cheek before settling behind me and pulling me close. Darkness reclaims me again, as do dreams of dragons.

CHAPTER
FORTY-SIX

A FAINT YELLOW GLOW BOUNCES OFF THE LAKE AS I TURN onto the colonnade lined with columns covered in green ivy and white flowers. I escaped Braxton's watchful eye to check on my dragons before the celebration banquet. They're still warming up to me, and I imagine it'll take some time to become fully in tune with each other, but we're in a sweet, curious stage. Which means I smile whenever they drop a dead animal carcass at my feet and congratulate them on their kill.

They acknowledge me as they soar above the lake filled with hundreds of floating candles but are far too enraptured by the sky to submit to the ground. A path of candles leading to a gazebo covered in the same ivy and white flowers as the pillars catches my attention, as does the movement inside. I kick off my heels and carry them in my hands, sinking my feet into the cool grass to investigate, and my heart propels me forward when I realize who the culprit is.

"Hello, beautiful," Cayden says, only turning to face me once he's done lighting a candle, and he extends his hand to lead me up the steps, my corset tightening with every slow footfall.

"What's all this?" I ask, taking in the enchanting display of a blanket decked with pillows and a basket filled with wine and pastries spilling out. The same kind I had in Imirath and adored. A fresh, elaborate bouquet of pink peonies, sunflowers, and starsnaps that must've cost a fortune sits in the corner.

"It was supposed to be a surprise," he mumbles, and draws my attention when he clears his throat and pulls on the collar of his black doublet.

"Cayden, are you nervous?"

"I've never done this"—he gestures between us—"so I'm not sure how to go about it. I apologize if I've overwhelmed you. Do you want a drink? I think I'm going to have—"

I frame his reddened cheeks with my hands and bring his lips to mine, snaking my arms around his neck while his mind shuts off. He sighs against my lips and slowly parts them, trailing his fingers up and down my spine. I fiddle with the ends of his hair and rest my forehead against his after we pull apart.

"You're going to spoil me, aren't you?"

"Absolutely rotten," he responds.

His eyes heat when I slide my hands down his chest and trail my tongue across my lips before dropping onto the blanket, arching my back a bit while I grab the chilled pink wine. His gaze moves from my hips to my lips when I wrap my mouth around the bottle and take a generous sip. "And if I want to be spoiled right now, Commander?" I set the bottle aside and drag my gown up my legs, spreading my thighs wide. "What then?"

He falls to his knees, eyes completely black like a depraved demon that wants to consume my soul. I must say, I quite like having the most dangerous man in Ravaryn wrapped around my finger. I press my foot into his chest when he tries to come closer, but he yanks my ankle up and rests my leg against him.

"Touch yourself." Our gazes remain locked while he undoes his sword belt slowly, and only part when I do as he commands. "Soaked for me already, angel?"

I nod, pumping my fingers, but it offers me little relief. He positions himself between my legs and sucks my fingers clean as he enters me. My back arches off the blanket but he remains still, pinning my hips in place when I try to move on him.

"You think you can part your legs and torture me without consequences, love? I was teetering on the edge of obsession before we kissed, but I'm a damned man now."

I pull on his hair, urging him to move, but he half laughs, half growls before skimming his lips down the sensitive skin on my neck and plunging neckline, driving me to madness. "We don't have a lot of time," I pant.

"Do you think I give a fuck about a dinner while you're under me?" He reaches down to rub my clit, and I whimper. "Have you finally let go of the notion that we're not good together?"

"I have!"

"Part of you wants us to get caught, don't you?" He begins moving slowly, and I try to bury my head in his neck so he can't see the truth written on my face, but he pins me by my wrists. "You want them to find me deep inside you, the commander fucking the princess he can't have while you have those damn flowers in your hair."

"More like the demon," I gasp as his thrusts increase. His feverish hands roam my body over the fabric, and I do the same to him before sliding mine beneath and digging my nails into his back.

He lifts my hips off the ground and drills into me, biting and sucking the sweet spots on my neck. I tilt my head to grant him more access. There's no teasing, no slow starts or gentle caresses, only pure need. "Demon, commander, criminal . . . they make no difference when you're saying them while I'm inside you."

They don't make a difference to me either. He's been told to stay away, and the irony of his king finding us is so sweet it nearly makes me shatter around his cock. I don't want a prince of Galakin or a lord of Vareveth, I want the commander riddled with darkness. I'm too far gone to worry about the consequences. We must look desperate and starved. Two forbidden lovers who didn't bother discarding their clothes because they would waste precious moments together.

My core clenches around him, and he cuts our kiss off with a deep groan as he looks to where our bodies are joined. "After this dinner, I want you on my bed with your legs spread so I can taste you for hours," he growls into my ear before nibbling on the lobe. "I want to make your legs shake. I want you to scream my name like a prayer." The memory of what his tongue can do almost sends me over the edge. "I plan on memorizing exactly how you look when you moan my name."

"You're awfully demanding," I say, tightening my legs around him to flip him onto his back. "Have you forgotten who I am?" I sink down onto his length until my body is flush with his and cry out.

"Gods, El," he pants, hands tightening on my hips as he lifts my gown. His chest moves unevenly beneath my hands, and I begin rocking my hips, staring down at him through hooded lashes and hazy eyes. "I can have you every day for the rest of my life and I will still die a starving man."

I move faster, bouncing my hips until spots dance in my vision and my body is begging for release. Bolts of pleasure travel through me like lightning as Cayden tilts me forward and thrusts beneath me, fast and hard, reaching a part that unleashes something in me. I bite down on his neck and suck, marking him before walking into the banquet. His moan vibrates my lips as I pull away and gaze down at him, meeting his hips in the middle.

"You're so pretty when you ride me, princess, but you look perfect when you come." Gods, his mouth. He reaches between us to play with my clit, and my mouth parts as I shatter around him and intense shards of pleasure pierce me. He flips us over again and loses all control, cresting my pleasure once more as his fierce thrusts decimate me. Our kisses become a clashing of tongue and teeth, and we're too lost to form words. The only sounds to be heard are moans and skin slapping until he finds his release and silences his shout with my lips.

He peppers kisses along my collarbone as he pulls out and tucks himself into his pants before fixing my gown for me. It's made of thousands of silver crystals that shimmer like a star-filled sky. The sleeves cling to my arms but pool around the underside of my wrists and stretch toward the floor. Cayden kisses up the high slit, winking at me as he places a kiss to my dragon dagger before wiping lipstick off his mouth.

I pick a pastry out of the basket and sink my teeth into the sweet raspberry and savory buttery flavors. "I don't want to go to the banquet. I want to eat these the whole night."

"Don't say that," he groans, and takes a bite of my pastry before I can move it away. "You know I'll give you whatever you want, and one of us has to be responsible here."

I tip the wine back and take another gulp, shrugging my shoulders. A few pink petals float to the ground around me while I rake my fingers through my hair and take out my knife to fix my makeup in the reflection.

"Are you all right?" he gently asks.

"I'm fine."

"El..."

I bite my tongue. Saying I'm anything other than fine has always been a struggle for me because I despise feeling like I'm burdening someone with my emotions. Plastering on a smile nobody will look too deeply behind because the façade is more palatable is simple. "I'm just... nervous about how Ailliard will react to the dragons. He blames them for my mother's death."

"I'll stay with you while you talk to him," he says.

"I should do it alone, but I'll find you once it's done." I sheathe my knife and get to my feet after slipping my heels on. It's for the best if I do this without Cayden, considering Ailliard will probably attack him once I reveal our change in status.

"Do I look all right?"

He doesn't look fully convinced but doesn't argue. "You look gorgeous."

He drinks in the color that rises on my cheeks. "And I don't look like we just..."

"Well, you are glowing." His lip curls in a half smile. "Try looking grumpier."

"I'll make sure to do my best impersonation of you." I peck his cheek before slipping out of his hold and dashing away from the gazebo with him hot on my heels.

CHAPTER
FORTY-SEVEN

———

Cayden and I swoop through the threshold, joining the array of generals and political advisors. The banquet is held in a hall with a gorgeous view of the lake—thankfully with no view of the gazebo. Every room in the castle is decadent yet ethereal. Smiling faces of those congregated beam in our direction as they mingle around the room, sipping drinks and listening to the harpist pluck the strings skillfully.

"Two more of our honored guests!" Eagor announces, stepping forward to shake Cayden's hand and kiss mine. "Seeing a dragon in my lifetime is more than I ever hoped for."

"They are quite magnificent," I reply, darting my eyes to the window in time to spot Delmira gliding close.

"Otherworldly," he says. "There is something I must discuss with you, Commander."

Cayden cuts his eyes to me briefly. "You can speak freely."

Eagor clenches his jaw, but I step in before this can escalate. "Ailliard is probably waiting for me."

Cayden leans down to kiss my cheek. "I'll find you."

"Of that, I have no doubt," I mumble, and smile when he glares.

I find Saskia and Ryder, but no Finnian yet, and Ailliard is briskly striding toward me. Relief floods through me as he wraps me in a hug and lifts my feet off the ground. My bruises ache, but the heat comforts me once he sets me down. I'm going to search Cayden's desk to find a list of magical shops in Ladislava, and then I'm spending the whole week exploring.

"You're not upset?" I ask.

"I'm just happy you're safe." He squeezes my shoulders and glances around the room. "Would you mind stepping into the sitting room so we can speak privately?"

"Of course, but have you seen Finnian? I thought he'd be here by now."

"Not yet, but I'm sure he's not too far behind. You know he's usually late." He guides us into the room off the banquet hall and shuts the door. "Did you enjoy Imirath?"

"I . . . suppose. Though that had more to do with the company." There was nothing *wrong* with Imirath, but it's not a place I'll crave to revisit.

"I often reminisce about the beauty of Zinambra." His eyes take on a dreamlike film as we sink onto the couch across from the fire. "I have news."

"Of Aestilian?"

"Of home," he replies. "We can finally return."

I laugh softly. "I must stay here to fight in the war, but you're not my hostage. You're free to leave if you wish."

"No." He shakes his head. "*Home.*"

Home.

Home.

The confusion on my face bleeds into utter disbelief.

He can't mean—

"Imirath." My stomach knots when he proclaims the word with such reverence. I press my elbow into my bruise to confirm I'm not dreaming.

I shift farther away from him and swallow the bile that rises in my throat. "I don't understand what you mean."

"King Garrick has rescinded the bounty on your head after you freed the dragons. I rode to the border to meet with Imirath soldiers under a white banner; your father wants you to come home and if the peace crumbles, we'll be on the right side of the war."

"My father would sooner put me back in chains than welcome me into the castle," I argue.

"That's all in the past." He waves a dismissive hand. "You'll find peace with it eventually."

"Tell me, when Garrick throws a bone, do you chase it with your tail wagging?" The torture I suffered is in his past because he's not the one who must live with the memories.

"He won't kill you, Elowen." His voice has taken on a defensive tone.

"I'm grateful you never had children if that's your standard of fatherhood." A dry laugh rattles through me. "I will sooner burn that castle to the ground before I ever take the throne and prolong the Atarah reign. My dragons will not return to their prison, nor will I."

"Those beasts are unstable and dangerous." He reaches for me as his eyes take on a soft note, but all it does is rouse my suspicion.

"What do you know?"

"Elowen, please be—"

"Don't you dare demand I alter my reaction to your treachery. The mask has fallen, I see you as you are." I rise from the couch to put distance between us. "What do you know?"

He sighs and rakes a hand through his beard, weighing the consequences of telling me now or telling me when I'm close enough to *his king* to burn him. "Your father never physically hurt the dragons. He opted to toy with their minds by hiring a mage to re-create your essence despite you being in the dungeon, and I imagine he continued doing so while you were in Aestilian. Garrick would give them a sense of hope and comfort before ripping it away, but he's not a bad man, Elowen. We all have blood on our hands."

Horror sinks into me when I recall the way the dragons' eyes softened in the chamber before Cayden entered. They were tortured to the point they attacked hope before it could touch them. I know they sensed my pain while I was in the dungeon, so they must know I didn't want to leave them when I disappeared.

"My hands are not nearly bloody enough, and will soon be covered in ash," I state. Garrick is my father. He's supposed to be the man in this world to protect me from others, not stain his own hands with my blood.

Ailliard stands and mirrors my position across from me, squaring his shoulders to appear larger. "You are an exiled princess. Aestilian cannot protect you against the kingdoms of this world. It was your choice to come out of hiding, and I warned you of your foolishness. Imirath will give you the security you need."

"I was chained when I was nearly five years old! Where was my security then?"

"He did it for the good of his kingdom!" Ailliard shouts. "The prophecy stated you could be the doom of Imirath. He chose to be a king first, and father second."

"What of Galakin? Is it not you who said I should entertain a marriage offer from them to put distance between myself and Imirath?" His condescension slams into me, and all I see is red. Anger bubbles in my blood, boiling my temper and sharpening my claws. "I set my dragons free from the walls he cowers behind. The walls you made me believe were impenetrable. You manipulated me to believe you were protecting me by keeping the details of the Imirath castle to yourself, that a rescue mission was pointless."

"You no longer need Galakin now that your father has rescinded the bounty," Ailliard growls. "You're being unreasonable."

"Personally, I would define locking a child in the dungeon on a whim as unreasonable. The prophecy was filled with possibility, but Garrick's fate has been sealed by his own actions. He's a pathetic excuse of a king, and he will meet death as the coward he is." I roll my shoulders, feeling my poisonous anger course through me with no antidote. "I'm glad my dragons killed Isira. They saved me the task."

"DO NOT SPEAK OF MY SISTER IN THAT MANNER!"

His body shakes, and his face is flushed to the point it looks like he'll explode.

"You knew everything that happened to me while it was going on." I laugh until it becomes shrill and manic as the truth becomes apparent. "You took me out of Imirath after she died for revenge against my father, and only regretted it once you realized how deeply the treachery ran from your moment of impulsivity. Oh, uncle, you're worse than spineless. You're a fool."

"You're coming back to Imirath even if I must force you. You will understand in time." He doesn't even deny what I accused him of because he can't. I was ignorant to think he loved me. I was nothing more than a poor investment and a misplaced mercy.

"You know everything those guards did to me and that my father condoned it, and you still want me to return."

It's not a question, but he answers it with no remorse. "Yes. King Eagor is informing Commander Veles of the change in plans. Do not assume opening your legs for him will ensure his loyalty."

I don't let the hurt show on my face. "You sound bitter. When you spread yours for Garrick, did it not yield the results you wished?"

He bares his teeth like a feral animal. "Your judgment is clouded. You're too enraptured with your life here, but it isn't real. This is not where you're meant to be. Cayden will not fight a war for one woman, and Finnian will benefit from the stability Imirath offers."

My father will use Finnian as leverage the first chance he gets. "You're even more ignorant than I suspected if you believe Garrick's fury can hold a flame to mine. I may have suffered him, but it's his turn to suffer me and my dragons. He will reap what he has sown."

"Let go of your hostility and see *reason*," he pleads, taking a step closer with desperation written across his features. "This quest for revenge is abhorrent. You cannot live to kill, and you need to be smarter than this, Elowen. Look to your future. Nobody can love a vile creature."

"Clearly," I say, hating that it comes out hoarse as I look into the eyes of a man I've grown up believing was on my side. He's never been my hero, that's always remained myself, but he was someone who fought beside me. It hurts to look at Ailliard, to hear his voice say these things.

"I do love you." Tears shine in his eyes. "But love alone isn't enough."

I blink rapidly, sinking my teeth into my cheeks to refrain from breaking. His betrayal burns me from the inside. It pummels me, drowns me, and bleeds me dry. I need to find Finnian before Ailliard intervenes. "I'll show you one mercy tonight. A life for a life. Don't go back to your room or Aestilian. Get on a horse and get the fuck out of my sight because our debt has been repaid, and the next time I see you I won't hesitate to bury a knife so deep into your back that I'll have to retrieve it from your charred corpse. You are to stay away from Finnian, Cayden, Ryder, and Saskia. In my eyes, you're already dead."

Ailliard stares at me from across the room, looking at me as if he doesn't know who I am anymore. But I'm still the same Elowen he has always known. It's he who has changed. The tension between us is so thick that I let it push me toward the door, taking one last look at my uncle before I'm forced to turn. I refuse to let him see the pain he caused.

My fingers graze the knob when a sharp, shooting pain travels through my ribs, and a gold candlestick clatters to the ground beside me as a firm hand grips me by the roots of my hair. Ailliard yanks me back and punches me in the ribs marred with bruises before shoving me to the ground.

"You're the princess of Imirath, and you're going to fulfill your duty to your kingdom," he growls while scrambling from the room. The lock clicks in place as I'm wiping the blood from the corner of my mouth and shoving myself to my feet. The dragons roar beyond the walls, most likely sensing my distress, and I calm them before they blow the castle to smithereens with everyone inside.

Discovering the method of their torture makes it harder to hold myself together. My presence has been dangled in front of them throughout their imprisonment until their first reaction was to harm me. Garrick couldn't break the bond, but he could try to condition them to kill me.

There's no alternative exit and no windows to escape from. I force myself to get to my feet and take in several measured breaths to calm my nerves. My skin is covered in a cold sweat, and I want nothing more than to run somewhere nobody can find me, other than my dragons and the people who walked into enemy territory and stood by me.

But I owe it to myself to fight. I'm far from who I was but have yet to become all that I am.

I break the door handle with the candlestick and shove it open as Ryder rounds the corner. He grimaces when he spots the blood trailing down my leg from my reopened wound and tosses a spare sword.

"A group of Imirath soldiers infiltrated the banquet," he says.

I grit my teeth and finish securing the sword around my waist. "How the fuck did they get past the guards? They're under Cayden's command."

Ryder swallows. "He sent me to find you."

"Why?"

"He couldn't leave the room." He licks his lips. "They're holding Finnian at knifepoint."

Glass shatters, and Venatrix's roar rumbles the hall.

CHAPTER
FORTY-EIGHT

Finnian is paler than usual, and on his knees before an Imirath soldier. Blood trickles from his lips and stains his white doublet. He looks at me across the hall like he wishes he could both run to me and run from me to keep the danger away. But I'll always chase him even if it means running into a war. My heart falls to the floor and suddenly we're children again, separated by a thief in the forest. It was the first moment I knew I'd throw myself in front of Finnian to take any blade aimed at him.

Not Finnian.

Not my Finnian.

Venatrix shattered the wall of windows, and her large body takes up half the hall. The other dragons remain close but can't fit in here no matter how tall the ceiling is. Cayden throws a knife into an advisor's neck, cutting his whispers to Eagor short, and Valia shrieks when the blood sprays her in the face.

Ryder escorts me to where Cayden, Saskia, Braxton, and several generals are gathered. The blood Cayden spilled feeds the garden of corpses he must've planted before I rejoined the banquet. He probably picked off several people after he sent Ryder to find me, and stopped once Finnian was ushered in at knifepoint. Venatrix moves behind our group, tucking her wings close to her body as her head towers above us.

"Princess Elowen." Eagor is the first to speak. "I know it may not seem so, but this is the start of a very long peace."

"Peace?" I echo. "You think to start peace by holding my brother at the tip of a knife?"

"It's merely a precaution."

I shake my head, too angry to form words as my eyes flash between Eagor and Finnian. The doors bang open and two Vareveth soldiers drag Ailliard's bloodied body between them before dropping him to the floor and joining our side. I'd think he was dead if he didn't begin crawling toward Eagor and Valia. His right eye is swollen shut, there's a gash on his forehead, and blood slides down the side of his face.

It feels strange to mourn someone who still breathes.

"I love what you've done with your face," Finnian says, and the guard holding him slams his fist into his cheek.

"Unhand him!" I demand. "Unhand him or my killing won't stop with the people in this room. I'll find where each one of you lives and I will burn your homes and families alive."

"You're not like your father," Ailliard spits. "You're worse."

"And yet she's still far better than you," Cayden says, scanning his eyes over the gathering across from us. "I've never been a forgiving person, and I don't intend to become one tonight."

"We have a chance at peace!" Eagor cries. "If we send her back to King Garrick, he will pay us a hefty sum and will ease off the borders."

"Eagor is an imbecile cursed with ignorance," Saskia mutters.

"We will do an exchange of prisoners," I announce. "Release him and you can have me." I'll find a way to fight my way out, or I'll die in dragon fire before they chain me again, but I will never condemn someone I love to the same fate.

"NO!" Finnian shouts as Cayden wraps his hand around my wrist.

"Do not keep me from him," I command. "I will not watch him die."

"He won't die," Cayden promises, lowering his voice so only I can hear. "I'm going to distract them. Finnian is smart, he'll wield it to his advantage. I'll do whatever it takes to get us out alive, but please know this isn't how I wanted to do this."

"Do whatever you must," I reply, too focused on getting Finnian away from the enemy to care about details and sending a warning to Venatrix to prepare herself.

"I promise I'll make you happy," he says before straightening up to address the crowd. "There will be no exchange."

"She's the princess of our kingdom, you'll hand her over or I'll cut this one open," sneers the guard holding Finnian.

"She's my queen," Cayden states, declaring his loyalty and sending a wave of suspicion crashing down on our enemies. "If you successfully sent Elowen to Imirath, which you've obviously and pathetically failed at, I would've started a war to get her back."

"You would start a war for one woman?" Eagor shouts incredulously. "You are the Commander of Vareveth, your loyalties reside with the crown!"

"You should be terrified of what I'll do for her," Cayden answers, his grip tightening on my wrist. Sweat collects at the base of my neck. "My loyalties do lie with the crown. I, Cayden Veles, Commander of Vareveth, invoke my right to challenge the throne, deeming the reigning monarchs unfit to rule."

The room erupts in chaos, and Finnian elbows the guard restraining him in his crotch. Venatrix hops over us and sends the guards reaching for him into the wall with her tail. I meet Finnian halfway and cover his back while returning to our side. He frames my face with his hands once we're safe.

"Never offer yourself to Imirath again," he growls.

I smile up at him. "Don't get captured and I won't have to."

Ryder slaps a hand on Finnian's shoulder and another general hands him a spare sword. Venatrix continues roaring to keep our enemies on the other side of the room as they try to charge. Ryder and Saskia are trying to get Cayden's attention, but his emotionless eyes are fixed on me, and what he declared to the room hits me.

He challenged the throne.

"What are you doing?" I almost whisper. He shouldn't be able to hear it over Eagor, Valia, and Ailliard shouting profanities, or the advisors and Imirath soldiers trying to maneuver around Venatrix, but he does.

"The Commander of Vareveth can challenge the throne if they marry someone of royal blood." He steps forward and steadies me when my knees buckle. "The clause was written into our laws after the civil war, to prevent another internal war in Vareveth by providing a way to legally overthrow the reigning monarchs with the support of the army."

"You knew about the clause this whole time?" The floor feels like it's shaking under my feet, about to crack and send me plummeting. A pained expression crosses his face, but Venatrix turns our attention when she rears her head back and the scent of smoke fills the room.

"If the room fills with flames, we won't be able to see people escaping," Saskia states, and I call Venatrix off. "We should fight them with blades. It'll be easier to gain allies in the war if you express restraint."

Everything is moving so fast and spinning around me. I feel as if I don't have enough time to take a breath, like I'm running just behind everyone as they near the finish line.

"I agree," I say, shoving Cayden's hands off me. He'll challenge the throne legally or illegally to keep me safe, but illegally will lead to all kingdoms of Ravaryn turning their backs or raising their blades on us. "I will marry you."

"El, I didn't fall for you because of a clause." He steps forward, and I step back. "Please, believe that."

"Spare me the details until we've dealt with this mess," I state.

His jaw clenches and he nods while unsheathing his sword.

By the gods... I can't believe I'm doing this. A life with him doesn't sound bad at all, but my mind is my own worst enemy, and it twists every interaction we've ever had. I can tell he practically feels my memory warping, turning every stolen glance in a crowded room into something calculated.

I command Venatrix to leave the hall, but she remains close by with the other dragons. The guards surrounding the room draw their swords and point them toward our enemies. I've come too far and sacrificed too much just to let power slip from my fingers now. I came from nothing, and now I have a kingdom ripe for my taking. I will shake the very stars the gods hung in the sky and crumble the mountains they forged on the earth.

Vengeance is a promise signed in blood.

"This is madness!" Eagor wails. "I am the king, you fucking bastards!"

Cayden tsks. "I would think a man of your standing wouldn't have to resort to using such vulgar language."

"You are nothing but a band of thieves," Valia growls as tears stream down her face. "No kingdom will respect a queen who whored her way to a throne or a king who committed regicide."

"Venomous words from a bitch that doesn't know how to hold a blade," I say. "I'm terrified, truly."

Cayden twirls his sword in his hands, and I let all arguments and noise fall away while zoning in on my targets. My heart slows, and I fall into the hypnotic trance of a battle. It's my chance to expel the rage, fear, confusion, and betrayal that churn inside me. I'm a wasteland of vexation and fury. I can't be in an open field, screaming until every emotion plaguing me relents, but I can kill my way to clarity.

"Charge!" Cayden commands, and both sides clash.

I throw my dragon dagger at an Imirath soldier advancing on me, killing him instantly while engaging with another. I swing my sword but let the advisor deflect it so I'm able to kick him in the groin and slice his neck open when he leans forward.

The hall is filled with the sounds of clashing steel, people gurgling on blood, and battle cries. Cayden cuts down the advisors surrounding Eagor and Valia, but Valia is already dead, and Cayden orders a soldier to restrain Eagor before he can kill himself.

I continue blocking the advances of a guard, but he kicks my wounded leg before I have the chance to maneuver away. It gives out, and I slide my blade down his stomach as my knees hit the floor in a pile of his entrails. My ribs throb and I cough blood onto my hand, using my sword to get back on my feet.

Finnian battles an advisor.

Ryder battles two, swinging his swords in an ancient dance of war.

Saskia slices through an Imirath soldier.

Movement registers in the corner of my eye before I have the chance to find Cayden, and I settle on Ailliard running through the blood and downed bodies. I track his target, and dread pools in my stomach as my heart crashes through the floor.

"Ailliard, stop!"

I feel every step he takes closer to Cayden in my bones. He's fighting three Imirath soldiers at once, all skillful, and all united against him. My fingers tighten around the hilt on my knife as I recall Ailliard throughout different phases of my life.

That Ailliard is dead. He's in the past and will forever remain there. My future has been rewritten in a language I can't yet read, but Cayden is in it; I could recognize him in any vernacular.

Cayden threw himself in front of a dragon for me, and Ailliard threw me to the wolves the second he heard a whisper from Imirath.

I throw my knife, piercing Ailliard between his ribs. Time moves slowly as I watch his body fall to the floor, head smacking against the polished tile. He used to be one of the strongest people in the world to me, and now he's scrambling to his knees, crying out from the blade I impaled in him. My gown drags through the blood and over the bodies littering the same path he took. I step over him, and my heels crunch in broken glass as I offer my back to the shattered windows.

"You were right, uncle." I call on Calithea and her shadow appears instantly, her silvery wings spreading on either side of me. He underestimated my ability to find solace in the flames. My eyes glow gold, and he gapes at me in horror. "Love isn't enough."

Calithea's flames shoot forward, encompassing Ailliard as his screams and the scent of burning flesh filter through the room.

CHAPTER
FORTY-NINE

I KILLED HIM.

I killed him.

Tears prickle my eyes, and a sob erupts from my throat that has no right to be there. I feel feverish, and ragged gasps flutter from my lips like butterflies metamorphizing through irrevocable actions. Calithea nudges me with her snout when I drop to my knees, avoiding the glass, and I turn away from Ailliard to rest my forehead against hers.

"This is real, sweetling," I sob. "Garrick can't manipulate your mind anymore."

I run my hand down her snout as another sob rips free and pull back to swipe the tears off my face. Ailliard is selfish for making me live with this, and yet I wouldn't have wanted anyone else to kill him. I don't understand how he could look me in the face and dream of the kingdom that tortured me.

"When your mother got pregnant, she thought you were her blessing. But I lived long enough to know you were her curse."

Ailliard's voice replays in my head.

My body shakes so hard I feel my teeth chatter together. He was going to kill Cayden. No matter how upset I am with him, I could never let that happen.

"You need to let go of your anger because no matter how much you fight, you'll never be strong enough to accomplish the things you wish for."

"Get out of my head." I screw my eyes shut and cover my ears with my blood-covered hands, but Ailliard's verbal assault continues. His insults are branded into my memory, and his corpse is engraved behind my eyelids.

"Your bond to those dragons was the worst thing that ever happened to me."

Hands wrap around my wrists, and I snap my eyes open. Cayden's concerned gaze bores into me, and his face is splattered with blood. His doublet is torn on his bicep, there's a slash on his chest, and blood trickles from the reopened wound under his eye. I try to make out what he's saying but can't focus on his lips. I can't concentrate on anything. Everything feels like it's too much to process.

Ailliard's betrayal.

Ailliard's death.

The marriage clause.

I rip my wrists out of his hold and shove him back. "You knew," I rasp.

"Elowen, please." Cayden reaches for me again, eyes pleading. "I just need you to breathe for me right now. We can talk about the rest later."

I shake my head, shutting my eyes against the dizziness. "Where's Finnian? Where's Finnian? FINNIAN!"

A pair of familiar arms spin me away from Ailliard's body, and Finnian shoves my head into his neck. "I'm right here, Ellie. Just breathe."

I suck in short, frantic breaths, but my head grows lighter as the seconds tick by. Finnian runs a hand through my tangled hair, whispering that everything is okay. I fist his shirt and pull him closer, breathing in his scent. I can't hold it back anymore—I sob into his neck. I scream and sob until my throat burns. Tears soak his skin and leave fresh trails down my face.

I pull back and search his watery eyes. "Please don't be scared of me."

"I could never be scared of you."

"I would never do this to you." I try to turn back to Ailliard, but Finnian keeps his hands firm on my shoulders. "Please, you must know I would never do this to you. Ailliard didn't love me, he . . . he . . ."

Finnian wipes my tears while cupping my face. "I know. You love me, and I love you. You're not a monster, Ellie."

Finnian is the only love I've ever known outside of Ailliard, but I've always known that the differences in the way they treated me were as clear as night and day. Ailliard would tell me he cared for me, but Finnian never had to, I just knew it. Blood travels from my fingers to my elbows and looks like I'm wearing crimson gloves. I turn my hands around, taking them in before I let my eyes travel along my stained gown. I wonder if any blood is Ailliard's. It pools around me, seeping into my soul, staining it more than it already is. My breathing picks up, and it causes the pain in my ribs to flare.

I bow my head, clutching my torso, doing my best to breathe through it. Cayden's before me in an instant, and I'm too exhausted to shove him away again. "Were your ribs hit?"

I nod. We're all maimed in some way. Finnian's left eye is swollen shut and his doublet is still stained from previous wounds. Saskia has a slash on her calf. Ryder clutches his side while she supports his weight and needs a healer immediately.

"I should stitch Ryder," I say.

"The court physician will come to the suite," Cayden says, brushing the hair out of my face.

I try to speak but press my lips together and pinch my eyes shut when another wave of pain surges. "Cayden . . ."

"I know, love. I've got you." He lifts me in his arms, careful to stay away from my bruises, and carries me from the bloodied banquet hall.

✤ ✤ ✤

Saskia slides her brush and fingers through my hair, braiding the wet strands down my back. I've never had someone brush my hair before, and I didn't realize how relaxing it would be. I close my eyes, wanting to remain present within the peace.

The tea Cayden sent has grown cold, and I'm surprised he's waited this long before appearing. He's blood free but looks both crazed and tortured as he leans against the doorframe. I watch him and remain silent as Saskia ties a lavender bow around the bottom of my braid to match my night-slip.

"Let me know if you want me to come back," Saskia says as she rises from the couch, her robe trailing behind her as she walks past Cayden, looking back at him with sadness.

I drop my eyes to my lap, but it matters little when he's kneeling before me within seconds. "El, please look at me."

It hurts to look at him, to feel the things I do when I wish to be burning in anger only. To be lost in this confusing sense of grief, craving his arms, but not knowing if I should. "Royals have marriages of convenience quite frequently."

He rests his hands on my thighs. "I never planned on invoking the clause, ever."

"But you did." I shove myself off the couch, stepping around him and toward the fire. My leg throbs painfully, but I stand my ground. "And you played it well."

"I'll happily be the villain for you if it ensures your safety. I'll watch this kingdom burn to the ground if it means you live. I've never wanted to be king, that's why I never told you about it." He strides toward me, stopping inches away and yet much too far. "You've been stuck in my head since the night we met, even before then, but I knew there was no going back for me once I met you."

Self-loathing enraptures me when helpless tears mist my eyes. "When did you find out about the clause?"

"The night of the alliance ball," he says, hands fisting at his sides to stop himself from reaching out to me. "Galakin approached you about marriage while we were sitting at the table, and I felt like I couldn't breathe."

"You deceived me for weeks!"

"I wanted something to offer you after we had time together, if you wanted something more than a commander, but I won't lie or apologize. I'm not a hero. This is who I am, Elowen, and I'm yours. All of me, every darkened part. Until the moon crashes into the sea and all the stars blink out of existence."

I shake my head, but he steps forward to frame my cheeks with his hands.

"I've always been yours, even if you weren't mine. There are no stipulations to the power you have on me. Even if you despise me, you'll always have me."

I fist his shirt but don't pull him closer. "You say everything I want to hear, but I don't know how to trust it." I may be mad at him, but I can't cut him out from where he embedded himself inside my heart. "You say you never wanted to be king, but you're now the king of one of the most powerful kingdoms in Ravaryn. You crave power, and I've seen the lengths to which you'll go to obtain it. The clause is a game, and you've made me your pawn."

"I crave *you*. You are my queen, always have been, even when it was treasonous," he says, brushing his thumbs over my cheeks before leaning down to kiss my forehead. When he pulls back, his eyes beg me to believe him. "They didn't want us in their world, so I made a new one."

I stare up at him and all words known to me vanish from my mind as if they never existed. My mind is a maze that even I don't always know how to navigate. I've been betrayed and abandoned so many times that antidotes morph into poison, honest words become riddled with ulterior motives. "You didn't betray me, but a lie of omission is still a sin."

"Please, my love."

"I need time."

"I'll give you whatever you need," he says, trying to give me a reassuring smile, but I've never seen him look so defeated. "And I'll spend the rest of my life proving I didn't do this for a crown."

"I'm not an easily convinced woman."

"I'm a man who loves a challenge."

A tear falls down my cheek, and I hate myself for it. "Perhaps my mind will be the one to finally best you. I don't know how to stop thinking. I don't know how to trust words. My life changed in an instant when I was a child, and I've tried to avoid another situation like that."

"I will quiet any doubt you have; you just need to tell me."

I shake my head, more tears falling from my eyes. I haven't known much kindness in my life, and whenever I've gotten emotional in the past it's been met with anger for feeling things that were inconvenient to others, but Cayden is being so gentle that I don't know how to perceive it. It's like I'm waiting with bated breath for him to lash out at me, so I can see who he truly is, but it never comes.

The events of tonight weigh on me like stones tied around my ankles dragging me to the bottom of the sea. I fight to get back to the surface, but it's little use. I step away from him, making myself feel worse, but I refuse to crumble in his arms. I feel like he's driven a wedge into my heart, but he's also the only one who can take it out.

I need him to understand that this isn't something I'll brush under the rug because his arms make me feel whole. I'd rather be broken and respected than loved and deceived. I need to be alone with my thoughts, even if they'll torture me, but one thing I know for sure is that I want the world to know that if they stand against us, they're lighting their own pyres or digging their own graves. We've taken Vareveth through conquest, and it's inevitable that other rulers of Ravaryn will feel threatened.

"I need you to send a message to the fire priestess," I say. "Our crowns and betrothal are drenched in blood, and war will come, but my dragons will be with us. That is all I want from you tonight."

He slides his hand down my braid, and I force myself not to break while I look up at him. "The reign of the demon king and dragon queen."

CHAPTER

FIFTY

THE SUN SETS BEHIND THE MOUNTAINS AS CAYDEN LEADS me to the shore beside the lake, walking between the parted crowd filled with nobles who have bent the knee and soldiers who were more than happy to proclaim their loyalty to us. Though I believe they always viewed Cayden as king. A war drum slowly beats, sending ripples through the water Eagor kneels in, and two bonfires bordering him burn every banner and tapestry with the Dasterian sigil. The smoke dances through dragon wings as they soar above.

His reign is over, but mine has just begun.

"Eagor Dasterian," Cayden begins. "You are hereby sentenced to death by order of the king and queen of Vareveth. Those who cannot hold on to power have no right to hide behind the façade of strength."

Eagor spits, but not far enough to reach us. His clothes bear no blood from the banquet, a clear sign he's never fought for his people. "The king-slayer and the whore."

His words don't faze me when he's on his knees at the mercy of the crown he once wore. I murdered my uncle and gained a kingdom; burning a puppet king is a simple task. Basilius swoops down, lavender scales glistening in the sun.

"Burn him," I whisper, and the flames pour down like rain as Eagor's screams echo through the sky. His body flails in the water, seeking a remedy for the excruciating pain, but Basilius blows until Eagor falls silent.

"Long live King Cayden and Queen Elowen," Ryder announces. "The Conquerors of Vareveth!"

The crowd echoes the statement as Cayden and I offer our backs to the flames, painting a ruthless picture to match the darkness within. His obsidian crown sits atop his head to match the black doublet stitched with crimson and a matching cape. My gown is a mirror; flames are stitched into the cape sewn to the straps and skirts that pool around me, and the golden dragon crown solidifies me as the queen I was always meant to be.

I want to be both light and dark, gentle and ruthless, soft and fierce. I am both an executioner and a healer. I wring dreams from despair and hope from hopelessness.

The bond pulls in my chest, and I turn my eyes to the sky, but my dragons are landing in the shallow water behind me, looking to me for reassurance. Golden light shimmers from my palms and crawls its way up my arms in long swirling swoops. It radiates into the air around me like tiny snowflakes.

Cayden turns to me, his features a mixture of awe and confusion. "The light has formed a crown. Are you doing this?"

"No." Gold wisps continue to shoot from my palms, wrap around my torso, and speckle the surface of the lake until it glitters like a jewel.

"*You sent for me, Daughter of Flames. I'm here to stoke the embers that live within you,*" a voice whispers in the wind, just as it did several months ago.

"The priestess is here," I whisper. "She's calling to me."

I spy a red hooded figure being led across the grass by Braxton before Cayden has the chance to respond, and we order the crowd to disperse until only Finnian, Saskia, and Ryder remain.

"*You have never feared the flames, Queen of Fire, but others will fear yours.*"

She pulls her cloak back to reveal chestnut curls and kneels at my feet, bowing to press my hand to her forehead. "I am honored you sent for me, Your Majesty. I go where the flames command, and all wind carries the flames closer to you."

"I was told priestesses have the ability to conduct bond-strengthening ceremonies," I reply, gesturing for her to stand.

"I do, my lady, but your bond isn't of this world. It transcends the ordinary." Her eyes cut to my left, watching the wisps swirl around Cayden's wrist and run through his tousled waves, tethering him to me. "How curious."

"What do you mean?"

She shakes her head, leaving my question unanswered, though it appears she doesn't have an answer to give. "I'll do my best to tap into the bond and mend what time stole, but I need to gather some supplies for the spell if someone could show me to the kitchens."

Braxton steps forward to offer his arm, and the priestess thanks him while fisting her robes and disappearing into the castle. The wisps continue flowing and latch on to the horns and wings of each dragon. I sink into the sand beside the others, happy to listen to their chattering while I wait for the priestess to return.

Trust me, I shoot down the bond. *I will never do anything to harm you.*

When she returns, Finnian squeezes my hand before I follow the priestess farther up the lake and sit across from her in the icy water that bites at my skin. She fills a large bowl and sets it between us. "To contain the spell," she says while reaching into a satchel and throwing ingredients in. "Salt for protection. Garlic to ward off dark magic. Basil to dispel evil. Water to balance you. It's your opposite, and yet you'll always feel a pull toward it for that very reason. It keeps you grounded."

She dips her dark-skinned hand into the bowl to mix it with her fingers and drags a line across my forehead. "Thank you for helping me," I say.

"You are my queen," she responds. "This is an honor."

"But I thought cults only swore fealty to the gods."

"Your soul is forged in flames and blessed by the gods. You're the only person who can share a link with those dragons. The fire of the gods resides in you."

I smile, not denying her words considering she's been nothing but helpful, but I've never been a believer. The fire of the gods does not reside in me—my own flames do. They were not given to me on a whim. I bow to nothing other than my crown and kneel to no god.

"I need five drops of blood," she says. "Cut your palm and let them drip into the water individually."

I unsheathe my dragon dagger and do as she says, squeezing my hand together above the bowl. The first drop falls, spiderwebbing through the water as the colors change to green and black.

Sorin, the wind whispers. He rises from the shore and takes to the skies as green and black glittery strands spill from the bowl like untamable roots.

The second drop falls and becomes a brighter shade of red, pink, and gold. Venatrix joins Sorin and her strands mingle with his. My bond urges me to continue. Lavender is next, and Basilius joins the others. Then sky blue and yellow, followed by silver and white. The strands shimmer and twine together like a braid, and a sharp, thunderous crack echoes through the air as color explodes around me. Wisps of all colors zoom across the lake and high into the air like shooting stars.

The dragons tumble and twirl through them like a fresh snowfall, roaring in happiness and hope. The bond hums happily in my chest, becoming a fullness I've never felt and don't know how I lived without. I float in the water and stare up at my dragons. To watch is a mundane task, but it becomes extraordinary when you watch someone you love. No matter how much I long for a calming, sated sensation to settle over me, it doesn't. Restlessness flutters in my belly as if a sixth dragon is flying inside me.

The dragons soar in a perfect circle and let out a synchronized roar before shooting flames to the center, colliding them above my head. I feel their fire in my soul. I've questioned where I was supposed to be so many times. I'm always contemplating my next move and looking toward the future. But right now, I know that everything that happened after I left Imirath happened so that I could be here.

But it doesn't feel quite right.

I crave more.

"Something isn't right," I say.

The priestess tears her wide eyes from the sky and wipes them while taking a few moments to collect herself before speaking. "I've done all I'm able, my lady, but the dragons may be calling to you through the bond. Trust it. A dragon and rider are one, intertwined in an unbreakable, unyielding way. It is a trust like no other. A foundation stronger than the earth we stand upon."

"A dragon rider," I mutter, walking back to the shore with my eyes glued to my dragons.

They begin flying in front of the waterfall beside the castle that spills down a rocky cliffside and into the river littered with sharp rocks. Venatrix stares me down, and it's like she's pulling me in, urging me to take the leap. I see my reflection in her red eyes. Two lost souls tethered together. The world falls away from me as I take the next step forward, and I ignore the protests of Cayden, Finnian, Saskia, and Ryder that I'm leaving behind.

I fist my wet gown and tear through the grass, not letting the heavy fabric slow me down. Time is a cruel thing. You don't know how much you have left until the end is staring you down and you're powerless against it.

But I was born to ride dragons, and I will not let fear stand in the way.

I make it to the edge of the cliff and jump.

The dragons dip and follow me as I plummet but don't move beneath me. Sorin flies upside down and stares into my panicked eyes with curiosity. Fear grips my lungs and squeezes until I can't even form a scream. The bond is a choice, and it's a choice I'm willing to die for. A true dragon rider places all their trust in a dragon, and there is no reward without risk.

I think of nothing but the dragons, quieting my mind and taking comfort in the bond pulsing through me like a second heart. I reach my hand out, stroking it along his snout and filling my eyes with the fire raging inside me.

Like calls to like.

Bravery does not come from chaining a dragon, it comes from riding one.

Sorin tucks himself below me and I slam onto his back, taking hold of two black horns and parting my legs around his neck. I'm yanked upward along the waterfall, and we soar over the cliff and swirl around the castle spires. It's a freedom like I've never known, and know nothing will ever compare. To be on the back of a dragon is to experience infinity.

Wind whips through my hair and my cape flows behind me as Sorin carries us higher into the sky, the other four quickly following. Basilius flies above us, and I reach up to stroke a hand down his neck. Sorin continues pumping his black-tipped wings until the skies fall silent for the dance of dragons.

I loosen my hands on his horns when he levels out and spread my arms wide, sliding my fingers through frothy clouds. This is *everything*. It's more than I dreamed it would be. I was riddled with homesickness for a home I never knew. Sorin chuffs happily beneath me, tilting his head to watch me.

I get to my feet, balancing myself before leaping onto Calithea's silver back. She roars when Venatrix gets too close. "You'll get your turn, Venatrix."

Calithea flies faster with Venatrix hot on her tail, but Venatrix is second fastest and Calithea is third. Venatrix flips and flies above Calithea and me, but I don't switch dragons just yet, wanting to make sure they all get enough attention. Basilius seems content to trail behind and spin in the clouds.

A crescent moon hangs in a sky littered with stars. So many have tried to kill me, and all failed. I've been imprisoned, tortured, and exiled, but I've never been nothing. Dragons have always lived inside me, and I them. I never found faith in the gods because my faith has always lain with these beautiful beasts.

I take hold of Venatrix and pull myself onto her as she flips. We sharply dive down, flying so fast that tears leak from my eyes. My heart pounds and I expel the betrayal and beatings from my body by letting out a scream so fierce it leaves my throat raw and mingles with five dragon roars. She sharply juts up and glides along the surface of the lake before landing at the top of the cliff I jumped from and roars at those gathered.

Cheers ring through Verendus, Ladislava, and everyone watching the dragon queen reborn from flight. Fire itself can't burn brighter than I am right now. Finnian and Saskia have tears streaming down their faces as Ryder and Cayden holler beside them, the latter pointing at me with his arm slung around Ryder, shouting, *"That's my girl!"*

I can't help but smile at the four people who walked this path with me. My life hasn't always been easy, but all darkness must pass.

The priestess steps forward and raises her voice. "May I present the first dragon-riding queen since the gods left us, Queen Elowen Atarah! Long may she reign!"

"Long may she reign!" echoes the crowd as Cayden takes several steps in front of the gathering, his eyes never leaving mine even when Venatrix growls. He continues his steady pace forward, and all eyes are on him to watch what he's doing.

But Cayden does something he's never done for anyone.

He unsheathes his sword from his waist and kneels in the grass, bowing his head and offering up his blade to me. It's a sign of respect and loyalty. He's announcing that his sword is not only commanded by himself, but also me.

"Bow before your queen or burn and bleed!" Cayden declares, sending a rippling effect throughout the kingdom until my eyes can't stretch further.

A united front.

Burn and bleed.

Together we reign.

Together we go to war.

ACKNOWLEDGMENTS

Writing the acknowledgments for *Fear the Flames* is surreal. When I self-published this book in 2022, I had no idea how much it would change my life. I'm forever thankful for this story and these characters. Elowen Atarah has been in my mind for so many years, and having the opportunity to go back to the start has been unexpectedly cathartic. Words have always been my light in the dark, and I hope you've found some light through the letters I've woven together.

First, I want to thank my family. Without their love and support, I wouldn't be able to do this. Mom, I don't know how to properly thank someone who has done more for me than I'll ever be able to articulate. No matter who doubted me, you never did, and you showered me in endless love until I believed in myself. Dad, no matter how old I get, I'll always be your sweetie. Thank you for always telling me I could do anything I set my mind to and for being there to help me in any way I needed. Andrew, you were my first best friend, and I'm so thankful you're my brother. No matter what's happened, I've always had you, and you'll always have me no matter what.

Tanner, thank you for believing in me even when I doubted myself. Opening my door when I was nineteen and finding you on the other side changed my life in the best way imaginable. I've loved you for five years, and I'll love you forever.

Next up is the dream team: Jessica and Shauna. Jessica, I'll never forget the day your email came into my inbox and I stared at a wall for the next two hours, wondering if I was dreaming. You're my superagent and therapist. Your faith in me and my work means more to me than I'll ever be able to say, and I'm so grateful we crossed paths. Shauna, my amazing editor. Trusting *Fear the Flames* with someone wasn't easy until I met you. I'm so thankful for the dedication and work you've put into making *Fear the Flames* what it is today. My spice-loving readers also owe you a thank-you for encouraging me to sprinkle a bit more pepper on the manuscript.

The beautiful map you see on the endpapers of the book was designed by Andrès Aguirre Jurado. Andrès, thank you so much for bringing my world to life, and for capturing the details in each and every corner of it.

To the lovely publishing team at Delacorte Press that worked on *Fear the Flames*, thank you so much for the love you've shown my work. It takes a village to finalize a book, and your enthusiasm has made this such an amazing experience. At the risk of sounding entirely cheesy, this is genuinely a dream come true.

I'd also like to thank a few friends who have been unyieldingly supportive not only of my work but of me. Ashely, my soul sister and favorite CEO. I've known you since we were fourteen, and growing up with you is something I'm eternally grateful for. No matter where you go in the world, you'll never be without me. Imani Erriu, my pookie author bestie. You came into my life completely unexpectedly but at the perfect time. Navigating our author journeys together has been so amazing, and I'm so thankful our readers pushed us together. Grace, I miss you every day. I always carry your love with me, no matter where you are. Not only do I write for myself, but I write for you, too. Sarah, thank you for being with me throughout this journey and for convincing me my literary agent wasn't pranking me when I got the email—you're a lifesaver for that! To thank every single person that's impacted me, I'd have to write a second book, so I just want to say a massive thank-you to everyone in my life who has walked this path with me.

My lovely readers, it is a privilege to write these stories for you and my greatest passion. Thank you so much to everyone who took a chance on me when I self-published this book, and welcome to all new readers. You all have a place in Ravaryn, no matter when you got here. I wouldn't be where I am today without your support, and I will never be able to truly express my love for you all within a paragraph.

Xoxo,
Olivia Rose Darling

ABOUT THE AUTHOR

OLIVIA ROSE DARLING split her time growing up between New York and Manchester, Vermont. She developed a passion for writing from a very young age, always scribbling poems onto napkins and short stories into her school notebooks. She earned a degree in English with a concentration in creative writing from Pace University. The Lord of the Rings was her favorite movie series growing up and formed her fantasy obsession. Becoming an author and living a life filled with words and magic has always been her dream. *Fear the Flames* is her debut novel.

oliviarosedarling.com
@itslivdarling